Blood of a Boss II

Lock Down Publications
Presents
Blood of a Boss II
The Streets Is Watching
A Novel by *Askari*

Lock Down Publications
P.O. Box 1482
Pine Lake, Ga 30072-1482

Copyright 2015 by Askari Blood of a Boss II

First Edition March 2015
Printed in the United States of America

Lock Down Publications
Like our page on Facebook: Lock Down Publications @
<u>www.facebook.com/lockdownpublications.ldp</u>
Cover design and layout by: Dynasty Cover Me
Book interior design by: Shawn Walker
Edited by: Shelby Lazenby

Askari

Dedications

This book is dedicated to the memory of my loving mother, Mrs. Edith Annette Farmer. This book is also dedicated to my beautiful children, Dayshon Kapone Farmer, Keyonti Nikkia Farmer, and Quamar Preston Adams.

Shout outs to my family: My grandmother, Jeanette Farmer. Pop Pop and Grandma Zetti. My pops, Earl "Bigg Dawg" Farmer. My aunt, Mary "Dee Dee" Broomer. My sister, Chrissia Lindsay. My brothers, Tyron and Shamar Farmer. My nephews, Kanye and Noah Lindsay-Green. My niece, Sahala Lindsay-Green. My uncles: Nate "Bubbles" Farmer, Robert "Suggie" Farmer, Anthony "Tone" Broomer, George "Russy" Lindsay Jr., James "Uncle Jim" Lindsay, Leonard Lindsay, and Daniel "Jap" Minor. My aunts: Cynthia Basketbill, Carol Minor, Trina Lindsay, Tina McLauren, Michelle Farmer, Drema, Yolanda Orlina, and Tanga. My cousins: Robert "Cheese" Basketbill (Cheese fought me...made me tougher, love you for that my nigga, no matter what brah), Sheena and Glen Morgan, Gina "GiGi" Basketbill, Kaleena and Kennedy Farmer, Sabrina Farmer, Anyae and Nydia Broomer, Munch, Nonnie, and Kizzy Canada. Jared, Danielle, and David Minor, Jim-Jim and Lance Lindsay, Tiana Lindsay, Reese and George "Tockie" Lindsay, Lenia and Lenette Lindsay, Gregory "Nyce" McLauren, Andre McLauren, and Journey McLauren. Ms. Mona Davis, Keisha, Shana, Chanel, Lexi, Kori and Breanna Eaglan (Bre, I love you baby sis). Rickina "Pooh Face" Binns, Kareem Acevedo(I love you, lil man. Hold ya head) and Diamond. The Canada Family, The Benjamin Family, and The Kent Family.

Shout outs to The Crease Legends: OG Winky (R.I.P.), OG Boston (R.I.P.), OG Sid (R.I.P.), Lil Ben (R.I.P), Justin Winstead (R.I.P.), Jimmy Ford (R.I.P.), Jeff Green (R.I.P.), and Richard Saunders (R.I.P.)

Shout outs to my homegirls: Destiny Taylor (I love you, baby girl, and I'm proud of you) Toyia and Ms. Tonya, Nicole "Mookie" Vaughn, Precious, Yarnell, Shante, Erica, Niesha, Quita, Angel, Atiya, Yannie (R.I.P.), Butter, Sheena Gordon, Chenoa, Jamie, Davita, Yah Yah, Tamara Bell, Barbie, Jesse, Ebony Butler, Diedra Wilson, Shakiera Wilson, Whup, Leena (Sweety Raw), Noobie, Shantiera, Teahona Adams (May Allah continue to bless you. Ameen.), Carol Adams, Kimberly Sizer, Ms. Bev and Kelly Scott, Angie, Syd, Michelle, Tamieka Jefferson, Margret, Kreesha, Dita (Ms. Sonyia), Meeka, Yolanda "Lala" Jackson, Sakina Jackson, Flo, Treasure, Puff, Khaliyah, Summer, Boog, Kyra, Krissy, Sharita, and Taneesha.

Shout outs to my DAY ONE NIGGAS: Micheal "Muk Millionz" Vaughn, Jason "Goon" Vaughn, Anton "Skeeny" Orlina, Marlow "Biggie" Hariston, William "Billy Bear" Taylor, Roy "Pretty Boy" Jolly, Eric "E" Stubbs, Bobby "Boner Bob" Canada, Deshay Canada, Uncle Stevie Canada, Joey Canada, Carson, Wayne "Wiggz" Johnson, Reggie "Reg" Johnson, Cutchie, Kut, Bliz, Rock, Black Sam, Marty, Spunk, Nate, Shawn Pinkney, Shawn Peppi, Jacquan "Nasty" Carter, J-Rizzy, Micheal Richards, Hasan, Mole, Raz, Kirby, Vinny Raysor, Coldplay Wu and Rell, Gerald, Nick Knowledge, Kyle Fisher, Uncle J, Kio, Mal and Quanny, Lil Toney, Eric and Rashid Camp, Lhamar Smith, Craig (Banga), Tone (Muff), Lil Eddie, Jermaine "Pete" Martin, Uncle Hick, Javon, Nate Nate, Ceez, Fudd, Jimmy Bean, Rahfiq, Man Man,

Tyrone "T.Y." Groomes (R.I.P.), Ryan and Todd Flamer, Rock, Joezell, WeeLee, Alvin, and Beetle (R.I.P.)

Shout outs to my North Philly Family: Uncle Sonny Blue (Pop), Uncle Reese, Nassideen, Marty Stacks (Cousin BEAST), Briz, Cousin Meatball (I still love you bul), Peedi Crakk, Indy 500, Freeway, C4, Cousin Heemy (R.I.P.), Omillio Sparks, Kyree (hold ya head homie), Horsey and Boo Boo, Nyce, Footy James, Malik, Tauphiq, Parkay, Buttah, Lil' Veezy, Stizzy Mac, Nips, Shokka Bop, Doe Boy, Cam, Cheeks, Keeny and Fonze, Ted (Saubir), Toot, Uncle June, Charlie Mack, Johnny Ahk, Spanky (Shiest), Dev, Gooch, Hollywood, Ant Ant (R.I.P.), Man Man, Don Don, Cheeze Mean Money, Day Day From J-Street (hold ya head bro). Reese and Susquhanna, 8th and Diamond, Franklin and Diamond, Fairhill and York, Marshall and Montgomery, 7th and Clearfield, Richard Allen Projects (RAM SQUAD), Fairhill Projects, Lil Pat, Lil Reese, Lil Marty, Rob (Sheed), Jameel Capers, Cousin Squeeze (R.I.P.), Geez and Lil Weezy. T-Mac (R.I.P), 12th and Huntingdon, 12th and Cumberland, Delhi and Dauphin, Delhi and Cumberland, Lee Street, 11th and Diamond, and Erie Ave.

Shout outs to Team LDP: Cash, Coffee, Reds Johnson, Kenneth Chisholm, Damion King, Lady Stiletto, J Peach, Tranay Adams, Royal Nicole, Chance, Frank Gresham, Walt Johnson, Linnea, and Sa'id Salaam.

400 Saulte to all my Block Boys!!! Tali Da Don, Sunshine, F.T., K.K., Melly Whispers, OG Rah Dollaz, Pizzy Bishop, Kali Budd (B.I.P). Bishop Love to all my Bishops. East to da West!!!

Last but not least, I wanna give a special shout out to all of the FANS AND SUPPORTERS of LDP!!! I thank y'all so much!!! Y'all are the best!!!! We around!!!!

Preface
The Moreno Family Legacy

My name is Gervin Moreno and I was born to be a gangster. My bloodline is West African and Sicilian, and I'm Gabriella Moreno's first child. My mother, an Afro-Cuban was rumored to be a descendent of Queen Nzinga. She was beyond beautiful. Her chocolate skin was reminiscent of her Angolan heritage, and her silky hair and aqua blue eyes were courtesy of the Spanish slavemaster who brutally raped her great-grandmother in the middle of a sugar cane field. I, too, have his eyes.

My father, Angolo Gervino, was a Sicilian-American. He had a rich olive complexion, wavy black hair, a chiseled face, and piercing black eyes. At 6'2", 195 pounds, he was full of charisma and his body language exuded power.

In 1939, my father and his friends migrated to Cuba. Fulgencio Batista was the president, and he welcomed these Sicilian and Jewish gangsters with open arms. With the government tucked away in their back pocket, my father and his friends were given free rein to capitalize on Cuba's underworld. In the Centro section, they extorted the small business owners, and had their hands in everything from prostitution to gambling. On the infamous Zanja Street, my father claimed ownership of The Bamboo Lounge, and it was there that he met my mother. The two of them fell in love, and I was born a year later.

By 1950, under the tutelage of a man named Lucky, my father and his friends became extremely wealthy. In Old Havana, they owned The Hotel Nacional, and on La Rompa they owned The Hotel Lincoln and The Hotel Biltmore. These hotels were the most extravagant in all of Cuba. I haven't laid eyes on them in over sixty years, but I can vividly remember

9

their opulence as if it were yesterday. They stood tall and prominent like Spanish castles, and were flanked by tall palm trees and elaborate gardens. American movie stars and famous athletes would frequent these hotels, and on my tenth birthday, at The Hotel Biltmore, my father introduced me to my idol, Mr. Mickey Mantle.

Life was sweet back then. My mother was pregnant with my little sister, Angela, and my father built our family a small palace from the ground up. He would often travel back and forth between Cuba and America, but whenever he was home, he showered our family with love and affection.

By 1952, I was known throughout the streets of Havana as Ang's boy. My father used to always tell me I had the blood of a boss, and that one day I'd be the boss of Havana. In order to make his dreams for me a reality, him and his friends taught me everything there was to know about being a gangster. They taught me rackets of all kinds, and the numerous ways of making and taking money excited me. His underboss, Micheal Picatti, was like an uncle to me. He trained me in hand to hand combat, and spent endless hours teaching me how to operate firearms. On Saturday nights, they would take me to their legendary poker games, and it was there that I met some very important men. I refuse to mention any names, but I'm quite sure that you've read about them and seen the movies that depicted their lives.

Essentially, Cuba made my father a powerful man, but toward the end of 1953, things began to change. A man by the name of Fidel Castro and his brother, Raul, were on the brink of a revolution. They openly despised the Batista regime and the American gangsters who controlled Cuba's underworld. They made numerous attempts to overthrow the government, and in the process, they placed murder contracts on my father and his friends. As a precaution, my father packed up our family and flew us to America.

When our plane landed in Philadelphia, the first thing to grab my attention was the snow and the freezing weather. In Cuba, the weather was always hot, and to us, snow was nothing more than a prop in a Hollywood movie. But there we were, in the middle of a Philadelphia snowstorm, freezing our asses off with snow up to our ankles.

My Uncle Mikey picked us up from the airport in a black Lincoln Continental. He drove us to a small row home in South Philly, and my father told us that this was our new house. I remember feeling confused. In Cuba, we lived like royalty, and now we were standing in front of a row home that appeared to be smaller than our garage. My father handed my mother an envelope full of money, and then turned his back as if he didn't even know us. We didn't know it at the time, but on the other side of Broad Street, in Little Italy, he had a wife and a son. From that day forward, my life as Ang's boy was over, and in my new country I was just another nigger. A light skinned, curly head, blue eyed nigger.

Initially, it was hard for my family to adjust. In Cuba, my mother was a famous singer, but here in America she could hardly keep a job. My father was long gone and the only person who helped us out from time to time was Uncle Mikey. I just turned thirteen, and as the man of the house, I was forced to take action. My only problem was that my peers considered me an outcast. Aside from my light skin, curly hair, and blue eyes, I spoke with a Cuban accent and mostly kept to myself. My only friend was next door neighbor, Russell Fitzgerald, and together we dealt with the constant bullying of some neighborhood kids who called themselves The 20th and Carpenter Street Gang. There leader was this stocky brown *skinned kid named Ant Man, and with his gang always around to back him up, he treated me and Russell like shit.*

On my fifteenth birthday, my life changed forever. It was July 3rd, 1955, and my mother bought me a new bike to help me with my paper route. I took it for a spin around the neighborhood, and when I reached the corner of 20th and Carpenter, I ran smack dab into Ant Man and his gang. Without saying a word, Ant Man cracked me upside the head with an empty wine bottle, knocking me to the ground. He kicked me in the ribs, and then rode off on my new bike.

About an hour later, I was sitting on my front stoop when Uncle Mikey pulled up in front of my house in his Lincoln. He hopped out of the car and approached me. I was embarrassed to say the least. After all the time he spent preparing me for combat, I should've handled myself better. I could've easily broken Ant Man's face, but for some strange reason I was afraid.

He pointed at the two inch gash above my right eye. "Gervin, what happened?"

I lowered my head. "I was playing basketball, and this kid elbowed me by mistake," I lied.

Uncle Mikey shook his head in disbelief. "Come on, Gervin. What am I friggin' idot ova here?" he asked in his Sicilian accent. "Tell me what really happened. And pick up your head while you're at it. Didn't I teach you to always look a man in the eyes when you're talkin' to him?"

"Yes sir," I said while lifting my head to lock eyes with him.

"Alright, now tell me what happened."

"It was this kid from the neighborhood named Ant Man. He hit me with a wine bottle," I shamefully confessed.

Uncle Mikey's face turned bright red. He reached behind his back and pulled out a nickel plated .357 Magnum. He handed me the gun. "Gervin, whenever a man is violated by another man, the man who was violated must do everything in his power to make sure that the man who violated him never violates again." He looked at me like I was pitiful, and then returned to his Lincoln. As he started the engine and pulled off, I examined the pistol that was clutched in my right hand. I knew what I had to do to earn my respect. In order for me to get my point across, it had to be done in front of my entire neighborhood.

The next day was the 4th of July, and The 20th and Carpenter Street Gang was hosting their annual block party. I decided to make an appearance. Dressed in a black T-shirt, a pair of black shorts, and my tattered Chuck Taylors, I posted up by the record player. The smell of barbecued chicken was in the air, and the sounds of Chuck Berry had the intersection jam packed with people dancing. Ant Man was in the middle of the street doing The Freak with this girl from the Tasker Projects. I sized him up. He was six inches taller, and forty pounds heavier than me, but with a .357 tucked in the small of my back I felt like a giant. His gang was scattered throughout the block, but due to the festivities none of them noticed me. After watching Ant Man from a distance, I decided to make my move. I cut off the music, and everybody stopped dancing. They looked in my direction and pointed. Ant Man took the bate. He stormed toward me and pushed me in the chest.

He screwed up his face. "What the hell is you doin' at my block party chump? I ought to whup yo' ass!"

Everybody laughed at me, but I smiled at Ant Man. This was my moment. I was determined to make every one of them mutha'fuckas remember my name.

Ant Man looked at me like I was crazy. "What the hell is you smilin' for, chump? Oh I get it, you must want another bottle upside yo' mutha'fuckin' head!"

Before he had the chance to utter another word, I pulled the .357 with my right hand, and grabbed the front of his T-shirt with my left. I pulled him towards me and placed the barrel underneath his chin.

Boom!

His brains burst out the top of his head, and he crumbled to the ground. Loud screams permeated the area and everybody scattered including his gang. They didn't even stick around to see his body drop. Enraged, I kicked him in the face, and then fired a few more rounds into his chest.

Boom! Boom! Boom!

The barrel of the gun was smoking. My hands were trembling. My chest heaved up and down. His warm blood was on my face and T-shirt. I didn't care. I'd made my point. The stage was set.

Later that night I was arrested and charged with Ant Man's murder. I was ultimately convicted, and the judge sentenced me to juvenile life. I took it in stride. To me, prison was a conduit to something much greater. While serving my time, I built up my body and developed my mind. I was exposed to the philosophies and opinions of Marcus Garvey, intrigued by the war tactics on Tsung Tsu, and infatuated with the will and ambition of Genghis Khan. But most importantly, I learned the teachings of the Honorable Elijah Muhammad.

In July of 1961, I was finally released from prison. I was twenty one years old, and my dreams were as big as the sky. When I returned to my South Philly neighborhood, I quickly discovered that my old friend, Russell Fitzgerald, was running the show. Apparently, when I went to prison for murdering Ant Man, Russell received all of the benefits. The entire South Philly knew we were best friends, and they assumed that just like me, he wouldn't think twice about blowing a mutha'fuckas head off. It didn't take long for Russell to figure this out, and he used my new rep to enhance his street credibility. The first thing he did was take over Ant Man's gang. After extracting the strong from the weak, him and his new crew opened up a number's house, a whore house, and flooded the streets of South Philly with a new drug called heroin. I didn't mind that Russell had made his bones off of my rep because when I came home he did the right thing. He blessed me with a brand new Cadillac, and even purchased a new house for my mother and my little sister. He also stepped down as the gang's leader, and rightfully handed me the position.

In two years, with the grooming I received as a child, I elevated our game to the next level. From Broad Street to 31st Street, from Center City to Oregon Avenue, we robbed, extorted, kidnapped, and murdered. I literally gripped up the black section of South Philly, and in turn the streets named me Grip.

Our territories began to expand. Our leather jackets and Jeff caps turned into full length minks and wide brim Stetsons. Our Cadillacs and Lincolns turned into Mercedes Benzes and Rolls Royces. Our South Philly row homes turned into mansions. Our legacy in Black Philadelphia was solidified.

On the east side of Broad Street, The Gervino Crime Family began to hear stories about the niggers from Carpenter Street. Initially, they paid us no mind, but when a story about a light skinned nigger with curly hair and blue eyes reached my father he sent for me. It was January 10th, 1963, and I was relaxing at The Reynolds Wrap Lounge on 18th and South Street. Russell was at the bar talking to a broad, and I was sitting at my private table drinking a club soda. My Uncle Mikey and another man entered the bar. I noticed them immediately and waved them over to my table.

"Whoa!" Uncle Mikey smiled at me. "Look at you. All grown up and takin' care of business."

I stood to my feet and embraced him with a warm hug. "Longtime no see Uncle Mikey."

"Aww, fugget about it!" He continued smiling, and then gestured toward the man standing beside him. He was around my height, an even six feet. He had a rich olive complexion, wavy black hair, and cold dark eyes. His face was that of my father's and I immediately recognized him as my brother. "I want you to meet your younger brother Little Angolo."

I extended my right hand, but just Little Angolo stared at it. He scowled at me, and then fixed his eyes on Uncle Mikey. "You gotta be shittin' Mike. He's a friggin' moulie."

My face turned to stone and Uncle Mikey noticed my demeanor. He knew what I was capable of doing.

"No," Uncle Mikey quickly checked him. "He's your brother, and it's time for the two of you's to sit down and talk business."

Reluctantly, Little Angolo pulled out a chair and took a seat at my table. Uncle Mikey sat down beside him, and gestured for me to do the same.

As I took a seat on the other side of the table, Uncle Mikey said, "Gervin, your father's been hearing some very good things about you. He wants to know if there's anything he can do to assist you."

I looked at him skeptically, knowing exactly what him and my father were up to. They were attempting to shake me down. I told him, "Listen, Uncle Mikey, I know what's going on and I respect it. As you can see," I took a sip of my club soda, allowing the diamonds in my pinky ring to gleam in their faces, "I'm doing pretty good for myself. I've never been a stingy guy so I don't mind sharing with the Family. Especially if my Family's willing to share with me."

"Family?" Little Angolo snapped. "You're not a part of this fuckin' Family! You're a fuckin' moulie!"

His words cut like a knife. The same Sicilian blood that ran through his veins was the same blood that ran through mines. Here in America, he was Little Angolo, but back in Cuba, I was Ang's boy. We both had the same father so at the end of the day, what made me so different? I calmed myself down and looked at Uncle Mikey.

"Those are my terms. If my father wants a piece of my empire, then he has to acknowledge me as a member of his Family."

"Listen, Gervin, your father…"

"No," *Little Angolo interrupted him.* "I'm sick of this shit Mike! You ain't gotta explain nothin! Fuck this moulie!"

At that point I lost it. I completely blacked out. I reached across the table and grabbed my brother by his throat.
"Looka here you little bitch! You disrespect me one more time and I swear to God, I'll seperate your soul from your fuckin' body!"

He struggled to get free, but my strength overwhelmed him. Uncle Mikey jumped to his feet and removed the pistol from his shoulder holster.

He aimed the barrel at my face. "Gervin, let him go!"

"What?" *I squeezed tighter and Little Angolo's face turned a pale blue.* "You heard the way this mutha'fucka was disrespecting me!"

"Gervin, I'm not fuckin' around. Let him go!"

Just as I was about to release my grasp, I looked around Uncle Mikey and saw Russell creeping toward him with a black .9mm clutched in his left hand. He stepped to Uncle Mikey and placed the barrel to the side of his face.

"Honkey, I'll blow yo' fuckin' brains out. You know good and goddamn well that mafia shit don't fly around here. Y'all better take that shit back across Broad Street."

Uncle Mikey trembled with rage. He lowered his pistol and scowled at me. "You's fucked up Gervin. You's fucked up bad."

"Shut the fuck up and lay the gun the gun on the fuckin' table!" I shouted at him. He looked at me with a pure hatred, but followed my orders nonetheless. I released my left hand from Little Angolo's throat and grabbed the pistol off of the table. I looked at Russell who still holding his gun to Uncle Mikey's face. In a calm, steady voice, I said, "Kill this mutha'fucka."

Russell smiled at me, and then squeezed the trigger.

Boc!

The bullet struck Uncle Mikey just below his right ear. He stumbled to his left and felt the wound with his right hand. He looked at me with a shocked expression, and then lunged toward me. I raised his pistol and fired.

Pow! Pow!

Two penny sized holes appeared on his forehead, and he dropped to the floor. I snatched Little Angolo out of his seat and placed the smoking hot barrel to his left cheek.

I said, "I want you to tell that father of yours, I said fuck his Family! I've got my own Family! The Moreno Family!"

Prologue

Fifty-One Years Later...

A white Mercedes Maybach was double parked outside of the Philadelphia International Airport. The hazard lights were blinking, and Muhammad was sitting behind the stirring wheel, anxiously awaitng Grip's arrival. He glanced at his Cartier watch and the platinum timepiece read 4:09 p.m. He knew that Grip's layover flight from Cuba to Miami was scheduled to land at 4:00p.m., so he was expecting his boss at any moment. He rolled down the 60" plasma that served as a partition, and looked into the back seat. Everything was set up just the way the boss liked it. A fresh box of Cohiba cigars were positioned on top of the center console, the mini refrigerator was neatly stocked with cranberry juice, and the sounds of Curtis Mayfield was drifting through the speakers.

"Yep," he said to himself. "Just the way he likes it."

He settled back in the driver's seat, and then looked out the window just in time to see Grip emerging from the airport's revolving glass door. A year and a half had passed since the don of *The Moreno Family* was forced to leave the country. But now he was back.with a vengeance!

Askari

Chapter One

November 23, 2014

The warm autumn rain had just finished falling and for the first time that day, Sonny rolled down the bulletproof windows on his Rolls Royce Ghost. He was at the *Ivy Hill Cemetery* in Uptown Philly, and after twenty months of procrastinating, he finally had the nerve to pay Riri a visit.

As he drove through the cemetery's winding roads, he nodded his head to the sounds of Aaron Hall's, *I Miss You*, and took slow pulls on his neatly rolled Backwood. When he finally reached the plot of land that held the remains of his first love, he grabbed the white long stemmed roses from his French vanilla passenger's seat, killed the ignition, and then climbed out the cherry red sedan.

After sidestepping a number of graves, he finally approached hers. A two foot high, pink marble headstone that was carved into the image of an angel. As he laid the roses against the base of her headstone, the sun fought its way through the clouds, giving him a comforting feeling. He knew that she was up in heaven smiling down on him. He could feel it. He looked up at the sky, and then returned his gaze to her headstone.

"What's poppin' ma? I know you're probably mad at me," he said with tears in his eyes. "I know I'm outta pocket for takin' so long to visit you, but a nigga just needed some time to get his mind right."

The pain in his heart began to overwhelm him, so to keep from breaking down, he thought about the one person who always managed to put a smile on his face. "Yo, you know I'm a daddy now, right? Yep," he nodded his head. "Me and my fiancé had a little girl, and we named her Keyonti Nikkia

Moreno. She just turned one, and she's the prettiest thing in the world," he continued, and then smiled at the thought of his little princess.

"I finally took your advice about going legit. Well at least I'm partially legit," he corrected himself. "Last year, with the help of my fiancé's real estate firm, I bought a nightclub and a sports bar. I named the nightclub, *Club Infamous*, and the sports bar, *Donkees*. So far, they've made over $700,000 in profits, and from the way it's lookin', they'll fuck around and do even better this upcoming year."

He reached inside of his Gucci cargos and retrieved a neatly spun Backwood and his solid gold lighter. He placed the spliff in his mouth, sparked it up, and took a deep pull. After inhaling and exhaling a thick cloud of Kush smoke, he continued their one sided conversation.

"Oh yeah, I saw ya mom the other day, and she snapped on a nigga something crazy," he said while slowly shaking his head from side to side. "She called me a coward and said I was less than a man because I failed to protect my family. I ain't gon' hold you Ri 'cause ya moms had me mad as shit. I couldn't really knock her though," he shrugged his shoulders and lowered his head. "It was my responsibility to protect you and the baby, and I fucked up," he shamefully admitted, and then broke down crying.

After regaining his composure, he took another pull on his Backwood, and continued talking. "But on a more positive note, everybody's good. My mom just opened up a hair salon on Broad and Montgomery, and her and my pops had their wedding vows renewed last month.

"Breeze and Erika are doin' good. They just had a lil' boy about three months ago, and they're supposed to be gettin' married in a couple of months.

"Sheed's locked up, but he should be home in a couple of weeks. Yo, you remember my young buls, the twins, Egypt and Zaire? Well, them lil' niggas is doin' they thing. They tearin' up the city in twin Panameras and fuckin' everything movin'."

He took another pull on his Backwood and continued talking as if she could hear him from her grave. "As for myself, I just bought a 10,000 square foot mansion in Montgomery County. It's got eight bedrooms and six bathrooms. A swimming pool with a built in Jacuzzi, a basketball court, a tennis court, an ATV track, and a six foot high stonewall that surrounds the perimeter of my property line. Actually, it's the same exact mansion that my pops bought us back in the day. He told me that he spent about $1,800,000 on that jawn back in '92, but my fiancé's real estate firm purchased it for $1,300,000.

"Yeah, I know what you thinkin'," he smiled. "Ya boy been gettin' at a dollar right? Well, yeah I'm sittin' on close to $6,000,000, but don't tell nobody." He chuckled and held his index finger up to his lips. "Ssh!"

He took one more pull on his Backwood, and then tossed it to the ground. "Well I love you lil' mama, and that's somethin' that'll never change. Oh yeah, and before I go, I need you to holla at God for me. In the words of my nigga Pac, *Tell Him I was a G, did the best I could, raised in insanity.* Once again, I love you Riri, and I miss you like a mutha'fucka." He kissed the top of her headstone, and then headed back to his Rolls Royce.

***

It was *Club Infamous'* first annual Retro Eighties Party, and the intersection of Broad and Erie resembled the *Gotham Nightclub* during Philadelphia's *YBM* era. Hustlers from all over the city were pulling up in the latest luxury vehicles and hopping out wearing all types of fashions from the late eighties. They had Cazel glasses, gold rope chains, four finger rings, and wore customized Dapper Dan sweat suits.

Flocks of women were standing in front of the entrance, and just like the men, they too sported fashions from the late eighties like spandex body suits, leather 8 Ball jackets, small rope chains, bamboo earrings, and anti-symmetrical hairstyles.

It was 10:00 p.m. when Sonny pulled up in front of the club in a customized '88 Mercedes Benz SL 500. The top was down and the sounds of Special Ed's, *I Got It Made*, was thumping from his Alpine system.

I'm your idol/ The highest title/ Numero uno/ I'm not a Puerto Rican, but I speak it so dat chu know.

His strawberry red BBS rims matched the car's paint job to perfection, and his white leather seats were covered in red Gucci print. The presence of the throwback Benz, coupled with the trunk rattling sounds of Special Ed's legendary baseline, made him the center of attention. *I'ma fuck 'em up wit'* this one, he thought to himself as he pulled out an old school Motorola flip phone and called Breeze, who was already inside of the club.

Ring! Ring! Ring!

"What's poppin', bro? I just pulled up. What's goin' on in there?"

"Yo, I can't hear you, Blood!" Breeze shouted through the phone. "The music's too loud! I'ma slide to the bathroom, and hopefully I can hear you better!" He stepped inside of the men's room, and resumed their conversation. "A'ight, now what was you sayin'?"

"I asked you what was goin' on in there?"

"Awww man, it's so many bitches in here that it don't make no mutha'fuckin' sense," Breeze bragged, and then took a swig from his bottle of Spades.

"Is everybody here?" asked Sonny.

"Yeah we all here. The twins is in here stuntin' as usual, and the last time I saw Uncle Easy he was on the dance floor wit' a crowd of bitches around him."

"A'ight," Sonny nodded his head. "But what about security, Mello got them niggas on point?"

"Without a doubt," Breeze confirmed. "You know that nigga on point."

"More or less, but dig though, I need you to get everybody together, and meet me in the Block Boy Room in like ten minutes."

Before Breeze could respond, a short, thick, brown skinned chick that reminded him of Remy Ma entered the men's room. She was dressed in a black body suit and a pair of black Reebok pumps.

"Aye yo, this the men's room, ma. The ladies room is next door," he informed her.

She looked him up and down, admiring his Louis Vuitton sweat suit and the bulge in his crotch. "Humph, my bad," she said as she turned around to leave. He noticed her thick juicy ass, and he gently grabbed her by the arm. "Damn sweetheart, where you goin'? You ain't gotta go nowhere."

She turned her head to face him, and the look in her eyes said it all. She was tipsy and trying to get her freak on. She led him to the last toilet stall and pulled him inside. She then, dropped to her knees, pulled his sweat pants down to his thighs, and started sucking him off.

"Hey yo Breeze, who you talkin' to Blood?" Sonny asked, oblivious to the events that were taking place inside of the men's room.

"Nah Blood, I was just talkin' to this lil'..."

Sonny pulled the phone away from his ear, and looked at it with a baffled expression. He held the box shaped phone back to his ear. "Yo Breeze, what the fuck are you doin'?"

"Yo, this lil' bitch got my dick in her, ohhh shit! Y—Y—Yo, I can't talk right now. Holla at me when you come inside," he laughed, and then disconnected the call.

Sonny chuckled and shook his head from side to side. "I don't believe this nigga just banged on me."

He killed the engine and then hopped out the car. If the people standing outside of *Club Infamous* thought that he was hurting them with the throwback Benz, then his clothes and jewelry was sure to be a head shot. His red Gucci valor was hands down the hottest in the vicinity. On his jacket, the chest, shoulders, and elbows were covered in white leather with red Gucci print, and the white leather strips that ran down the sides of his pants had the same. His white on white Nike Cortez's were fresh out the box, and his jewelry was like a crack house, nothing but rocks! His 35" platinum chain was smothered in white diamonds and his customized *BBE* charm was littered with VS1s and red rubies. The iced out four finger ring on his right hand spelled *Coke* and the matching ring on his left hand spelled *Money*. An iced out bracelet was wrapped around his right wrist, and a diamond bezzled, big face Rollie decorated his left.

When he strolled through the club's entrance, he smiled at the sight of his jam packed dance floor. Everyone seemed to be having a good time. The bartenders were serving drinks nonstop, and every hustler in the building had their hands wrapped around a $500 bottle of champagne. He glanced up at the elevated stage where Peedi Crakk was performing his remake of DJ Jazzy Jeff and The Fresh Prince's, *Brand New Funk*. Schooly D was directly behind him. He was tearing up the ones and twos, and the crowd of hip hop lovers were going crazy.

As Sonny headed toward the back of the club where a staircase led to the second floor, he spotted Meek Mill lounging in the V.I.P. area. He was accompanied by three beautiful women, and two two bodyguards. A case of champagne was sitting on his table, and he was thumbing through a stack of hundred dollar bills. He acknowledged Meek with a head nod, and then approached Rahmello, who was guarding the double doors that led to the staircase.

"What's poppin', brozay? You good?"

"Yeah, I'm good," Rahmello assured him as he embraced him with a brotherly hug.

As Sonny walked through the double doors and headed up the stairs, Rahmello sparked up a Backwood and thought about the night that he first met his older brother.

February 10th, 2013

He was sitting in his bedroom, bagging up a pound of weed when his mother shouted his name from the bottom of the stairs, "Rahmello!"

"What?" he shouted back.

"Boy, don't you be whatin' me! Now bring ya ass down these goddamned stairs!"

"Damn man, she always fuckin' naggin," he complained.

He laid down the scissors he was using to chop up the buds, and then stashed the aluminum turkey pan full of weed underneath his bed.

When he came downstairs and entered the living room, he was surprised to see the man that he'd just robbed sitting on his mother's couch. A smug expression was written on the man's face, and a black book bag was clutched in his hands.

27

"Dizzamn, this pussy caught me slippin'," he said to himself. He spun around and attempted to run up the stairs, but his mother gripped the back of his shirt collar and pulled him toward her.

"Ahn ahn, ya lil' ass ain't gettin' off the hook that easy."

"Come on mom! What the fuck is you doin'?" he snapped at her. "You try'na get me killed!"

She released his shirt and looked at him as if he was crazy. "Do you even know who this is?" she asked while pointing at Sonny.

"Naw, I never seen this nigga a day in my life."

Sonny got up from the couch and approached him. "Oh, so I guess you ain't rob me then either?"

Frustrated, Rahmello shook his head. "A'ight man fuck it," he shrugged his shoulders. "Yeah, I robbed you, but you ain't gettin' none of ya shit back."

Sonny screwed up his face. "Nigga, I ain't come over here for no chump change and some punk ass jewelry." He threw him the book bag. "I came over here to give you the $100,000 that was stashed in my trunk. If you was really 'bout ya work you woulda took that too."

Rahmello was confused. He looked inside of the book bag, and just like Sonny said, it was filled with money. "I don't get it. I jammed you and smacked you upside the head with my burner, but now you givin' me all this money. Why?"

Sonny smiled at him. "Because you're my lil' brother, that's why."

"Ya lil' brother?" Rahmello echoed, and then looked at his mother for clarification.

"Yeah it's true," she nodded her head in the affirmative. "This is Sontino, your dad's first son."

Still confused, he returned his gaze to Sonny.

"Well, if you're really my brother, how come I never seen you before?"

"It's a long story," Sonny replied while cracking his knuckles. "All I know is that my pops was outta my life since I was seven years old, and it wasn't until last year that we reconnected. That's when he told me about you and our sister Nahfisah.

"I ain't sure whether you know it or not, but back in the day our pops was a major nigga. Somehow he got hooked on crack and my mom cut the nigga off. After that, he hooked up wit' ya mom and they had you. I'm assuming he was puttin' y'all through the same shit he was puttin' me and my mom through, and ya mom cut his ass off too."

"Damn," Rahmello shook his head from side to side. "That's some deep ass shit. I can't even front, now that I'm lookin' at you, we definitely look alike."

Sonny nodded his head. "And that's why I was lookin' at you like that when you was robbin' me. I knew you was my brother. Matter of fact, I came around here looking for you a couple weeks ago, but ya mom said that she ain't seen you in like a month."

"Damn dawg, I never even knew I had a brother. Let alone a sister," Rahmello replied in a somber voice. "And speakin' of our sister, where she at? Why ain't she come over here wit' you?"

Sonny took a deep breath and flexed his jaw muscles.

"Man, I ain't seen Nahfisah and our niece, Imani in over six months."

Rahmello thought about Easy. "Damn yo, I don't even know my pop. I ain't seen that nigga since the first grade."

Sonny embraced him with a brotherly hug. "Trust me, I know the feeling lil' bro. I went through the same exact shit, *but everything's different now." He released his embrace and straightened out the wrinkles in Rahmello's shirt.*

Rahmello looked at his mom, and then reverted his gaze back to Sonny. "I'm sayin' though, now that I know you're my brother," he shrugged his shoulders, "where we 'posed to go from here?"

Sonny smiled at him. "Let's just say that you ain't gotta rob niggas no more. Especially a nigga like me." He looked him square in the eyes to convey the seriousness of his next statement. "If you was anybody else I woulda downed you!"

Rahmello smirked at him. "Yeah right! I had the drop on ya ass!"

"Yeah, you definitely caught me slippin'," Sonny admitted. "But at the same time, ya lil' ass ain't have no bullets in ya gun!"

"Damn," Rahmello chuckled. "How the fuck you knew that?"

"Because you had a revolver, and when I looked down the barrel, I could see the empty chambers in the cylinder."

He reached behind his back and pulled out a black Desert Eagle with an extended clip. "Now, if you woulda had some shit like this," he smiled at his younger brother, "it mighta been a different story!"

From that day forward, Sonny bridged the gap between him and his younger brother. He reconnected him with Easy, and the three of them established a bond that would last forever. Easy gave him his loft apartment in Center City, and Sonny bought him a brand new Aston Martin. He also made his younger brother an official Block Boy and appointed him as the second in command.

Back To November 23rd, 2014

After reminiscing about the night that he met his big brother, he stubbed out his Backwood and continued looking around the club for any signs of a disturbance.

***

The Block Boy Room was a V.I.P. area on the second floor. It was strictly designated for Sonny and his crew, no exceptions. The cherry red walls were sound proof, affording them the luxury of being inside of a nightclub, while at the same time, feeling as though they were in their own world. A black leather sectional was positioned in the far corner of the room and directly in front of it, there was a 60 inch flat screen, a Bose sound system, and an XBox One. A small, customized bar was positioned in the opposite corner, and a regulation sized pool table was positioned in the center of the room. The best feature, however, was the picturesque glass front window that provided a bird's eye view of the entire club.

When Sonny walked through the door, he spotted Easy, Breeze, and the twins sitting on the sectional. The television was showing the last season of *The Wire*, and the four men were hunched over the coffee table, counting and wrapping rubber bands around large bricks of money.

"Soowoo," Sonny stated, announcing his presence.

"*Bang! Bang!*" Everybody replied, except for Easy.

Easy was an old school Philly nigga, and to him the concept of gang banging held no relevance. Sonny looked at him and smiled. "What's up pops? How much money did we make tonight?"

"About $42,000," Easy replied. "And that's just the money from the champagne. By the end of the night, we should see about $7,000 from the liquor, and another $5,000 from the door."

"That sounds about right," Sonny said as headed toward the picturesque window. He looked down at that crowded dance floor, and a euphoric smile spread across his face. Despite the fact that he'd lost so much at the hands of the game, at the age of twenty five, he was the undisputed *King of Philadelphia.* After running Grip out of the country and inheriting Mook's empire, Easy plugged him in with Columbian Poncho, and the rest was history. Just like his former boss, he had the best quality of cocaine and the best prices. The dope boys loved him. From Philly to Virginia, whether directly or indirectly, a vast majority of the hustlers became Block Boy's clientele. Not only did they appreciate him for getting rid of Grip, they relished the fact that he only charged them $35,000 a brick when he could've easily charged them anywhere between $40,000 to $45,000. He left the window and walked toward the bar. "Y'all want somethin' to sip on?"

"Naw we good," they replied in unison.

He went behind the bar and grabbed a bottle of Deleon Tequila from the liquor shelf. After pouring himself a double shot, he took a sip and then sat down beside Easy on the sectional. "Yo Zai, hand me the remote to the television."

Zaire handed over the remote control, and Sonny pressed the *pause* button.

"Yooooo!" Easy exclaimed. "The young bul was just about to kill Omar's faggot ass, and here you come with the bullshit!"

Sonny ignored him and took another sip of his Tequila. "Yo, y'all know Sheed went to court yesterday right?"

"Yeah we know," they replied in unison.

"Aight," Sonny continued. "Well, I holla'd at Savino this morning and he told me that Sheed should be home in a couple of weeks. They had a suppression hearing and the judge threw his case out. He ruled that the initial traffic stop was illegal, and as a result, he suppressed the gun and the work that they found in Sheed's Benz."

"Now, that's *gangsta!*" Zaire smiled and hopped up from the sectional. "It's about time Savino spanked somethin'! Other than beatin' the case that you caught at the hospital when you popped off on the cops, this nigga ain't been doin' nothin' but collectin' money every month and that's for cases that we ain't even catch yet."

"Yeah, that's definitely a good look," Egypt concurred. "But if the homie spanked his case, why the fuck is he still locked up?"

"He's gotta wait until he sees the parole board," Sonny informed him. "Aside from the case he just beat, he was still serving 23 months for a gun case he caught back in 2012. He already served 20 months, so Savino gon' get him time served with   3 months of unsupervised probation."

"Damn, Blood, that's good fuckin' money," said Breeze. "I hope these couple of weeks fly by because the faster this nigga come home, the faster we can stop dealin' wit' Pooky's grimy ass."

At the mention of Pooky, Easy gritted his teeth and folded his arms across his chest. Just like the rest of the men in the room, he'd been hearing stories about Pooky doing everything from beating up crackheads to selling his customers watered down work. Basically, he was a bad reflection on their organization, and Easy wanted nothing to do with him. "Hey Sonny, that nigga Pooky's bad money. He's hot headed and he's stupid. He's arrogant and most of all, he's a pain in my mutha'fuckin' ass," Easy stated, using his fingers to count off the numerous ways that Pooky made him uncomfortable.

Pooky was Sheed's older brother, and after being released from prison a few months ago, Sheed suggested that he take over his part of their operation. Sonny agreed and started hitting him off with bricks. Initially, Pooky was playing his part. He had a direct line to Sheed's clientele, and in less than two weeks, he was turning over bricks like cartwheels. Everything was going smooth, but for the past couple of weeks, he'd been nothing less than a fuck up. For instance, just earlier that day somebody complained to Sonny about Pooky selling them some fucked up work. According to the customer, he purchased a kilogram of coke and after cooking up the work, he only recouped 900 grams. Upon hearing this, Sonny decided that Pooky had to be stretching his work. This was something that he strictly forbade. He made it very clear to everyone at his roundtable that his product was not to be tampered with in any way shape or form. His work was 75% pure, so if a customer purchased a kilogram and loss 108 grams in the cooking process, then something wasn't right.

After listening to Easy express his concerns for the thousandth time, Sonny said, "Listen pops, I understand where you're comin' from and all dat, but at the end of the day that's Sheed's brother. So if Sheed wants him to hold down his side of the family until he comes home, then the only thing I can do is respect his wishes."

"I'm tellin' you, Sontino, that's a bad move," Easy continued his protest. "The whole city knows this nigga be fuckin' wit' us. So therefore, every time this mutha'fucka tries to pull off some nut shit, it's a bad reflection on the whole family." He took a deep breath and massaged his temples. "At the very least, you need to holla at Sheed and tell him to talk some sense into his brother. We've worked too hard and came too far. I'll be damned if I let him or anybody else fuck up this movement."

34

Sonny glanced around the room and from the looks on everyone's face, he could see that they harbored the same exact feelings. He grabbed his glass of tequila from the coffee table, and then stood to his feet. "Don't worry about Pooky," he assured them. "I'ma talk to this nigga myself, and I'ma give him two options. Either fall back and play the game how it's 'posed to be played, or sit his ass on the fuckin' bench. It's as simple as that."

As he headed toward the door, Easy asked him, "So what about the turkey giveaway? Are you comin' or do you want us to handle it?"

"Yeah I'ma be there," Sonny replied while opening the door. "I've got *Power 99* comin' through, and we gon' do it real big."

He looked at the diamond bezel on his Rolex, and then pointed at the stacks of money on the coffee table. "Make sure that you collect all of the money from the party and take it to the bank first thing in the mornin'. Don't forget to holla at Suelyn. She needs to know exactly how much money we made so she can add it to the ledger."

Easy nodded his head. "Don't worry 'bout it baby boy, I gotchu."

Askari

Chapter Two

It was a little pass 2 a.m. when Sonny returned to his Upper Dublin estate. As he drove through the security gate and up the horseshoe driveway, an eerie feeling washed over him. For some strange reason, he had the notion that somebody was watching him. Even worse, he felt that somebody was watching his family. He parked behind Daphney's Mercedes Benz G63, and then killed the ignition. After taking a few seconds to peep his surroundings, he reached under the driver's seat and pulled out his FNH handgun. He cocked back the hammer and cautiously climbed out the car.

With the .45 cocked and ready to fire, he spent the next hour or so meticulously searching the premises. He didn't find anything, but yet and still, his intuition remained. Somebody was watching him, but who could it be? As far as he knew, outside of his immediate family, nobody knew where he lived, not even his homies. So who was watching him? Could it be Grip? Maybe, but that was highly unlikely. Nobody had seen or heard from him since the day he left the briefcase full of money at the warehouse. Could it be the feds? Possibly, after the fall of Ace Kapone and Big Meech, he knew they could be gunning for him next. Could it be a hater trying to stick him for his bread? Doubtful, but at the same time, he remembered what Jay Z said in his smash hit, *The Streets Is Watching,*

Kidnap niggas wanna steal ya/ Broke niggas don't want no cash, they just wanna kill ya/ For the name/ Niggas don't know the rules/ Disrespecting the game/ Want you to blow cool/ Force ya hand, of course that man's plottin'/ Smartin' up nigga, the streets is watchin'.

After all of these questions and scenarios ran through his mind, he searched the premises once more, and then entered the house through the back door. As he stepped into the kitchen, he was immediately greeted by Rocko, his 120 pound Rottweiler. This was a clear indicator that no intruders were inside the house. Had that been the case, then either Rocko would have been dead, or his black and brown fur would have been covered in the intruder's blood.

Still acting off intuition, he tightened his grasp around the handle of the FNH .45, and began searching the house.

After thoroughly inspecting the basement and the entire first floor, he crept up the right side of his dual staircase and continued his search. His first stop was his daughter's room, the same exact room that belonged to him as a child. When he stepped through the cracked door, the first thing to grab his attention was the aroma of Baby Magic lotion. Cautiously, he glanced around the room, and then settled his eyes on his daughter. The sight of his baby girl sound asleep with her left thumb stuffed in her mouth, made his heart melt. She was beyond beautiful. Aside from inheriting the blues eyes that ran in his family, she was the spitting image of Daphney. As he approached her bed with Rocko trailing closely behind, he silently thanked God for the birth of his little princess, and then gently smothered her chocolate face with kisses.

After leaving her room, he crept across the hallway and headed toward the bedroom door of her six year old brother, Dayshon. He slipped inside of the room and saw that the little boy was bundled up under his Transformer blanket. Dayshon was Daphney's son from a previous relationship, but that didn't stop Sonny from loving him as if he were his very own. He approached the full sized bed, and gently kissed his little man on the forehead. He remembered a conversation that he had with Daphney earlier that day when she informed him about Day Day losing another baby tooth, so he reached inside of his Gucci sweats and pulled out a thick wad of hundred dollar bills. After peeling away two of them, he reached underneath the little boy's pillow, and swapped the money with his tooth.

Finally, his nerves were at ease. He holstered the FNH, and then headed down the hallway toward the master bedroom. After a long stress filled day, he was more than ready to spend some quality time with his queen. He opened the bedroom door, and the sight of her lying on their black and gold Versace bed set in nothing but her chocolate birthday suit, made his dick rock hard. Her thick thighs were slightly spread apart, giving him a sneak peak of her Brazilian waxed pussy. The light from the moon was beaming through the balcony's glass door, illuminating her chocolate skin, and all he could do was shake his head from side to side. *Damn, I love this lil' mutha'fucka,* he thought to himself as he admired her natural African beauty.

After taking off his Gucci valor, he climbed on top of the bed and placed soft kisses on her left foot. He then, slid the tip of his tongue along the length of her leg.

"*Ummm!*" she moaned in ecstasy. "Daddy, watchu doin'?"

"Whatchu think?" he softly replied, and then buried his tongue inside of her juice box.

***

Up The Block From Sonny's Estate

A pearl white Mercedes Benz Maybach 62 was parked along the side of the road. The headlights were turned off, but the engine was running. In the back seat, relaxing behind a curtained window, Grip was sipping on a glass of Grand Marnier and nodding his head to The Isley Brothers. After spending the past year and a half in Cuba, he was back with a vengeance. It was time for old scores to be settled, and this time around he would show no mercy. He rolled down the partition and locked eyes with Muhammad in the rearview mirror. Nothing needed to be said. He tapped the brim on his Bossalini, and his trusty driver pulled away from the curb.

"Where to Mr. Moreno?"

"South Philly," Grip instructed. "We need to visit an old friend."

***

At An Undisclosed Location In South Philly

Carmine Gervino, the new boss of *The Gervino Crime Family*, was seated at the head of his dinner table. His underboss, Alphonso Picatti, was seated at the other end of the table, and six of his capos were seated in between. After fifty two years of bad blood and hostility, Carmine had managed to do what his grandfather and uncle couldn't. He crippled their enemy. At the young age of thirty three he was sharper than most, but to the older members of his *Family*, he had much to prove. Despite taking an oath of loyalty to his grandfather, Angolo *Little Angolo* Gervino, these old school gangsters resented the fact that Carmine was the new boss. They couldn't have cared less about his bloodline. To them, he was nothing more than a snot nosed pretty boy and they openly despised Angolo for handing him the position.

Carmine stood to his feet and looked around the table with a weird smile on his face. His black hair was slicked back, and his cold dark eyes were tucked behind his gold Versace frames. He knew that some of the older members of his *Family* were waiting for him to fail and that a few of them even wanted his spot. Tonight, however, their felonious aspirations would prove to be detrimental.

"So this is the thing," he addressed them in his thick Sicilian accent. He grabbed the bottle of champagne that was sitting in front of him, and held it up with his right hand as he continued speaking. "I wanna propose a toast to me and the new generation of this *Family*."

His capos looked at one another with smug expressions. Once again, their so called, *Boss*, was getting beside himself.

"Awww, come on guys," Carmine chuckled. "Why the funny faces?" He glanced at his Audemars Piguet. "In about six hours, a 38 count indictment is comin' down, and the moulinyan that you old fucks couldn't control is finally gettin' his just due."

Luca Andolini, his sixty two year old capo from South Jersey was livid. His over tanned face became bright red and he couldn't control his tongue. "The nerve of this fuckin' kid," he said to Junior Dillagio, the sixty year old capo of the 6th Street crew.

Junior shook his head in contempt, and then looked up at Carmine. "What's da matter wit' you? This was supposed to be celebration ova here. Where's your friggin' manners?"

"That's right Junior. You tell him," Tony Bruno, the capo of the 27th and Morris Street crew encouraged him.

Carmine took a swig of his champagne, and then slowly walked around the table. When he approached Luca, he stopped walking and stood directly behind him. He placed his left hand on the old man's shoulder, and then looked around the room. "You know what gentlemen, it's time for a moment of truth." He swung the champagne bottle and cracked Luca on the right side of his head.

Crash!

The bottom of the bottle shattered to pieces and Luca's face slammed into the table.

"Carmine!" Tony Clemetti, his capo from Camden, New Jersey shouted as he hopped up from the table. "What the hell are you doin'?"

"Shut the fuck up!" Carmine snapped. "You shut the fuck up and you watch!"

He banged Luca's face into the table, and repeatedly stabbed him in the neck with the rigid edge of the broken bottle.

"Carmine, that's enough!" Junior bellowed. "You're gonna friggin' kill him!"

Carmine smirked at him, and then stabbed the old man once more, burying the broken bottle deep in his neck. Luca slid from his chair and fell to the floor. As he rolled around in pain, Alphonso stood to his feet and removed the black .10 millimeter that was tucked in the small of his back. He aimed the large barrel at Junior's face and squeezed the trigger.

Pow!

The bullet ripped through the old man's forehead and a bloody mist erupted from the back of his skull. He rocked backwards, and then slumped forward before melting to the floor.

Carmine looked at his remaining four capos, wishing that one of them would make a move. His chest heaved up and down, and his nostrils flared like a bull. "You's thought I wouldn't find out about this shit? Thought you's could go behind my back complainin' to my fuckin' grandfather? Well, here's a fuckin' news flash!" He reached inside of his suit jacket and removed the Colt .45 that was nestled in the small of his back. He looked down at Luca, who was still rolling around in pain. He aimed the nickel plated beauty at the old man's face and fired.

Boca! Boca! Boca! Boca!

"If I ever—"

Boca!

"Hear some shit like this again—"

Boca! Boca!

"I'll kill every last one of you motherfuckers!"

Boca! Boca! Boca! Boca!

"You's got that?"

Terrified, the four old men looked at him with pleading eyes, but neither one of them said a word.

"Good," Carmine continued in a calm voice. "Now, clean this shit up."

Askari

Chapter Three

For the past twenty months, former Detective Adam Smith enjoyed the fact that he avoided prosecution for attempted murder and police corruption. The only thing that rubbed him the wrong way was that his downfall came at the hands of his own partner. He often thought of the night that he gunned down Sheed on the corner of 5th and Cumberland. Although it was nearly two years ago, the look of confusion that covered the young man's face, still gave him an intoxicating feeling. He could still smell the gunpowder that hung in the air, and he vividly remembered the thoughts that ran through his mind at that very moment. His first thought was to shoot him in between the eyes, his second thought was to make a clean get away, and the third thought was wrapped around the money that Grip would pay him for eliminating one of his problems. Unfortunately, things didn't go as he anticipated. As he hovered over Sheed, preparing to separate his soul from his body, he was blindsided by his own partner. After being shot in the leg and placed under arrest, he sold his soul to the devil and the price was cheap.

As a result of being on Grip's payroll for the past twenty years, he had more than enough information to put the old gangster behind bars for the rest of his life. He provided a signed statement that covered everything from tax evasion to murder. As a result, he was given immunity, with the condition that he testify before a federal grand jury. An hour ago, he received a phone call from U.S. Attorney, Andy Clavenski.

According to Clavenski, his case against Grip and *The Moreno Crime Family* was going before the grand jury in the morning, and his testimony was needed.

As he prepared to take a shower and get ready for bed, the incessant barking of his German Shepherd deterred his plans. Irritated, he stuck his head out the bedroom window, and shouted at the large K9.

"Goddamnit Wolfy! Wouldja knock it off!"

Roof! Roof! Roof!

"You're not comin' in the house, so don't even think about it! Now, shut the hell up, and go to sleep!"

Roof! Roof! Roof! Roof!

"Wolfy, I swear to Christ if you make me come down there I'm gonna kick the shit outta ya! Now, knock it off!"

Roof! Roof! Roof!

"Alright!" he continued his rant, and then threw on his bathrobe and a pair of house shoes. "You asked for it!"

He ran down the stairs and darted out the back door, only to find that Wolfy was still barking.

"Goddamnit Wolfy! Just what in the hell are you barking at?" he questioned, realizing that the dog was desperately trying to break his leash and get to the shed on the other side of the yard. Smitty looked at the shed, but the only thing he saw was a stray cat running away at top speed. He returned his gaze to the large German Shepherd.

"You've gotta be shittin' me! All of this fuss over a friggin' cat?" He shook his head from side to side, and then burst out laughing. "I swear to Christ, if you weren't the only family that I had left, I'd chop you to pieces, and sell you to a Korean restaurant." He patted Wolfy on the head and smiled at him. "Now, settle down and go to sleep. I've got a long day ahead of me."

As he turned around and headed toward the house, the bone chilling sound of Wolfy shrieking in pain stopped him in his tracks.

Urn!

He spun around and couldn't believe his eyes. Wolfy was laying on his side and a Bowie knife was protruding from his neck. On instinct, he reached for the .38 that usually occupied his waist, only to discover that the gun wasn't there.

"Goddamnit!" He cursed himself for leaving the house without his pistol. A mountain of fear permeated his heart, and his body began to shiver. "W—W—Who's there?" He stuttered while frantically looking around the back yard. "I—I—I'm a cop, and I'll lock your ass up!"

A dark figure emerged from behind the shed and slowly walked toward him. Whoever it was, they were dressed in all black, and their face was covered with a ski mask.

"Y—Y—You stay right there, and don't take another step!" He turned around, attempting to run, but a Louisville Slugger crashed into the side of his head.

Whack!

He stumbled backwards and another blow landed across his back.

Whack!

He fell to the ground and curled up in a ball. Another blow crashed into the back of his head and everything went black.

Approximately fifteen minutes later, he was awakened by the warm sensation of a tongue massaging his dick. He looked in between his thighs, and was surprised to see a beautiful Spanish woman going up and down on his shaft. He tried to push her away, but he couldn't move. His naked body was strapped to his dining room chair, and his hands were tied behind his back. He his head was throbbing and warm blood trickled down the right side of his face.

"W—W—What the hell is going on? What are you doing to me?"

Murder lifted her head, and made a slurping noise as she released his four inch dick. "Ay yi yi," she smiled at him seductively. "Take it easy papi. My boss will be wit ju in a minute."

"Your boss?" he shouted at her. "Who the hell is your boss? And what the fuck does he want with me?"

Murder smiled at him and stood to her feet. She kissed him on the forehead, and then walked toward the kitchen where Malice was standing at the stove boiling a pot of water.

"Goddamnit! Will somebody tell me what the hell is going on? If it's money you want, you can have it! I've got a quarter mil' stashed away, and if you let me go it's all yours!" He pleaded while desperately trying to free himself from the chair.

After a thirty second struggle, he calmed down and searched his mind for answers. He quickly put two and two together, and the image of an old, light skinned man with piercing blue eyes and a salt and pepper beard invaded his thoughts, *Grip!*

No sooner than he came to this dreadful conclusion, the front door opened, and Grip strolled into the house as if he paid the mortgage. He was dressed in a white Prada button up, beige Prada slacks, and a pair of brown, wing tipped Alligator shoes. A mocha colored Kiton topcoat was draped over his shoulders, and his brown Fedora was slightly cocked to the right. He closed the door behind him, and then walked over to Smitty.

Smitty bucked back and forth, but he couldn't break free. He looked at Grip and began to cry.

"M—M—Mr. Moreno! T—T—They had me by the balls!"

Grip towered over top of him, and looked at him with a blank expression. In his deep voice, he said, "Now, you know I'm disappointed in you, right?"

"J—J—Just gimmie some time to make it right!" Smitty pleaded with him. "I promise you, Mr. Moreno, I can make this shit go away!"

"Oh, is that right?" Grip shrugged his shoulders and fiddled with the diamond ring on his right pinky. "And how the fuck do you plan on doin' that?"

"All they have is me. If I recant my statement and refuse to testify, they'll never secure an indictment."

Grip reached inside of his Prada slacks and pulled out a Cohiba cigar and a gold cigar cutter. After clipping off the ends of the stogie, he held it to his nose, and inhaled the sweet tobacco scent.

"So, let's get this straight," he said while placing the cigar in his mouth. "You said they had you by the balls, huh?"

Smitty nodded his head fervently. "They left me no choice, Mr. Moreno. I didn't wanna do it, but those cocksuckers in the DEA's office, they made me."

Grip nodded his head as if he understood Smitty's position, then in the blink of an eye he swooped down and grabbed his shriveled up dick.

"Oh my God! W—W—What are you doing?" Smitty bitched up.

"Didn't yo' funky ass just tell me that they had you by the balls?" Grip snarled. He placed the head of Smitty's dick through the hole in the cigar cutter, and added a little pressure. "Well, now I got you by the dick!"

"Please, don't do this, Mr. Moreno! I'm begging you!"

Snip!

"*Aaaggghhhh!*" Smitty screamed in pain as the head of his dick fell to the carpet, and blood decorated his thighs. He looked at his decapitated penis and began to shiver. The gory sight, coupled with the excruciating pain, made him pass out.

After releasing the grasp that he had around Smitty's shriveled up dick, Grip reached inside of his back pocket, and pulled out a white handkerchief. He wiped the blood away from his hand, and then reached inside of his coat pocket and pulled out his gold lighter. He held the blue flame to the tip of his cigar, and a cloud of smoke quickly appeared in front of his face. "Murder! Malice!" he called for his beautiful enforcers. "It's about that time!"

A couple of seconds later, they emerged from the kitchen with Malice leading the way. She was carrying the pot of boiled water, and the liquid was so hot that beads of sweat trickled down her light brown face. As they approached Smitty's naked body, Murder smacked him in the face with the back of her hand.

Whack!

He regained consciousness and looked at her skeptically.

"Ahn ahn papi," she waved her index finger in front of his face. "No sleeping! De best is yet to come."

Smitty shook away his dizziness, and then looked at Malice. For a split second, he wondered why she was holding a pot of boiling water, and then reality set in.

"Oh my God!" he cried out. "For the love of Christ, I'm begging you! Don't do this!"

Splash!

"*Aaagggggghhhhh! Somebody wake me up from this fucking dream!*" His pale white skin turned beet red, and starting at the top of his head, it slid down his face like melted cheese on a hot pizza. As he continued to scream, he bucked so hard that the chair tipped over and he crashed to the floor.

Grip looked at him and flexed his jaw muscles. He knew that this day was coming, and now that it was finally here, he refused to waste any more time. He looked at Murder and slightly nodded his head. Without an ounce of hesitation, she pulled a .357 Magnum from her Birkin bag, and aimed it at Smitty's forehead.

Boom!

Askari

Chapter Four

The Following Morning...

At the federal building on 6th and Arch, Clavenski was staring at his Cartier watch, and nervously tapping his ink pen against his desktop. It was 10:00 a.m., and former detective Adam Smith had yet to arrive at his office. He was scheduled to appear before Judge Johnson and a federal grand jury over an hour ago, but so far his star witness was a no show. After persuading Judge Johnson to grant him a two hour recess, he sent DEA Agent Terry Long to Smitty's South Philly residence, and with ten minutes left on the clock, he still didn't have his witness.

"Goddamnit Terry, where the hell are you?" he asked himself while subconsciously fiddling with his Purple Label necktie.

Just as he was about to call it quits and prepare himself for the embarrassment of standing before the court unprepared, his Blackberry vibrated on the desktop. He picked it up and saw that the caller was Agent Long.

"Terry where the hell are you? Please tell me that you've located Smith, and that the two of you are just now pulling into the parking lot."

"I wish that was the case, but it's not," Agent Long sighed. "Me and Monica are standing in front of Smitty's house, and the crime scene unit won't let us back inside."

"Crime scene unit? What the hell are you talking about, Terry?"

"I'm talking about Smitty. We found him about forty five minutes ago. I should've called you sooner, but..."

"You've gotta be shittin' me!" Clavenski rudely interrupted him. "Goddamnit! I knew we should've put him in witness protection!" he continued shouting, and then banged his fist on the desktop. "Do you realize how bad this is? He was all we had, Terry!"

"You're absolutely right, Andy," Agent Long admitted, "but we can still build a case against *The Moreno Family*. All we gotta do is redirect our investigation. Let's shake a few trees, and see what we can come up with. For now, I just need you to have a little patience"

"Patience? Really Terry? You want me to have patience. Fuck patience! I want Gervin Moreno! Do you hear me Terry? You bring me Moreno!"

Click!

***

In North Philly

Pooky was inside of his trap house on Delhi Street. He was weighing cocaine in denominations of four and a half ounces, and packaging the work in sandwich bags. As he sat at the dining room table with his eyes glued to a digital scale, he felt the energy of someone else in the room. He looked up and noticed that Heemy, the seventeen year old son of the crack whore who owned the house was standing on the other side of the room with an aluminum baseball bat clutched in his right hand. The young man was scowling at him with a burning rage, and his body language exuded hostility. He was sick and tired of Pooky taking advantage of his mother's addiction. Crack head or not, she was still his mother, and he was determined to keep dudes like Pooky away from her.

Pooky looked at him and started laughing. "Yo Heemy, you better put down that mutha'fuckin' bat, and go play somewhere."

Heemy didn't budge. Instead, he gripped the bat with both of his hands and casually closed the distance between Pooky and himself.

Pooky got up from his seat, and removed the titanium .38 that was tucked in his shoulder holster. "Let's try this again. If you don't put down that bat and go play some damn where, I'ma clap ya lil' ass!"

At the sight of the .38, Heemy stopped in his tracks.

"Oh, so, it's like dat? You gon' pull ya lil' hamma out on me? Yo, I *knew* you was a bitch ass nigga!" He smiled and shook his head from side to side. "Try'na walk around on the hood wit' dat fake ass husky shit. Nigga, you's a *pussy*!"

Pooky was hot. "Oh, so I'ma pussy now?"

"Yeah you's a pussy," Heemy repeated. "And if you put that ratchet down, I'ma knock you the fuck out."

Pooky couldn't believe his eyes and ears. At 6'3" and 240 pounds, he was two inches taller and seventy pounds heavier than Heemy. Yet and still the young man appeared to have no fear. He knew the reason that Heemy was mad, and because of that, he decided to give the young man a proposition.

"A'ight young bul, I'll tell you what. I know you feel some type of way about me servin' ya mom, and hustlin' out y'all crib," Pooky smiled at him. He refused to take the young man seriously. "If you want me stop, then you gotta show me that you're man enough to make me stop. If you're not man enough," he shrugged his shoulders and smiled mischievously, "then I get to do whatever I want around this mutha'fucka."

"A'ight," Heemy nodded his head. "But only if I get to keep my bat."

"Nigga, I don't give a fuck about no goddamned bat!" Pooky shouted, attempting to intimidate his young opponent. "I just did eighteen years upstate! I was knockin' out niggas wit' swords in they mutha'fuckin' hands! What the fuck I care about a…"

Crack!

The tip of the baseball bat crashed into the side of his head, knocking him backwards. As he fought to regain his balance, Heemy took another swing, but missed his head by centimeters. Pooky reached out with both hands and gripped him up by the neck. He hoisted his lanky body in the air, and yelled at him.

"You lil' bitch! You gon' hit me while I wasn't even ready!"

Again, Heemy swung the bat, but due to the close proximity between Pooky and himself, he was unable to land a solid blow. After another failed attempt, he dropped the bat, and desperately tried to pry Pooky's hands away from his neck.

"Get off me, pussy! Lemme go!"

"Naw, fuck that!" Pooky growled at him. "Ya lil' ass wanna act like grown fuckin' man, so now I'ma treat you like one!" He slammed Heemy to the soiled carpet, and released his right hand from around his neck. He balled his hand into a fist, and then cocked his arm back. "Nigga, I oughta break ya fuckin' face!"

Heemy struggled to free himself from Pooky's grasp, but Pooky was too strong. *Damn*, he thought to himself, realizing that he'd lost any chance of winning this battle. *Fuck it! I ain't goin' out like a bitch!* Instead of giving his enemy the satisfaction of hearing him beg for mercy, he conjured up a thick wad of phlegm in the back of his throat, and then spat in Pooky's face.

When the slimy mucus splashed against Pooky's forehead, he wiped it off with the back of his hand, and then returned a lougie of his own. The snotty saliva landed in Heemy's mouth, and he went ballistic.

"Agh! Pussy I'ma kill you!" he screamed. He bucked so hard that he nearly escaped Pooky's strength.

"What the fuck is y'all doin' down there?" Treesha, Heemy's mother, yelled from the top of the steps. "I'm up here try'na get my groove on, and y'all mutha'fuckas is down there makin' all that mutha'fuckin' noise!" she continued yelling while descending the stairs.

When she entered the living room in her four sizes too big T-shirt, she was sweating profusely. A can of Natural Ice beer was clutched in her left hand, and a crooked Newport 100 dangled from the corner of her mouth. Her worn out weave was sticking out the bottom of her oily headscarf, and she was so skinny that her gray tights looked like parachute pants. "What? Y'all mutha'fuckas ain't heard what the fuck I just said? What the fuck is y'all doin' down here?"

"Treesha, you better get ya son 'fore I fuck his ass up!" Pooky warned. He was still choking Heemy with his left hand, and his right fist was still cocked in the air.

Treesha looked at Heemy, and gritted her teeth. "Boy, get ya ass off of that goddamned floor."

"I can't!" Heemy yelled at her. "Don't you see he's got me pinned down?"

"Let him up, Pooky," she lowered her voice a few octaves.

"A'ight," Pooky nodded his head. "But I'm tellin' you right now, if I let him go and his lil' ass gets crazy, I'm fuckin' up both of y'all."

He released his grasp from Heemy's neck, and they both jumped to their feet.

Treesha looked at Heemy and sucked her teeth. "Boy, bring ya ass over here," she demanded.

"Come over there for what?" Heemy retorted.

"Don't be askin' me no mutha'fuckin' questions," she spat, and then pointed at the carpet directly in front of her. "I said bring ya ass here!"

He shook his head, and reluctantly walked toward her. The second he came within arms distance, she cocked back and slapped him across the face.

Whack!

"The next time you call ya'self disrespectin' my man I'ma fuck that ass up myself! You got that?"

A demonic raged spread throughout his body. He was tired of coming second to the man who fed her drug addiction and treated her like shit. His hands began to tremble and warm tears fell from his eyes. He wanted to smack her face off, but he didn't. Instead, he darted out the front door and swore that he would never return as long as Pooky was still in the picture.

***

Donkees Sports Bar was in full swing when Kev strolled through the front door. The patrons were enjoying a college football game between LSU and Michigan State, and scantily dressed waitresses and bartenders were serving food and drinks. The jukebox was playing Rico Love's, *They Don't Know*, and despite the law that prohibited people from smoking in public places, weed and cigar smoke hung in the air.

As he glanced around the bar's interior, the only thing he could do was shake his head in disbelief.

"Damn, this nigga's on that Blood shit fa'real!" He said to himself.

He was referring to the red and black colors that decorated the bar. The walls were painted in the image of a red bandana, and aside from the red tables and black chairs, four pool tables were positioned throughout the bar. Each had a black frame and a bloody red canvass with a black five point star in the center.

He walked over to the bar and took a seat. The bartender was a thick, Puerto Rican mami. She had a short haircut and a light brown complexion. Her face was that of an angel's, and everything about her was sexy. She was wearing a black T-shirt that was cut just below her breast, and her red booty shorts revealed the fat camel toe that was wedged in between her thick thighs. The *Donkees* logo was printed across the back of her shorts in black letters, and across her shirt in red letters.

She looked at Kev, smiled, and then asked, "Can I get you somethin' papi?"

"Yeah," he smiled back and licked his lips seductively. "Lemme get a shot of Henny and a Corona wit' lemon."

"Cool papi, I gotchu."

After reaching under the bar to grab a shot glass, she spun around and grabbed a bottle of Hennessey from the liquor shelf.

Damn, mami bad as shit, he thought to himself as he admired her body from head to toe.

"Yo, what's ya name, mami?"

Before she had the chance to respond, a deep masculine voice spoke up from behind him.

"Bianca and she's already spoken for."

Kev spun around to face the voice, and when he discovered that it belonged to Sonny, a huge smile spread across his brown skinned face.

"My fuckin' boy! What it do, Ike?" He greeted him in his Pittsburgh accent. He extended his right hand, and Sonny accepted the gesture.

"Ain't shit Kev. I ain't seen you in a while, my nigga. Whatchu been up to?

"Aww man, I'm wearing cashmere from last year that ain't comin' out 'til next year, you feel me? Trips to Vegas wit' my bitch just to gamble at the *Palazzo*. Give the bitch a hunnid racks so she can tear up *Blvgari* while I'm tearing up the craps table. After that, we on the third floor eating cannoli's at *Carlos'*."

Sonny burst out laughing. "Yeah, I hear you nigga, talk dat shit." He reached out and grabbed the iced out lion's head that hung from Kev's necklace. "I see you shinin', but you ain't never holla at me. What's up wit' that?"

"Shit nigga, you tell me!" Kev shot back, stretching out his arms for emphasis. "I called you the day we was supposed to link up, but ya phone was disconnected. Then I holla'd at Diamondz, and he told me about the situation wit' ya girl. I just assumed you was fallin' back."

Refusing to talk about Riri, Sonny changed the subject. "Yo, speakin' of Diamondz, I heard that him and Shiz got booked for a body out in Cincinnati. What happened?"

"Nah dawg, that shit happened in Cleveland. I brought them niggas out Pittsburgh wit' me, and somehow they linked up wit' these Cleveland niggas. Long story short, they went out Cleveland to set up shop, shit got crazy, and from what I'm hearing, they spanked a nigga," Kev explained. "Matter of fact, I went to visit them niggas a couple of weeks ago, and they both sayin' they gon' beat the case. Hopefully they do, 'cause the time they givin' niggas for bodies these days—"

"Yo, I need they info so I can reach out to 'em, and see if I can help," Sonny said in a somber voice. "Especially Dia. Me and that nigga been rockin' wit' each other since we was young buls."

Kev nodded his head. "I got you. I should be back in Philly in a couple of weeks to holla at my connect. After I handle my business and get right, I can meet up witchu, and make sure you got all the info you need."

"Your connect?" Sonny looked at him like he was crazy. "You mean to tell me that you been comin' to Philly to grab work, and you ain't holla'd at ya boy?"

Kev shrugged his shoulders, and then gulped down his Henny. "I'm sayin' though, I ain't have no way to get in touch witchu. Plus, the Italians in South Philly been holdin' a nigga down somethin' crazy."

"*The Italians*!" Sonny scrunched up his face. "Who you talking 'bout, Carmine and them fake ass mob niggas? Come on dawg, you know them spaghetti eating mutha'fuckas ain't try'na show a nigga no love. What they chargin' you?"

"$42,000."

"$42,000?" Sonny chuckled. "For some shit that's been stepped on more times than a crack house floor? Nigga my shit's raw, straight from Columbia to Mexico to me," he bragged, giving up way too much information. "I'll tell you what," he rubbed his hands together, blinding Kev with the sparkle of his 5 carat pinky ring. "All you gotta do is grab at least 10, and I'll let em' go for $35,000 a whop."

Kev perked up and subconsciously fiddled with his iced out lion's head. "Shit nigga, you got a deal! I just wish I woulda ran into you sooner. I just finished copping off them niggas, and I ain't gon' be ready for at least another two weeks."

Sonny waved him off.

"Yo, don't even worry about that shit, fam. Whenever you ready to get right, just holla at me." He reached inside of his Calvin Klein slacks and pulled out a business card. "Here," he handed him the card.

Kev examined the black and red card, and noticed the *Donkees* logo.

"Damn Ike, I ain't know this was ya bar! This mutha'fucka's off the hook! Especially these lil' bitches you got workin' up in here!"

"It's a'ight," Sonny replied in a nonchalant manner. "But as far as these bitches go, which one you feelin' the most?"

Kev looked at Bianca, and then turned his attention to the two Brazilian waitresses, Toya and Gabby. He then, fixed his gaze on Kelly, the thick brown skinned waitress who was leaned over the first pool table, preparing to knock the 8 Ball in the right corner pocket. Just as he was about to select the brown skinned beauty, a petite, Black and Korean woman emerged from the door that led to Sonny's office. She was dressed in a black Valentino business suit, and a pair of black Cavalli pumps. Her silky black hair was pinned into a bun, and her slanted eyes were tucked behind black Donna Karan frames. A suede Bottega Veneta handbag was strapped over her right shoulder, and her sexy walk was full of attitude.

"Damn Ike," Kev whispered in his Pittsburgh accent. "Who the fuck is that?"

Sonny smiled. "That's Suelyn, my accountant."

"Oh yeah," Kev replied while licking his lips. "I'm try'na see what's up wit' her."

Sonny shrugged his shoulders because he doubted that Suelyn would give him any play, but he called her over anyway. "Hey Sue, come here real quick. I wanna introduce you to somebody."

Chapter Five

Later That Night...

Grip was relaxing in his home theater. He was sipping on green tea, and his eyes were glued to CNN. News stations from all over the country were covering the latest events out of Ferguson, Missouri, and it was just announced that the grand jury had declined to issue an indictment in the Michael Brown case. The City of Ferguson was in an uproar. Large crowds of protesters were looting and setting the city ablaze, and the local police were trying to slow them down with rubber bullets and tear gas.

"Typical American bullshit," Grip said to himself.

He knocked down the last of his green tea, and then sparked up a Cohiba cigar. After taking a slow drag and releasing a cloud of smoke, he lounged back in his chair and closed his eyes. He massaged his temples and thought about a day that he'd never forget.

August 25th, 1964

It was the civil rights era, and just like the majority of the inner cities throughout America, Philadelphia was a racial ticking time bomb. The blacks in the city were sick and tired of being oppressed by the police, and their response was a three day riot that plagued the streets of North Philly.

It was during this time that the blacks in the city were beginning to recognize The Moreno Crime Family as The Black Mafia. They admired Grip for standing up against the Italians in an all out war, and in some ways this was the motivation behind their revolution. No longer were they afraid of the white powers that be, and they were determined to make city hall feel their power.

When the word traveled to South Philly that the blacks in North Philly were tearing up Columbia Avenue, Grip wanted to see it for himself. He stopped by The Reynolds Wrap Lounge on 18th and South Street, and gathered up two of his captains, Eddie Kyle and Russell Fitzgerald. The two men climbed inside of his Cadillac Deville, and they headed up 18th Street towards North Philly. When they reached the corner of 18th and Columbia, they couldn't believe their eyes. The Philadelphia Police Department, under the order of Mayor Rizzo was out in full force. Their mission was to put an end to the vandalism and destruction of the white owned businesses in the area. They were savagely attacking the blacks with service batons, water hoses, and K-9s. The blacks, however, fought back. In a fit of rage, they defended themselves with pocketknives, broken bottles, and anything else that they could use as a weapon.

After making a right turn, the steel gray Caddy cruised down the block at a calm 5 m.p.h. When they approached the corner of 17th and Columbia, Grip spotted a white street cop, who unbeknownst to Eddie and Russell was on his payroll. The skinny white man was accompanied by another cop. The two of them were inconspicuously tucked behind a large dumpster and viciously attacking a young black man. After easing the Caddy to a halt, Grip threw the transmission in park, and then hopped out the driver's side door.

"Yo Johnny, what the fuck are you doing?" he shouted while jogging toward the two police officers.

Johnathan Ferraci, a ten year veteran on the force was just about to land a devastating blow to the back of the young man's head when he heard Grip's voice. He looked to his left, and as sure as the sky was blue, the Black Mafia don was standing there in a white linen dress shirt, gray slacks, and a black pair gators. His wide brimmed Stetson was slightly cocked to the left, and a red feather was stuffed inside of the band.

"Grip," Officer Ferraci nervously replied. "Look at what these son of a bitches are doin' to their own friggin' neighborhood," he complained in a thick Italian accident.

His partner, Vincent Marco, was disgusted. He stopped kicking the young man, and then looked at Ferraci as if he were crazy. "Hey yo Johnny, am I friggin' missin' somethin' ova here? Since when did we start explainin' ourselves to moulies?"

Officer Ferraci looked at his partner with pleading eyes. He tried to tell him to take it easy, but before he could utter a single word, Grip removed the .357 that was tucked in the small of his back and fired a single round.

Boom!

The bullet struck Officer Marco in his right eye, and he tornadoed to the ground.

Eddie ran up on Ferraci and held a switchblade to the side of his neck. "Lemme do him Grip!"

Ferraci pissed in his pants and began to tremble. He glanced from right to left, praying that amidst the chaos one of his fellow officers would look behind the dumpster and come to his rescue. Terrified, he looked at Grip and pleaded for his life. "Don't kill me Grip. Please."

"Naw Grip," Eddie said in a cold voice. "Lemme do us all a favor and put this honky out his misery." He gripped Ferraci's hair with his free hand, and then applied pressure to the switchblade. "You know what I'm talking 'bout? Carve his punk ass up somethin' nice!"

Grip shook his head from side to side. "Naw Eddie, drop the blade." He looked to his left where Russell was helping the *bloodied young man to his feet. "Say youngblood, you ever killed a mutha'fucka?"*

"N—N—Naw suh," the young man answered in a southern drawl.

"That's good 'cause I ain't want you to kill him no way." He looked at Ferraci and flexed his jaw muscles. "I will, however, insist that you shoot this honky in his funky white ass!"

"Awww shucks," Ferraci whined. "Isn't there another way we can settle this?"

"Shut up and turn your punk ass around," Grip demanded. "And poke your ass out so the lil' brotha can get off a clean shot."

Reluctantly, Ferraci did as he was told. He leaned forward, and then peeked over his shoulder as Grip handed the young man his pistol. The feel of the pearl handle was something that the young man had never experienced before. He looked at Ferraci and took a deep breath.

Grip noticed his apprehension, and felt the need to talk him through it. "Just take your time, youngblood. Nice and easy," he nodded his head. "Nice and easy."

The young man looked at Grip for reassurance, and then returned his gaze to Ferraci. Begrudgingly, he steadied his aim and fired.

Boom!

"Agh!" Ferraci screamed as he fell to the ground and reached for his backside. "You fucking bitch!"

Grip towered over him. "That'll teach your funky ass about abusin' your authority. And I swear to God Johnny, if I hear one goddamned word about this shit I'ma murder your whole fuckin' family." He reached inside of his slacks, and pulled out a wad of cash. After peeling away $500, he crumbled the bills into a ball, and then threw them at

Ferraci's head. "For your trouble." He turned his attention to the young man and retrieved his pistol. "You cool, youngblood?"

"Yas suh."

"Is you able to walk?"

He nodded his head up and down. "I think so, suh"

"Alright, follow us back to my car, and I'ma take you wherever you need to go."

After climbing inside of the large sedan, Grip threw the transmission in drive, and then cruised down Columbia Avenue at a moderate pace. He looked in the rearview mirror and locked eyes with the young man. "Say, what's your name youngblood?"

"Gregory Johnson, suh."

"Well say now Gregory, you talk like you from big foot country. What you doin' all the way up in Philly?

"I's from Nawth Ca'lina. My momma sent me up nawth to attend school. I's a freshman at Temple University, suh."

"A college boy, huh?" Grip smiled.

He immediately thought of the numerous ways that an educated black man could help him with his criminal endeavors. From that day forward, he paid Gregory's college tuition and insisted that he attend law school. His investment paid off big time. Fifty years later, young Gregory Johnson from Nawth Ca'lina was Federal District Judge Gregory Johnson, and above all else, he was Grip's best kept secret.

Back To November 24th, 2014

"Uncle G, you good?"

"Huh?" Grip responded.

He looked up and saw that his nephew Gangsta was standing in front of him. Gangsta gestured toward the burning cigar stub that was wedged in between his thumb and index finger. "Yo, lemme find out you try'na burn the house down," he chuckled.

Grip stubbed out the cigar and wiped the ashes away from his housecoat. "I must've zoned out for a minute." He returned his gaze to his nephew and smiled at him. Gangsta was the son of his sister Angela and his best friend Russell Fitzgerald. When the two of them were murdered back in 1975, Grip inherited his one month old nephew and raised him to the best of his ability. He never wanted Gangsta to be a part of the criminal lifestyle, and he did everything to deter him from it. He sent him to boarding school, college, and even the military. Unfortunately, none of these things could trump the Moreno and Fitzgerald blood that ran through his veins. He was destined to be gangsta.

At 6'2" and 180 pounds, he was the spitting image of Russell. He had a strong build, medium brown skin, a chiseled face, and dark brown eyes.

"So nephew, what's goin' on?"

"Everything's goin' according to plan," Gangsta answered while plopping down in the chair beside him. He pointed at the Sony projector screen and asked, "Whatchu watchin'?"

"This bullshit down in Ferguson, Missouri. The grand jury refused to indict that cracker ass cop who killed that young bul, and now the whole city's goin' *ape shit*." He pointed at the screen where a local pastor was trying to get the people to calm down. "Now, look at this mutha'fucka right here. He's supposed to be a leader, but he's leading the people in the wrong direction."

Gangsta shrugged his shoulders. He didn't care one way or the other, but out of respect for Grip, he expressed a fake concern. "How's that?"

"Because," Grip continued. "The whole concept of marching and protesting is only a facade. It'll never produce long term results, only a temporary pacifier. The only way to fight against this type of injustice is through the local elections. You see, our people have a misconceived notion when it comes to the voting process. When it comes to voting for the president, we'll show up in record breaking numbers, but when it's time to vote for local officials from the governor down to the district attorney, the majority of us won't lift a goddamned finger. I mean, how can we as a people be so misdirected and irresponsible. We've made ourselves obsolete by neglecting to use our voting power within our local governments, and as a result, our local governments can treat us in any manner they see fit without the threat of any political backlash. This is why the cops can kill us and get away with it, and why the courts can unjustly give us a million years. It makes no goddamned sense."

Gangsta sparked up a Newport and leaned back in the suede theater chair. "That's the reason we move the way we move. We put political pieces in certain political places, and that way we're always two steps ahead of these mutha'fuckas." He took a drag on his Newport, and then quickly changed the subject. "I looked into that situation on Delaware Avenue, and just as we expected, Carmine's been conducting business on the docks." He took another drag on his cigarette, and exhaled a cloud of smoke. "Ever since you left for Cuba he's been shakin' down everything from the drugs to the casino. Any and everything that's been coming into the city from the Delaware River, he's been taking a percentage. Our percentage."

"I figured that," Grip replied. "When the big dog's away, the cats are gonna play. It's the nature of a pussy." He looked Gangsta square in the eyes. "This is what I want you to do.

Get with Murder and Malice, then report back to me. We're gonna send these mutha'fuckas a *gee* mail."

Gangsta nodded his head, and then stood to his feet. "Just gimmie a couple of days to handle the other situation and after that I'm on it."

"Alright," Grip replied. "We can't afford any mistakes so be careful."

"I already know," Gangsta assured him. "Is there anything else that we need to discuss before I leave?"

"No, just tell Muhammad to get Gregory on the phone."

Gangsta left the theater room, and a couple of minutes later, Muhammad appeared in the doorway. He was dressed in a black suit and a cell phone was clutched in his left hand. "May I enter, sir?"

Grip gestured for him to enter the room, and Muhammad handed him the phone. "Brother Gregory," Grip addressed his old friend. "I'm assuming that everything worked out according to plan."

"For now," Judge Johnson sighed. "It's that goddamned Clavenski. I've never seen a prosecutor so hell bent on taking down a specific individual. This is like Guiliani and Gotti all over again."

"Humph!" Grip chuckled. "Gotti couldn't have touched me with a ten foot pole, and Clavenski isn't half the prosecutor that Guiliani was. He's too soft."

"But yet and still," Judge Johnson countered. "He's got a hard on for you that you wouldn't believe."

Grip laughed. "He's reaching for straws. There's nothing he can do to me at this point. No Smitty, no case."

"I'm telling you, Gervin. That son of a bitch is up to something."

Grip chuckled. "Tell me something I *don't* know!"

Chapter Six

The Following Day...

On Columbia Avenue, from 19th to 22nd Street, the Block Boy Turkey Giveaway was more like a block party. The music was blasting, and the strip was full of people dancing. A *Power* 99 truck was parked up on 19th Street, and news van were parked on 22nd. An 18 wheeler was parked in front of the King Center, and the cargo bed was filled with frozen turkeys. Dressed in mink coats, Sonny and the Block Boys were standing behind the 18 wheeler. A large group of people were crowded around, and eagerly waiting to get their hands on a free turkey.

"Yo, what's goin' on? Everybody good?" Sonny asked with a smile on his face. He was happy to be doing something positive for his community. "We got enough turkeys for everybody so calm down and stop pushin' each other," he announced.

His words were pertaining to the two old ladies who were standing in front of the crowd shoving one another.

"Ahn ahn Sonny. This heifer try'na act like she next. She ain't fucking next. I was standing here first," the younger of the two hissed at him.

"Bitch, I was standin' here first." The second woman staked her claim, refusing to back down.

Sonny laughed. "Hold up y'all. This ain't that type of party. We showin' love out here today. This that North Philly love right here. We ain't doin' none of the drama." He looked down and smiled at the little boy that was standing beside the first old lady. "Ain't that right lil' man?"

The little boy smiled back and nodded his head up and down.

Sonny looked into the back of the 18 wheeler where Easy was bagging up turkeys. "Pops double up two of them bags for me."

Easy nodded his head, and then placed two Butterball turkeys inside of two separate bags. He handed them to Sonny, and Sonny handed each of the old ladies a bag. "Y'all have a Happy Thanksgiving."

As the two old ladies walked away from the crowd, Sonny was approached by a middle aged black man and a camera crew. "Hello, I'm Roland Rushin, the news correspondent for Channel 10 News. Everyone's telling me that you're the guy who's responsible for all of this. Sontino Moreno, right?" He extended his right hand and Sonny accepted the gesture with a firm handshake.

"Yeah, I'm Sonny Moreno. What's poppin'?"

"Well, I like what you're doing for the community and I was hoping that you would give me an interview for the one o'clock news."

Sonny looked him up and down, and then shrugged his shoulders. "A'ight, but just for the record, I'm not doin' this for publicity. I'm doin' this because I know how it feels to be trapped in the hood, fucked up, and lookin' at the world like don't nobody give a fuck about you."

The reporter looked at his black waist length mink, his iced out Rolex, and the VS1 diamonds that smothered his *BBE* charm. "Yeah, I'm sure of it," he replied sarcastically. He motioned for his cameraman to start filming, and the fat white man aimed the lens at him and Sonny. In true to the hood fashion, everybody crowded around, desperately trying to get their faces on the news.

"Good afternoon Philadelphia. This is Roland Rushin, and I'm reporting to you live from the Martin Luther King Jr. Center in North Philly, where people from all over the city are here to receive a free Thanksgiving turkey. Standing to my right is the man who's responsible for this event, North Philly's own, Mr. Sontino Moreno."

He held the microphone to Sonny's face. "Mr. Moreno, what's the motivation behind your philanthropy?"

"My what?" Sonny shot back, looking at him like he was crazy.

Roland Rushin smiled at him. "What's the motivation behind you giving to charity?"

"Oh," Sonny shrugged his shoulders. "I just do it on the strength of those who are less fortunate."

"Well, you seem to be doing pretty good for yourself young man. May I ask what you do for a living?"

"I'm co-owner of *Donkees Sports Bar*, and aside from being the manager at *Club Infamous*, I just started a record label, *Block Boy Entertainment*." He held up his *BBE* charm and the diamonds shined bright.

"I see," the reporter said. "Now, a large number of these people were out here marching last night, protesting the grand jury's decision in Ferguson, Missouri. Do you have anything to say about that situation?"

"Naw, not really," Sonny quickly shot back. "But since we talkin' politics," he looked into the camera. "Free my nigga Sean Sean. Free my Uncle Tone. Free my cousin Cheese, and free my nigga Tali Da Don."

Roland Rushin shrugged his shoulders. "Well, I'm assuming that's all of the political talk we're going to get from Mr. Moreno." He scratched his head, and then looked at Sonny skeptically. "Moreno? You wouldn't happen to be related to the Infamous Gervin Moreno? The reputed boss of the Black Mafia because maybe that would explain your extravagance," he continued, then nodded toward Sonny's *BBE* charm.

Sonny's face turned bright red and he flexed his jaw muscles. "Mello, get this silly mutha'fucka outta my face."

Rahmello mugged the reporter on the side of his head, and pushed the cameraman in his chest. "Get the fuck outta here!" he snapped while reaching for the Glock .9 that was tucked in his waistline.

Roland Rushin noticed the gesture and hurried back to his news van. Still fuming, Sonny threw on a fake smile and continued handing out turkeys.

***

Up the block, sitting behind the tinted windows of a navy blue Ford Excursion, Agents Terry Long and Monica Brown were surveying the entire scene. Agent Long was watching The Block Boys through a pair of binoculars, and Agent Brown was taking pictures nonstop.

"So," Agent Brown said after snapping her final picture of Sonny. "Do you think Clavenski's gonna get behind our investigation?"

"Absolutely," Agent Long confirmed while nodding his head up and down. "He'll do anything to get his hands on Grip, and if taking down Sontino is our only option, he'll support us."

Agent Brown returned her focus to Sonny. He and Rahmello were leaned against his Rolls Royce, laughing and joking with the people of North Philly. It appeared as though the two brothers didn't have a care in the world, and this was one of the many reasons she hated drug dealers.

"So, what's the status on the meeting with Clavenski and the other agents?" she asked without taking her eyes off their target. "Did you schedule a date?"

"Yeah, it's scheduled for next Saturday," said Agent Long. "I sent an email to Clavenski and made it clear that the meeting was pertaining to the Gervin Moreno case."

Agent Brown sighed, and continued watching Sonny through the tinted window. "It hasn't been a full two years and the streets are treating Sontino like he's a fucking legend."

"What else would you expect?" Agent Long stated. "Aside from running Grip out of the city, he inherited a multi-million dollar drug empire. Michael Brooks' death was the best thing to ever happen to this guy, and he appears to be handling himself accordingly."

"Well, do you think we have enough information to persuade Clavenski to sign off on the buy money?" she asked.

Agent Long caressed the iced out lion's head that hung from his platinum necklace. "We've got more than enough."

***

At Club Spontaneous

Carmine was sitting in his office counting the kick up money that he collected from his capos the night before. A black money counter was positioned in front of him, and piles of money were scattered around his desk. As he removed a stack of hundred dollar bills from the tray, a soft knock sounded from the door.

Knock! Knock! Knock!

"Who the hell is it?" he shouted. "I'm friggin' busy ova here!" He hated to be disturbed when he was counting money, and today was no exception.

Alphonso stuck his head inside of the office. "Yo Carmine, are you watchin' the news?"

"No, Why?"

Alphonso entered the office and walked toward the television. He pressed the *ON* button, and then turned to the Channel 10 news.

Carmine looked at the 50" screen and saw two black guys handing out turkeys to a crowd of people. Hardly impressed, he shrugged his shoulders. "What the fuck is this?"

Alphonso pointed toward the screen and replied, "The dude in the black mink is Sontino Moreno, and the guy standing beside him is his younger brother, Rahmello. They're Grip's grandsons."

Carmine waved him off, and returned his attention to the digital screen on the money counter. He fed the machine another stack of hundreds, and after sifting through the bills the digital screen read 100. He nodded his head and removed the money from the tray. He secured the stack with a rubber band, and then grabbed his ink pen and jotted down $10,000 in his notebook. Without looking up he said, "Fuck 'em. They're nobodies."

"I'm not so sure about that," Alphonso disagreed. "Sontino's been makin' his bones all over the city. He's responsible for most of the cocaine between Philly and South Jersey, and he's gaining a lot of power in the process. I think it's time that we send for him."

Carmine loaded the tray with another stack of hundreds, and then settled back in his chair. "You know what Phons, I *did* hear about this kid. Romey Noodles was tellin' me about him. He's supposed to be the reason that Grip left the country. Can you believe it?" He chuckled and pointed at the television. "This sonofabitch tried to whack his own grandfather. Kudos to you kid." He saluted with his right hand and started laughing. "You got a lot of friggin' balls!"

"Exactly," Alphonso nodded his head. "That's the reason I think we outta send for him. We haven't had a presence in

North Philly since your Uncle Joey was dealin' with those niggers in the Richard Allen Projects."

"And we all know how that turned out," Carmine reminded him. "That fuckin' T. Hill made a fool outta Uncle Joey, and 'til this fuckin' day our friends in New York won't let him forget about it. Now, consider everything that's goin' on within the family. By me being the new boss, I can't afford that type of shit. These moulies are great earners. I'll give you that, but at the same time they're rats waitin' to happen."

"But Carmine," Alphonso started.

"But nothin'," he interrupted his underboss. "I can't afford that type of heat. Speakin' of Romey Noodles, you need to have a talk wit' him. This is the second time this month that he came short wit' my fuckin' money," he said while gesturing toward the stacks of money on his desk. "I did him a favor by givin' him the docks, and this is how he repays me? By not payin' me my fuckin' money."

Alphonso began to perspire. He was the one who petitioned for Romey Noodles to get the docks, and he knew that Carmine would hold him responsible.

"Don't just stand there lookin' stupid," Carmine antagonized him. "He's makin' every bit of fifteen grand a week, and all I wanted was a measly 30%. Last week he brought me $2,500 and last night he dropped off $3,000. You tell that degenerate fuck that I want my goddamn money. That's $3,500 he owes me."

"Listen Carmine, I'm not exactly sure about what's goin' on, but he did tell me that the money's been comin' in slower than usual," Alphonso spoke up on his behalf.

"Slower than usual?" Carmine banged his hand on the desktop. "The docks are one of our best money makers! You tell that fuckin' hump to get his shit together, and that's the end of it!"

As Alphonso lowered his head and left the office, Carmine's cell phone rang. He grabbed it from the desktop, and noticed that the caller was his grandfather. "Yo gramps! What's goin' on?"

"This Miami weather, fugget about it!" Little Angolo chuckled. "But listen Carmy, you did a good job with Luca and Junior. Respect comes from admiration and fear, and in order for this family to move forward, it was something that needed to be done."

"Alright," Carmine nodded his head. "But I can tell from the sound of your voice that somethin' ain't right. So, quit the bullshit and lay it on me."

Little Angolo sighed. "There's not gonna be an indictment."

"There's not gonna be an indictment? What do you mean there's not gonna be an indictment? This was supposed to be water under the friggin' bridge."

"Gervin's back, Carmy."

"How? I thought he was in Cuba?"

"That's what we thought, but he's back. He whacked Smitty, and the entire case was based on his testimony. I told Andy to put Smitty in a witness protection program, but he didn't. He dropped the fuckin' ball," Little Angolo explained.

Carmine jumped to his feet and swiped everything off his desk. "Andy did what? You tell that Jewish piece of shit that I'll rip off his fuckin' balls! He's got one month to fix this shit! One!"

**

At SCI Graterford

Daphney's father, Alvin Rines, was sitting in his cell with his eyes glued to the pages of Cash's debut novel, *Trust No*

Man. A hot cup of coffee was clutched in his right hand, and the Super III radio that sat on his desk was tuned into Power 99. He wasn't really paying attention to the radio, but when the music stopped and the disk jockey mentioned Sonny's name, he laid down the book and turned up the volume.

"So Sonny, it seems like you popped up from outta nowhere," said Mo Jeezy, the top disk jocky in Philly. "Go 'head and tell the city who you are, and let 'em know what you been up to."

"No doubt," Sonny's voice eased through the speakers. "For those of y'all who don't know me, I'm straight out the Bad Landz and I been doin' my thing for a while now. I just kicked off my record label, *Block Boy Entertainment*, and my first artist is Coldplay Wu."

"Yo, that's what's up," Mo Jeezy shot back. "Coldplay Wu, that's the young bul from Uptown. I've been seeing him on those Smack DVDs. He's definitely bringing that heat."

"Without a doubt," Sonny cosigned. "My mission is to make him the next best thing to come outta Philly since Meek. Shout to Meek Mill by the way."

"Alright now what's the motivation behind this turkey giveaway?"

"This was somethin' that my big homie Mook used to do back in the day, and I wanted to honor his memory by keepin' up wit' the tradition. I also wanted to do somethin' positive for the hood."

"Well, congratulations brotha. Keep up the good work, and make sure that I'm the first one to get a copy of Coldplay's album."

"No doubt, Mo, and thanks for covering the event."

Alvin shook his head from side to side, and then took a deep breath. "This nigga's doin' too much," he said to himself.

He grabbed a pen and a sheet of paper, and began to write Sonny a letter.

Chapter Seven

A Week Later...

In the basement of an undisclosed location, Sonny, Easy, and Rahmello were sitting at separate tables using money counters to double check the buy money for their November shipment. This was their ritual ever since they linked up with Poncho. They would get together on the first Saturday of the month, count the buy money, and then drive to Poncho's bodega in three Cadillac Escalades. Easy and Breeze would lead the convoy, Zaire and Egypt would take the rear, and Sonny and Rahmello would ride in the middle with the buy money stashed inside of a hidden compartment. After purchasing their monthly shipment of 100 kilos, they would return to the stash house, and breakdown the work. Specifically, they would remove 9 ounces from a 100% pure kilo, and replace the weight with a liquefied cut. Next, they would place the kilo inside of a mixing kettle, and blend it to a thick paste. After that, they would pour the paste into a hydraulic compressor, and compress the kilo back together. In the end, they would have 132 kilos with 75% purity and 1 remaining kilo with 100% purity.

The 1 kilo with a 100% purity was put aside for Sheed, and 100 of 132 was given on consignment for $30,000 apiece, generating $3,000,000. Breeze, Egypt, and Zaire each received 30 keys, and Pooky received 10.

The remaining 32 were distributed on the street corners at $35 per gram, generating a total of $1,128,960. They had four corners, and each corner was manned by a caseworker, two runners, and two shooters. Each worker received a weekly payment of $2,000, and Easy took care of them every Sunday.

In conclusion, the net from every shipment was roughly $1,468,000, and they split the proceeds three ways.

After counting the buy money and confirming that it was $2,500,000, they loaded the money in two briefcases, and then left the house. Their destination was *Papi Land*. It was time to see Poncho.

***

In Northeast Philly

The Philadelphia Industrial Correctional Center, also known as PICC, was the most violent jail in the state of Pennsylvania. Unfortunately for Sheed, for the past twenty months this desolate environment was the place he called home.

"Food cart on the block! Food cart on the block!" Corrections Officer Jasmyn Logan announced over G Unit's intercom.

She was a beautiful fusion of Black and Cambodian, and could easily pass for the R&B singer Cassie. She had a high yellow complexion, slanted eyes, a sharp nose, rosey red cheeks, and juicy pink lips. She was 5'4", petite, and had the cutest little bubble butt that Sheed had ever seen. As a single mother who received her job through a welfare program, since her first day on the job, she made it extremely clear that if the money was right, she was willing to make moves. She knew about Sheed's reputation for getting money, so obviously he was her first target. They struck a deal that required her to bring him a weekly package of Newports and weed, but somewhere along the line they fell in love. Despite the fact that he was sitting in jail, he paid her bills and spoiled her with everything from Chanel sandals to Birkin bags.

As the inmates stepped forward to receive their food tray, she looked down the tier and saw Sheed standing in front of his cell. "Sheed come here for a minute!"

Upon hearing his name, he strolled toward the center console with a dope boy swag written all over him. He was freshly dressed in a brown and beige Louis Vuitton pajamas set, and gold framed Louis Vuitton eyeglasses decorated his chiseled face. As he approached her, he licked his lips and adjusted the semi-erection that formed in his pajamas pants.

"What's up, ma?"

She smiled at him and fanned an envelope in front of his face. "I found this when I was cleaning under the console. It's a letter addressed to you. It must've fell under there when I was passing out the mail yesterday. Here," she handed him the envelope. "And just so you know, I'm about to go on my lunch break so you know what that means."

"Facetime!" they laughed in unison.

This was their thing. Every day on her lunch break, she would go into the faculty bathroom, and use the Skype ap on her iPhone to give him a sexual performance.

He examined the envelope and saw that it was a letter from Pooky. He placed it in his back pocket, and then looked Jasmyn in the eyes. "I'm sayin' though, a nigga try'na taste that. What's up?"

"Taste that?" she looked at him like he was crazy. "Daddy, you know we can't do that with all these cameras watchin'. Plus, we only got one more week until you come home. You can wait."

Sheed chuckled. "I'm sayin' though, all you gotta do is play wit' ya pussy real quick, and then let me taste ya fingers."

A mischievous grin appeared on her face as she glanced around the dayroom. Satisfied that none of the inmates were watching, she slipped her right hand inside of her pants. After sliding her G-string to the side, she dipped her index and middle fingers inside of her honey pot, and swirled them in a circular motion until they were coated with her juices.

Sheed's semi-erection was now a fully loaded hammer. He loved the fact that his woman was a freak. "Yo hurry up, I'm try'na taste them jawns," he encouraged her.

She removed her hand, and he couldn't believe how drenched her fingers were. She spread her nectar across his mustache, and then slipped her fingers inside of his mouth.

"Damn Jas! Ya pussy smell like water and taste like chicken!"

"Boy, you's a mess," she laughed and playfully smacked him on the shoulder. "Now, go to ya cell and get ready. I'm goin' on my break."

As she left the cellblock, he went to his cell, and told his cellie to give him some private time. After locking the door and covering the window with his towel, he pulled the envelope from his back pocket and began reading.

Dear Lil' Bro,

How you holdin' up in there? I apologize for not coming to see you last week, but shit been a lil' hectic out here for me. After sittin' in a cell for 18 years, I'm still try'na adjust to the ways of streets. I took a lil' loss, but don't worry about it, I'ma bounce back on the next flip.

Oh yeah, I put Rahman in position, and we set up shop on Chew and Locust. That Germantown money ain't as fast as this North money, but you know how that go.

Anyway, hope you beat that mutha'fuckin' case next month. It's fuckin' me up that after 18 years, I finally made it home, and now you're the one that's locked up, and facin' 15. SMH!

Just stay strong and stay focused, lil' bro.

One Love, Pooky G's

After reading the letter, a huge smile spread across his face. "Fuck a 15 year bit!" he said to himself. "Big bro gon' be fucked up when I touch down next week!"

He placed the letter on his footlocker, and then plopped down on his bunk. He imagined his first day back on the streets. First, he would surprise Pooky and Rahman. Second, he would pay a visit to Sonny and pick up the $875,000 that he was holding for him. Finally, he would spend the rest of the day eating his favorite foods and making love to Jasmyn.

His Samsung vibrated through the pillow, snapping him out of his daydream. He reached inside of the slit and retrieved the rectangular shaped phone. *Damn, I love this lil' bitch,* he thought to himself while staring at her image on the LED screen. He grabbed a bottle of Jergens from his shelf, and then accepted the call. Let the games began!

***

In The Fairhill Projects

Heemy was awakened by the cold sensation of the .32 snub that was pressed against his forehead. He opened his eyes and was surprised to see that his best friend, Twany was the one holding the gun. "Yo Twany, what the fuck is you doin' dawg? Stop playin' all time!"

Twany laughed. "Nigga, stop bitchin'." He removed the gun from Heemy's forehead and held it in the air. "It ain't even loaded."

Twany lived a block away from Heemy in the Fairhill Projects on 10th Street. Just like Heemy, he was 17 and came from a broken home. His father was long gone and his mother was a heroin addict. The only person who loved him enough to look after him was his 21 year old brother Nipsy.

Basically, Heemy and Twany were two peas in a pod. They fought together. They stole together. They skipped school together, and most recently, they started selling weed together. Every day after school they would go to 7th Street and sell weed for Nipsy. Their shift was from 3-11 p.m., and at the end of the week they both received $250. Everything was going smooth until last week when Heemy arrived on the block with tears in his eyes. He told Twany and Nipsy about his altercation with Pooky, and Nipsy invited him to stay at their house with him and Twany. Obviously, Heemy accepted. Why wouldn't he? The living conditions at Nipsy's house were ten times better, and most importantly, he wouldn't have to worry about Pooky and his bullshit.

"Yo Twany, where you get that ratchet from?" Heemy asked while sitting up on the top bunk. "I know it ain't yours."

"I stole it from the Timberland box in Nipsy's closet," Tawny bragged. "That nigga's got so many burners that he probably won't even it's know it's missin'." He looked into the full length mirror on the back of his bedroom door, and aimed the gun at his reflection. "Yo, this that Dirty Harry shit right here," he started laughing.

"Lemme see that jawn," Heemy requested, and then held out his hand.

Twany handed him the .32 and a powerful feeling washed over him. It was a feeling that a 17 year old boy should never experience. It was the power of knowing that with this small piece of iron he could play the role of God and decide another man's fate.

"Yo, Nipsy ain't got no bullets for this jawn?"

"Yeah, he got bullets," Twany answered. He reached inside of his pocket and pulled out a handful of Winchesters.

"I got 'em right here." He handed Heemy the bullets, and gave him a funny look. "What you need bullets for? You ain't gon' shoot nuffin."

"Yah huhn," Heemy shot back as he tried to figure out how to load the revolver.

"Man, you don't even know what you doin'," Twany teased him. "Here, give it to me so I can show you."

Heemy handed him the gun and the bullets, and like a trained expert, Twany opened the cylinder with ease. He loaded the pistol, and then handed it back to Heemy. "A'ight, it's loaded. I bet you $20 you ain't got the heart to shoot somethin'."

"Yes I do!" Heemy perked up, and stuck out his chest. "Come outside and I'ma show you!"

They left the house without washing their faces or brushing their teeth, and posted up in front of the projects.

"A'ight, we out here. Whatchu gon' shoot?" Twany challenged. He folded his arms across his chest, and looked to Heemy for an answer.

"You got fiddy cents?" Heemy asked in a calm voice.

"Fiddy cents?" Twany looked at him like he was stupid. "What the fuck fiddy cents gotta do witchu shootin' somethin'?" He shook his head from side to side, and then fell out laughing. "Nigga, you pump fakin'! Ya ass ain't try'na shoot nuffin!"

"Nigga, you got fiddy cents or not?" Heemy snapped.

"Yeah, I got fiddy cents!" Twany shot back. He reached inside of his pocket and pulled out two quarters.

"A'ight, go in the Chinese store and get me a pack of cupcakes."

"A pack of cupcakes?" Twany teased. He leaned forward and stretched out his arms. "What the fuck you gon' do, go and shoot a pack of cupcakes? Nigga I'm hungry as shit! We can eat them jawns!"

Heemy pushed him in the chest. "Just buy the fuckin' cupcakes, damn!"

Still not understanding his best friend's logic, Twany strolled across Cumberland Street, and walked into the Chinese store. A couple of minutes later, he returned with a pack of chocolate cupcakes in his hand. He tossed them to Heemy. "A'ight cupcake killa. Whatchu gon' do now?"

Instead of responding, Heemy walked down the block toward the abandoned row house that was parallel to his backyard. Together, he and Twany crept around the side of the house, and approached the rusted fence that separated the two properties. Again, Twany questioned Heemy's logic. "What you gon' do, stick the cupcake in the fence and shoot 'em? Man you gon' fuck around and shoot up the back of ya house."

Heemy checked him. "Yo, chill the fuck out dawg. I know what I'm doin'." He whistled and called out for Pooky's pitbull. "Animal! Come here, boy!"

The muscular, tiger striped pitbull emerged from his doghouse, and trotted toward the fence. He looked at Heemy, and began to growl. His cropped ears stood at attention, and white foam dripped from his mouth. He rammed into the fence head first and desperately tried to bite through the rusted wire.

Twany nervously stepped back. "Damn, Heemy, how ya own dog comin' at you like dat? If it wasn't for this fence, he woulda fucked you up."

"He ain't my dog. He's Pooky's dog, and I hate his ass just as much as I hate Pooky," Heemy spat. He pulled the .32 from his waist, and then handed Twany the cupcakes. "Open these and hand me one."

Twany did as instructed, and Heemy placed one of the cupcakes on the barrel of the pistol. He then, grabbed the second cupcake and pressed it against the rusty fence. Animal stopped barking and sniffed the chocolate cupcake. Once he was satisfied that the cupcake was edible, he stuck out his tongue and licked the pastry.

Heemy smiled at him. "That's right boy, eat it all up," he encouraged him.

He pushed the cupcake through the fence, and continued smiling as the pitbull wolfed down the sweet chocolate. As soon as Animal was finished eating, he spotted the second cupcake, and pressed his nose against the fence. Heemy raised the .32 and gently pressed the cupcake against the fence. As Animal greedily licked the chocolate icing, Heemy squeezed the trigger.

Pow!

The bullet traveled through the pit bull's mouth and burst through the back of his skull. He fell on his side, and his muscular body began to twitch.

Stuck in somewhat of a trance, Heemy just stood there with the .32 still aimed at the fence. His nostrils flared and a single tear fell from his right eye. The sadistic feeling that spread throughout his body was exorbitant. He never imagined that taking a life would feel so intoxicating. He turned to Twany and saw that his comrade was staring at the mutilated dog with a devilish grin on his face. He handed him the pistol and told him to turn his head in the opposite direction. He then, pulled out his rock hard dick and urinated on Animal's dead body.

***

When Pooky pulled up in front of his house on 67th and Ogantz, he was nodding his head to Oshino's latest mixtape and puffing on an Optimo. After four weeks of doing what he considered to be hustling, he finally had the $300,000 that he owed Sonny for the 10 keys he received at the beginning of the month.

Eight months ago, when he was released from prison, Sheed supplied him with 24 keys, and made it clear that he expected to receive half of everything he made. He also provided Pooky with the cell phone that he used to serve his clientele. Initially, Pooky was on point, and in six months he had amassed a bankroll of $550,000. However, instead of sitting half of the money aside for Sheed, he fucked it all up. Due to his reckless spending habits and degenerate gambling, the only things he had to show for the money was his house, a silver Range Rover Sport, an extensive wardrobe, and a little over $75,000. His situation became so bad that two months ago, he explained the circumstances to Sheed, and begged his younger brother to hook him up with Sonny. Sheed had known all along that Pooky wasn't a hustler, and that's why he only supplied him with the 24 keys that he'd taken from Nahfisah. He wasn't really worried about the money because he was sitting on a little over $875,000. He just wanted to give his big brother the opportunity to shine. After giving Pooky a brief lecture about staying focused, he plugged him into Sonny, and Sonny offered to front him 10 keys for $30,000 apiece. The only condition was that Pooky couldn't tamper with quality of the work. When Sheed broke the news to Pooky, he was somewhat disappointed. He knew that even if he sold the keys for $35,000 a piece, after paying Sonny his $300,000, he would only make a $50,000 profit. In his mind, that wasn't enough. He expressed his concerns to Sonny, and on the strength of Sheed, Sonny gave him three corners, 10th and Susquehanna, Franklin and Diamond, and Delhi and Cumberland. Unfortunately, in Pooky's mind that still wasn't enough. He went against Sonny's orders, and stretched 5 of the keys to 10, and sold the watered down product to his weight customers.

As he sat behind the stirring wheel, he noticed a canary yellow 2014 Corvette Sting Ray parked across the street. A huge smile spread across his face, and he climbed out of the Range Rover. *Damn, she's right on time*, he thought to himself as he headed toward his house.

When he walked through the front door, Jerimiah's, *Birthday Sex*, was blasting from the second floor and the aroma of lavender scented candles permeated the air. He locked the door behind him, and then headed up the stairs. "Yo Flo, where you at?"

Instead of a response, the only thing he could hear was the music. He continued walking up the stairs, and the closer he got to the second floor, he could hear the sound of his headboard slamming against his bedroom wall.

"What the fuck?" he said to himself in disbelief. "I know this bitch ain't got another nigga in my mutha'fuckin' spot."

He removed the Glock .40 that was tucked in his waistband, and approached his bedroom door.

"Ummm! Fuck me baby! Right there! Keep it right there!" Flo shouted in pure ecstasy.

Infuriated, he pressed the muzzle of the Glock against the door, and slowly pushed it open.

"Oooooohhhh shit," he said to himself, completely caught off guard.

Instead finding another man in his bed, a cinnamon complexioned woman was fucking Flo from the back with a strap on dildo. He didn't recognize the woman, but her beautiful face made him hornier by the second. She had honey brown dreadlocks that were wrapped up in a crown, almond shaped eyes, full lips, and a broad nose that was decorated with a diamond stud. They made eye contact and she welcomed him to the party with the flick of her pierced tongue.

He stepped inside the room, and closed the door behind him. As he laid the Glock on his dresser, Flo must've felt his energy. She lifted her head from the pillow and smiled at him. Aroused by his presence, she bounced her ass against Miss Cinnamon's pelvis, and then reached in between her thighs to rub on her swollen clitoris.

"Now, that's what the fuck I'm talking 'bout!" Pooky encouraged them. He approached the bed and stood directly in front of Flo. The top half of her body was hanging off the bed, but the firm grasp that Miss Cinnamon had around her waist wouldn't allow her to fall. He unbuckled his belt, and his Prada slacks fell to the carpet. He pulled his dick through the slit in his boxer briefs, and slowly caressed her face with his anatomy. Miss Cinnamon thrust her hips and the dildo hit the bottom of Flo's pussy. Her response was a deep moan that was more akin to a soft cry. She pulled her hand away from her pussy, and then reached for Pooky's dick. She cradled the head between her thumb and index finger, and then pushed it against his pelvis. After tilting her head sideways, she leaned forward and used her tongue to massage his balls.

The look of ecstasy that was plastered on Pooky's face gave Miss Cinnamon the urge to put her own dick sucking skills to work. She removed the cum drenched dildo from Flo's pussy, and then crawled to the edge of the king sized mattress. After nuzzling her body beside Flo's, she grabbed Pooky's dick away from Flo's grasp, and placed it inside of her warm mouth.

After 10 minutes of getting his dick sucked and his balls licked at the same time, Pooky tapped out. "Damn, y'all gotta chill for a minute," he buckled under pressure. "Y'all got a nigga goin' crazy in this mutha'fucka."

Miss Cinnamon came up for air, and removed the strap on from around her waist. After tossing it on the floor, she looked at Flo and smiled. "Come on boo, let's take this nigga for a ride."

Flo smiled back, knowing exactly what Miss Cinnamon was referring to. Pooky didn't know it yet, but he was about to find out. Flo stood up on the mattress and told him to lie on his back. She then, straddled his face, giving him a mouthful of twat. Simultaneously, Miss Cinnamon hopped on his shaft, reverse cowgirl style, and together they rode him like there was no tomorrow.

***

An Hour Later...

Pooky emerged from the bathroom with a Polo towel wrapped around his waist. He had a neatly rolled Optimo dangling from his mouth, and he was higher than a fat man's blood pressure.

This was the fifth time that he'd done the unthinkable, and slept with Sheed's woman. It all started about a month ago when the two of them returned from a visit with Sheed. During the visit, Sheed informed them that he was considering a 15 to 30 year plea agreement. To Pooky's grimy ass, that was music to his ears. With Sheed out of the way, not only would he be able take over his business, he'd also have the opportunity to take from his younger brother the one thing that he'd wanted since the day he was released from prison, Flo.

After the visit, Pooky put his plan into action. He explained to Flo that with Sheed doing all of that time, the lifestyle that she'd grown accustomed to was over, and that the

Gucci and Fendi designs that she loved so much would soon be a memory. He promised her that he was man enough to hold her down, and he did everything in his power to prove it. That following week, he laced her with diamonds, money, and a brand new wardrobe. Initially, the love and loyalty that she had for Sheed outweighed Pooky's gestures, but eventually her greed turned the scales.

It also didn't hurt that Pooky's muscular frame, caramel complexion, wavy hair, and dope boy swag was a constant reminder of Sheed. In the end she abandoned her inhibitions, and just like Jay Z, she was on to the next one!

When Pooky entered the bedroom and saw that the room was empty, he went downstairs and found Flo sitting at the dining room table. She was smoking a Newport and stuffing the $300,000 that he owed Sonny inside of a black duffle bag. He looked around for Miss Cinnamon, but found no traces of her.

"Yo, where ya homie at?" he asked while using her Newport to light the tip of his Optimo. "I was hopin' we could go a few more rounds."

"A few more rounds?" she chuckled. "Nigga that was a one shot deal. You know I'm a stingy bitch when it comes to my man."

"Whatever," Pooky smiled as he took a seat at the table. He looked at the duffle bag, and then returned his gaze to Flo. "It came out to $300,000, right?"

She nodded her head. "Yeah. You said that every stack was $10,000, and I counted a total of 30 stacks."

Before he had the chance to respond, the cordless phone that was lying on the table began to ring. He picked it up, and held it to his ear.

"Who dis?"

"Hey yo Pook I need to holla at you about somethin'," his young bul Mar-Mar stated in a slow, Jadakiss type voice.

"Well holla at me. What's good?"

"Yo, that lil' nigga Heemy killed Animal."

"What?" Pooky snapped. "What the fuck you mean he killed Animal?"

"The lil' nigga shot him."

"Hold the fuck up, you mean to tell me that you just stood there, and let this bitch ass nigga shoot my fuckin' dog?"

"Nizzaw! I wasn't even here when it happened," Mar-Mar quickly explained. "I just pulled up on the block a couple of minutes ago. When I got out the car, Beaver Bushnut told me what happened. He said that him and SMD was out here waitin' on me when they heard a gunshot in the backyard. He said they went around back to see what happened, and that's when he found Animal wit' his shit pushed back."

"Well, how the fuck did Bushnut know that Heemy was the one who shot him?"

"Yo, you ain't even let me finish," Mar-Mar complained. "He told me that Heemy and Twany was creepin' from the back of the house, and that Heemy had a burner in his hand."

"A'ight man, damn!" Pooky retorted. "If you see them lil' niggas, keep em' close til' I get there!"

Askari

Chapter Eight

It was a little pass 2:30 p.m. when three triple black Escalades pulled up on the corner of Marshall and Tioga, and blocked off Poncho's bodega. The first truck parked along the edge of Tioga Street, the second truck parked at the bend in the corner, and the third truck parked along the edge of Marshall Street.

Easy hopped out the first truck, and Zaire hopped out the third truck. Both were strapped with an MP5, and together they scoped the area looking for any sign of suspicious activity.

Sitting behind the stirring wheel of the second truck, Sonny checked the safety on his FNH .45, and then gazed through the tinted window to read Easy's body language. After receiving a head nod, he grabbed the two briefcases from the back seat, and then him and Rahmello exited the SUV.

When they walked inside of the bodega, the first thing that grabbed their attention was the loud Spanish music that played over the intercom and the distinct aroma of the Goya products that filled the air. They approached the cash register where Olivia, Poncho's 19 year old daughter was reading a Hip Hop Weekly magazine and using her index finger to twirl her hair in a circular motion. The young woman was beautiful to say the least. She had a light brown complexion, green eyes, a pointed nose, thin lips, and a petite frame. Everything about her was exotic, and if one were to compare her to anybody, it would have to be the actress Zoe Saldana. She looked up from the magazine and smiled. "What's up Sontino? You here to see papi?"

"Yeah," Sonny responded, admiring her natural beauty.

She looked at Rahmello. His baby face, blue eyes, and wavy hair was driving her crazy. *Damn papi, you lookin' good as shit*, she thought to herself, admiring the way his soft yellow Dolce & Gabbana linen set was lying on his muscular body. She locked eyes with him for a brief moment, and then grabbed her cell phone from the counter. After dialing the numbers to the apartment on the second floor, she held the phone to her ear.

Poncho answered on the third ring. "Hola Oli."

"Papi, Sontino is here to see you."

"Okay, Oli. Send him up," he replied, then disconnected the call.

She looked at Sonny. "Papi said for you to come upstairs," she nodded her head toward the back of the bodega. "You know the way."

Sonny looked at Rahmello and gave him a look that said, *Be on point*. He then, headed up the aisle toward the door that led to Poncho's apartment. He knocked about four times, and a few seconds later he could hear footsteps descending the stairs on the other side. The door swung open, and a short Columbian man that he'd never seen before was standing there with a smug expression. He was extremely thin, and he appeared to be in his late forties. He looked Sonny up and down, and then gritted his teeth. "Ju packin' papa?"

"Am I packin'?" Sonny screwed up his face, wondering why the man would ask such a stupid question. "Yo, where ya boss at? He's expectin' me."

"I said is ju packin'?" The little man raised his voice.

Sonny looked at him like he was crazy. "And I said... where the *fuck* is ya boss at?"

"Chee-Chee!" Poncho yelled from the second floor. "He okay! Let him up!"

Chee-Chee gritted his teeth, and then stepped to the side. He gestured for Sonny to walk in front of him, but Sonny just

Blood of a Boss II

stood there shaking his head. "Nizzaw, you go first and I'ma follow you."

When they reached the apartment on the second floor, Poncho and another man were sitting on the sofa watching a soccer match. *Yo, what's up wit' this nigga?* Sonny questioned himself. *I've got two point five on me, and this nigga got me around two mutha'fuckas that I never even seen before. This nigga trippin'!* Subconsciously, he tightened his grasps around the handles of the briefcases.

Poncho got up from the sofa and extended his right hand. "Sontino, how ju doing?"

Sonny sat the briefcases down on the carpet and accepted the gesture with a firm handshake. At the same time, he attentively kept his eyes on the two strangers. "I'm a'ight."

Poncho could tell what he was thinking, and a huge smile spread across his face. "I want for ju to meet my brother Juan." He ushered him over to the sofa. "Juan, dis is Sontino. Easy's boy."

The second Sonny realized that the light brown skinned Columbian was Juan Nunez, a chill ran up his spine. He'd been hearing stories about him for the past year and a half, and he knew that Juan was the real deal. Juan and Poncho grew up in Columbia with Pablo Escobar, and in the mid-eighties, they came to America and flooded the states with the best cocaine that the country had ever seen.

"Sontino, it's nice to finally meet ju," Juan smiled and shook his hand. "I been hearing some very good things about ju, and I was hoping ju could help me and Poncho out with a small problem."

"Oh yeah," Sonny nodded his head. "What type of problem?"

The Al Pacino look alike reached inside of his trousers and pulled out a picture of a young Spanish man sitting on the

99

hood of a Pepsi blue Lamborghini Superleggra. He was wearing a white tuxedo and huge diamonds decorated his ears. He handed the picture to Sonny.

"His name is Roberto Alverez, but ju may or may not know him as *Mexican Bobby*. He's from Isla Mujares, but now he's in Philadelphia."

Sonny shrugged his shoulders. "A'ight, but I still don't understand the small problem that you're speakin' of, and on top of that, what makes you think that I can help you?"

Poncho stepped to Juan and whispered something in his ear. Juan nodded his head up and down, and then cleared his throat.

"Our problem is dat he's an informant. He testified against a friend of ours, and now he's rubbing it in our faces."

"How?" Sonny asked.

Juan looked at Poncho, and Poncho handed Sonny a mug shot of Mexican Bobby. He examined the picture and couldn't believe his eyes. On the right side of the man's neck, as clear as day, there was a tattoo of a rat eating a piece of cheese, and directly above were the words *La Ratta*.

"The rat?" Sonny questioned. He looked back and forth between Juan and Poncho. "Yo, this is a joke right?"

Juan just stared at him.

"Damn," Sonny shook his head from side to side. "This nigga told on a mutha'fucka, and then had the nerve to get a tattoo of a rat on his neck?"

Juan nodded his head. "Ju see my point? I want him dead within 48 hours. Can ju handle dat?"

"Yeah I can definitely handle that, but what's in it for me? This ain't no meatball shit. If one of my homies gets locked up or hurt in the process, then what?"

"We understand ju concern," Poncho interjected, "and to show our gratitude we are willing to give ju an opportunity dat we only give to a chosen few." He pointed toward the coffee table where 200 kilograms of cocaine were neatly piled one on top of one another. "Not only are we willing to increase ju monthly shipment to 200 keys, we'll drop de price from $25,000 to $20,000 a key. How ju feel about dat?"

Sonny contemplated his offer, and then nodded his head in agreement. "You know what Poncho, you can count me in. Consider it done."

Poncho smiled at him, and one by one, him and Juan shook his hand. Poncho placed his hand on Sonny's shoulder. "Ju made de right move Sontino lemme tell ju, but dere's one more thing. I need for ju to bring me de tongue dat he used to speak evil, and de hands dat he used to point out our friend from de witness stand. Ju got dat?"

"He's a done deal, Poncho. You have my word."

Juan nodded his head and smiled at him. He then directed his attention to Poncho. "Ju and Chee-Chee help Sontino carry de yahyo to his car."

"Naw, don't even worry about it," Sonny quickly interjected. "My lil' brother's downstairs. We can handle it. As a matter of fact, speakin of the work, I only brought two point five wit' me to pay for my usual 100. So how we 'posed to work this out with the extra 100?"

"Don't worry about it," Juan assured him. "We'll just call it a gesture of our appreciation. A gift from us to ju."

After stuffing the 200 keys inside of four duffle bags, Sonny placed a bag over each shoulder. Poncho and Chee-Chee grabbed the remaining two, and they left the apartment. When they descended the stairs and entered the bodega, they could see that Olivia was leaned over the counter smiling at Rahmello. Poncho became red with anger, and Sonny noticed his demeanor. He also made a mental note to tell his younger brother to stay away from her. Although the young woman was drop dead gorgeous, she was Poncho's daughter, and based on his body language, he obviously didn't approve of them being an item.

As they approached the cash register, Sonny removed the duffle bags from his shoulders, and handed them to Rahmello. He then, collected the remaining bags from Poncho and Chee-Chee. "I appreciate the opportunity, Poncho."

"I'm sure of it Sontino. Just make sure dat we hear from ju in a couple of days."

Sonny nodded his head in the affirmative, and then gestured for Rahmello to lead the way outside. When they emerged from the bodega, they noticed that Easy and Zaire were at full attention.

"Pops, is everything good?" Sonny asked.

Easy nodded his head. "Everything's good. A cop car drove pass a couple of minutes ago, but other than that, everything's good."

After glancing up and down the block, Sonny headed toward the back of his Escalade and opened the cargo doors. Rahmello hopped in the driver's side and quickly got to work. He started the engine, pumped the brake pedal three times, and then set the air conditioner to 65 degrees. The side panels in the back of the truck slid open, and Sonny filled the hidden compartments with the cocaine.

After everything was secure, him, Easy, and Zaire hopped back in their designated SUVs and headed back to the stash house.

"So," Sonny said to Rahmello as he settled into the passenger's seat. "What's up wit' you and lil' buddy?"

Rahmello smirked at him. "Who you talking 'bout? Oli?"

"Yeah, I'm talking 'bout Oli. You know that's a no-no, right?"

"A no-no?" Rahmello scrunched up his face. "Whatchu mean that's a no-no? We feelin' each other, and we try'na make somethin' happen. What's wrong wit' that?"

"She's Poncho's daughter, that's what's wrong."

"And," Rahmello shot back.

"And she's off limits. We never mix business with pleasure," Sonny stated with a no nonsense tone of voice. "We need Poncho right now, and we can't afford no bullshit behind you fuckin' his daughter. I refuse to let dick and pussy games stand in the way of this money. So, therefore," he paused for a couple of seconds to let his words sink in. "You gon' leave her lil' ass alone and focus on gettin' this mutha'fuckin money."

At the end of the day, Rahmello knew that Sonny was right. Unfortunately, him and Olivia had been secretly dating for the past six months and not only were they deeply in love, she was five weeks pregnant with his baby. *Man, fuck what this nigga talking 'bout. Ain't no mutha'fuckin way I'm turnin' my back on Oli and the baby.*

"Rahmello?" Sonny continued, interrupting his thoughts. "Did you hear what I said?"

"Yeah brozay, I heard you. She's off limits."

***

At The Federal Building

"What the hell is *Operation Block Boy* and how does it tie into the Gervin Moreno case?" asked Clavenski. He was seated at the head of a conference table, and accompanied by a room full of DEA agents. Based on their facial expressions, he had the strange notion that up until this point he was the only person in the room who didn't know what was going on.

Agent Long got up from his seat and approached the projector screen that was fixed to the front wall. He grabbed the remote control from its holder, and aimed it toward the projector box that was hanging from the ceiling. He pressed the on button, and a picture of Sonny appeared on the screen. He was wearing a black waist length mink and leaning against the hood of his Rolls Royce Ghost.

"Who the hell is this?" asked Clavenski.

"This is Sontino *Sonny Money* Moreno," Agent Long spoke with conviction. "He's the protégé of a slain drug lord by the name of Michael Brooks. After Brooks was murdered a year and a half ago," he pointed at the projector screen, "this is the guy who took over his multi-million dollar operation. We've been watching him for nearly two years, and we know for a fact that he's responsible for mass quantities of cocaine coming in and out of Pennsylvania."

Clavenski sat still with his arms folded across his chest. "I've never heard of this kid, and I'm beginning to feel as though I wasted an entire Saturday afternoon on some bullshit." He rubbed   the stubble on his chin, and then took a deep breath. "Will someone please tell me how this ties into the Gervin Moreno case?"

Agent Long simply smiled. "He's Gervin's grandson."

"Wait a second, you mean to tell me that this kid," he pointed at the projector screen, "is Gervin Moreno's grandson?"

"That's right," Agent Long confirmed. "And trust me Andy, I've been watching this guy for some time now. He's the real deal."

"The real deal?" asked Clavenski. "Just what do you mean by that?"

"In over fifty years he's the only one to legitimately hold his own against Gervin Moreno, and *The Moreno Crime Family*. In fact, the word on the street is that he's the reason that Gervin's been laying low. Some of our sources even went as far as to say that Gervin's afraid of him."

"Hold up Terry, you're confusing me. Didn't you just say that he was Gervin's grandson?"

"He is, but according to the Philadelphia Police Department, Sontino and Gervin bumped heads when Gervin killed Brooks. Allegedly, Sontino responded by killing at least ten of his men."

Clavenski's mind was traveling at the speed of light. "Well, if this kid is everything that you say he is, then why am I just now hearing about him?"

"I've *been* tellin' you about him Andy! You were so caught up in the Gervin Moreno case that you didn't pay me any mind!"

"What?" Clavenski protested, refusing to accept the fact that he was slacking in his performance.

"Listen Andy," Agent Long spoke in a softer voice. "Just look inside of your files. Trust me he's in there."

Clavenski turned his attention to the beautiful woman that was seated at the opposite end of the table. " Agent Brown did you know about this?"

"I sure did," she replied. "I've been working this case for over a year now."

"I see," Clavenski nodded his head. "Well, go inside of you're file and hand me some paperwork on this guy."

Agent Brown chuckled to herself. Like the rest of the agents in the room, she utterly despised Clavenski. Aside from the fact that he always gave the agents a hard time, he walked around the federal building as if he owned it, and he had a chip on his shoulder the size of Mt. Everest. "I already have it," she held up a manila envelope, and then slid it across the table.

She then lounged back in her chair, and gave him a look that said, *Yeah, Mr. I'm Smarter Than Everyone Else, had you been on top of your game, you would've known this shit already!*

He noticed her body language, and scowled at her. *Bitch!* He opened the envelope and removed its contents. After a few minutes of reading, a huge smile spread across his face, and he looked at Agent Long. "Based on this information, I'm thinking we can build a case for a continuing criminal enterprise. In fact, this kid could be the only opportunity that we have to stick it to Gervin. I mean shucks he is a Moreno. Therefore, every piece of evidence that we can gather against him we can attribute it to *The Moreno Crime Family.*

"You know," he held up both of his hands and used his fingers to indicate quotation marks, "make it a *Family* thing!"

"Exactly!" Agent Long agreed. "I told you we could still stick it to the Moreno's. All we had to do was think outside of the box."

"Alright, so what's the next move?" Clavenski asked him. "Is there anything I can do?"

"It sure is," Agent Long stated while handing him a white piece of paper. "It's a formal request for $350,000."

"$350,000?" Clavenski cringed. "For what?"

"Buy money," Agent Long replied. "Sontino's finally ready to do business with me."

***

Later That Night
At The Docks On Delaware Avenue

Romey Noodles was standing in front of his warehouse when a navy blue Excursion pulled into the parking lot. The high beams were on, and the lights were so bright that he couldn't identify the driver. He was expecting a visit from Alphonso to discuss the money that he owed Carmine, but Alponso didn't drive a dark colored SUV, he drove a white BMW.

"Who the fuck is this?" he nervously stated. He held up his right hand to shield his eyes from the bright light, and then reached behind his back with his left to grip the handle on his 9mm.

When the truck pulled up in front of him, the tinted driver's side window rolled down, and he was surprised to see a beautiful woman sitting behind the stirring wheel. He released his grasp from the butt of his gun and seductively licked his lips. "What's up sweetheart? Can I help you with something?"

Malice smiled at him and nodded her head. "I hope so, papi. I was supposed to be performing at *Club Spontaneous*, but my GPS is acting up and I can't find de club," she explained in her Cuban accent.

Romey Noodles looked at her skeptically. His warehouse was stationed by the edge of the Delaware River, about mile away from the strip nightclubs that lined Delaware Avenue. Therefore, it was highly improbable that she could have made it this far up the avenue without laying eyes on the infamous strip club. Malice picked up on his apprehension. "I noticed all of de clubs back dere, but I didn't see *Club Spontaneous*."

She opened the driver's side door and climbed out the Excursion in a black cat suit and knee high boots. Romey Noodles damn near passed out. Aside from her thick thighs, curvy hips, and flat stomach, the nipples on her coconut sized titties were popping up like turkey testers. He examined her body from head to toe, and then inconspicuously adjusted the erection that was forming in his pants.

"Y—Y—You shoulda seen it," he stuttered. "*Club Spontaneous* is the big gray building with the bright pink lights, and the club's sign," he stretched out his arms for emphasis, "is the biggest sign on the strip. It's the one with the image of a broad twerkin' her ass."

Malice pouted her juicy lips, and then spoke in a whiny voice. "Dis GPS system," she pointed inside of the SUV. "I was so focused on try'na fix it dat I musta missed de sign dat ju speak of."

Romey Noodles gently grabbed her by the arm. "I'll tell you what, how 'bout I take a look at your GPS system, and instead of you performin' at *Club Spontaneous* you can come inside and perform for me." He released her arm and stuck out his right hand. "The name's Romey."

She accepted his gesture with a feminine handshake. "My name's Malissa and I don't know about dat papi. I drove all de way from New York and de guy who owns de club is expectin' me."

"The owner's a good friend of mine," Romey Noodles chuckled. "He'll understand. Trust me."

"Ju know Carmine?"

He looked at her like she was crazy.

"Do I know Carmine?" He laughed and then waved her off. "Fugget about it."

She laughed at him. His swag reminding her of the mob movies that she loved so much. "Dis is what we can do, if ju can fix my GPS ju got a deal."

"Now we're gettin' somewhere," he smiled. "I'll have it fixed in no time." He rolled up the sleeves on his Armani sweater, and then approached the Excursion. She stepped aside, and he stuck his head in the driver's side door. "Hey," he called out over his shoulder. "How do I turn on the dome light? It's darker than a friggin' cave in here."

"I got a light for you," a masculine voice spoke up from the backseat.

Gangsta flicked his lighter, and the truck's interior lit up like a jack o'lanter. Romey Noodles couldn't believe his eyes. Murder and Gangsta were sitting in the back seat, and they both had a gun aimed at his face.

"What the fuck is goin' on?" he asked. "Did Carmine send you? Whatever he's payin', I'll double it."

Neither of them spoke a word. Malice slid up behind him and removed the .9mm that was tucked in the small of his back. "Take it easy, papi. Ju move and ju die."

***

Approximately Thirty Minutes Later...

Aside from the dark SUV that was used to kidnap Romey Noodles, the historical Walt Whitman Bridge was completely deserted. The moon was shining down on the water below, and the orange blaze of a burning trash can could be spotted from a distance.

Romey Noodles was barely conscious. Initially, he suspected that Carmine was the one pulling the strings, but he quickly realized that this was far from a traditional mafia hit. This was something different. Something far more sinister. His arms were handcuffed behind his back, and a thick chain that was fashioned into a harness was strapped to his chest and torso. His naked body was doused in gasoline, and his eyes were nearly swollen shut from the pistol whipping that he just received from Gangsta.

The weather was a chilly 48 degrees, and although he was shivering, his naked body was burning hot. Cold sweat covered him from head to toe, and warm steam rose from his body like fresh dog shit in the middle of winter. He could barely stand on his own two feet so to keep him erect, Malice held him up by his right side, and Murder held him up by his left.

Gangsta was off to the side weaving the chain through the railing of the bridge, and a money green Escalade was parked behind the SUV that was used to kidnap him. The headlights were turned off, and Grip was seated comfortably in the passenger's seat.

"Please," Romey Noodles whispered. "Just tell me what the I did to deserve this shit."

His request fell on deaf ears as Gangsta just looked him and laughed. After securing the chain with a deadbolt lock, he approached the Escalade and opened the passenger's side door.

"Uncle G, you ready?"

Grip nodded his head, and then climbed out the Cadillac truck. A gray trench coat was draped over his black suit, and his trademark Bossalini hat was cocked to the side. He walked toward the edge of the bridge and positioned himself in front of Romey Noodles. The battered Italian looked him in the eyes, and then regretfully lowered his head. It was then that he realized the root of his fate.

"Mr. Moreno," he whispered. "It ain't my fault. I told Carmine to stay away from the docks, but he wouldn't listen."

Grip didn't respond. Instead, he reached inside of his suit jacket and pulled out a Cohiba cigar and his gold cigar cutter. After clipping off the ends of the stogie, he gestured for Gangsta to give him a light. Gangsta lit the tip of the cigar and a cloud of smoke appeared in front of his face. He took a couple of puffs, and then looked at his nephew. "Gangsta," he said in his deep voice. "Sit his ass up on the railing."

Gangsta grabbed Romey Noodles by the waist, and with the help of Murder and Malice, he lifted him off his feet and sat his body on top of the steel railing.

Grip took a step closer and blew a thick cloud of smoke in Romey Noodles' face. He looked the Italian dead in the eyes, and slowly shook his head from side to side. "In this life Romey, some shit is just necessary." He tossed the burning cigar on Romeys' gasoline drenched body and the chubby Italian burst into flames. He fell off the railing and dropped about fifteen feet before the chain that was linked to his harness jerked him to a stop.

"*Agggghhhh!*" he screamed like a banshee, and struggled to free himself from the harness. He kicked his feet and wiggled his shoulders, but none of these movements could deter his fate. He continued to scream as his burning body swung from right to left.

As Grip turned around and headed back to his Escalade, Gangsta leaned over the railing and shouted at the burning pendulum. "Don't take it personal, Romey Rome! It's only business mutha'fucka!"

Askari

Chapter Nine

The Following Morning...

Sonny was awakened by the soft kisses that Daphney and Keyonti were placing on his face. This was their daily ritual. Every morning, Keyonti would wake up, crawl out of bed, and then slip inside of her parent's bedroom. She would wake up Daphney, and together they smothered Sonny's face with kisses. Today was no different.

"Cocoa Fat-Fat!" Sonny greeted his daughter with the nickname he'd given her. "Whatchu doin' to dada?"

The little girl giggled, and then wrapped her arms around his head. "Fat-Fat lub dada!"

He lifted her in the air and twisted her body from side to side. "Ahn ahn. You don't lub dada," he challenged her.

She nodded her head and playfully shouted at him.

"Fat-Fat lub dada! Momma lub dada! And D-Day lub dada too!"

"Yep!" Daphney chimed in. "We lub you, dada." She kissed him on the neck, and then inconspicuously stroked his dick under the satin sheets. "Guess who else lubs dada?"

"Rocko," Sonny smiled, knowing damn well she was referring to something else.

"And who else?"

"I don't know," he smiled. "Who?"

"Ya pussy lubs you," she whispered is his ear, and then gently bit down on his earlobe.

It was times like this that made him appreciate life. He had a beautiful family, a beautiful home, a loyal team, and more money then he'd ever imagined. Most of all, he had a hustle inside of him that just wouldn't quit. He truly loved his life, and aside from what happened to Riri and their unborn child he held no regrets.

As he turned to kiss Daphney on the lips, Dayshon and Rocko entered the master bedroom, and Keyonti went into a frenzy. She absolutely adored her big brother, and anytime he was in her vicinity, she lit up like a Christmas tree.

"D-Day! D-Day!" She pointed toward him. "Look, dada it's D-Day!" She wiggled away from Sonny's grasp, and crawled to the edge of the king sized mattress. "Up, up, D-Day! Up, up!" she demanded with her arms stretched out.

Dayshon picked her up and hoisted her small body in the air. "Fat-Fat, you so pwetty!" he said in a baby's voice. He spun her around, and she laughed uncontrollably. Feeling left out, Rocko hopped up on the bed and nestled his muscular body next to Sonny's feet.

"Rocko!" Daphney shouted at the large Rottweiler. "If you don't get ya ass off my goddamn bed!"

Defiantly, he looked at her, and then shifted his gaze to Sonny. "Ahn ahn, don't be lookin' at Sontino!" she continued shouting. "You heard what I said!"

Rocko pouted, and then hopped off the bed and laid down on the carpet. Keyonti noticed that her second best friend was sad, and she demanded that Dayshon put her down. "Down down, D-Day. I want Wacko!"

He sat her down on the carpet, and she cuddled up beside the large K-9. In turn, he rubbed his nose against her face, and licked her left cheek as if it were a chocolate ice cream cone. She giggled and wrapped her arms around his massive neck. "Fat-Fat lub Wacko."

Roof!

Dayshon laughed at the odd couple, and then sat down beside Sonny on the bed. Sonny placed him in a headlock and gave him a light noogie. "What's poppin' lil' homie? You good?"

"Yeah I'm good," the little boy smiled. "I'm hungry, though. Can you make us some cheese eggs and turkey bacon?"

"I wish I could, but I ain't got the time." He looked at Daphney and smiled before throwing her under the bus. "But your mom does."

She playfully scowled at him, and then threw a barrage of punches at his chest and shoulders.

"Agh shit!" He laughed, and then curled up in a ball. "Come on Daph stop playing! I got a lot of stuff to do this morning!"

She climbed off the bed, and then leaned forward to pick up Keyonti. "Come on y'all. Let's go downstairs so mommy can make y'all something to eat."

As they left the room, Sonny's iPhone vibrated on the nightstand. He picked it up and saw that the caller was Pooky.

"Yo bul."

"Sonny, what's up wit' it? It's about that time, you dig."

"Yeah," Sonny sighed. "It's definitely about that time, and I need to holla at you about some serious shit."

"What's good?" Pooky quickly replied. "Holla at me now."

"Nizzaw, you know I don't fuck wit' these phones like that. Just meet me on Delhi Street around 5 o'clock, and I'ma holla at you then."

Click!

He laid the phone back down, and then grabbed the pack of Newports that were lying beside his alarm clock. He removed one from the pack, and then searched around for his lighter.

"Damn, what the fuck I do wit' dat jawn?"

He looked on the side of his nightstand and spotted the lighter on the floor. Directly beside it, a white envelope was lying face down. He snatched up both of the items and instantly realized that the envelope was a letter addressed to him from Daphney's father. He got up from the bed and walked toward the intercom box that was positioned on the wall beside to the door. He pressed the *kitchen* button, and asked Daphney about the letter.

"Yo Daph, why you ain't tell me I got a letter from ya pop?"

"Damn, that's right. It came in the mail yesterday, and I forgot to tell you. What's he talking 'bout?"

"I don't know," he replied while eyeing the envelope. "I didn't read it yet."

"Well open it, and find out what's up wit' him."

"A'ight." He lit the tip of his cigarette and accessed the situation. Daphney's father was a legend on the streets of Philly. In the late eighties and early nineties, he was the boss of the infamous *Young Black Mafia*. His crew of young drug dealers were known for terrorizing the city, and they made millions of dollars in the process. Their drug of choice was cocaine, and their marketing strategy was simple. Either you did business with the *YBM* or you didn't do business at all. Unfortunately, a questionable chain of events landed him in prison with a life sentence, and after spending the past 23 years in SCI Graterford his chances of seeing the light of day were slim to none. *Damn*, Sonny thought himself. *I wonder what this nigga's up to.*

This was the first time that Alvin had ever written him a letter, and aside from him and Daphney taking the kids to visit him every month, their relationship was cordial at best. He opened the envelope and began reading the letter.

116

Dear Sontino,

First and foremost I salute you young brother, and I hope and pray that this letter reaches you in the best of health. I've never been the type to beat around the bush so I'ma make a fat girl skinny. It's imperative that I speak to you in person. I need you to visit me as soon as possible, and please do not bring Daph and the kids.

Respect, Loyalty, and Love,
Alvin Rines

PS. In the absence of humility, a man is destined for failure.

After reading the letter, his iPhone vibrated on the nightstand and the LED screen indicated that the caller was Easy.

"What's up, pops?"

"I was just callin' to let you know that everything turned out as expected, and I'm ready to get things rollin'," Easy informed him. He was referring to the shipment of cocaine.

"A'ight, just get everybody together, and meet me at *Donkees*. We got some important shit to talk about."

"What about Pooky?" Easy asked. "You want him there too?"

"Naw," Sonny quickly replied. "I'ma holla at dude later on today. Dig though, I just got a letter from Alvin sayin' that he needs to talk to me about somethin' important, and that he wants me to visit him as soon as possible."

"Oh yeah, I wonder what that's about," Easy stated, wondering what Alvin had up his sleeve.

"I don't know pops, but I'ma definitely find out," said Sonny.

"Yeah, you make sure you do that. Alvin was a stand up nigga, but at the same time, that's a crafty mutha'fucka. I ain't sayin' he on some other shit or nothin' like that, but be careful what you say to him. Information is power, and you never wanna give a nigga like Alvin more than what's needed."

Sonny nodded his head. "I feel you pops. Look, I gotta make an important phone call, so I'ma holla at you later."

"Say no more," Easy replied. "Tell Daph and the kids that I send my love."

"I got you," Sonny assured him. He disconnected the call, and then scrolled down his call log until he reached Savino's number. He pressed the call button, and held the phone to his ear.

Ring! Ring! Ring!

"Hello," Savino answered.

"Mario, what's up? It's Sontino."

"Sontino, what's up? Is everything okay?"

"Yeah everything's straight. I'm callin' because I need you to holla at your private investigators. I need to have somebody located."

"That's not a problem," Savino assured him. "Just give me a name and a possible location?"

"Roberto Alverez a.k.a. Mexican Bobby. He's originally from Mexico, but he's livin' somewhere in Philly."

"Is he a citizen or an illegal immigrant?"

"I'm not sure."

"Do you know what kind of car he drives?"

"Yeah," Sonny confirmed. "A blue Lamborghini."

"Consider it done," Savino assured him as he wrote down the details.

"And Mario, I need to know his whereabouts by tonight."

Savino chuckled. "Don't worry about it. This is the reason you pay me the big bucks. Trust me, I'm all over this shit."

***

Later That Day...

When Sonny pulled up on the corner of Delhi and Cumberland, he couldn't believe what he saw. Mar-Mar was standing in the middle of the street aiming his gun at Beaver Bushnut. He killed the ignition, and then hopped out the Escalade.

"Yo, Mar-Mar, what the fuck is you doin'?" he shouted while walking toward the chubby, dark skinned young man.

When Mar-Mar glanced over his left shoulder and saw that the voice belonged to Sonny, he almost shit in his cargos. "Naw Sonny, it's just a BB gun," he quickly explained. "Bushnut ain't have no money so he said that I could shoot him wit' my BB gun if I gave him a free blast."

Sonny ice grilled him. This was hands down the dumbest shit that he'd ever heard in his life, and he wanted to get to the bottom of it. He fixed his scowl on Beaver Bushnut, who at one point in time was considered to be the sharpest pimp and con man in the city. "Hey yo Bushnut, what the fuck is up witchu ol' head?"

"Nah ahn, Sonny Money!" The shabby light skinned man began his protest. "Me and the youngin' done already struck us a deal so you gon' have to fall back and let ol' Bushnut do what the fuck he gotta do!" he continued in his raspy voice. A huge smile spread across his face, he began to do the *Cabbage Patch* dance in the middle of the street. "The youngin' gon' gimmie a bazoomski," he bopped from side to side, "for every time I let him shoot me wit' dat dere BB gun." He spun around, did a split, and then came back up like James Brown. "Now, think about it Sonny Money, that ain't shit to a nigga like Bushnut." He wiped the sweat from his dusty brow, and continued pleading his case. "Bushnut done been shot, stabbed, set on fire, ran up in the church, and stuck up the choir," he bragged. "Now, Bushnut know you's a stone cold killah. He know it. But you gon' let ol' Bushnut get his paws on dem dere bazoomskis!"

Sonny looked at him like he was crazy, and then burst out laughing. He hadn't dealt with a crack head in over two years, and he forgot how obnoxious they could be. Especially when it came to getting a free blast. He looked at Mar-Mar and shrugged his shoulders. "Fuck it, if that's what he wants, give it to him."

A mischievous grin spread across Mar-Mar's chubby face as he aimed the BB gun and squeezed the trigger.

Put! Put! Put!

"Awww mutha'fucka goddamn!" Beaver Bushnut shouted as he hopped up and down, clutching his right ear. "You done shot ol' Bushnut in the goddamned ear!"

Sonny and Mar-Mar burst out laughing. As bad as Sonny wanted to conceal his amusement, he couldn't help it. The shit was just too funny.

"Now just what in the fuck is y'all laughin' at? This shit ain't funny!" Beaver Bushnut snapped on Sonny and Mar-Mar, making them laugh even harder. He walked up to Mar-Mar and held out his hand. "You done shot ol' Bushnut three times so now you owe him three dimes, and if I was you, I'd be payin' up! 'Cause if you don't," he raised his right knee and held up his arms like the Karate Kid. "Shit gon' get ca-razy out this summa-muh-bitch!"

Mar-Mar handed over the three bags of crack, and Sonny questioned him about Pooky's whereabouts.

"Yo where this nigga at? He was supposed to meet me out here."

Mar-Mar nodded toward the trap house. "That nigga upstairs wit' SMD."

"SMD?" Sonny asked, not familiar with the name. "Who the fuck is that?"

"Oh, that's the lil' bitch that be runnin' around wit' Bushnut," Mar-Mar informed him. "We call her SMD. It's short for *Sucka Mean Dick*," he laughed. "No bullshit Sonny, this bitch can suck a jar of peanut butter through a Twizzler. She be suckin' us off and lettin' us fuck for five dimes and a pack of Newports."

"Yo, hold the fuck up," Sonny screwed up his face. "You mean to tell me that Pooky's in there right now trickin' a smokah?"

"Hell yeah!" Mar-Mar bragged. "And I hope he hurry the fuck up! I'm try'na get my shit off too!"

Sonny shook his head in disbelief, and then headed toward the house. When he walked through the front door, the smell of cat piss and dog shit invaded his nostrils, causing him to gag. He glanced around the cluttered living room, and couldn't believe his eyes. The soiled carpet was littered with dog shit and on top of the coffee table, a congregation of cockroaches were spilling out of a Chinese food carton. *Yo these triflin' mutha'fuckas is outta pocket!* he thought to himself as he stood there with his left hand covering his nose and mouth.

He looked in the dining room where two women were sitting at a picnic table smoking crack from a glass stem. "Yo Treesha," he addressed the woman who owned the house. "Where Pooky at?"

She attempted to answer his question, but was too geeked out to speak. Her eyes were as big as golf balls, and her bottom jaw was sporadically moving from side to side. He looked at the other woman and reiterated his question.

"He—He upstairs," she managed to mumble, and then pointed toward the stairs.

As he carefully made his way up the stairs, desperately trying to avoid piles of dog shit, the sounds of moaning and groaning made his stomach turn. "Yo, this dirty dick ass nigga is really up here fuckin' a crack head!" he said to himself as he reached the second floor. He approached the room where the sounds were coming from, and banged on the door.

Boom! Boom! Boom!

"Pooky its Sonny! Open the door!"

On the other side of the door, the woman continued moaning, and Pooky continued grunting.

"Hey yo, Pooky!"

"Hold up dawg! I'ma be done in a minute!" Pooky shouted back.

"What?" Sonny snarled. "Nigga, open this fuckin' door!"

The woman stopped moaning, and a couple of seconds later the door creaked open. Pooky stuck his sweat covered face through the crack in the door, and the egregious odor of what seemed to be cat piss and corn syrup smacked Sonny dead in the face. The odor was so strong that he coughed a couple of times, and then hurled up his lunch. As he wiped his mouth with the back of his left hand he looked at Pooky. "Yo what type of freak shit is you into?"

Pooky looked at him with an irritated expression. "Sonny, what the fuck is you talking 'bout?"

"What I'm talking 'bout? Nigga, you up in this triflin ass house, fuckin' a crack head!"

Pooky gritted his teeth. "Yo, why you up in my business Sonny? I'ma grown ass man. You ain't got nothin' to do wit' the way I'm handlin' mines."

"Pussy, I'm up in ya business 'cause you a reflection of my mutha'fuckin' team!" Sonny shot back. "And ya nut ass got the nerve to be runnin' around the city sellin' niggas fucked up work, and now I'm the one that gotta make shit right! I swear to Blood if it wasn't for Sheed—"

"If it wasn't for Sheed what?" Pooky interrupted him. He snatched the door wide open, and then got up in Sonny's face. "Nigga, you ain't the only one that put in work! I get my mutha'fuckin' hands dirty too!"

In the blink of an eye, Sonny whipped out his FNH and pressed the barrel against Pooky's abdomen. "So what the fuck is you sayin' then nigga?"

Before Pooky had the chance to react the woman who was inside of the room shouted, "Sontino, don't do it! He ain't worth it!"

Sonny looked over Pooky's shoulder, and when he realized who the voice belonged to, it felt like he'd been stabbed in the heart with a dagger. It was his little sister, Nahfisah. The wear and tear on her body was evident. . Her once shapely frame was now a bag of bones, and although her beautiful face was still intact, her skin was covered with acne.

"Nahfisah?" he asked in a shaky voice. "What the fuck is you doin' in here?"

Pooky smirked, completely unware that Nahfisah was his sister. "Nigga, what you think? She in here suckin' and fuckin' for a rock!"

Sonny scowled at him, and then hit him in the nose with a short left hook that folded him like an envelope. He placed the FNH back in its holster, and then returned his focus to Nahfisah.

In a compassionate voice he said, "Yo Nah, what the fuck is you doin'?"

Embarrassed, she shamefully lowered her head.

"Yo, put some clothes on. I'm gettin' you outta here."

Reluctantly, she got up from the pissy mattress and did as he instructed. Her hands were trembling and tears were falling from her blue eyes.

When they emerged from the house, they were immediately greeted by the horrific sounds of Beaver Bushnut's voice. He was standing in front of the stoop doing his best rendition of Bobby Womack's, *If You Think You're Lonely Now*. He was singing into an empty can of Natural Ice beer as if it were a microphone, and slowly bopping from side to side. Just as he was about to begin the second verse he noticed that Nahfisah was following Sonny toward his Escalade.

"Ahn ahn bitch! Just where in the fuck you think you goin'?" He pulled a switchblade from his trench coat pocket, and flipped it open. "Don't you know Bushnut a carve yo' mutha'fuckin' ass up! I'ma mutha'fuckin' pimp, goddamnit! I don't play that shit!"

He ran toward her, but stopped in his tracks when Sonny pulled out his gun. He scowled at the young hustler. "Sonny Money, this ain't got nothin' to do wit you youngin'. This is between Bushnut and that funky lil' bitch right there," he pointed the blade at Nahfisah.

The thought of Beaver Bushnut pimping and violating his little sister infuriated Sonny. Although him and Nahfisah were raised without knowing that they were siblings, the bond they shared couldn't have been any closer. He aimed his FNH about an inch away from Bushnut's head, and let off a shot.

Boom!

"Oh shit goddamn!" Beaver Bushnut shouted as he turned to run. "This mutha'fucka's shootin'!"

"Nigga, you take another step, and I'ma air you the fuck out!" Sonny shouted.

124

Beaver Bushnut stopped running and dropped his switchblade in the middle of the street. "You and me is better than this, Sonny Money! It's only pimpin'! If the bitch chose, then she chose! I ain't gon' knock yo' game, playa!"

"Pussy, shut the fuck up!" Sonny continued shouting. "Matter of fact, bring ya dirty ass over here!"

Beaver Bushnut dropped his head and nervously walked toward him. When he came within arms distance, Sonny smacked him on the side of his head with the FNH.

Whop!

The blow caught him by surprise and he crumbled to the ground. Warm blood trickled down the side of his face and before he could wipe it away, Sonny grabbed him by the back of his collar. He dragged his body to the edge of the cracked sidewalk, and placed the barrel of the gun to the back of his head.

"Pussy, put ya mouth on the curb!"

Beaver Bushnut looked at him like he was crazy. "Put my mouth on the curb?" he questioned. "What type of barbaric, prehistoric, caveman shit is *you* on?"

Sonny fired another shot just centimeters away from his head.

Boom!

The bullet ricocheted off the curb, and then burned a hole into the fender of an abandoned station wagon. Obviously, that was enough to persuade Beaver Bushnut. Begrudgingly, he bit down on the cool concrete.

"Nahfisah!" Sonny shouted at the visibly shaken woman. "Come over here and stomp this nigga in the back of his fuckin' head!"

"I—I—I can't!" she cried while backpedalling toward his SUV. "I can't do that to him! I just can't!"

He scowled at her. The rage inside of him was so intense that his nostrils began to flare. He raised his Timberland boot and with all of his might, he stomped the washed up pimp in the back of his head.

Crunch!

A puddle of blood formed beneath his head, and his broken teeth littered the sidewalk.

Sonny turned his attention to Mar-Mar, and aimed the FNH at his face. "You and Pooky is cut the fuck off! Ain't no more hustlin'! Ain't no more nothin'!"

He kicked Beaver Bushnut in the ass, and then walked toward his Escalade. He looked at Nahfisah through the windshield and butterflies filled his stomach. She was sitting in the passenger's seat crying her eyes out, and he knew that he had to do something to help her.

While climbing inside of the truck, he noticed that Heemy and Twany were standing across the street staring at him. Previously, they were chilling around the corner when they heard the thunderous sounds of the FNH. Intrigued by the sound, they ran around the block just in time to hear Sonny screaming at Mar-Mar. They heard enough to know that Sonny was kicking him and Pooky off of the block, but they didn't understand why Beaver Bushnut was laid out with a puddle of blood around his head. Sonny looked at Heemy, and waved him over to the Escalade. "Yo, lemme holla at you."

Heemy looked at Twany, and then returned his gaze to Sonny. He knew who Sonny was, and he'd seen him around the neighborhood a million times. However, this was the first time that Sonny had ever acknowledged him. He took a deep breath, and slowly walked toward the truck. "What's poppin' Sonny?"

Sonny didn't respond. Instead, he reached inside of his pants pocket and pulled out a wad of money. He peeled off two thousand dollars, and showed Heemy the money. "Young bul, you ain't no rat is you?"

"Naw I ain't no mutha'fuckin' rat!" Heemy quickly confirmed.

Sonny looked across the street at Twany. "What about ya homie over there? He a rat?"

"Nizzaw. We don't do no rattin'," Heemy insisted. He lifted up the front of his hoody and showed off the .32 that was stuffed inside of his waistband. "We geed up."

Sonny looked at the little pistol and smirked. "Well here," he held the money out the window. "You take half, and give ya man the other half."

Heemy looked at the money, and then took a step backwards. He stuffed his hands in his pockets, and said, "Naw, Sonny, we don't want ya money."

"You don't want the money?" Sonny asked in a confused voice. He sized him up from head to toe, taking notice of his scuffed up Timberlands and faded hoody.

"Naw, we don't want ya money," Heemy reiterated his position. "All we want is ya respect."

"My respect?"

"Yeah, you heard me," Heemy nodded his head up and down. "Nothin' more. Nothin' less."

Sonny chuckled. "Damn, them some big ass words for such a lil' nigga."

Heemy shrugged his shoulders. "Maybe I'm the biggest lil' nigga you ever seen."

Sonny nodded his head. "More or less." He reached inside of his glove compartment and pulled out a prepaid cell phone. "Here," he handed Heemy the phone. "Take this, and wait for me to call you."

As Heemy stuffed the phone in his hoody pocket, Sonny rolled up his bulletproof window, and casually pulled away from the curb.

Chapter Ten

A Half An Hour Later...

Sonny and Nahfisah were riding up Germantown Pike, heading for the Eaglesville Rehabilitation Center. He glanced out the corner of his right eye, and refused to see a run down crackwhore. Instead, he saw the beautiful little girl who at the age of seven became his best friend. He desperately wanted to tell her that they shared the same father, but he decided that now was not the time.

"Yo what's up witchu Nah? What are you out here doin' to yourself?"

"They took Imani from me, and I lost it," she cried. "I couldn't function without my baby, and I needed something to take away the pain."

"They took Imani from you? Who?"

"DHS. They came and took her away from me," she continued crying and curled up in a ball.

He pulled over on the side of the road, and threw the transmission in *park*. "What the fuck they do that for?" The thought of his niece and goddaughter being stuck in the system was rubbing him the wrong way.

"Man, I don't even know why I'm talkin' to you," she sobbed. "I already know you gon' kill me."

"*Kill you*?" Sonny said as he screwed up his face. "Why the fuck would I do somethin' like that? I love you."

She coughed, and then used the back of her hand to wipe away the snot that was leaking from her nose. "No you don't. Tommy told on y'all, and y'all was try'na kill us!"

Hearing Tommy's name made the hairs on the back of his neck stand up straight. "Hold the fuck up. First of all, if I was gon' kill you, I woulda did it when we was back at that dirty ass crack house. Secondly, whatchu know about Tommy tellin' on us?"

"I went to visit him when he got locked up, and he told me everything. I wanted to come talk to you, but Tommy told me that the cops had you on a wiretap talkin' about killin' me and Imani to get back at him for tellin' on y'all. Then the next thing I knew, I got a call from his grandmom sayin' that he was tortured and murdered in his cell."

He looked at her and couldn't help but feel sorry for her. Aside from the fact that she was his sister, he'd always known her to be a stand up chick. Unfortunately, like countless other stand up chicks in the hood, her only crime was that she fell in love with a dude who turned out to be a rat. He reached over and gently massaged the back of her neck. "Look Nah, that nigga Tommy was a fuckin' liar. I love you and Imani, and deep down you know that I would never do nothin' to hurt y'all." He cracked his knuckles and took a deep breath. "Listen, all I wanna know right now is how my goddaughter ended up in the system, and how you ended up on the streets."

Her mind traveled back to the day that she lost her daughter, and her hands began to tremble. "After Tommy was killed, me and Imani moved to Logan to live with my grandmom. One day, she asked me to pick up her medicine from the drug store. When I came back from the store, Sheed popped up from outta nowhere and he—"

"Sheed?" he cut her off mid-sentence. "What about Sheed?"

"He crept up behind me, and put this big ass gun to the back of my head. He forced his way inside of the house, and made me give him the twenty-four keys that—"

"Twenty-four keys?" he interrupted her once more. "Nah, what the fuck is you talking 'bout?"

"I'm talking 'bout the coke that Tommy left me before he got locked up," she quickly replied. "It was twenty-four keys. I had 'em stashed at my grandmom's house, and Sheed took 'em!"

Yo, hold the fuck up! Sonny thought to himself. *This nigga ain't never tell me about no twenty-four keys! Lemme find out this pussy been tuckin' on me!*

After gathering his thoughts, he continued his interrogation. "I'm sayin' though, what does any of this have to do wit' DHS takin' Imani?"

"Because," she whined. "Before he took the work he fucked up my grandmom, and tried to drown Imani in the toilet."

"That nigga did what?" Sonny snapped. "Yo, please tell me that you're buggin' right now, and that Sheed ain't do no shit like that!"

"He did Sontino! I swear to God! And after he left the house, my grandmom called the cops and told them everything. When they asked me who he was, I wouldn't tell 'em his name. So to get me back for not tellin' they called DHS, and they came and took my baby from me."

She leaned her head against the passenger's side window and continued crying. Sonny was furious. How could Sheed do something like this? He knew that Nahfisah was his sister, but yet and still he chose to violate. Not just her, but her grandmother and Imani as well. To make matters worse, he never told Sonny about the 24 keys. Disloyalty was a crime that was intolerable, and if Sheed was guilty of committing such a crime this presented a major problem.

He leaned over the center console and embraced Nahfisah with a brotherly hug. "Don't cry Nah. Everything's okay now. I gotchu."

"But how?" she sobbed. "How is everything okay when I don't have my baby?"

"Listen Nah, this place that I'm takin' you to will help you wit' your addiction. All you need to worry about is completing this program, and I'ma take care of the rest."

She stopped sobbing and gazed in his eyes. "You promise, Sontino?"

He wiped away her tears, and then kissed her on the forehead. "I promise."

***

Back In North Philly

For the last hour or so, Heemy and Twany were sitting on Heemy's stoop watching the steady flow of crackheads who came through the block looking for Pooky and Mar-Mar. When they discovered that the two hustlers were no longer welcome on the block, they turned their attention to Heemy and Twany. "Well damn nephew, is *y'all* doin' something?"

"Naw," they replied.

The young men were both seventeen, but appeared to be a little younger. Heemy was brown skinned with a baby face, tall and lanky. Twany on the other hand was short and chubby. He had a light complexion and a thin mustache. Both were clearly in their mid to late teens, but yet and still the crackheads assumed that they were out there slinging crack.

Twany looked at Heemy and shook his in disbelief.

"You should've took that money."

"Come on dawg, you gotta look at the big picture," Heemy told him for the thousandth time. "That couple of dollars wasn't shit. If we woulda took that money, we woulda been the furthest thing from Sonny's mind. By doin' what I did, I made him see us in a different light."

"Yeah, and how you figure that?" Twany asked, holding out his arms for emphasis.

"Because the average young buls woulda took that money, and we didn't. That nigga know we ain't got no mutha'fuckin money, and that's why he was lookin' at me like that when I turned him down," Heemy continued, and then sparked up the Dutch Master that was clutched in his right hand. "In his world, that couple of dollars ain't shit. Niggas like Sonny drop that type of bread on a pair of shoes. To him, that couple of dollars wasn't nothin' but crumbs. I don't want us to have no mutha'fuckin' crumbs," Heemy declared. "I want us to have our own mutha'fuckin' cake. Trust me Twany, a nigga like Sonny can make it happen for us. That's why I kicked that respect shit to him. Dudes like him appreciate that kinda shit."

Twany looked at him skeptically. "Man, how you know?"

Heemy thought about it for a second, but couldn't come up with an answer. He shrugged his shoulders, and looked his best friend square in the eyes. "I just know."

***

In Germantown, on the corner of Chew and Locust, Pooky and Mar-Mar were sitting in Pooky's Range Rover waiting for his cousin Rahman. Pooky called him after his altercation with Sonny, and just as he anticipated Rahman offered his assistance.

As they sat in the smoke filled SUV, a black Mazda MPV pulled up behind them. Two men exited the minivan dressed in black Islamic garbs. The man who climbed out of the driver's side was Rahman, and the man who climbed out of the passenger's side was his Muslim brother Jihad.

Rahman was 6'2" and 240 pounds. Aside from his dark complexion, he had a lazy right eye, a baldhead, and a thick bushy beard. Jihad was 6'4" and 265 pounds. He was light skinned with short wavy hair, and he also had a long curly beard. They each had a *jailhouse physic* with bulky tops and legs like baseball bats. They cautiously walked toward the Range Rover, and judging from the bulges under their garments, the conclusion that they were packing heavy artillery was inescapable.

"As Salaamu Alaikum," they greeted Pooky and Mar-Mar as they hopped in the backseat of the Range Rover.

"Wa-Alaikum Salaam," they replied in unison.

"Dizzamn!" Rahman laughed. He was referring to Pooky's two black eyes and swollen nose. "Main man caught you wit' a good one, huh?"

Pooky was livid. "Man, that bitch ass nigga snuffed me. It ain't like we was rippin'. We had some words, and the next thing I know this bitch ass nigga socked the shit out me."

Rahman settled into the leather seat and ran his fingers through his large beard. "A'ight lil' cuz, gimmie some info on this dude."

"You ever heard of the bul Sonny from the Bad Landz?" Pooky asked him.

"I don't know," Rahman shrugged his shoulders. "If he wasn't upstate wit' us, then I probably wouldn't know him. Especially if he wasn't makin' noise in the eighties and nineties." He looked at his companion. "Haddy, you been home for a few years. You ever heard of this nigga?"

"Yeah," Jihad answered in a deep voice that was sounded like Barry White's. "He's a young bul Rock. I don't know the nigga personally, but I knew his ol' head Mook. Matter of fact, remember that retro eighties party at *Club Infamous*?"

"Yeah I remember."

"A'ight," Jihad nodded his head. "Well that was the bul's party, and word in the streets is that he owns the club. This lil' nigga's killin' the city, and the last time I seen him, he was pushin' a red Ghost. I was at the Dr. J Classic in West Philly, and this nigga pulled up in a fuckin' Ghost. He shut down the whole shit."

"Fuck all dat," Rahman hissed. "My lil' cuz got beef wit' this nigga so we got beef wit' him too. Fuck his bank account. The majority of niggas who get that type of money be straight up bitches. All they do is hide behind niggas like us. The real gangstas." He turned toward Pooky, but his lazy eye was directed at Mar-Mar. "So what's up lil' cuz, you ready to ride?"

"Huh?" Mar-Mar questioned. He assumed that Rahman was talking to him because his lazy eye was fixed on him. "Rock you talkin' to me?"

Rahman spun in his direction and scowled at him. "No, I'm not talkin' to you," he snapped, and then turned his face back to Pooky. "So what it is, lil' cuz? You down to ride on this nigga or what?" He lifted the bottom of his garb, and showed off his stockless AK-47. The massive assault rifle was equipped with a 50 round magazine, a night vision scope, and a shoulder strap. He looked at Jihad, and the large light skinned man pulled out an AR-15 that was equipped with the same exact features.

A lump formed in the back of Mar-Mar's throat, and goose bumps covered his skin. He quickly realized that he was out of his element, and he silently prayed that Pooky would decline the offer.

Pooky noticed the look of concern on Mar-Mar's face, and deep down he felt the same way but how could he turn back now. Contrary to Rahman's assumptions, he knew that Sonny and the Block Boys didn't play any games when it came to putting in work, but at the same time he refused to look like a coward. "Yeah, we can ride on this nigga. I just don't know where he at right now."

"A'ight, well tell me where this nigga be layin' his head," Rahman demanded.

"I don't know," Pooky admitted. "All I know about is *Club Infamous* and *Donkees*. I ain't never been to his crib."

"Well goddamn, lil' cuzzo. We gon' need a lil' more information than that."

Pooky shrugged his shoulders. "That's all I know."

Rahman shook his head in disbelief. "You been gettin' money wit' this dude for a few months now, and you don't know nothin'? At the very least, you should be able to tell us where the nigga be movin' his work."

"Yeah, I know where he movin' his work," Pooky nodded his head, and then used his fingers to count off the drug corners that Sonny owned. "He got Fairhill and York, 24th and Somerset, 25th and Master, and Percy and Pike."

"A'ight, well dig this," Rahman rubbed his hands together. "Haddy said the bul be ridin' around in a red Ghost. Is that what he was drivin' earlier today?"

"Naw," Mar-Mar interjected. "He was divin' a black Escalade."

"A'ight, well now we workin' wit' somethin'." Rahman nodded his head, and then climbed out the Range Rover. "Come on y'all. We gon' take the MPV. This truck's too flashy."

Pooky and Mar-Mar nervously glanced at one another. "I'm sayin' though," Pooky bitched up. "We don't even know where this nigga at."

Jihad smiled at him. "And that's why we gon' ride around North Philly until we see that Escalade," he stated in his deep voice. "And when we do, we gon' tear his ass up."

***

After admitting Nahfisah into the rehabilitaion center, Sonny drove up Germantown Avenue in silence. In the back of his mind, he realized that the only thing strong enough to turn a sweet innocent girl into a crackwhore was the streets. He would never admit it, but deep in his heart, he was ashamed of the role that he played in the entire situation. As he continued driving, he looked at his left hand and examined the scar that brought him and his sister together on that fateful night. A tear slid down his right cheek, and butterflies filled his stomach. An image of Keyonti appeared in his mind, and he promised himself that no matter what, he would never let the streets get a hold of his daughter the same way they did Nahfisah.

***

Back In North Philly

Pooky, Mar-Mar, Rahman, and Jihad were patrolling the streets looking for Sonny's Escalade. They were cruising down Broad Street when Jihad scrolled through his iPod and selected The LOX's song, *Breathe Easy*. He cranked up the volume, and together they rapped along with the gritty lyrics.

We gonna R-U Double-F R-Y-D-E/ Revolvers, semi-automatics in the P.G., hooptie/ Get away driver, breathe easy/ Explain things further, murder or get murdered.

Rahman reached inside of the glove compartment and pulled out an ounce bottle of dust juice. He motioned for Pooky to give him a cigarette, and Pooky handed him a pack of Newports. Rahman removed four cigarettes from the pack, and then one by one he dipped them in the light brown oil. "Here," he handed each of them a sherm stick.

"This is that shit right here."

"What the fuck is this?" Mar-Mar asked while examining the oil laced Newport. "This shit stinks like a mutha'fucka."

Jihad looked at him with an annoyed expression. "It's a dipper. Now, stop askin' so many goddamn questions, and smoke that shit." He leaned back in the passenger's seat, and sparked up his dipper. A huge flame erupted from the tip of the cigarette. It flickered a few times, and then settled into a burning cherry.

When they approached a red traffic light at the intersection of Broad and Susquehanna, a black Escalade with tinted windows pulled up alongside of them.

"Yo, there he go right there!" Jihad shouted and pointed out the passenger's side window.

"Oh shit, that *is* him!" Pooky insisted. He was high out of his mind. "Bitch ass nigga wanna talk all that gangsta shit, but look at him now! This pussy don't even dig it!"

The traffic light turned green, and the Escalade pulled away from the corner.

"Rock, follow this nigga," Jihad dictated from the passenger's seat. "The second he stop drivin', we gon' hop out and park his dumb ass!"

"I got you ahk! I got you!" Rahman shouted. The music was so loud that they could hardly hear one another.

As Rahman cruised behind the Escalade, he rocked back and forth and squeezed the stirring wheel. His eagerness to catch wreck, coupled with the effects of the dust juice had him in warrior mode. This was the type of shit that he lived for!

They were a couple of feet behind the Escalade when it stopped at a red light on Broad and Columbia. They pulled up on the left side of the truck, and Jihad cracked the passenger's side door.

"No! No! Fuck no!" Mar-Mar shouted at the top of his lungs. He was the only one in the MPV with a sober mind.

Unbeknownst to Pooky, Rahman, and Jihad, he never smoked his dipper. Instead, he secretly switched it with a regular Newport. "We can't shoot right here! Y'all nigga's trippin! Y'all don't see all these mutha'fuckin' Temple cops?"

"Fuck!" Jihad shouted, exuding his frustration. He slammed the passenger's side door, and then settled back in his seat. "I had this pussy!"

The traffic light turned green, and once again the Escalade took off down Broad Street.

Jihad was fuming. "Yo, fuck all dat! The next time this nigga stop drivin', we gettin' busy!" He looked into the backseat where Pooky was puffing on his dipper and nodding his head to the music. "Me and you is the only ones hoppin' out, so you mines well go 'head and crack the side door!"

"A'ight!" Pooky shouted back. They were so high that they didn't even realize they were shouting.

As they approached the intersection of Broad and Girard, the traffic descended from green, yellow, to red. The Escalade eased to a halt and the MPV pulled up behind it. The passenger and side doors swung open, and both men hopped out of the mini-van. As they ran up on the SUV, Pooky caught a glimpse of the factory rims, and realized that it wasn't Sonny's truck. He lowered his pistol and looked at Jihad. "Naw Haddy, chill!"

He was too late. Jihad was already squeezing his trigger.
Bdddddddoc! Bdddddddoc! Bdddddddoc!

In less than five seconds, the Escalade was surrounded by smoke, and the smell of burnt gunpowder hung in the air. Bullet holes as big as nickels covered the left fender and driver's side door, and broken glass and empty shell casings littered the street.

"What the fuck, Ahk? I told you to chill!" Pooky shouted with his hands covering his ears. His eardrums were ringing and he could barely hear himself talking.

"What?" Jihad shouted.

"I told you to chill!" Pooky shouted back. "That's not him!"

When Jihad realized what Pooky was saying his high quickly descended. He looked through the shattered driver's side window, and couldn't believe what lay before him. A middle aged black woman was slumped over the center console. The left side of her face was blown away, and what appeared to be her intestines were protruding through her blood soaked blouse. He returned his gaze to Pooky, and shook his head from side to side. "Yo Pooky what the fuck? I thought you said it was him?"

"Man, fuck all dat!" Rahman shouted from the minivan. "We gotta bounce 'fore the cops come!"

Without saying another word, Pooky and Jihad hopped back in the MPV, and sat in silence as Rahman sped away from the scene.

***

When Sonny reached the intersection of Germantown and Erie, he stopped at a red light, and looked across Broad Street where *Club Infamous* was in full swing. It was *Sexy Sunday*, and the line outside of the club was full of beautiful women and young hustlers. The traffic light turned green, and he veered right onto Broad Street. His iPhone vibrated in his pocket, interrupting his thoughts of Nahfisah. He retrieved the phone and saw that the caller was his lawyer. "Mario what's good? Whatchu got for me?"

"I'm calling with the information you requested. According to my investigators, Roberto Alverez, a.k.a.

Mexican Bobby, is Mexico's Welterweight Boxing Champion. He's scheduled to make his American debut at *The Blue Horizon*, and for the past two weeks, he's been training with Danny Garcia."

"A'ight," Sonny anxiously replied. "But where's he staying? Do you have an address?"

"I'll do you one even better," Mario chuckled. "As of right now, my lead investigator's following him up Old York Road. He's driving a blue Lamborghini, and he's traveling with a bodyguard."

"A'ight," Sonny nodded his head. "Tell your investigator to keep a tail on him, and I'ma hit you back in an hour."

Click!

He laid the phone on the center console and continued driving down Broad Street. Up ahead, he noticed a congregation of red and blue lights, and assumed that there must have been some type of car accident. However, the second he spotted the shot up Escalade in the middle of the taped off intersection his heart dropped into his stomach. "Yo, please tell me this ain't one of my niggas!" he said to himself as he pulled into the gas station on Broad and Girard.

As he hopped out the truck and fixed his gaze on the crime scene, a wave of relief washed over him. He spotted the Escalade's factory rims, and realized that the truck didn't belong to any of his peoples. After a few seconds of watching the crime scene unit conduct their investigation, he returned to his truck and rolled up a Backwood.

As he placed the spliff in his mouth and sparked the tip, a pearl white Mercedes Maybach 62 pulled into the gas station and parked at the first gas pump. *Damn, who the fuck is that?* he thought to himself as he admired the plush automobile. *It's probably either Meek or Gillie. Whoever it is, they gettin' it off on me right now!* He smiled, and then started the ignition. *It's*

141

cool though. I got somethin' for these niggas. Just wait 'til the summer. Me and Mello pullin' out the Bat Mobiles!

Little did he know, the plush sedan was carrying his archenemy, and the shot up Escalade was an attempt on his life. Shit was real and he didn't even dig it!

Chapter Eleven

When Sonny pulled up in front of *Donkees*, he could tell from the vehicles in the parking lot that everyone was there. Easy's triple black Jaguar XF was parked in between Breeze's silver Maserati and Rahmello's snow white Aston Martin Virage. A couple of parking spaces down, he spotted Egypt and Zaire's twin cherry red Porsche Panameras.

He entered the sports bar and approached Easy and Breeze who were shooting a game of pool. Easy was dressed in a white Versace dress shirt with gold buttons, black Versace slacks, and a pair of black crocodile boots. The diamonds in his Presidential Rolex shined bright, and the ice in his wedding ring shifted with his every movement. Breeze on the other hand was dipped in Chanel For Men, and from his ears to his wrist, his jewelry was covered in VS1 diamonds.

Sonny looked at his father and shook his head in contempt. He didn't say anything, but deep in his heart he blamed Easy for everything that was happening to Nahfisah.

Easy looked at him skeptically. "What's wrong, Sonny?"

"I'ma holla at you later," Sonny replied, and then looked at Breeze. "What's up wit' Mello and the twins? Where they at?"

"They chillin' in ya office," Breeze said as he knocked the 3-Ball down the right side pocket. "You want me to go get 'em for you?"

"Naw," Sonny shook his head and waved him off. "We about to go back there anyway." He approached the bar where Bianca was serving a customer. "B, when you finish his order pour me a double shot of Henny."

She smiled at him and nodded her head. "I got ju papi."

After receiving his drink, they headed straight for Sonny's office. When they stepped inside of the large room the first thing they noticed was that Rahmello was sitting behind Sonny's desk rolling up a Dutch Master. The twins were sitting on his suede sectional, sharing a Backwood, and playing Madden on his X Box One.

"Yo, turn that game off," Sonny said to the twins. "And you," he pointed at Rahmello. "Get ya ass outta my seat."

Without saying a word, Rahmello got up from the desk and joined the twins on the sectional. Breeze took a seat on the edge of Sonny's desk, and Easy leaned up against the door.

Sonny sat down in his swivel chair and got straight to business. "A'ight, so this is the situation," he sparked up the Dutch Master that Rahmello left on his desk and took a deep pull. After exhaling a thick cloud of Kush smoke, he fixed his gaze on Breeze and the twins. "From here on out, we're changin' the way that we conduct business. Instead of coppin', the usual 100 bricks at the beginning of the month I'ma start coppin' 200. I'ma drop y'all consignment price from $30,000 to $25,000. So therefore, y'all can keep y'all prices at $35,000, and make an extra $5,000 off every brick. At the same time, I'ma start frontin' y'all 50 bricks instead of the usual 30, so y'all gon' have to step y'all game up." He paused for a few seconds and examined them closely. "At the end of every month I'ma need $1,250,000 from each of y'all. Can y'all handle that?"

They nodded their heads in unison, but Breeze was the only one to verbally confirm.

"Yeah we can handle it."

Sonny looked at Easy. " Pops, you ready for 'em?"

"Yeah," Easy nodded his head, and then headed toward the closet. He opened the door, and one by one, he handed them a duffle bag full of bricks.

"A'ight," Sonny continued, then exhaled another cloud of Kush smoke. "Now, for the second order of business." He reached inside of his pocket and pulled out the two pictures of Mexican Bobby. He passed them around the room, and then lounged back in his swivel chair. "This nigga gotta die tonight, and as a favor to Poncho we gon' be the ones to park him. According to Poncho, this nigga pissed off the wrong people and now he's gotta go. As we speak, I've got people watchin' his every move, and we need to have him parked by the mornin'. No mistakes." He looked at Breeze. "I need you and the twins to stash that work at Mello's apartment, and then wait for me to call wit' further instructions."

"Say no more," Breeze replied.

He stood to his feet, and motioned for the twins to follow him out of the office.

Sonny turned his attention to Rahmello, who was secretly texting back and forth with Olivia.

"Lil' brozay, I need you to go to *The Swamp* and put shit in motion. I already holla'd at *The Butcher* so he's expectin' you." He pointed at Breeze and the twins who were leaving the office. "They should be there in the next couple of hours."

Rahmello smiled, then eagerly hopped up from the sectional. It had been months since the last time he'd caught some wreck, and he was happy that Sonny was finally allowing him to do what he did best. Murder shit!

"Brozay," Sonny called out, stopping him in his tracks. "I need you to bring me his hands and his tongue."

Rahmello nodded his head, and then followed Breeze and the twins out of the office.

Easy approached Sonny's desk, and sat down across from him. He knew his oldest son like the back of his hand, and he could tell that something was bothering him. "Alright Sontino, tell me what's bothering you."

Sonny stubbed out his Dutch Master, and then cracked his knuckles one by one. "I had to pop off on Pooky earlier today."

"On Pooky?" Easy shot back in disbelief. "Naw, not Pooky?" he chuckled. "You're the main one who's always stickin' up for him! What happened?"

Sonny took a deep breath. "Them niggas violated, and I popped they fuckin' tops."

"Them niggas?" Easy squinted his eyes and leaned forward. "I thought you was only talking 'bout Pooky! Who else you killed?"

Sonny scowled at him. "First of all, I ain't killed nobody! I should have, but I didn't. It was Pooky and Beaver Bushnut. I had to fuck them niggas up."

"Beaver Bushnut?" Easy couldn't believe his ears.

His old running mate was a crack head bum, slumming around the city, pimping crackwhores. What the fuck was Sonny doing bumping heads with the likes of him?

"Yeah nigga, you fuckin' heard me!" Sonny snapped, and jumped to his feet. "And it's all your mutha'fuckin' fault!"

"All *my fault*?" Easy retorted, and then stood to his feet. "How the fuck is this my fault? I ain't tell you to be out there rollin' around in the dirt, fightin' mutha'fuckas! Fuck is you talking 'bout?"

"Nigga it *is* ya fault!" Sonny continued shouting. "If you woulda been a man, and not thrown ya daughter to the mutha'fuckin' wolves none of this shit woulda never even happened!"

Easy screwed up his face. "Thrown my daughter to the wolves? Sontino, what the fuck are you talking 'bout?"

"Pussy, I'm talking 'bout Nahfisah! You remember her? Ya mutha'fuckin' daughter?"

At the mention of Nahfisah Easy's body became rigid. "What happened to her?"

"The streets!" Sonny barked at him. "That's what the fuck happened to her! She was out there smokin' crack, and her daughter's in a mutha'fuckin' foster home!"

Tears welled up in Easy's eyes. He was more than familiar with the effects of crack cocaine, and throughout his years of getting high, he'd seen a gang of young women fall victim to their addiction.

"Listen man, I'm sorry."

"Yeah, you sorry a'ight," Sonny antagonized him. "Had you been a man about this shit from the jump, it woulda never happened. How you gon' turn ya back on ya daughter? I woulda never did that to Fat-Fat!"

"But Sonny, I—"

"But nothin'!" he interrupted. "Get the fuck outta my office!"

Easy searched for the words that would express his feelings, but he couldn't find any. Disgusted with himself, he lowered his head and left the office.

Sonny sat back down and retrieved his Dutch Master from the ashtray. As he rekindled the cherry, his iPhone vibrated in his pocket. He pulled it out and saw that the caller was Mario.

"Mario, what's poppin'?"

"As of right now our little Aztec warrior is spending way too much money on champagne and lap dances. And to think, this guys supposed to be training for a fight."

"Aztec warrior? Champagne and lap dances? Yo, Mario, whatchu talking 'bout?"

"Mexican Bobby. He's partying at *Club Spontaneous*."

"A'ight, say no more." He disconnected the call, and a soft knock sounded the door. "Who is it?"

"It's me," Suelyn responded as she cracked the door open and stuck her head inside of the office. "I need to download a file from your computer. Tax season is right around the corner, and I need to make sure that everything's in order."

He got up from the desk and motioned for her to come inside. "That's cool. I'ma be at the bar so just holla if you need me."

"Okay," she smiled, and then took a seat at his desk.

As the door closed behind him she reached underneath his swivel chair and removed the listening device that she planted earlier in the week. She kissed the small black box, and then quickly placed it inside of her bra.

***

At The Eaglesville Rehabilitation Center

After taking a shower and throwing on the new underwear and sweat suit that was given to her by the program director, Nahfisah was standing in the bathroom looking at her reflection in the mirror. She hardly recognized herself. Her blue eyes had bags underneath them, and she was so skinny that she could clearly see her jaw and cheekbones.

Damn Fisah, what the fuck were you thinking? she questioned herself. Her hands began to shake, and a migraine headache appeared from out of nowhere. Images of Imani invaded her thoughts and she broke down crying.

A soft knock sounded the door and her drug counselor, Ms. Mary stuck her head inside of the bathroom.

"Nahfisah is everything okay?" the beautiful Puerto Rican woman asked her. When Nahfisah didn't respond, Ms. Mary stepped inside of the small bathroom and wrapped her arms around her. "Just let it out baby. Just let it out," she repeated. Her words full of compassion and wisdom. She gently pulled

Nahfisah out of the bathroom and led her toward the bed. "Here honey just sit down."

Nafisah fell on top of the bed, and curled up in the fetal position. Ms. Mary caressed her back and spoke to her in a compassionate, motherly voice. "Go on and cry, baby. You gotta let it out." Her eyes began to water and her heart grew heavier by the second. The young woman who lay before her reminded her so much of her own daughter. "Listen baby," she said in a cracked voice. "I have to leave right now, but I'll be back to check on you."

As she got up to leave the room she reached inside of her pocket and pulled out a small piece of paper. With trembling hands, she looked at the picture of Riri and broke down crying.

***

At Club Spontaneous

Carmine was sitting behind his desk in total silence. Alphonso and Tony Bruno were standing on the other side. They just told him the news about Romey Noodles, and now they were anxiously awaiting his response.

"It was that fuckin' Grip," Carmine snarled through clenched teeth. "I fuckin' know it."

"Carmine, I really think we can benifit from this situation," Alphonso suggested. "Between the five *Families* in New York, and the old fucks in our own *Family*," he turned to Tony Bruno, "No disrespect to you Tony, but they're all waiting for us to fuck up," he continued as he returned his attention to Carmine. "We could use this beef with Grip to establish ourselves as the new generation of this *Family*."

Carmine looked at him, and then fixed his eyes on Tony Bruno. "What about you, Tony? You think we should finish this moulinyan once and for all?"

Tony Bruno's palms began to sweat and a cold chill ran up his spine. He'd been a soldier in *The Gervino Crime Family* for over thirty years and he was well acquainted with the caliber of drama that Grip was capable of bringing.

"Well don't just stand there with a thumb in your ass," Carmine spat. "Say somethin'."

Tony Bruno wiped the sweat from his brow and shrugged his shoulders. "I don't know what to say. Do you want me to be honest?"

"No, I want you to friggin' lie to me," Carmine responded sarcastically. "Of course I want you to be honest."

Tony took a deep breath and sighed. "I think a war with the Moreno's is the last thing we need right now. Grip's too strong. I've never seen anything like him."

Carmine listened to Tony Bruno express his feelings, and although he wouldn't admit it, he knew that the old man was right. A war with *The Moreno Family* was pure insanity.

"Leave me," he stated in a low tone of voice. "I need to get my thoughts together."

As they left the office he grabbed his cell phone and called Little Angolo. "Gramps it's me. I need you to come back to Philly."

Chapter Twelve

After receiving the word from Sonny that Mexican Bobby was partying at *Club Spontaneous*, Breeze and the twins were heading up Delaware Avenue in Breeze's triple black Hummer H2. Breeze was driving, Egypt was in the passenger's seat, and Zaire was sitting behind him watching *State Property* on the 8 inch screen that was built into the headrest.

When they arrived at the strip club, they circled the parking lot, and just as they expected, they spotted Mexican Bobby's Pepsi blue Lamborghini. Breeze parked the H2 directly beside it, and then looked at Egypt.

"Go inside and see what's poppin'. Sonny said the nigga was posted up in the V.I.P. Here," he handed him the two pictures of Mexican Bobby. "This way you can't miss him. Sonny said he was wearin' a wife beater and a pair of beige slacks. As you can see from the pictures, he's light skinned, about 5'6", and 160 pounds. Oh yeah," he smirked, "and this is the funniest shit ever. This bird ass nigga got the nerve to have a tattoo of a rat on the left side of his neck."

"A rat?" Zaire questioned from the backseat.

"Yeah," Breeze nodded his head up and down. "And above the rat it says *La Ratta*, which means *the rat* in Spanish. This nigga's bugged the fuck out."

"Yo that's crazy!" Zaire laughed. "I'ma have fun watchin' this rat ass nigga beg for his life!"

"Me too," Egypt chuckled while climbing out the Hummer and heading toward the entrance.

As soon as he walked through the door he was greeted by the sounds of T-Pain's new hit.

Booty going up...down/ I ain't got no problem spending all of my money/ I'm try'na see what's up...now/ I can do this all day like it ain't nothin'.

The interior of the club was flooded with neon lights, and a plethora of naked women were prancing back and forth flaunting their God given and surgically augmented body parts. He spotted a Black and Cambodian chick that he used to smash and gently grabbed her by the arm.

"Damn, Jas, let me holla at you real quick."

"What's up, Egypt?" she replied while chewing on a piece of gum. She was standing still, but her ass was moving to the music as if it had a mind of its own.

"Ain't shit. Just try'na spend a couple of dollars witchu." He pulled out a wad of hundreds and peeled away five of them. "I'm try'na slide through ya spot later on tonight so I'ma pay you right now." He extended the $500, but all she did was look at it. "Damn Jas, why, you actin' like that? What my money ain't good no more?"

"Naw Egypt, it ain't that. You know I fucks witchu. It's just that my boo is comin' home next week, and this is my last night dancing. I'm really try'na get my shit together, and fuckin' niggas for bread is no longer an option."

"More or less." He shrugged his shoulders. She walked off, and he smiled at yhe sight of her ass jiggling. He posted up at the bar and ordered a double shot of Patron. As the topless bartender prepared his drink, he looked toward the V.I.P., and ice grilled Mexican Bobby. The little Mexican was standing on a chair, throwing 100s in the air and watching them rain down on some Spanish girl's naked body. His 6'8", 295 pound bodyguard was standing beside him with his massive arms folded across his pumped up chest. His eyes were scanning the club and his facial expression was stone cold.

"Goddamn!" Egypt shook his head in amazement. "This nigga looks like a Mexican Andre The Giant!"

The bartender handed him his drink, and he slid her a hundred dollar bill. He returned his gaze to Mexican Bobby. He was still throwing money in the air, and watching it rain down on the woman's body. *Fuck it*, he laughed to himself. *At least he got to have some fun before he died.*

An hour later, after knocking down a few shots of Patron and smoking half a pack of Newports, he was happy to see that Mexican Bobby and his bodyguard were finally making their way toward the exit. He knocked down the rest of his drink and followed them from a safe distance.

"Aww man!" Mexican Bobby slurred. "I love America! We shoulda crossed de border a long time ago, mijo! De chicas in dis country, mijo. Dey are tigers!" He laughed, and then stumbled into his large companion.

He was so drunk that he didn't even realize he'd pissed himself. The bodyguard positioned himself behind his client, and did his best to keep the little man on his feet. Unknowingly, Egypt was a few feet behind them, sending Zaire a text message.

Yo, Be On Point. They Komin' Y'all Way!

Sitting behind the H2's tinted windows, Breeze and Zaire looked to their left, and sure enough they spotted the large bodyguard supporting Mexican Bobby's weight with his large hands positioned under his armpits. Egypt closed the distance between himself and the two Mexicans.

"Excuse me big guy. I think you dropped somethin'."

"Huh?" the bodyguard said as he turned his head to face the dark-skinned man with the shoulder length dreadlocks. "Dropped what?"

"This!" Egypt pulled out a stun gun and squeezed the trigger.

Ttttttttat! Ttttttttat!

The taser darts sprang from the barrel and bit into the bodyguard's muscular chest causing him to release his hands from Mexican Bobby's armpits. As his client melted to the pavement, he stumbled backwards and desperately fought the 7,500 volts of electricity that spread throughout his massive body. He staggered forward, attempting to wrestle the stun gun away from Egypt, but before he could reach him Zaire hopped on his back and put him in a tight chokehold. His body shook feverishly and globs of saliva ran down the sides of his mouth. The volts of electricity were taking its toll, but somehow he managed to rock backwards and slam Zaire against the grill of the Hummer.

"Goddamn!" Breeze said to himself as the Hummer rocked from side to side. "What the fuck, he on steroids or somethin'?"

As Zaire fall to the ground with the wind knocked out of him, Breeze grabbed his .45 from the center console and jumped out the truck.

As the bodyguard staggered toward Egypt with his hands reaching for the stun gun, Breeze slid up behind him and aimed the .45 at the back of his head. Just as he was about to squeeze the trigger, the electordynamics of the stun gun decimated the bodyguard's will to fight and he crashed to the pavement.

After controlling his breathing Zaire hopped off the ground and ran toward the bodyguard in a fit of rage. Savagely, he stomped the man's head into a bloody pulp.

Breeze approached Mexican Bobby, who was laying on the ground in a drunken stupor. He placed his hands behind his back, and then looked at Zaire. "Yo, stop kickin' that nigga, and bring me them zip ties!"

Zaire kicked the bodyguard one last time, and then grabbed the zip ties from his back pocket. He tossed them to Breeze, and Breeze tied them around Mexican Bobby's wrist. Breeze picked the little man off of the ground and hoisted him over his right shoulder. He hurried toward the back of the Hummer and called out to Egypt, "Yo, start the truck and pop the the back door."

Egypt did as he was told, and thirty seconds later they were driving up Delaware Avenue, heading for I-95.

***

The Swamp as they called it was a country house that was situated on a 10 acre farm in Doylestown, Pennsylvania, about thirty minutes on the outskirts of Philadelphia. The house and land belonged to a 51 year old white man called *The Butcher*, and he was one of Easy's oldest friends.

Back 1988, while Easy was doing bit in the Bucks County Prison, he was placed in a cell with the man that The Philadelphia Daily News referred to as *The Bucks County Butcher*. Allegedly, The Butcher found his wife and his best friend in bed together. He beat them to death with his bare hands, and then one by one he carried their mutilated bodies to the in-house butcher's shop that was located in the basement of his house. The shop was built by his father in the late 1950's, and it was there that The Butcher prepared his signature cuts for the customers who purchased whole pigs from his pig farm. Unfortunately, on that dreadful afternoon pork wasn't the meat of choice. Instead, he hacked up his redheaded wife and his pot bellied best friend, and piece by piece he fed their body parts to his massive sized hogs. He was eventually convicted for the murders and given the death penalty. After serving five years on death row, the Pennsylvania Supreme Court overturned his conviction and awarded him with a new trial. He was transferred from a state prison back to the county jail, and it was there that he met the man who would help him get his life back.

When Easy approached his cell for the first time he'd never heard of The Butcher, and therefore, he had no apprehensions about sharing a cell with the 6'5", 280 pound white man. In fact, after ten months of occupying the same space the two became close friends. When Easy heard the news about The Butcher's case he paid his high powered attorneys to represent him at his new trial. The Butcher was eventually acquitted on all charges and to show his gratitude, when Easy was released from jail, The Butcher became his go to man whenever he needed someone to turn up missing. Up until now, The Butcher had never disappointed him.

***

It was a little pass 8:00 p.m. when Egypt turned off of Route 611 and drove up a long dirt road that lead to a white colonial style house. Up ahead he spotted Rahmello's Aston Martin. It was parked beside a brown pick-up truck, and he knew that they reached their destination. In the past, him and Zaire had heard stories about The Swamp and The Butcher, but they'd never been here before.

As the H2 cruised up the dirt road, Egypt noticed a huge barn that was surrounded by oak trees, and despite the fact that the windows were rolled up, a rancid odor invaded the SUV.

"Damn, which one of y'all niggas bust y'all ass?" Egypt asked while covering his nose with his right hand. "Whoever it was, y'all need to change y'all mutha'fuckin' lifestyle! Y'all insides is doin' bad right now! Nigga need to go vegan or somethin'! Damn!"

Blood of a Boss II

Breeze laughed at him. "Nah Blood, ain't nobody bust they ass! That's just the way it be smellin' out here."

Zaire gagged and coughed. "Damn yo, how the fuck this nigga be livin' out here wit' this shit smellin' like that? This nigga's outta pocket!"

Breeze pointed out the pigpens that were scattered through the property. "The majority of whatchu smellin' is comin' from them," he pointed at the pigs. "But *The Butcher* be havin' all types of shit out here. Y'all already know about the pigs, but this nigga be havin' alligators, snakes, lizards, hawks, eagles, and gamecocks. That's just the shit that I know about. Ain't no tellin' what else he's got stashed around this mutha'fucka. He fuck around and have a hippo out this bitch."

"Or maybe a dinosaur," Mexican Bobby slurred, oblivious to the fact that he'd been kidnapped.

Zaire, who was still sitting in the back seat, spun around and was surprised to see the little Mexican sitting up in the cargo compartment, smiling from ear to ear. "Pussy shut ya rat ass up!" he snapped, and then punched him in the face, knocking him unconscious.

Egypt parked the H2 beside Rahmello's Aston Martin, and they climbed out the truck. As they approached the house, the front door swung open and The Butcher appeared in the threshold. He was dressed in a black one piece Dickies suit, and a weird expression was written on his face. His long orange hair fell to his shoulders and his long orange beard looked like a baby orangutan was hanging from his ears. His chest heaved up and down, and his piercing blue eyes burned holes through the three men standing on his front porch.

Zaire discreetly tapped his twin brother on the leg and whispered, "Fuck is up wit Sonny? He got us way out in east bumble fuck wit' this big ass white bul. This nigga's trippin'."

157

Breeze shook his head from side to side, and then walked up to the massive man and shook his hand.

"What's up Butchie? You ready for us?"

"Yeah," The Butcher responded in a high pitched squeaky voice. "Rahmello's in the barn. He's got everything you guys are gonna need."

Egypt and Zaire looked at one another dumbfounded. Without saying a word their twin intuition said, *Damn, how the fuck this big ass white bul gon' have the nerve to sound like Freeway?*

Breeze released his grasp from The Butcher's hand, and then gestured toward the twins. "Butchie I want you to meet the twins, Egypt and Zaire."

"Hey guys!" The Butcher smiled and waved. "It's nice to meet ya! Heard a lot about ya!"

The twins nodded their heads. "What's up?"

"Everything's fine," The Butcher replied. "Like I just told Breeze, everything's in the barn with Rahmello. It's a good thing Sontino called when he did. I was just about to feed 'em," he said, referring to his pet alligators. "Alright guys, I've gotta finish preparing this package for one of my customers so if you need me I'll be downstairs in the butcher's shop. Oh yeah, If you're hungry, I've got some fresh pork jerky for ya."

Breeze cringed. "Nah Butchie, we good. You helped us enough already. Good lookin' though."

"Suit yourself." The large man shrugged his shoulders, and then disappeared inside of the house.

Breeze turned his attention to the twins. "Grab rat boy out the back of the truck and bring his ass to the barn. I'ma holla at Mello, and let him know we here."

Inside of the barn, Rahmello was sitting on a workshop bench smoking a Black & Mild. About thirty feet in front of him, two alligators were crawling around the bank of a makeshift swamp. It was a ten foot deep ditch with a three hundred foot perimeter, and was filled with muddy water and broken tree logs. It smelled something awful, but Rahmello couldn't have cared less. He loved the two reptiles that he nicknamed *T-Rex* and *Godzilla*. T-Rex was 13 feet long and weighed close to 1,400 pounds. Godzilla was 11 feet long and weighed approximately 1,300 pounds. Their powerful jaws and long teeth intrigued Rahmello, and ever since Easy introduced him to The Butcher he would often travel to The Swamp and spend some quality time with his prehistoric friends.

Breeze entered the barn followed by Egypt and Zaire who were carrying Mexican Bobby's unconscious body.

"Damn Blood," Egypt complained while screwing up his face. "How the fuck is you in here chillin'? It smells like ten fat bitches was in here mud wrestling for three days straight."

Rahmello got up from the workshop table and approached them. "It ain't nothin'. It used to bother me at first, but now," he shrugged his shoulders, "I kinda like the smell. It reminds me of power."

"Power?" Zaire asked while laying Mexican Bobby on the ground. "What the fuck does power have to do wit' this stinkin' ass barn?"

Rahmello smiled. "Come wit' me over to the fence. I wanna show y'all somethin'."

Egypt and Zaire followed him to the edge of the makeshift swamp and were blown away when they locked eyes on the massive reptiles.

"Goddamn!" Egypt looked at Rahmello, and then pointed toward the alligators. "Yo, them jawns big as shit!"

Rahmello directed their attention to T-Rex. A deep groan escaped his body and he wagged his tail back and forth. He groaned once more, and then stretched his mouth wide open. He paused for a few seconds then in the blink of an eye he forcefully clamped his jaws together.

Clap!

"Yizzeah," Rahmello smiled and nodded his head up and down. "Now, that's what the fuck I call power!"

"Hey yo, Crocodile Dundee!" Breeze called out in a sarcastic tone. "Where you want me to put this nigga?"

Rahmello pointed at the workshop bench. "Lay his ass right there and put his head in between the vice grips. I'll be over there in a minute." He returned his attention to the twins. "I know y'all gon' help me feed 'em, right?"

"What?" Egypt asked. He looked at Rahmello like he was crazy, and backed away from the fence. "Yo, you buggin' right now scrap. I ain't got no problems when it comes to blowin' a mutha'fucka's face off. But feedin' niggas to alligators," he shook his head from side to side. "You can count me out, Blood. I'm good."

Rahmello laughed at him, and then looked at Zaire. "What about you?"

"Nigga, I'm wit' it."

They approached the workbench where Breeze was strapping down Mexican Bobby's naked body. Rahmello reached under the table to grab the blowtorch and sparker that The Butcher gave him. He pressed the lever on the blowtorch and placed the sparker directly in front of the barrel. He squeezed the sparker, and like magic the blowtorch came to life. He looked at Breeze. "Yo, wake his ass up."

Slap!

"W—W—What de fuck homes?" Mexican Bobby slurred. He was still oblivious to the fact that he'd been kidnapped. He glanced around the barn, and then one by one, he looked into the faces of his captors. "Yo, homes! What de fuck is this? Where's Chico?"

Instead of responding, Rahmello caressed his abdomen with the blue flame.

"Aaagggghhhh! Ay dios mio! What de fuck homes!"

The skin on his stomach bubbled up and blackened, and the aroma of burnt flesh added another element to the barn's funky odor.

Rahmello removed the flame from its target, and then looked at Breeze. "Reach under the table and grab the pliers and the box cutter." He then returned his gaze to the Mexican. "It's niggas like you that got the game turned upside down Bobby. Jails is gettin' packed 'cause of niggas like you, and the cops ain't even gotta do they jobs no more. Y'all rattin' ass niggas is doin' all the work for 'em!"

"Please!" Mexican Bobby cried. "Don't do me like dis homes! I'm not a rat! I swear to God!"

Rahmello smiled at him. "I don't know about that, Bobby. There's some important people who say otherwise." He grabbed the pliers from Breeze, and then waved them in front of Mexican Bobby's face. "This is what we gon' do, you gon' open ya mouth and stick out ya tongue, and if you don't," he shrugged his shoulders, "I'ma torch ya whole body." He aimed the torch at his dick. "Startin' wit' that."

"No!" the little Mexican screamed.

Rahmello chuckled. "Well, I guess we have an understanding."

Begrudgingly, Mexican Bobby stuck out his tongue and cringed when Rahmello squeezed it with the teeth of the pliers.

"Agggghhhh!"

"Pussy shut the fuck up! If anything I'm doin' ya ass a fuckin' favor! It's ya tongue that got you in this shit in the first place! You should be thankin' me!" He handed the blowtorch to Egypt. "Start cookin' this nigga! My young buls like to eat they rats well done."

Mexican Bobby screamed in pain as the blue flame sizzled the lower half of his body. All the while, Rahmello was still holding his tongue with the pliers. He motioned for Breeze to hand him the box cutter, then reached inside of Mexican Bobby's mouth, and severed the pink piece of flesh.

The little man's eyes blinked rapidly as he slipped in and out of consciousness. Rahmello handed the tongue to Breeze, and Breeze placed it inside of a zip lock bag. Thereafter, he placed the tongue inside of the cooler that was sitting on the ground beside the workbench.

Rahmello removed a Smith & Wessin .40 from the small of his back, and then passed the gun to Zaire.

"Rock this nigga."

Zaire aimed the barrel at Mexican Bobby's forehead and squeezed the trigger.

Boc!

Instantly, a black hole appeared in between his eyebrows and crimson red blood eased from the wound. The aroma of burnt flesh and fresh blood drove the alligators into a frenzy. Their huge lungs produced moans and groans that Breeze and the twins had never heard before, and their long tails splashed against the surface of the muddy water.

"Settle down!" Rahmello shouted at the alligators. "I'll be over there in a minute."

He walked over to the coat rack and grabbed The Butcher's work coat. It was a rubber yellow trench coat, and its sole purpose was to shield a butcher from the spraying of blood while chopping up meat. He slipped inside of the coat and threw on a pair of goggles. He then grabbed an electrical saw from the tool shelf, and returned to the workbench.

"Y'all need to back up a lil' bit," he said while starting the motor on the saw. "It's about to be blood everywhere."

They did as he suggested, and watched him from a safe distance as he put the saw to work. The time that he'd spent around *The Butcher* was evident, and he sawed through Mexican Bobby's wrist with such precision that if they didn't know any better they would've swore he worked in a butcher's shop.

After severing his hands, Rahmello placed them inside of a zip lock bag and laid them in the cooler beside his tongue. Next, he motioned for Breeze to loosen the restraints that held him to the table, and together they carried him over to the swamp where T-Rex and Godzilla were anxiously waiting. They tossed his mutilated corpse over the fence, and the hungry alligators wasted no time. T-Rex gripped his head, shoulder, and torso with one bite, while Godzilla locked on his waist. Simultaneously, their powerful bodies, propelled by their tails violently spun in opposite directions, ripping Mexican Bobby in half.

"Ooooohhhhh shit!" the twins stated in unison.

They couldn't believe how easily the man was ripped in half. Breeze cringed from the sounds of snapping bones and tearing flesh.

Rahmello, on the other hand, was smiling at the alligators like a proud poppa. He sparked up a Black & Mild and took a deep pull as the two reptiles disappeared under the murky water with Mexican Bobby locked in between their jaws.

Askari

Chapter Thirteen

The day had finally arrived for Sheed to be released from the county jail, and Jasmyn was a nervous wreck. For the past two weeks she'd been doing everything in her power to welcome him home accordingly. She cleaned her small apartment from top to bottom, bought him a new wardrobe, and stocked up on sexy lingerie. Now that the day was finally here, she was parked across the street in front of the beer distributor, nervously anticipating what she presumed to be the end of her career. It was a cardinal sin for a corrections officer to be involved with an inmate, and if anyone saw her picking him up, not only would this verify the rumors that the two of them were an item, it would also be the infraction that earned her, her walking papers.

***

It was 10:00 a.m. when Sheed emerged from the intake room and walked through the front gate. *Damn, a nigga finally up out this mutha'fucka!* he thought to himself as his eyes scoured the free world. The early December leaves were a bright yellow orange, and the grass a dark green. He couldn't believe it. Something as simple as the sight of a baby squirrel running behind its mother was enough to make him enjoy his newfound freedom. He looked across the street and spotted Jasmyn's forest green Mazda 929. It was sitting in the parking lot of the beer distributor, and he began walking in her direction. The closer he got to the car he could see that she was crouched down in the driver's seat, hiding behind her tinted windows. He approached the driver's side door and gently tapped on the window.

"Damn," he smiled and held out his arms for emphasis. "No hug? No kiss? No nuffin?" he teased her.

She pouted at him through the window. "Come on boo, stop playin'. If somebody sees me I'ma fuck around and lose my job."

"Your job? What job?" He continued smiling, then pointed behind him toward the jail. "Oh, you mean that c.o. shit? Yo, that's over wit' ma." He opened the driver's side door and gently pulled her out of the car. He then, removed her oversized Chanel shades and gave her a passionate kiss. Despite her soft moans, she smacked him on the shoulder.

"Stop it, Rasheed. You're gonna get me fired." No sooner then she said it, a black Cadillac ATS pulled up beside her 929, and the tinted driver's side window rolled down. It was her supervisor Lieutenant Brown. He looked Sheed up and down, and then scowled at Jasmyn.

Sheed ice grilled him. "Fuck is you lookin' at, dawg?"

Lieutenant Brown didn't respond. Instead, he just shook his head from side to side, rolled up his window, and pulled off.

"See Sheed!" Jasmyn whined. "Fuckin' wit' you I'ma lose my job!"

He gently grabbed her by the chin and gazed into her eyes. "Yo, what's the matter witchu?"

Her face turned bright red and she began to cry. "I'ma get fired for this. Me and my daughter need this job, and obviously you don't give a fuck. I'm so stupid for fallin' in love witcha ass."

"Baby girl," he replied in a soft tone, "do I look like the type of nigga that would let my wifey work inside of a prison?" Defiantly, she folded her arms across her chest, and looked away. He guided her face back to his. "Again, do I look like the type of nigga that would let his wifey work inside of a prison?"

"No," she answered. "But—"

166

"But nuffin," he interrupted her. "You wit' me now."

"And what's that supposed to mean?"

"It means that you ain't gotta do nuffin but look beautiful and help me spend this bread."

"Whatever Sheed." She climbed back in the car and slammed the door. Sheed chuckled, and then walked around the front of the car and climbed in the passenger's side.

"Look Jas, just know that I love you and that I'ma hold you down. You'll never have to look no further than me."

She shook her head in disbelief, and then started the car. "Like I said, whatever Sheed."

He leaned over the center console and kissed the side of her face. "You gon' have to relax and start trustin' me. I said I got you, right?"

His smooth words lightened the mood, and she turned to face him. "Are you sellin' me a dream or are you really gon' be there for me?"

"First of all, I don't sell no dreams. Especially to the people I love. Just to show you how much I love and care about you, I'ma cop you a new whip 'cause this ol' ass 929 ain't cuttin' it. After that, sometime this week I want you to start lookin' for a new house."

A huge smile appeared on her face as she pulled out of the parking lot and made a right turn on State Road.

"Do you still need me to take you to Germantown to see ya brother?"

"Yeah," he reclined back in the leather seat and sparked up a Newport, "and after that you already know."

She licked her lips, and then reached over to massage his dick through his pants. "So whatchu sayin'? Is it gon' be *Mr. Nasty Time*?"

He closed his eyes and exhaled a cloud of smoke. "Umm! Girl you better stop playin' wit' me."

***

In Upper Dublin, Pennsylvania

Sonny was seated at the island in the middle of his kitchen. He was finishing his breakfast and reading the Philadelphia Daily Newspaper. The front page displayed an image of the shot up SUV from the night before, and he was surprised to find out that the victim was the mayor's personal assistant. This was obviously the talk of the city. Every local news station was covering the murder, and even Nancy Grace, the correspondent from CNN had weighed in on the topic.

As he took a swig from his glass of orange juice he heard the click clack of Daphney's Christian Louboutin pumps walking down the hallway. He looked up from the newspaper just as she was entering the kitchen. Her silky black hair was pulled back in a ponytail, and her black Fendi frames added an elegant look to her beautiful face. Her gray Fendi business suit hugged her curvaceous body just right, and her Chanel 5 perfume was intoxicating. "I'm on my way to the office," she stated, and then gave him a juicy kiss. "And don't forget about tonight," she reminded him of their dinner date at *Applebee's*.

It was the anniversary of their first date, and to celebrate they made reservations at the restaurant where they shared their first meal.

"Come on ma, you know I'm on point," he said as he reached inside of his bathrobe pocket and pulled out a white envelope. "I need you to drop these off to Savino. It's copies of Imani's birth certificate and social security card."

He handed her the envelope and she stuffed it inside of her crocodile skin handbag.

"I gotchu, daddy. I've been workin' on it ever since you told me about it last night. It's a good thing you already had this information because if you didn't it might've made things a lil' harder."

"I know," Sonny nodded his head. "Giving me these papers and making me Imani's godfather was the best thing that Nahfisah could've done. Make sure you tell Savino that I want my niece outta that foster home a.s.a.p. No excuses."

Daphney took a piece of turkey bacon off of his plate and placed it inside her mouth. "I gotchu, bae. Just so you know, ya daughter's in the living room watching *Dora The Explorer* so keep an ear out for her." She leaned forward to kiss him, and then headed toward the back door. "And when you drop her off at your mom's house, let her know that I'll be droppin' Dayshon off around 4 o'clock."

"I gotchu, love." He knocked down the rest of his orange juice and admired the way her ass jiggled as she headed toward the back door. "Daph, don't forget to start the paperwork on the house for Nahfisah."

She blew him a kiss, and then walked out the door. He grabbed his iPhone from the counter and called Easy.

Ring! Ring! Ring!

"Hello," Easy answered.

"What's up, pops? You good?" he asked, referring to their argument from the night before. Easy took a deep breath and exhaled. "Yeah I'm alright, but how's your sister?"

"She'll be a'ight. I admitted her to the rehab center in Eaglesville, and I got Savino pushin' the paperwork to get Imani out of that foster home."

"Alright, well whatever I can do to help out just let me know," Easy replied in a somber tone.

"She's goin' through a lot right now, and I didn't wanna make shit more complicated than it already is. That's the reason I didn't tell her that she was my sister. At this point I just need her to get better."

"That definitely sounds like a plan," Easy encouraged him.

"A'ight pops, now lemme change the subject real quick. What's up with the package? Did Mello drop it off last night?"

"Yeah, it's outside in the garage. I told him to put it in the deep freezer."

"A'ight well look, I got a lot of shit to do today, so I'ma need you to take that package to Poncho for me."

"Come on Sontino," Easy complained. "You always findin' a way to throw a monkey wrench in the game. Me and your mom had plans to spend the day with Fat-Fat and D-Day."

"Pops," he responded in a stern voice. "I need you to make that happen."

"Alright man, damn! But it's gon' have to be later on tonight."

"Good lookin', pops."

He disconnected the call, and then dialed the number to the prepaid phone that he gave to Heemy.

Ring! Ring! Ring! Ring! Ring!

"Hello," Heemy finally answered. "Sonny?"

"Yeah this me, lil' homie. Where you at?"

"Damn dawg, you caught me at a bad time," Heemy stated, shaking his head in disappointment. This was the call that he'd been waiting for, and now that it finally came through he wasn't in the position to do anything. "I'm at school right now."

"School huh? That's good shit. I can definitely respect it. What time you gettin' out?"

"At 2:30," he quickly replied.

"A'ight, I'ma pick you up. What school you go to? Franklin or Penn?"

"I go to Benjamin Franklin."

"Say no more. I'll be there at 2:30 and make sure you got ya man witchu."

Click!

After disconnecting the call he placed his scraps on the kitchen floor, and then called out for Rocko. "Where you at boy! Come eat!"

A couple of seconds later, the large Rottweiler followed by Keyonti entered the kitchen. Sonny patted him on the head and smiled at his little girl. Her thick dark hair was plaited into four pigtails with pink barrettes on the ends, and she was dressed in a pink Polo jumper and a white long sleeved Polo shirt.

"Up up, dada! Up up!" she demanded with her arms stretched in the air. He picked her up and covered her face with kisses. "You wanna go see mimaw and paw-paw?"

"Yesh!" she smiled from ear to ear, and then nodded her head up and down. "Fat-Fat want mimaw and paw-paw!"

Sonny laughed. "A'ight lil' mama. Dada gon' take you to see mimaw and paw-paw."

She kissed him on the forehead and wrapped her arms around his neck. The man who she loved so much was wrapped around her little fingers and she enjoyed every minute of it.

***

At The Federal Building

Clavenski was sitting in his office with his old college buddy, Philadelphia District Attorney, Steven Williams.

"So Steve," he sipped from his coffee mug then sat it back down on his desktop. "I heard from a little birdie that I'm the laughing stock of the Criminal Justice Center because I dropped the ball on the Gervin Moreno case."

"Aww come on Andy," D.A. Williams smiled. "It was just an in-house joke! Everyone knows you gave it your best shot. This shit happens from time to time. We've all had that airtight case that we knew we'd win, and outta nowhere had the carpet snatched from under us. Get over it. It happens," he continued, attempting to ameliorate his best friend's embarrassment.

"Oh yeah," Clavenski smiled. "Well, since you state guys have so much to gossip about, the next time you decide to have an in-house forum," he used his fingers to indicate quotation marks, "be sure to mention that a new judge, Justice Arroyo, just signed off on my Title III wiretaps."

D.A. Williams playfully punched him on the shoulder. "Atta boy Andy!" He smiled, and then took a sip of his coffee. "So what's next? I'm assuming you're gonna tap Gervin's cell phone?"

"Nope," Clavenski beamed. "This time around I've got a completely different Moreno in the midst of my crosshairs."

"Oh yeah," D.A. Williams folded his arms across his chest. "Who? The only Moreno I know that's worth mentioning is Gervin." He looked at Clavenski skeptically, eager to hear about the Moreno he was referring to. "You mean to tell me there's another Moreno? A son or a nephew?"

Clavenski reached inside of his desk drawer and retrieved a manila envelope. He opened it and pulled out a picture of Sonny sitting on the hood of his Rolls Royce Ghost.

"Here," he handed the picture to D.A. Williams.

"Who the hell is this?" D.A. Williams asked while examining the 10 x 12 inch picture. "He looks like a friggin' rapper or somethin'. Is this that kid from Berks Street?"

"Nope," Clavenski smiled. "He's Sontino Moreno. Gervin's grandson."

"No shit?" D.A. Williams exclaimed.

172

"And get this," Clavenski continued to smile, "him and his crew *The Block Boys* are the biggest thing since Alvin Rines and the *YBM*. The only difference is that Alvin made his competition *Get Down Or Lay Down*," he stated while using his fingers to indicate quotation marks. "This kid, he laid down the top dog, his own grandfather, and as a result the rest of the dealers in the city got down willingly."

D.A. Williams rubbed his chin and examined Sonny's picture from his jewelry to his Rolls-Royce.

"Interesting. I want you to keep me posted on this one, Andy. A kid with this type of power and influence may very well be the missing link in a slew of my unsolved murder cases."

***

About Forty Minutes Later...

Pooky and Mar-Mar were parked in front of Rahman's house on Locust Street. They were delivering the four and a half ounces of crack that he ordered earlier that morning.

"So Pook, what we gon' do about gettin' some more work? After this," he held up the four and a half ounces, "we only got 9 ounces left, and wit' Sonny on his bullshit, where we 'posed to cop from?"

"I don't know," Pooky answered while shrugging his shoulders. "I guess I'ma have to holla at Sheed, and let him know what's goin' on."

"Well you better hurry up and make that happen 'fore Sonny throw some shit in the game." Mar-Mar suggested, and then passed him the Optimo he was smoking.

"Man, fuck Sonny! Sheed wasn't even feelin' that nigga 'fore he got locked up. He was about to branch off and do his own thing, anyway." He rolled down the driver's side window to pluck the ashes off the cigar, and out of nowhere a forest green Mazda 929 pulled up beside his Range Rover. When he looked down and spotted Sheed sitting in the passenger's seat with a huge smile on his face, he couldn't believe his eyes. "Yo, get the fuck outta here!" he shouted.

Sheed told Jasmyn to park in front of the Range Rover, then he hopped out to embrace his brother. This was the first time that the two of them had been on the streets together in over eighteen years. As he walked over to give Pooky a hug, he noticed his swollen nose and two black eyes. "Yo, what the fuck happened to ya face?"

Embarrassed, Pooky lowered his head and stuck his hands inside of his pockets. Sheed reiterated his question, but this time around his words exuded anger. Pooky took a deep breath, and then looked him square in the eyes. "Ya man Sonny snuffed me out yesterday."

"Sonny snuffed you out? Fuck you mean he snuffed you out?" He flexed his jaw muscles and balled up his fist. "What happened?"

"This nigga came through Delhi Street to pick up his bread, and—"

"And you had his money right?" Sheed asked, cutting him off mid-sentence.

"Of course I had the money, but the nigga went crazy when he caught me fuckin' the lil' bitch Nahfisah from 8th and Diamond."

"Nahfisah?" Sheed screwed up his face. "Nahfisah Thompson? Tommy's baby mom?"

"I don't know who baby mom she is, but if she's from 8th and Diamond, then that's the Nahfisah I'm talking 'bout. This nigga came in the spot, and the second he realized I was fuckin' this bitch, the nigga snuffed me."

174

"Pooky you better not be lyin' to me. You sure all of this happened over a bitch?" Sheed asked, completely overlooking the fact that Nahfisah was Sonny's sister.

"What the fuck I gotta lie for?" Pooky shot back and held out his arms. "Matter of fact, you can ask Mar-Mar." He pointed at the Range Rover and the chubby young man climbed out the passenger's side door.

"Yo Sheed, that's real shit," Mar-Mar said, backing up Pooky's play. "The bul was on some real live goofy shit. He even ran down on Beaver Bushnut, and threw a couple shots at me. I ain't gon' hold you, I was about to park him, but the only reason I gave him a pass was on the strength of you."

Sheed scowled at him. He could tell that Mar-Mar was exaggerating. Irritated, he returned his attention to Pooky. "Yo, gimmie ya phone."

Pooky reached inside of his hoody and grabbed his cell phone. Sheed snatched it fom him and called Sonny.

Sonny answered on the second ring. "Stop callin' my phone, Pooky."

"This ain't Pooky. It's Sheed. Where you at? I need to holla at you."

"I'm rippin' and runnin' right now, but we definitely need to talk. Meet me at the barber shop around 5:30."

"More or less," Sheed replied, and then disconnected the call. He returned to Jasmyn's car and tapped on the driver's side window. She rolled it down, knowing he was about to ditch her. "What Rasheed?"

"Bae, it's some important shit that I gotta take care of so I'ma have to get witchu later on tonight."

"I had the whole day planned out for us, and here you go wit' the nut shit," she complained.

"I know, but some unexpected shit just popped up. I really need to take care of it before it goes too far."

She looked into his hazel eyes, and her heart throbbed for him. "A'ight," she sighed, "but you better bring dat ass home tonight and I'm not playin' witchu!"

He leaned inside of the window and kissed her. "I'ma be there. I promise."

When she pulled off, he looked at Pooky. "Go in the house and tell Rock that I'm out here. Tell him to bring me a burner." He looked at Mar-Mar. "I need you go back to Pooky's house and bag up whatever work y'all got left. We gon' meet back up witchu later on tonight."

***

It was 2:28 p.m. when Sonny pulled up in front of the Benjamin Franklin High School. He'd just left the car wash, and the paint job on his Ghost, coupled with the sparkle of his rims, made the large sedan appear as if it were glowing. The early December weather was a warm 65 degrees so he rolled down his windows and blasted French Montana's, *I Ain't Worried 'Bout Nothin.*

Strapped up wit' that work, riding 'round wit' that Nina/ Two bad bitches wit' me, Molly and Aquafina/ Huhn, I ain't worried 'bout nothin.

As the students exited the building, they couldn't help but to stop and stare at the shiny Rolls Royce. The school's security guard was standing by the exit scowling at the plush automobile. Sonny noticed his demeanor and smiled.

He looked at the old man and rapped along with Frenchie, "I ain't worried 'bout nothin'."

When Heemy and Twany emerged from the building, they immediately noticed the pandemonium that Sonny was causing, and their faces lit up like Christmas trees. As cool as an ice cream Snickers bar, they strolled toward the Roll Royce and made sure that all of their classmates could see them.

Sonny looked at them and laughed. He could vividly remember the days when Mook would pick him up from school in his Bentley.

When they opened up the suicide doors, and climbed in the car Sonny said, "Yo, y'all know y'all pussy rate just shot through the ceilin' right?"

"Yeah," Heemy chuckled. "I was thinkin' the same exact shit." He was sitting in the passenger's seat and Twany was behind him.

"Me too," Twany chimed in. "But yo, I ain't even gon' front, this mutha'fucka look like a big ass candy apple. How much this mutha'fucka cost?"

"A couple hunnid," Sonny replied. "But next year, I'm hoppin' in somethin' bigger. I heard Meek and Spade been tearin' up the city in back to back Phantoms, so I'ma have to step it up on these niggas," he continued while heading toward Roosevelt Boulevard. "So what's up wit' y'all niggas? Y'all ready to get this bread or what?"

"Hell yeah!" they replied in unison.

"A'ight," Sonny nodded his head. "From here on out, y'all gon' hold down Delhi Street. Tomorrow, my lil' brother Rahmello gon' bring y'all a brick of raw. That's 1008 grams. Every gram gotta get bagged up, and he's gonna show y'all how to do it. I'ma need y'all to move 'em at $35 apiece, and y'all should move every gram in about three days. When y'all done, I'ma have Mello bring y'all another one. Every Sunday, I'ma pay y'all $2,000 piece." He looked at Heemy. "You're the case worker, so your job is to manage the block, and Twany," he looked in the back seat, "I'ma need you to be one of the runners. In a day or so I'ma send y'all another runner and two shooters to secure the block. Y'all each gon' make the same amount of money so it's no need to feel like it's a competition. We all playin' for the same team. So what's up? Y'all good wit' that?"

"Yeah," Heemy replied for the both of them, "but its one thing I'm not feelin'."

"Oh yeah," Sonny looked at him skeptically, "and what's that?"

"Twany's big brother, Nipsy. That's our ol' head, and we want him to be the caseworker. We wouldn't be loyal if we didn't include him in our plans. So without Nipsy," he shrugged his shoulders, "ain't nothin' jumpin'."

Sonny nodded his head and smiled. Loyalty. This was one of the words that Mook had drilled inside of his head since a little kid. *Everything's based off of loyalty*, Mook would often say. *And before you can be loyal to a mutha'fucka, you gotta love a mutha'fucka, and you'll never truly love a mutha'fucka until you respect a mutha'fucka. These three words are the key to life, Sontino. Respect. Loyalty. Love. Without respect there's no love, and without love, there's loyalty. In this life, this is the only way to measure the integrity of a mutha'fucka. This is the standard that must be applied when you judge the character of the niggas in ya cypha. The second one of 'em falls short when it comes to these three words, you cut his ass off. Quick!*

He continued smiling, and then turned to look at Heemy. "A'ight young bul, I respect ya position. Ya ol' head can manage the block and you and Twany can do the runnin'. The only thing left is the shooters. I'ma send y'all two."

"Naw Sonny," Twany interjected. "All you gotta do is send us two runners. Me and Heemy gon' be the shooters."

"Oh yeah!" Sonny laughed. "And what y'all gon' shoot wit'? That lil' ass .32 that Heemy flashed on me the other day?"

Embarrassed, they both remained silent.

"Don't even sweat that shit," he assured them. "I'ma have Mello bring y'all some real heat to hold it down. Two Mack lls, two Glock 40s, and a sawed off shotty. In any event, y'all don't know how to use 'em, trust me he gon' make sure y'all niggas is good."

They nodded their heads in unison.

"More or less," Sonny nodded his head, and then sparked up a Backwood. "Yo, y'all know where we goin' right?"

"Naw," they replied.

"First, we gon' hit up Roosevelt Boulevard to visit my connect at the dealership and see about gettin' y'all some new whips. Then, I'ma take y'all clothes shoppin' and get y'all niggas fresh. After that, we goin' to the barber shop. Y'all wit' it?"

"Hell yeah!" they replied in unison.

"More or less."

He turned up the music and French Montana told them all about his days of hustling raw throughout the streets of The Bronx.

Askari

Chapter Fourteen

It was a little past 5:30 p.m., Sonny pulled up in front of the *Philly Finess Barbershop* on Broad and Rockland. Heemy and Twany were behind him in their new whips. Heemy was pushing a jet black 2008 Chevy Impala and Twany was right behind him in a snow white 2009 Buick Lacrosse. Both cars were equipped with 22 inched rims and their backseats and trunks were filled with shopping bags from the *Cherry Hill Mall*. They parked behind Sonny's Ghost, and hopped out their new whips feeling like a million bucks. When they entered the barbershop Sonny greeted his barber.

"Ted, what's up, big bro?"

"Sonny, what's goin' on, him?" the stocky, light brown skinned man replied with a smile on his face. Ted was from 12th and Huntingdon, also known as *Beirut*, and his entire swag North Philly personified. At first glance, his charismatic nature and bright smile would lead one to believe that he was the nicest dude in the world, but in all actuality he was a certified goon. His dark, cold eyes told a story of hardship, struggle, and pain, and under the right circumstances he wouldn't hesitate to put something in the cemetery. He came from behind his barber's chair and embraced Sonny with a brotherly hug.

"What's up wit' Daph and the kids? They good?"

"Yeah they good," Sonny smiled. "As a matter of fact," he glanced at his Rolex. "I need to hurry up 'cause me and Daph got plans for later, and I still gotta get dressed.

"Say no morzies!" Ted replied in his trademark comical slang. "Just let me finishin' cleaning these clippers, and I gotchu him."

Sonny looked at Heemy and Twany, and then returned his gaze to Ted. "Damn, my bad bro, these my young buls right here," he introduced them. "They from up ya way too. On Delhi Street."

"What's goin' on, him?" Ted greeted them.

"Ain't shit, ol' head," they replied in unison, then shook his hand.

Sonny walked over to the empty station next to Ted's, and began brushing his hair in the mirror. While stroking the waves on the left side of his head the thumping sounds of 50 Cent's, M*any Men,* interrupted his movements. He glanced out the front window and spotted Pooky's Range Rover double parked beside his Ghost. Sheed was hopping out the passenger's side door, Pooky was walking around the front of the truck, and a husky dark skinned man with a baldhead and a Sunni Muslim beard was climbing out the backseat.

The three men barged inside of the barbershop and Sonny could feel their hostility. Heemy and Twany could feel it as well. Heemy quickly stood to his feet and inconspicuously gripped the handle on his pistol. He looked at Pooky and ice grilled him.

Sheed approached Sonny. "Damn Blood, how you call ya'self puttin' ya hands on my brother?"

Sonny laid his brush on the counter and looked at him with pure hatred in his eyes. "Nigga, how the fuck you call ya'self puttin' ya hands on my sister and my niece?"

"What?" Sheed asked, completely caught off guard.

He then remembered the night when Sonny told him about Nahfisah being his sister.

"Nigga, you heard what the fuck I said!" Sonny shouted at him. "And what about them 24 bricks you took from her? When was I 'posed to hear about that?"

Feeling guilty and embarrassed, Sheed quickly down played the situation."Man fuck dat! How the fuck you gon' pop off on my brother?" He snapped. "So that's what we doin' now? We puttin' hands on each other's family?"

Sonny took a step forward, closing the distance between them. "Nigga, I know you ain't just threaten my mutha'fuckin' family?"

"A threat?" Sheed retorted. "Nigga, fuck a threat! We pass that already! You shed the blood of my brother!" He threw a right hook, but Sonny slipped it and caught him with a straight right. The punch burst open his lip and he stumbled backwards. Rahman reached for his .45, but stopped when Heemy aimed the .32 at his face. "Pussy, I wish you would," the young man snarled through clenched teeth. Rahman raised his hands in a defenseless posture. "Nah, you got it young bul. You got it."

Sheed wiped his mouth with the back of his left hand, and then examined the blood. Infuriated, he took another swing at Sonny's face but Sonny tucked his chin, and blocked the punch with his left shoulder. He then, countered with a right jab and a left hook. Sheed crashed to the floor and reached for the Desert Eagle that was tucked in his waist. As he went to pull it out, Twany ran over and kicked him in the side of his head.

Pooky and Rahman ran toward Twany, but stopped in their tracks when Sonny aimed his FNH in their direction. Ted followed his lead and pulled a Glock .40 from under his smock.

"Yo, I ain't gon' hold you him," Ted said as he waved his Glock between Pooky and Rahman, "if y'all don't leave my mutha'fuckin' shop, I'ma start twistin' shit."

Slowly, Sheed stood to his feet and ordered Pooky and Rahman to fall back. He massaged his jaw and looked at Sonny with tears in his eyes. "After all the shit we been through this is how you treat me?"

"Naw, nigga, this is how you treated me when you violated my mutha'fuckin' family! That ain't even considering the fact that you tucked all that work on me," Sonny stated in a cold voice. He threw up his set. "Word to Bishop! If it wasn't for the love and respect that I got for Mook and his memory, I woulda blew ya fuckin' head off!"

"So what, we ain't brothers no more?" Sheed asked with tears falling from his eyes. "We at war now?"

"Brothers?" Sonny looked at him like he was crazy. "Nigga, we ain't brothers! If we was brothers, you woulda never did what the fuck you did! We ain't nothin'!" he spat. "And as far as a war? Come on fan, we both know you ain't built for that!"

The pain that exuded from Sheed's eyes quickly turned into hatred. "So I guess it is what it is."

"Pussy, it's whatever you want it to be," Sonny fired back, and then waved the FNH back and forth between him and Pooky. "Y'all niggas is done in Philly. Both of y'all!" He aimed the large pistol at Rahman. "That goes for ya cross eyed ass too! Now, get the fuck out my face 'fore I start ringin' this mutha'fucka! Matter of fact, drop them fuckin' hammas and put y'all hands in the air. Heemy and Twany," he called out. "Grab them hammas off the floor and pat them niggas down."

They did as they were told, and further took it upon themselves to remove the money that Pooky and Rahman had their pockets.

After being relieved of their belongings, the three men backed out the barbershop and hopped in the Range Rover. When they pulled off, Sonny sat in Ted's chair and laid the FNH on his lap.

"Ted, lemme get my usual," he said as if nothing had ever happened. "A one and a half wit' the grain." He then, reached inside of his pants pocket and pulled out a sandwich bag of

Kush and a pack of Backwoods. He tossed them to Heemy. "Yo, roll somethin' up for me."

***

Later That Day...

Sheed, Pooky, and Rahman were sitting in Pooky's living room, plotting their revenge. "Damn lil' cuzzo, I knew we shoulda ran up in that mutha'fucka and started blazin'!" Rahman snapped. He was pacing from one side of the room to the other and puffing on a Newport 100. "I can't believe I let these bitch ass niggas get it off on me!"

"I feel you Rock, but dude was like my brother," Sheed explained. "Me and this nigga came up from nuffin, and our ol' head Mook always taught us to move as a unit. We done got money together, partied together, fucked bitches together, and went to war together. I couldn't just run down on him and treat like some random nigga in the streets. That was my mutha'fuckin' man."

"Well damn bro," Pooky interjected, "from the way this nigga was actin', he obviously ain't feel the same way about you!" He looked at Rahman for support. "Is it just me or was the bul about to start blastin'?"

Rahman nodded his head in agreement, and then sat next to Sheed on the sofa. "Listen lil' cuz, I know the nigga was ya homie but we gotta respond," he stated in a leveled voice. "The streets is watching and you know how they operate. If we give this nigga a pass, everybody gon' think we soft. I'm tellin' you Sheed, we gotta do somethin'."

Sheed took a deep breath. "I dig where you comin' from Rock, but at the same time we ain't built for a war right now. If we make a move it's not just Sonny we gon' have to worry about." He laid back on the sofa and stared up at the ceiling.

"We gon' have to go to war wit' the entire *East Coast Bishop Blood Family*, and trust me my nigga that's a whole 'nother monster. You talking 'bout New York niggas, Jersey niggas, Pittsburgh niggas, South Carolina niggas, Georgia niggas, and Miami niggas. Trust me Rock, that's a war we can't win right now."

Just as Rahman was about to respond, they could hear the sound of keys jingling against the front door. A second later, the door swung open and Flo stepped inside of the house with shopping bags in both hands.

"Pooky where you at daddy?"

She was texting on her cell phone, and didn't notice the three men sitting on the sofa. As she walked toward the dining room, she spotted them out the corner of her left eye. Specifically, she spotted Sheed. He scowled at her, and then turned his attention to Pooky. "Damn big bro, you got my bitch callin' you daddy now?"

"N—N—Naw Sheed. It ain't even like that," Pooky tried to explain.

Sheed chuckled. "Yo, don't even sweat that shit." He returned his gaze to the woman that he used to love more than himself. "What's poppin' Flo? I'm glad you stopped by, you saved me a trip. I was just about to stop by ya house and pick up my Sting Ray. My new bitch needs to get her shit upgraded."

Begrudgingly, she removed the Corvette key from her key ring, and threw it at him. "Fuck you, Sheed!"

"Nah bitch, don't fuck me! Keep fuckin' my brother!" he snapped, and then spit across the room. His snotty saliva landed on her fur coat and her face turned bright red.

"I fuckin' hate you!" she shouted before running out the front door.

Pooky got up to run after her, but Sheed gripped him by the back of his shirt. "Nigga, sit ya ass back down! We talkin' business right now! Fuck that bitch!"

Pooky returned to his seat and folded his arms across his chest. Sheed looked at Rahman, and snapped. "You know what, fuck Sonny! Him and whoever he got ridin' wit' him! That pussy ain't build this shit by hisself! Mook was my ol' head too! So, at the end of the day, half of this shit is rightfully mines!"

"Now that's what the fuck I'm talking' bout!" Rahman instigated. He jumped off the sofa and snatched up the AK-47 that was lying on the coffee table. "Let's ride on this mutha'fucka!"

"Naw, not yet," Sheed replied in a calm voice. "Before we do anything, we gotta get my paper back in order. Like I said, half of everything this nigga owns belongs to me so we gon' take back what's rightfully mines. First, we gon' take over his blocks. Then after that, we gon' shutdown *Donkees* and *Infamous*." He looked at Pooky. "How much work you got left?"

"A little over 9 ounces."

"A'ight," Sheed said as he got up from the sofa and headed for the front door. "Tomorrow mornin' I'ma bring you a brick. Break it down to grams, and then take it to Delhi Street."

"But Sonny said - "

"Fuck what Sonny said," Sheed cut him off. "That's my mutha'fuckin' block!"

***

It was 7:30 p.m. when Sonny arrived at the *Applebee's* on Old York Road. As he cruised through the parking lot, he noticed that the only cars in the vicinity were Daphney's Benz,

Easy's Jaguar, Breeze's Maserati, Rahmello's Aston Martin, and his grandmother's Navigator.

"What the fuck is she up to?" he wondered as he parked beside her SUV.

He hopped out the Ghost and examined his reflection in the tinted windows. He was dressed in a black tuxedo with diamond cuff links, and a black Burberry London trench coat was draped over his shoulders. Satisfied with his appearance, he casually strolled toward the entrance.

When he stepped through the door and entered the restaurant, he couldn't believe his eyes. The large dining room was transformed into a wedding chapel. The tables and windows were covered in white silk and lavender fabrics and crystal chandeliers decorated the ceiling. A plethora of white chairs was positioned on both sides of the room. A purple carpet ran down the aisle and stopped at the altar, where Daphney was waiting for him in a pearl white Vira Wang. A white veil covered her face and the only thing he could see was the large diamonds that decorated her ears. Standing to her right, Annie, Erika, and her best friend Tasha were draped in lavender gowns from The House Of Versace. They were smiling at him from ear to ear, and they each held a single white rose.

Reverend Johnson, his grandmother's pastor, was standing beside Daphney. Off to his left, dressed in black tuxedos, Easy, Breeze, Rahmello, and Dayshon were standing at attention. All of them waiting for him to take his rightful place beside his bride.

A familiar baseline erupted from the sound system, and the R&B group, Jagged Edge emerged from the kitchen area. They were dressed in white suits and singing their classic hit, *Gotta Be*.

Don't wanna make a scene/ I really don't care if people stare at us/ Sometimes I think I'm dreaming/ I pinch myself just to see if I'm awake or not.

"Damn, my baby went all out for a nigga," he said to himself.

As he began to walk toward the altar, a light tug on the back of his tuxedo made him stop and turn around. Behind him, his grandmother was smiling like a little kid on Christmas morning. She was standing beside Keyonti, and the little girl was reaching out for him.

"She's givin' you away," his grandmother giggled, and then placed Keyonti's hand inside of his. She then nodded her head toward the altar. "Go on now. Your queen is up there waitin' on you."

He looked down at his daughter and couldn't keep the tears from rolling down his face. She looked so beautiful in her white gown and diamond studded tiara. She looked up at her father's wet eyes, and slowly shook her head.

"No cry dada. Look," she pointed down the aisle toward her mother. "Mama lub dada." She smiled at him, and then gently tugged him toward the altar.

When they approached Daphney, Keyonti connected his hand with her mother's, and then wrapped her arms around his leg.

Slowly, he lifted the veil away from Daphney's face and saw the warm tears that dripped from her brown eyes. He leaned forward and kissed her on the lips. He then kissed her tears away one at a time

"I love you, Sontino."

"I love you more, ma."

Together, they turned toward Reverend Johnson, and before God they became united as one.

***

After experiencing their first dance together as a married couple, Easy approached them with a white envelope clutched in his right hand.

"Here," he handed Sonny the envelope. "It's two first class plane tickets to the Bahamas. Me and your mom made reservations for y'all at the *Atlantis Beach Towers*. It's a five star resort on Paradise Island. The plane is scheduled for lift off tomorrow mornin' at eleven o'clock, so be on point. As far as Dayshon and Keyonti, me and your mother are gonna keep 'em for the week."

"Good lookin' pops. We appreciate it!" Sonny smiled at him, and placed the envelope in his back pocket.

Easy kissed him on the forehead, and then leaned forward to kiss Daphney on the cheek. "I love y'all."

"We love you too," they replied in unison.

Easy returned his gaze to Sonny and reached out to straighten his bow tie. "A'ight Sontino, I'm 'bout to slide. I gotta go handle that situation wit' Poncho. Enjoy y'all honeymoon and I'ma see y'all when y'all get back."

Chapter Fifteen

It was 10:47 p.m. when Easy pulled up in front of Poncho's bodega. He killed the ignition and climbed out the Jag. After glancing up and down the block, he popped the trunk, and then looked around once more. Satisfied that nobody was watching, he grabbed the red Cambryo and closed the trunk.

When he entered the store, Poncho's wife Marisol was standing behind the cash register. She looked at him and squinted her eyes. Although she hadn't seen him in over twenty years, she immediately recognized the face of the man who was once her husband's best customer.

"Easy!" she smiled at him. "How ju doing? It's been a long time since I seen ju last!"

"Yeah Mrs. Nunez it sure has," he returned her smile, and then glanced around the store. "Is Poncho here? He's supposed to be meetin' me tonight."

She nodded her head toward the back of the store.

"He's in his office. I'll let him know ju are here."

"Thanks," he said.

As she called Poncho to let him know that Easy was there to see him, Easy walked down the center isle and approached the two wooden doors that occupied the back wall. He gently tapped on the door to his left and waited patiently. About thirty seconds later, the door swung open and Poncho was standing there with a smile on his face. He was dressed in tan slacks and a worn out wife beater. Tattered Payless shoes adorned his feet and a straw hat rested on his head.

"Easy my friend! How ju doin'?" he continued smiling as he shook Easy's hand. He looked at the Cambryo that was clutched in Easy's free hand, and then motioned for him to step inside of the office.

"Considerin' all the circumstances, I'm doin' pretty good," Easy replied while looking around the pantry that Poncho called his office. It amazed him that after two decades, the small room looked the same as it did back in 1985 when they first met. There was a wooden picnic table that he used for a desk, a 13 inch black and white television that was sitting on a file cabinet, and a liquor shelf on the right wall.

"It's exactly the way you and Juan wanted it," Easy said as he handed over the cooler.

Poncho looked inside and was pleased to see that Mexican Bobby's hands and tongue were neatly packaged in two separate zip lock bags. He closed the Cambryo and motioned for Easy to take a seat. "Sontino's a good boy, Easy. Ju raise him right."

"Thanks Poncho, I appreciate that," Easy smiled. "He wanted to bring this to you personally, but he just got married today and him and his wife are getting ready for their honeymoon."

"Young love," Poncho sighed, and then shook his head as if he were reminiscing about a love from his past. "Speaking of which, my Olivia and ju son," he waved his hand dismissively, "de other one. What his name?"

"Rahmello," Easy quickly answered. "What about him?"

"He been snooping around my Olivia, and I do not like it," he complained. "I need for ju to talk to him. Ju tell him to keep away."

Just as Easy was about to respond, the door cracked open and a young Spanish man who appeared to be in his early twenties peaked his head inside of the office.

"Papi, Fernando said that he needs to see you."

"Okay," Poncho looked at him with an irritated expression, "but ju do know how to knock on a door, no?"

The young man smiled. "Si papi. My bad."

"Easy, dis is my son Estaban. Estaban, dis is my old friend, Easy," he introduced them.

When they shook hands, Estaban recognized Easy as someone from his past. The only difference was that this time Easy wasn't aiming a gun at his face. *What the fuck? This is the nigga that killed Angelo and Gordo*, he thought to himself as he remembered the day that his older brother and cousin were gunned down on Indiana Street. He looked at his father and in Spanish he informed him that Easy was the man responsible for the murders of his brother and cousin. Poncho looked at Easy and smiled.

"Hey yo Poncho, you know how I feel about you talkin' that Spanish shit around me," Easy reminded him.

Poncho chuckled. "Don't ju worry my friend. Estaban was just informing me about a family issue. It's nothing," he waved him off, and then returned his gaze to Estaban. "Beta Busca Chee-Chee."

"Si papi."

The young man scowled at Easy, and then left the office. Poncho approached the liquor shelf and grabbed a bottle of rum. "Ju want something to drink?"

"Nah, I'm good," Easy answered. He was slightly uncomfortable from the look that Estaban gave him before he left the office. "I'm still waitin' on you to tell me about my son snoopin' around your daughter."

Poncho looked at him with a blank expression. The office door swung open and Chee-Chee was standing in threshold with a double barrel shotgun clutched in his palms. Confused, Easy hopped out of his seat and looked at Poncho. "Yo, what the fuck is this?"

Poncho trembled with rage. "Ju remember de day ju robbed 4th and Indy?"

"What?" Easy asked, completely dumbfounded.

"Ju don't remember robbing my corner a couple of years ago?" Poncho shouted. "And killing my son and my nephew?"

Instantly, Easy remembered the day that he robbed and killed the two Spanish men on the corner of 4th and Indiana. "Fuck!" hHe reached for his gun, but before he could pull it out, Chee-Chee squeezed the trigger on his shotgun.

Boom!

The blast lifted Easy off of his feet and he landed on the picnic table. Despite the gut wrenching wound to his abdomen, his adrenaline was in overdrive and he felt no pain. He grabbed his Glock .19 from his shoulder holster, and then he staggered to his feet. Sluggishly, he attempted to let off a shot but once again Chee-Chee beat him to the punch.

Boom! Boom!

The bullets ripped through his chest and right shoulder, flipping him over the picnic table. As he lay on the floor, struggling to breathe, Poncho removed a .44 Bulldog from the small of his back. He cocked the hammer and aimed the barrel at Easy's head. "Ju fucked up. I never shoulda trusted ju."

Just as he was about to pull the trigger, Olivia pushed pass Chee-Chee and stormed inside of the office. "Papi, what happened?" she asked in a shaky voice. No sooner than she asked the question, her eyes locked on the crimson red blood that decorated the back wall. She then looked behind the picnic table where Easy was twisted on the floor. "Ay dios mio!" she screamed. "Ay dios mio!"

Poncho snapped at her. "Leave Olivia! Beta!"

"But papi," she cried.

"Escucha me!"

She lowered her head and turned around to leave. As she closed the door and began walking toward the front of the bodega, the thunderous sound of another gunshot pierced her soul and the only thing she could think about was Rahmello.

***
The Following Morning...

Gladys Miller, the fifty year old block captain for the 500 block of Glenwood Street was leaving her house when she noticed the black Jaguar that was parked on the corner. "I know good and goddamned well these motherfuckers ain't out here slinging them rocks again," she said to herself, assuming the vehicle belonged to a drug dealer.

For the past ten years she relished over the fact that she played a part in cleaning up one of the most notorious drug corners in North Philly, and now that 5th and Glenwood was relatively drug free, she planned to keep it that way.

She glanced up and down the block looking for any signs of the car's owner, but the only person she saw was a scrawny little Spanish man dressed in blue overalls. He appeared to be loading up the bread truck that was parked in front of the corner store. She looked inside of the truck and realized that another Spanish man was sitting in the passenger's seat. He was watching her like a hawk, and his cold eyes sent chills down her spine. Defiantly she locked eyes with him for a few seconds, and then headed toward her car.

The man who was loading the bread truck slipped inside of the corner store, and for some strange reason Glady's intuition was telling her that something was wrong. She glanced at the Jaguar one last time, and then climbed inside of her car. *I don't know what's going on, but something ain't right*, she thought to herself.

As she started the engine she noticed that smoke was seeping from underneath of the Jaguar.

"What the hell is—"

Ka-Boom!

The loud blast lifted the sedan off the ground sending scrap metal and broken glass flying through the air.

***

In Upper Dublin, Pennsylvania

Sonny was awakened by the warm sensation of Daphney deep throating his dick. He looked down and the only thing he saw was the shape of her head underneath the silk sheets. She was going up and down on his shaft, while moaning and slurping.

"Well goddamn, Mrs. Moreno. That's how you feelin' this mornin'?"

She kissed the tip of his dick, and then pulled the sheets away from her body. She then spun around on her hands and knees, and arched her back, giving him a back shot view of her pussy. "I wanna get fucked by my husband," she insisted.

He smiled at her. "Oh, is that right?"

She turned back look at him and slowly twerked her ass. "And you *better* fuck me hard."

"Hard huh?"

"Umm hmm," she purred while popping her ass one cheek at a time. "If it ain't rough, it ain't right!"

"Say no more." He positioned himself behind her and used the tip of his dick to play with her clitoris and pussy lips.

"Ummmmm! Damnit daddy!" The feeling of his dick going up and down her slit was driving her crazy. "Daddy, you better stop playin and put that mutha'fucka in me!"

He laughed at her. "Nah," he teased. "I was layin' here mindin' my own business. So now," he dipped his 9 and a half inches inside of her, and then quickly pulled out, "ya ass is on my time!"

"Yo, stop playin'," she whined.

196

He smacked her on the ass and continued to tease her. Again, he used the head of his dick to caress her clitoris and her pussy lips. She rocked backwards, attempting to get him inside of her but he laughed at her and pulled back.

"Sontino!" she whined like a spoiled baby. "Stop playin' all the time!"

"Ain't nobody playin'!"

Wham!

He rammed his dick inside of her and she damn near jumped off the bed.

"Nah, don't run!" he grabbed her around the waist, and then quickly pulled out.

"Oh my God!" she continued to whine like a baby. "Why the fuck are you teasing me like this?"

"Shut the fuck up!" He rammed his dick back inside of her and stroked so hard that she came instantly. "Yes baby! Just like that!" she encouraged him. "Fuck me like that!"

After fifteen minutes of nonstop pounding, he exploded inside of her and together they collapsed on the bed. He looked at the alarm clock on the nightstand and saw that it was 6:15 a.m.

"Damn, I gotta hop in the shower and get dressed. Can you twist somethin' up for me?"

"I gotchu. Just hurry up because we have a lot to get done this mornin'. Aside from packing our luggage, we gotta visit my daddy, and make it to the airport by at least ten o'clock.

"I already know Mrs. Moreno," he replied in a sarcastic tone of voice. "We ain't even been married for a whole 24 hours and you try'na boss me around *already*!."

"Don't front. You know it turns you on when I boss you around," she laughed, and then twisted her beautiful face into an ice grill. *"Now get ya sexy ass in the fuckin' shower 'fore I fuck you up!"*

"Damn," he chuckled as he leaned forward to kiss her on the lips. "What's up wit' all that bass in ya voice?"

Never mind me," she said in between kisses. "That's just my boss voice."

Sonny laughed. "Oh, that's ya boss voice huh?"

"Yup."

His iPhone vibrated on the nightstand, and the screen indicated that the caller was his mother. He accepted the call and held the phone to his ear. "What's up, beautiful? How you feelin' this mornin'?"

"Is your father over there?" Annie asked in a concerned voice.

"Naw. Why would he be over here?"

She sucked her teeth and sighed. "I don't know. He didn't come home last night and I was thinking that maybe he stopped over there to take care of somethin' before you and Daph left for the Bahamas."

Confused, he scratched his head. "Naw mom. I ain't seen him since the weddin'."

"Alright, well can you call around and see if you can track him down for me. I'm starting to get worried."

"Aww man, you always worried about something," he laughed trying to lighten the mood and lift her spirits. "I'm sure he's a'ight. He's probably at one of the spots or somethin'. I'ma find him, and as soon as I talk to him, I'ma have him call you."

"Alright baby, you do that because I'm really starting to get a wierd a feeling."

"Just calm down, I gotchu. I'm sure that everything's okay."

"I hope so," she replied, and then disconnected the call.

He called Rahmello.

Ring! Ring! Ring!

"Yo," Rahmello panted. "Sonny, what's poppin' brozay?"

"You already know," Sonny replied. He listened closely and heard the sounds of a woman moaning and speaking in Spanish. "Yo, who you wit'?"

Rahmello hesitated. "Umm, Umm, you don't know her," he lied. He held his index finger up to his lips, signaling for Olivia to be quiet.

Sonny shook his head in disbelief. "Yo, you wit' Olivia ain't you? And you better not lie."

"Come on bro, you buggin' right now."

"Nigga, answer the question!"

Rahmello sighed. "A'ight man, fuck it. Yeah I'm wit' Olivia!"

Sonny was steaming. He specifically told Rahmello not to fuck with this broad, and what does he do, he fucks with her anyway!

"Listen Mello, you lucky I gotta plane to catch, 'cause if I didn't I'd be over there fuckin' you up! But you better believe when I get back to the states, we gon' sit down and talk about this shit."

"A'ight man, whateva."

"Yeah, I gotcha a'ight man whateva," Sonny shot back. "But dig though, I need you to stop whatever you're doin' and pay close attention."

The phone went silent for a few seconds, and then Rahmello's voice eased through the receiver. "What's up, brozay? Holla at me."

"You seen or heard from pops this mornin'?"

"Nah, I ain't seen him since last night. Why, what's up?"

"My mom just called and told me that he didn't come home last night."

"He's probably at the stash house," Rahmello suggested. "I gotta shoot over there in lil' bit so I'ma see what's up."

"A'ight, get on top of that," Sonny replied. He sparked up the freshly rolled Backwood that Daphney just handed to him. "Oh yeah, and before you leave the spot grab one of them piggies that we turned into bacon bits and drop it off wit' the young bul Heemy."

"Heemy? Who the fuck is Heemy?"

"The young bul from Delhi Street."

"A'ight," Rahmello nodded his head. "Say no more. I gotchu."

Chapter Sixteen

It was 8:35 a.m. when Sonny and Daphney pulled into the parking lot of SCI Graterford. He'd been calling Easy's cell phone for the past hour, but to no avail. A concerned expression was written across his face, and like his mother he was beginning to suspect that something was wrong. He handed Daphney his phone.

"Keep callin' him while I go in here to holla at ya pop." He climbed out the Ghost and looked up at the 40 foot wall that surrounded the prison. "Damn," he said to himself. "This some ancient history, King Author type of shit."

As he headed toward the entrance an eerie feeling washed over him, but he shook it off and entered the building. After handing over a fake driver's license and going through a metal detector, his left hand was stamped with an invisible ink, and he was escorted to the visitor's house.

About twenty minutes later, the corrections officer at the front desk announced, "Alvin Rines! The visitor for Alvin Rines, report to the front desk!" Sonny got up from his seat and headed toward the officer. The fat white man gave him the once over, and then shook his head in contempt. "Look at this fuckin' asshole," he said to himself. He was referring to Sonny's flamboyant appearance. Aside from his powder blue YSL sweater, his Seven Jeans, and his navy blue Mauri's, his customized jewelry was more than enough to make the flashlight cop green with envy.

"Devin Scott?" the C.O. questioned while glancing at his clipboard.

"Yeah, that's me," Sonny lied.

"Alright, go through the door right there," he gestured toward the door that led to the visiting room. "One more thing Mr. Scott," he pointed back and forth between Sonny's watch and necklace, "you wouldn't happen to be a professional athlete or some kinda of entertainer would ya?"

Sonny picked up on the officer's insinuation and scowled at him. "Nizzaw. Just know that the tax money I pay is the money that pays for your salary."

When he stepped inside of the visiting room he immediately attracted everyone's attention. His diamond earrings, Rolex, and *BBE* charm resembled a light show, and the clarity of his VS1 diamonds spoke volumes with the slightest movement. He paid his spectators no mind and scowered the large room looking for Alvin. He spotted him sitting in the last row of chairs directly in front of the vending machines. As he walked toward him, the muscular, brown skinned man stood to his feet. He was dressed in a cocoa brown, one piece jumper, and a pair of cream Pradas. His body language was somewhat tense, and behind the lenses in his gold framed Prada glasses, Sonny could see that sonething was bothering him.

"What's up Alvin? Is everything good?"

Alvin embraced him with a fatherly hug, and then placed his hands on his shoulders. He looked Sonny square in the eyes. "First, lemme start by sayin' congratulations and welcome to the family." He noticed Sonny's confused expression, and smiled. "Yeah I know right," he shrugged his shoulders, "word travels fast around here. Speakin' of which, I've been hearin' a lot of stories about you." He removed his hands from Sonny's shoulders and returned to his seat.

"A lot of stories?" Sonny replied as he sat down beside him. "About *me?*"

"Yes," Alvin shook his head, "about you. Look around and tell me what you see."

Sonny looked around the room and shrugged his shoulders. "I don't know. Mutha'fuckas is lookin' at me. What's new?"

"Exactly!" Alvin nodded his head. "Your whole style Sontino, it's too loud. Anytime a man can walk into a room full of people visiting a family member that they haven't seen in a while, and he becomes the center of attention that's a major problem." He gestured toward his *BBE* charm. "Man, look at this shit. That's every bit of a $100,000, and that's not including them big ass diamonds in ya ears and that dumb ass Rolex."

"What?" Sonny screwed up his face. "Yo, I *know* you ain't have me come all the way out here just to tell me this dumb ass shit?"

"Naw," Alvin shook his head from side to side. "I asked that you come because I'm worried about the welfare of my daughter and my grandbabies," he said in a sincere voice.

"Ya daughter and ya grandbabies? What the fuck my jewelry gotta do wit' Daph and the kids?"

"It has *everything* to do wit' them," Alvin fired back. "If these mutha'fuckas is sittin' in this visiting room watchin' you, then what the hell do you think the feds are doin'?"

"The feds?" Sonny chuckled. "All of my shit's legit, and if it really comes down to it I can cover all my assets wit' my 1099. My sports bar's poppin'. My nightclub's poppin' and together they make about a $700,000 a year so fuck the feds."

Alvin removed his Prada frames, and shook his head in disappointment. "Yo, this is deja vu like a mutha'fucka."

"Deja vu?" Sonny countered. "Ol' head don't take dis the wrong way, but you had your turn and now its mines. Just because you fell, that don't mean I'ma fall. I'm not you," he said while slowly shaking his head. "I'm Sonny Moreno, not Alvin Rines.

Alvin chuckled. "Are you sure you're not me or at least who I used to be? Sontino, the only difference between you and me is the money! You probably count yours and me but I had to weigh mines."

Sonny laughed at him and clapped his hands together. "A'ight, ol' head, talk that shit!" The laughing stopped and he looked Alvin dead in his eyes. "That might be true, but all dat YBM, *Get Down Or Lay Down*, shit is over. The only thing you weighin' up these days is some old ass memories."

Alvin was heated. Every fiber of his being wanted to smack fire out of Sonny's face, but somehow he managed to keep his cool. "Dig right, I'ma let that slide because my intentions don't revolve around you and me bumpin' heads. Rather my only concern is my daughter and my grandchildren. It's bad enough that I can't be there to love and protect them, but you Sontino, you have the opportunity to be the man that I'm incapable of being right now." He took a deep breath and fiddled with his Prada frames. "All I'm askin' you to do is to quit while you're still ahead. I mean shit, you even said it yourself, you have two businesses that are doin' extremely well and when you couple that with the real estate company that I left to Daph, y'all should be more than straight."

Sonny remained quiet. He recognized the bald truth of Alvin's statements, but he also remembered what happened the last time he attempted to take his foot off the gas pedal. He lost Riri and their unborn child.

"Listen ol' head, I feel where you're comin' from and all dat. So this what I'ma do, I'ma take some time to figure out what's best for me and my family."

"Yeah you do that," Alvin encouraged him. "And while your at it, I want you to think about Daph. I I I want you to think about the way that she looks at me toward the end of every visit. Think about the pain in her eyes. It's the pain of a daughter who has to live with the reality of her daddy never comin' home again. All of her pain and suffering," he shamefully lowered his head and took a deep breath, "it burns through her eyes Sontino. I've been lookin' at those tortured eyes for over 20 years now." He stood to his feet and Sonny did the same. "I need you to think about Keyonti. I need you to imagine her growing up in this cold world without the love, protection, and support of her father. Then I want you to ask yourself if you're man enough to look that little girl in the eyes and tell her that her daddy's never comin' home again?"

The impact of his word hit Sonny like a ton of bricks. He thought about the streets and how they affected the women in his family. Then he thought about Keyonti and what seemed to be inevitable. He attempted to speak, but Alvin waved him off. "It's no need to talk about it. Just be a man and do what your family needs you to do."

As Sonny turned to leave, Alvin stopped him in his tracks, "And Sontino, whatever you do," he paused for a second, "you better believe the streets is watching."

***

Back In Philly

Agents Terry Long and Monica Brown were riding down Broad Street when Agent Long received a phone call from Detective Sullivan. "Terry, where are you?"

"Monica and I are heading toward the office. Why? What's going on?"

Detective Sullivan chuckled. "Everything's okay, well for us anyway. Unfortunately, I can't say the same for *The Moreno Family.*"

"Oh yeah," Agent Long replied. "What makes you say that?"

"Well, we found a body this morning."

"Did Sontino catch up to Gervin?"

"Nope."

"Well did Gervin kill Sontino?"

"Nope."

"Well what the fuck happened, Sully?"

"It's Ervin *Easy* Moreno, Sontino's father. We found his body this morning and whoever killed him, they got his ass good."

"What's your location?"

"Were on the corner of 5th and Glenwood."

Agent Long made a U-turn at the intersection of Broad and Spring Garden. "We're on our way."

***

When they arrived on the scene the first thing they noticed was a burnt up Jaguar that was sectioned off by yellow crime scene tape. The paint job was scorched to a crisp, and light strands of smoke were rising from the car's surface. The crime scene unit was conducting their investigation, and the uniformed police officers were doing their best to keep the neighbors at bay.

Agent Long parked the navy blue Excursion a few feet away from the corner, and beeped the horn to elicit Detective Sullivan's attention. The middle aged black man opened the back door, and smiled at Agent Brown.

"Hello Monica," he greeted the Black and Korean beauty. "You're looking radiant this morning."

Agent Brown scowled at him playfully. "Don't waste your time try'na flatter me, Sully. Just give up the goods."

He reached inside of his beige trench coat and pulled out a miniature sized notepad. "So this is the scoop, at approximately 7 o'clock this morning, we received a 911 distress call from a woman by the name of Gladys Miller." He pointed across the street toward an elderly black woman. She was standing on her stoop going over the details with another detective. "Apparently, as she was sitting in her car, preparing to leave for work when she witnessed the explosion.

"By the time we arrived on the scene, the car was engulfed in flames. The fire department put out the blaze and it was then, that we discovered Easy Moreno's body in the trunk of the car. Aside from being severely burned, there was unequivocal evidence that he suffered from multiple gunshot wounds to his face and torso. We're assuming he was dead before the blast, but we won't know for sure until we get the final word from the medical examiner."

"Well, if the corpse was severely burned," Agent Brown interjected, "how was it determined that the victim was Ervin Moreno?"

"Easy," Detective Sullivan laughed, while using his fingers to indicate quotation marks. "Pun intended!"

"Stop being such an asshole," Agent Long checked him. "How did you know it was Easy Moreno?"

Detective Sullivan reached inside of his trench coat pocket and pulled out a zip lock bag that contained a soot covered gold Rolex. "Aside from the fact that the car was registered under his name, we found this." He held up the zip lock bag and twisted the watch around until he was able to see the inscription on the back of the bezel. He held out the zip lock bag so the agents could have a better view. "It says, and I quote, *To Pops. From Sontino.*"

He handed the zip lock bag to Agent Brown. She examined the timepiece, and then handed it to Agent Long.

"Alright," Agent Long looked at Detective Sullivan, "did anybody break the news to the family?"

"Nope, not yet," Detective Sullivan smiled. "Detective Phoenix and I were just about to pay them a visit."

Chapter Seventeen

In Upper Darby, Pennsylvania

Annie was chain smoking Newport 100's, and pacing back and forth from the living room to the dining room. A silk scarf was wrapped around her fresh hairdo, and she was dressed in her pajamas from the night before. The hot cup of coffee that she poured herself over an hour ago was now a luke warm liquid. It was sitting on the dining room table and she was so stressed out that she forgot she'd even poured it. *Is he gettin' high again?* she wondered. *Is he cheatin' on me? Is he in jail? Or God forbid, is he hurt, and layin' up in a hospital somewhere?* These were the questions that ran through her mind.

She felt a light tugging on the bottom of her pajamas pants, and looked down to see an agitated Keyonti. "Mimom, Fat-Fat wan' eat, eat."

Annie picked her up and gently kissed her on the cheek. "Aww, Mimom sorry baby! Her forgot she had the babies over here. Where's D-Day? Did he wake up yet?"

"D-Day sleep," the little girl answered. She looked at Annie's scarf, and then pulled it off of her head. "Mimom pwetty like Fat-Fat," she giggled, and then wrapped her tiny arms around Annie's neck. Annie hugged her back, and then called out for Dayshon.

"D-Day, wake up and get ready for breakfast!"

A couple of minutes later he descended the stairs in his blue and gray Polo pajamas set.

"What's up Mimom? Is breakfast ready?"

"No, D-Day," Keyonti answered like she was the big sister and he was the younger brother. "Her no make eat, eat yet."

He smiled at his baby sister, and then gave her and Annie a big hug. He didn't want to say anything, but he was well aware that Easy hadn't come home night before. He also knew that Annie was worried sick.

"Miiiiimom," Keyonti said in a sarcastic voice. "No eat, eat yet!"

Annie and Dayshon fell out laughing. "Girl, you are something else," Annie continued to laugh, happy that her grandchildren were taking her mind off of Easy. "Come on y'all, let's go in the kitchen and see what Mimom can put together for her babies."

As they headed toward the kitchen, they were interrupted by the chiming of the doorbell. Annie carried Keyonti over to the door and looked through the peephole. "Damn," she said to herself as she examined the two black men standing on her front porch. The younger looking man was wearing a gray suit, and his companion was draped in a tan trench coat. They each had a silver badge hanging from their neck, and their overall body language exuded authority. She opened the door. "Can I help you gentlemen?"

"Yes," Detective Sullivan answered in his preppy voice. "I'm Detective Sullivan, and this," he gestured toward his partner, "is Detective Phoenix. Ma'am, would it be okay if we stepped inside to speak with your for a minute?"

Annie looked at him like he was crazy. Her husband and son were two of the biggest drug dealers in Philadelphia, and for the majority of her life, she'd been a part of the street culture. Therefore, inviting the police inside of her home was utterly out of the question.

"I'm sorry detective, but unless you have a search warrant, whatever you need to say, you can say it from there," she replied with a hint of attitude.

The detectives looked at one another and shrugged their shoulders. "Suit yourself," Detective Sullivan shot back then reached inside of his pocket and pulled out his notepad. "Ma'am, is your name Annette Moreno, and are you the wife of Ervin Moreno?"

"Yes," she nervously replied. "Why? Is he okay? Is somethin' wrong?"

Detective Sullivan reached in his pants pocket and pulled out the zip lock bag containing Easy's Rolex. "Ma'am, does this watch belong to your husband?"

She examined the Rolex, and despite the fact that it was covered in dark soot she knew that it was Easy's.

"Y—Y—Yes, that's my husband's watch," she stuttered, knowing what the goofy looking black man was about to say next. She handed Keyonti to Dayshon. "Baby take her in the kitchen, and make y'all some cereal. I'll be there in a minute."

With tears in his eyes, he lowered his head and replied, "Yes, ma'am."

After watching her grandchildren leave the room, she turned back around to face the detectives. "Just tell me how it happened."

Detective Phoenix cleared his throat. "Earlier this morning, we found his body in the trunk of his car. Apparently, he suffered multiple gunshot wounds to his head and torso. After that, whoever killed him, they stuffed him inside the trunk of his car, and then used what believe to be a pipe bomb to blow up the vehicle."

Annie was crushed. Everything inside of her wanted to breakdown, but she couldn't. She had to be strong. Not just for her sake, but the sake of her family.

"Will that be all detective?"

"Just about," Detective Phoenix answered. "The only thing we're gonna need from you at this point is a positive identification." He pulled out his cell phone and showed her a picture of Easy's mutilated corpse. "Is this your husband?"

She glanced at the picture, and then quickly turned away. "Yes, that's him."

"We thought so," Detective Sullivan interjected. "We're still going to need you to come down to the M.E.'s office to make an official identification. But this is something that can wait until later." He handed her his business card. "If there's anything that we can do to help, just give me a call. Especially if it's anything pertaining to our investigation."

Slowly she shook her head from side to side, and then closed the door.

***

When Sonny emerged from the prison, he walked toward the parking lot with a heavy heart. The thought of being locked away from his young family had him in a trance. He realized that Alvin was right. Between him and Daphney, they had three businesses that annually grossed over a million dollars, and aside from Nahfisah and Imani, his entire family was situated. He had $3,000,000 stashed away in a Swiss bank account, a $1,875,000 stashed in the basement of his Reese Street row house, and after his last shipment he was sitting on 375 kilograms of cocaine. He imagined himself in Alvin's shoes, and the thought of being locked away with Keyonti having to grow up without him pierced his soul. He thought about Nahfisah and her current condition, and dreaded the possibility of Keyonti going through the same struggle if he wasn't there to protect and guide her. Thoughts of Riri and their unborn child struck him to the core and tears began to fall from his eyes.

"Damn, this shit is bugged the fuck out," he said to himself. He examined his wedding ring and took a deep breath. "Fuck the bullshit. I gotta do what's right for my family."

As he approached the driver's side of his Rolls Royce, he noticed the dark rain clouds that blocked out the sun. He could hear the soft rumblings of an oncoming storm, and a weird feeling invaded his spirit. When he climbed inside of the car, he noticed that Daphney was talking on her iPhone and jotting something down on a piece of paper.

Who's that?" he asked. He leaned over the center console and kissed her on the cheek. "Is it my pops?"

She held up her index finger, signaling for him to wait a second and continued writing on the small piece of scrap paper. After disconnecting the call, she looked at him. "That was Savino. He was calling about Imani. He said he did the best he could do, and he got us a court date for next month."

"That's good money," he said while starting the ignition. "But what about pops? Did he ever return my calls?"

She frowned at him and used her left hand to massage the back of his neck. "Nah bae, he didn't."

No sooner than she said that, his iPhone vibrated in her hand and she handed it to him. He glanced at the screen and saw that the caller was his mother. "What's up, mom? Is he home yet?"

Daphney stared at him attentively, and when he dropped the phone in his lap and laid his head against the stirring wheel her intuition was confirmed. She knew that Easy was dead.

***

Back In North Philly

Rahmello had just finished showing Nipsy, Heemy, and Twany how to operate their new guns, and now he was telling them how to operate the block.

"It's a gram of raw inside every one of these baggies," he said, showing them the four bags in the palm of his hand. "I know this block is known for bein' a crack spot, but trust me, them same smokas that was coppin' off of Pooky and Mar-Mar are gonna love this shit. Why? 'Cause they can cook it they self and bring it back just the way they want it."

"A'ight," Nipsy nodded his head, and then took a pull on his Dutch Master. "So how much of this shit is you expectin' us to move? Is there a quota or somethin'?"

"Yeah," Rahmello answered, and then exhaled a cloud of Kush smoke. He passed his Backwood to Heemy then returned his gaze to Nipsy. "Y'all should move about two bricks a week. Every three days, my pops gon' drop off a bird and collect the money from the last one. Every Sunday, he's gonna pay y'all two racks apiece."

"Yo, what about the runners?" asked Heemy. "Sonny said he was gon' send us two runners. Where they at?"

"Don't worry 'bout that right now," Rahmello assured him. "They'll be here tomorrow." He handed Heemy the four baggies of cocaine, and then looked each of them square in the eyes. "I need y'all to pay close attention because I'm only gonna tell y'all this shit one time. If you get snatched by the cops," he paused for second, "don't, say, shit. We got top notch lawyers and all the bail money y'all need. Y'all ain't gotta come outta pocket for none of that shit. We got y'all. Just shut the fuck up and wait for the lawyer."

"That's a bet," Twany smiled as he gave Nipsy and Heemy some dap.

Rahmello looked at him and squinted his eyes. "Now, that don't give y'all niggas a free pass to be out here doin' all types of nut shit. This is a business so y'all gotta keep shit professional."

"Don't worry Mello, we got you," Nipsy said while shaking his hand. "But what about Pooky and Mar-Mar? What if they come back?"

"Park 'em," Rahmello answered without a hint of hesitation.

"Park 'em?" Nipsy asked, not expecting Rahmello to answer so harshly. Like so many others, Rahmello's boyish looks, light skin, and blue eyes, gave Nipsy the impression that he was pretty boy playing the role of a gangster. "Just like that, though?"

"Ain't that what the fuck I just said," Rahmello fired back with his voice full of aggression. "We ain't playin no games 'bout this mutha'fuckin' money! So if anybody and I mean anybody, call they self gettin' money out here," he pointed from Cumberland Street to Boston Street, "y'all better park they ass!"

Nipsy was confused. "Kill 'em, and then what?" he asked, while scratching his head. "Just leave they body out here and make the block hot?"

"Nah," Rahmello shook his head from side to side, "just drag they ass to one of these vacant lots, and then call me. I swear to Blood, nobody will ever see or hear from them niggas again."

"Speakin' of Blood," Heemy interjected, "we been thinking 'bout it and we wanna know what we gotta do to be *Block Boys.*"

Rahmello looked at him skeptically but before had the chance to respond, his cell phone vibrated in his jacket pocket. He glanced at the screen and saw that the caller was Sonny. "What's poppin, brozay? You hear from pops yet?"

"Nah," Sonny replied in a shaky voice. "They found his body on 5th and Glenwood. Somebody rocked him."

"What?" Rahmello snapped. "Fuck you mean somebody rocked him?"

"The cops," Sonny continued in a shaky voice, "they found him in the...Yo, they found him in the trunk of his Jag," he managed to say. "Whoever did it, they hit him in the head, stuffed him in the trunk, and then blew the mutha'fucka up."

"Yo, who the fuck did it?" Rahmello shouted through the phone. "Where these niggas at?"

"I'm not sure, bro. I've got an idea, but I'ma bring you up to speed when you get here. I'm at my mom's spot. Drop whatever you're doin' and get ya ass over here."

"Word to Blood!" Rahmello continued snapping. "Whoever killed pops, I'ma murder they whole fuckin' family!"

Heemy, Nipsy, and Twany looked at one another with a shocked expression. They tried offering their assistance, but Rahmello didn't even look there way. Instead, he hopped in his Aston Martin and sped away.

***

In Bala Cynwyd, Pennsylvania

Grip was finishing his daily workout in his indoor pool. His powerful chest and arms were propelling his third lap of breaststrokes and just as he was about to begin his forth, Muhammad entered the large room and cleared his throat, "Ah, em!"

Grip swam to the edge of the pool and grabbed the white towel that was hanging from the diving board. He wiped the water away from his face, and then looked at his personal assistant.

"Yes Muhammad, what is it?"

"You have a telephone call, sir. It's Alvin." He handed Grip the phone, and then stood there with his hands folded in front of him. Grip held the phone to his ear. "Brother Alvin," he greeted his former protégé. "How was the visit?"

"Based on my perception, I'd say he got the point," Alvin replied. "I just hope and pray that he's smart enough to listen."

"Well, did you let him know that the feds are watching him?"

"Nah, not exactly. I did, however, give him a few things to think about in that regard. He reminds me so much of myself when I was younger, and by him being family I gave him the game the way I wished someone would've given it to me. It's like, you and me we had conversations about this shit, but your main concern was for me to secure and maintain political alliances. Now don't get me wrong, that was definitely some good advice, but what I really needed was for somebody to tell me that I was movin' too fast. Maybe then I would've pumped my breaks."

Grip sighed. He loved Alvin like a son, and he still regretted the day that his young protégé was slaughtered in the courtroom like a sacrificial pawn. It was 1992, and under his tutelage, Alvin and his crew were on trial for making the city, *Get Down Or Lay Down*. The district attorney at the time was Andrew Clavenski, and after years of trying to dismantle *The Moreno Crime Family*, he turned his aggression toward Alvin. He charged him with a double murder, and assumed he could use the flamboyant hustler from West Philly to testify against his mentor in order to save himself. He was wrong. Alvin was as real as they came, and he gladly accepted a life sentence rather than be labeled a rat.

"Alvin listen, I love you to death, and I apologize for the way things turned out. I owe you my life, young brother."

"Nah, Mr. Moreno, you don't owe me nothin'. I'ma man with morals and a firm believer in death before dishonor. If you owe anybody, it's Sontino. Don't let them people do to him what they did to me."

Grip wiped the last of the water away from his face, and then reached out to hand Muhammad the towel. "Muhammad, can you throw this away for me?"

As the tall, slender man bent forward to take the towel, Malice burst through the door. "Mr. Moreno, ju watchin' de news?"

Grip looked at the beautiful young woman and shook his head. "No, why?"

She grabbed the remote control from the edge of the pool and aimed it at the 60" screen that was fixed to the back wall. She turned to the Channel 10 news where a mug shot of Easy was plastered on the screen. "Ju see?"

"Hey Alvin, I can't talk right now. Call me later on tonight." He climbed out the swimming pool and approached the television. "Malice, turn up the volume."

She did as she was told, and then the screen switched from Easy's mug shot to news reporter, Roland Rushin. He was standing in front of a burnt up Jaguar and a microphone was clutched in his right hand.

"We're broadcasting live from the corner of 5th and Glenwood, at what appears to be the scene of a gangland murder. The victim in this incident was positively identified as Ervin *Easy Money* Moreno, the son of Black Mafia Don, Gervin *Grip* Moreno. The victim was shot multiple times, and then stuffed inside the trunk of this Jaguar."

Chapter Eighteen

Later That Day...

Annie's house was filled with family and friends. In true African-American fashion, each of them arrived with a soul food dish, attempting to ameliorate the pain that was surely caused by her husband's murder. In the basement, Sonny, Rahmello, Breeze, and the twins were chain smoking Sour Diesel, and desperately trying to figure out who killed Easy.

"Yo, I think it was Sheed," Sonny propounded.

"Sheed?" they replied in unison, looking at him as if he'd lost his mind.

"Naw Blood, you buggin' right now," Breeze added. "This is the homie you're talking 'bout. That nigga wouldn't go against the fam."

"Oh, is that right?" Sonny quickly replied. "I guess he wouldn't steal from us either."

"Steal from us?" Egypt asked. "Yo, whatchu talkin' 'bout?"

Sonny took a deep breath, and then wiped away the tear that fell from his left eye. "Nahfisah told me that before Sheed went to jail, he ran up in her grandmom's spot and took the 24 keys that Tommy left her. In the process, he put a gun to her head and he tried to drown Imani."

"Nizzaw!" Zaire interjected, shaking his head from side to side. "Everybody know Sheed's a wild nigga, but I ain't got him doin' all dat! Especially, when he knew Nahfisah was your sister!"

"Trust me Zai, it's official. I talked to this nigga yesterday, and when I asked him about it, he didn't even try to deny it. He just changed the subject and kept asking me why I fucked up Pooky."

"Hold up," Egypt waved his hands in the air, signaling for him to pause for a second. "You popped off on Pooky? When the fuck did all this happen? Why you ain't never say nothin'?"

"Truthfully," Sonny replied, "this bitch ass nigga was the furthest thing from my mind. I was plannin' to tell y'all about the Sheed situation, but then Daph surprised me wit' the weddin', and that shit threw me off a lil' bit."

Breeze took a deep breath and cracked his knuckles. "I'm sayin' though," he shrugged his shoulders, "don't none of this got nothin' to do witchu thinkin' that Sheed killed Uncle Easy."

Sonny took another pull on his Backwood, and then stubbed it out in the ashtray. "When me and Sheed was havin' words the nigga felt some type of way about me puttin' my hands on Pooky, and he said some shit about puttin' his hands on my family. You know me, I punched the nigga in his fuckin' mouth!"

Breeze hopped off the sofa and placed his hands on his head. "Yo, you popped off on him? And what the fuck happened after that?"

"He had Pooky and another nigga wit' him. A dark skinned nigga wit' a baldhead and a Sunni beard. Anyhow," he shrugged his shoulders, "I punched him in his shit, and then Pooky and the other nigga was try'na get froggy, but Heemy and Ted pulled the heat out."

Breeze shook his head in disbelief. "Yo, this is bad Sonny. This is Sheed we talking 'bout! This ain't some random ass nigga."

"Fuck Sheed!" Rahmello snapped as he got up from the sofa. "That bitch ass nigga threatened my mutha'fuckin' family, and now my pops is dead! Fuck that nigga!"

Breeze glanced at him, and then returned his gaze to Sonny. "I'm tellin' you Blood, I just can't see him doin' nothin' like this."

"So what the fuck is you sayin' then Breeze?" Rahmello continued snapping. He balled up his fist and closed the distance between them. "You ain't gon' ride?"

"Fuck no!" Breeze shot back. "We ain't no every day, just do whatever you want type of mutha'fuckas! Nigga, we Bloods! It's rules to this shit! You can't make that type of move without havin' all the facts!" He knew Sheed, and above all else he knew the love that Sheed had for their family. To him, none of this made any sense, and he knew that he had to find a way to calm things down before they went any further. "Look Mello," he lowered his voice a few octaves, "all I'm tryna say is that Sheed ain't have no reason to kill ya pops. I can understand that he was mad about the situation between Sonny and Pooky, but that ain't enough for him to just say fuck it, and go from zero to sixty like that." He looked at Sonny, "Come on bro, you're smarter than that. And deep down we both know I'm right.

Sonny considered his position, and in some ways it actually made sense. However, the fact that Sheed had already crossed the line was something that he refused to let slide. "Listen fam, I'ma put it like this, the nigga violated my sister and my niece. He stole from us, and in so many words he threatened my family." He pointed toward the ceiling. "My family's upstairs cryin' their eyes out, and at the end of the day I gotta bury my pops. Not my homie. Not my girl. I'm talking 'bout my mutha'fuckin' *pops*." He flexed his jaw muscles, and then turned his attention to Rahmello. "With that being said, I want you to put a team together, and go kill this nigga."

***

At The Creek Side Apartments In Bensalem, Pa.

Sheed was laying on Jasmyn's bed in nothing but his boxer briefs. He'd just finished watching the news, and the segment about Easy's murder left him with mixed feelings. He couldn't deny the fact that he felt sorry for Sonny and his family, but in the same vein he felt as though Sonny shitted on him. As he lay there debating whether or not he should give him a call and express his condolences, Jasmyn entered the small bedroom in her correctional officer's uniform. She turned on the stereo and the hypnotizing sounds of R. Kelly's, *Half On A Baby*, eased through the speakers. One by one, she lit the lavender scented candles that were positioned throughout the room. She closed the window blinds, turned off the lights, and after that she grabbed a pair of his Timberlands from the closet.

Sheed sat up in the bed and looked at her with a confused expression. "Yo, what you about to do with them?" he pointed at the boots.

She smiled at him, and seductively bit her bottom lip. "You gon' take off them boxer briefs, throw these Tims on, and then fuck me like a gangsta!"

"Oh yeah," Sheed chuckled. He got up from the bed and removed his underwear. "You like that gangsta shit, huh?"

"You better know it." She threw him the boots, and then tapped the badge that was pinned to her shirt. "I'm the law around here and I gave dat ass a direct order, so you *better* comply."

After lacing up his boots, he pushed her against the bedroom door. "So you the law around here, huh?" He kissed her on the lips, and then ran the tip of his tongue along the side of her neck.

"Umm hmm," she moaned. The anticipation of feeling him inside of her was driving her crazy. "I want you so bad."

He dropped to his knees and unbuckled her pants. After easing them down to her ankles, he kissed the front of her Victoria Secret thong, and used the tip of his nose to massage her clitoris through the sheer pink fabric. She smelled so good, and the warmth of her pussy was heating up his face. He pushed her thong to the side, and then ran his middle finger up and down her slit. Her breathing became heavy and she grinded her pussy against his finger.

"Umm baby. Damn, this shit feels so good." She grabbed the back of his head with both of her hands and pulled him toward her. "Suck my pussy."

He slipped his index and middle fingers inside of her and massaged her G spot. "Is that a direct order?"

"Boy, you better stop fuckin' wit' me," she purred, and then she mashed her pelvis against his face and grinded her pussy against his lips. Sheed laughed, but followed her orders nonetheless. Slowly, gently, passionately, he flicked his tongue in and out of her slit, and then wrapped his lips around her clitoris. He sucked it, released it, and then sucked it again. Simultaneously using the tip of his tongue to massage her love button in a circular motion.

"Eat this pussy baby! Eat this pussy!" She cried out and closed her eyes in sheer bliss. Sheed couldn't believe what he was experiencing. Her pussy was so wet that in a matter of seconds not only his chin, but his neck and chest were covered in her juices.

"Umm! Fuck!" she shouted. "Baby, what are you doin' to me?" Her knees buckled and she fell on top of him, knocking him backwards. She climbed on top of him and kissed him passionately. Her kisses went from his lips to his chin, to his chest, and to his pelvis. Then in one swift motion, she deep throated his entire eight inches. As her mouth went up and down on his shaft, he positioned her body in the 69 position, and continued sucking the juice out of her honey pot.

"Umm!" she moaned on his dick. The vibrations of her vocal cords was driving him crazy. She focused on the head of his dick and used both of her hands to jerk his shaft. After five minutes of riding his face and sucking him off at the same time, she hopped up, spun around, and began riding him.

"Damn Jas, ya pussy so good it don't make no mutha'fuckin' sense," he groaned, and then squeezed her ass with both of his hands. She gently bit him on the side of his neck, and whispered in his ear. "Whose dick is this?"

The question caught him off guard. "Huh?"

"I said," she violently thrust her hips, "whose dick is this?"

"Damn Jas, it's yours! Shit."

She giggled and slowed her pace to a smooth ride. "It better be my dick," she warned. "And since you said the right answer," she smiled mischievously, "I'ma give you somethin' special."

She reached in between her thighs and removed his dick from her pussy. She then eased it inside of her ass hole.

"Oh my fuckin' God!" he shouted. Her ass was so tight and wet from her pussy juice that he went in and out of her with ease. "This shit is fuckin' crazy!" he continued shouting.

"Oh, you like that huh?" She dropped her ass against his pelvis, gripped his shaft with her anal canal. She twirled her hips in a circular motion and scratched his chest with both of her hands. "Ahhh fuck!"

His toes began to curl and sperm erupted from his balls. The warm juice coated her insides and she hastened her pace. Her body locked up and her legs began to shake. "I'm cummin' baby! I'm cummin'! Ahhhhhh shit!"

After releasing her orgasm, she rested her head on his muscular chest and he used his left hand to massage her scalp. "Damn Jas, I woulda never thought a woman so beautiful could be such a freak."

She lifted her head and smiled at him. "Shit, if you thought that was somethin', just wait until you see what I can do wit' a bottle of K.Y. Jelly!"

***

In North Philly

Twany was sitting in his Buick Lacrosse rolling up a Backwood, when two crackheads tapped on his passenger's side window. "Hey nephew, y'all got them grams of powder out here?" asked the dingy looking black man. He was standing beside a dirty white woman with blotched skin and oily hair.

Twany rolled down the window. "Yeah, we got grams of raw for $35. How many you want?"

"I got a buck fifty, nephew. Can I get a play for 5 of 'em?"

"Naw," Twany replied. "My shit go for $35, and that's the best price around. Take it or leave it." He looked at the white woman. She was bouncing from side to side, and nodding her head as if she could hear music playing. When she noticed that Twany was looking at her, she smiled at him and seductively licked her lips insinuating that she was willing to trade sexual favors for the cocaine. Twany cringed. "Yeah right."

"Huh nephew?" the man asked, assuming that Twany was talking to him.

"Naw unc, I ain't givin' no plays," he reiterated his position. "So what's up? You spendin' that bread or not?"

The man nodded his head. "A'ight nephew, well here go a buck forty," he said, and then handed Twany the crumbled up bills through the window.

Twany counted out the money, and then handed him four baggies.

As the crackheads walked away from his car, Heemy pulled up in his Impala and parked in front of his mother's house. He hopped out the car with a bag of Chinese food clutched in his right hand, and then plopped down on his mother's front stoop. Twany climbed out of his Buick and sat down beside him. "Did you get my shrimp and mixed vegetables?" he asked.

Heemy reached inside of the bag and pulled out a white carton with a thin metal handle. "It's right here. I got you a couple of spring rolls too."

Twany grabbed the carton and the wax bag full of spring rolls. "Good lookin' bro. I ain't eat nuffin' all day. That shit wit' Sonny and Rahmello's pop had a nigga feelin' fucked up."

"Yeah, I know," Heemy agreed with him. "Them niggas gon' paint the city red behind that shit. Just wait and see." He took a bite of his fried chicken wing sprinkled with garlic salt, and then used a napkin to wipe the corners of his mouth. "I'm sayin' though, you think Pooky and Mar-Mar had somethin' to do wit' what happened?"

"I don't know. For all we know anybody coulda parked the ol' head," Twany stated with a mouth full of food. "All I know is this," he paused for a second and looked Heemy square in the eyes, "if Sonny and Rahmello give us the green light, we movin'."

"Without a doubt," Heemy shot back. He took   another bite of his chicken wing, and then tossed the bone in the vacant lot that was next to his house. "But on another note, where Nipsy at?"

"He went to grab us some more work," Twany answered. "Rahmello wasn't bullshittin'. As soon as word got around that we was movin' grams of raw this shit been poppin' non-stop. Matter of fact," he pointed down the block toward Boston Street where a scruffy looking black man was riding toward them on a ten speed bicycle, "here comes Quiet Storm right now. He musta heard about the shit too."

"Yo Heemy where Pooky at?" Quiet Storm inquired as he brought the ten speed to a halt. "I heard he had them yams out here."

"Nizzaw," Heemy shook his head from side to side. "Me, Twany, and Nipsy got them grams out here. Fuck Pooky and Mar-Mar. Them niggas can't come around here no more."

"Well shit nephew, I heard that," Quiet Storm chuckled. He reached inside of his pants pocket and pulled out four twenty dollar bills. "Can I get 3 yams for eighty?"

"Naw," Twany shook his head. "But you can get 2 of 'em and $10 back."

"Well come on wit' it," Quiet Storm smiled. "I kinda figured y'all wasn't givin' out no plays, but fuck it," he shrugged his shoulders, "you can't knock a nigga for tryin'"

He handed Heemy the four twenty dollar bills, and Heemy added the money to the large knot he pulled from his pocket. After handing Quiet Storm his $10 in change, he pulled out a sandwich bag full of grams and extracted two of them. "Here you go," he said as he handed over the chunky white rock.

Quiet Storm examined the cocaine, and then nodded his head in approval. "A'ight nephew, y'all are safe out here." He stuffed the work inside of his pocket, and then pedaled away on his ten speed.

As Heemy stuffed his money back in his pocket, Pooky's Range Rover turned the corner and parked at the bottom of the block. Pooky was sitting behind the stirring wheel, and Mar-Mar was sitting in the passenger's seat.

Twany looked at Heemy. "Damn bro, what we gon' do? Should we chop on these niggas, or what?"

"Naw," Heemy replied in a calm voice, and then went to work on another one of his chicken wings. "As long as they ain't out here try'na hustle, they good. But the second they try to serve somebody or get outta pocket it's on."

"I'm sayin' though," Twany looked at the Range Rover, "them niggas is just sittin' there watchin' us. I'm tellin' you Heemy, them niggas is up to somethin'."

"Well I guess we gon' find out," Heemy replied, and then casually gripped the handle of his Glock.

Inside of the Range Rover, Pooky and Mar-Mar were smoking a Kush filled Optimo, and nodding their heads to the sounds of Yo Gotti.

"Look at these lil' bastards," Pooky chuckled. "I should take off my belt and whip they lil' asses for killin' my goddamn dog. They lucky I'm chasin' this paper right now."

"I feel you," Mar-Mar cosigned as he flicked the ash from the tip of the Optimo.

A green mini-van pulled up in front of Heemy and Twany, and a fat Spanish man rolled down the driver's side window. "Papi, y'all doin' something?"

Twany glanced up and down the block, and then returned his gaze to the customer. "Yeah papi, we got grams of raw for $35, but we don't walk up on cars. So you gon' have to hop out if you try'na cop somethin'."

The man opened the driver's side door and climbed out the mini-van. He reached inside of his pocket and pulled out three twenties and a ten dollar bill. "Lemme get 2 of 'em."

When Pooky realized what was happening, he damn near lost his mind. Him and Mar-Mar jumped out the Range Rover, and stormed toward Heemy and Twany. "Yo, what the fuck y'all think y'all doin'?" He snapped. "I know y'all lil' mutha'fuckas ain't out here hustlin'!"

The Spanish man was confused. He looked back and forth between them, and then settled his gaze on Twany.

"Papi, I don't know what's goin' on, but I ain't try'na be in the middle of y'all beef."

Twany looked to Heemy for guidance. Heemy laid his bag of food on the stoop, and then stood to his feet. "Go 'head and serve him."

Twany shrugged his shoulders, and held out the cocaine. As the customer went to grab the two baggies, Pooky smacked the work out of Twany's hand. Twany ice grilled him.

"Pussy you ever touch me again, I'ma fuckin' kill you!"

The Spanish man could see what was about to happen, and he wanted no parts of the confrontation. Empty handed, he hopped back in his mini-van and pulled off.

The front door to Heemy's house swung open, and Treesha appeared in the doorway. She scowled at Heemy, and then turned her attention to Pooky. "What's goin' on Pooky? I know his lil' ass ain't out here showin' off."

Pooky took his eyes off of Twany, and looked at Treesha.

"Bitch, you knew these lil' mutha'fuckas was out here hust —"

Boc! Boc! Boc!

Three bullets from Heemy's Glock .40 blazed through Pooky's chest, and the velocity of the slugs knocked him backwards. He stumbled into Mar-Mar, and then dropped to the ground. Mar-Mar was terrified. He reached for his P89, but Twany was already squeezing the trigger on his Glock.

Boc! Boc! Boc! Boc!

The bullets struck him in the chest and left shoulder, knocking him to the ground. He tried to crawl away, but Twany was already standing over top of him.

Boc!

The bullet blazed through the back of his head and burst out the front of his face.

"R—R—Raheem," Treesha stuttered, totally surprised by his actions. "W—W—Why did you do that?"

Heemy looked at her with a blank expression. He then looked down at Pooky, who was laying on his back struggling to breathe. He aimed the Glock .40 at his head, and then returned his gaze to Treesha. "Do what? This?"

Boc!

Pooky's head jerked sideways and a red air bubble sprouted from the nickel sized wound in the center of his forehead. Treesha clutched her chest and passed out in the doorway.

Heemy laid the Glock on the stoop, and then carried his mother inside of the house. After laying her on the sofa, he emerged from the house and shut the door behind him. He picked up his Glock and looked at Twany. "Yo, gimmie that burner."

Twany handed over his Glock and Heemy wiped away their fingerprints. He then stashed the pistols in the abandoned station wagon that was parked across the street.

They weren't worried about any nosey neighbors calling the cops because every house on the block, except for Heemy's was either condemned or abandoned. Therefore, they had more than enough time to stash the bodies in a vacant lot, contact Rahmello, and wait for further instructions.

***

After receiving a phone call from Heemy, Rahmello called The Butcher and told him not to feed the alligators. He also called Sonny and told him about the situation on Delhi Street. Sonny offered his assistance, but Rahmello declined. "Naw brozay, I got it covered. The fam needs you right now. Just chill at ya mom's spot and make sure everybody's good. I got this."

"A'ight," Sonny conceded. "But what about Breeze and the twins? They at *Donkees* right now. Want me to send 'em ya way?"

"Nizzaw. I'ma take the young buls wit' me. Them lil' niggas need to earn some stripes."

"More or less," Sonny replied, and then disconnected the call.

Rahmello waited until nightfall, then he drove to Delhi Street in a black utility van. When he arrived on the block, he drove pass Pooky's Range Rover and parked the van directly in front of Heemy's house. His eyes searched up and down the street for any nosey neighbors, but he quickly realized that except for Heemy's house, the block was essentially deserted. The only thing that made him uncomfortable was the orange streetlight in the middle of the block. It provided enough light for anyone driving or walking down Germantown Avenue to look across one of the lots and see him. He hopped out the utility van and removed his Glock .19 from his shoulder holster. He aimed at the orange light and fired off a single round.

Boc!

The light went dead and broken glass rained down on the cracked sidewalk. Satisfied that nobody would be able to see him, he pulled out his iPhone and called Nipsy.

Ring! Ring! Ring!

"Mello," Nipsy answered, "did you get here yet?"

"Yeah I'm out here. Where the fuck is y'all at?"

"We around the corner on 10th Street in front of the projects. We comin' around there right now."

"A'ight, hurry up."

Click!

Rahmello looked down and noticed a trail of blood from the sidewalk to the vacant lot beside Heemy's house. He shook his head from side to side and chuckled to himself. "Amateurs!"

Just as he was about to follow the trail, the three men turned the corner dressed in all black. They walked up to Rahmello and one by one, they shook his hand.

"Yo, we sorry to hear about ya pops," Heemy expressed their condolences. "Whatever you and Sonny need us to do, we all over that shit."

Rahmello stared the young man in his eyes. He was looking for any signs of weakness, but all he could see was loyalty and determination.

"Right now, I need you to run in the house and get a pot of cold soapy water." He pointed at the bloodstained sidewalk. "We can't leave this like that."

"Say no more," Heemy nodded his head, and then ran up the steps and disappeared inside of the house.

Rahmello went to the back of the utility van and opened the back door. He motioned for Nipsy and Twany to join him, and then he handed each of them a roll of carpet. "Yo, use these to wrap them niggas up."

As they ran toward the lot where the bodies were stashed, Rahmello heard a snapping noise from across the street. In one swift motion he spun around with the Glock .19 clutched in his right hand. The block was so dark that he could only see a few feet ahead of him. He cautiously made his way across the street with the gun aimed in the direction of the noise. As he approached the abandoned house that was adjacent to Heemy's, he noticed that the front door and windows were boarded up. He looked to his right and examined the vacant lot that was next door. Out of nowhere a large rat sprang from underneath the rubble and scampered across the street.

"A fuckin' rat," he shook his head in amusement. "How ironic is that?" He holstered his weapon, and then returned to the van where Nipsy and Twany were stuffing the bodies in the back compartment.

A few minutes later they were sitting in the van watching Heemy do his best to clean up the blood. As soon as he was finished, he climbed inside the van and looked at Rahmello.

"So how we 'posed to get rid of these niggas?"

Rahmello started the ignition, and then slowly pulled away from the curb.

"We taking 'em to The Swamp.

***

When the black utility van left the block, a dark shadowy figure emerged from the vacant lot where Rahmello heard the snapping sound. The dark figure was wearing a dingy trench coat and the top of his head was wrapped in a white gauze. A wrinkled Newport 100 dangled from the corner of his mouth and a can of Old English 800 was clutched in his left hand. He staggered across the street toward Pooky's Range Rover and opened the driver's side door. He climbed inside of the SUV and began rummaging through Pooky's belongings. He opened the glove compartment and found a zip lock bag that was filled with cocaine. Quickly, he stashed the bag in his pocket. He looked in the backseat and noticed a black gym bag lying on the floor. He grabbed the bag and opened it slowly. *Oh my mutha'fuckin' God! This shit cannot be happenin' to ol' Bushnut! Anybody but you Bushnut! This shit*

233

can't be real! he thought to himself as he thumbed through the stacks of money. Unbeknownst to him, he had stumbled across the $300,000 that Pooky owed Sonny for his last shipment. *Bushnut, you back babyboy! You back!*

As he sat there gloating and referring to himself in third person, he heard a distinctive humming noise.

Vrrrrm! Vrrrrm!

He looked down at the center console and saw the illuminated screen on Pooky's cell phone. He picked it up and saw that the caller was Sheed. The word was already out that Sheed was home from jail, and that him and Sonny were beefing. Being the shady individual he was, Bushnut used this information to his advantage.

"Thello," he managed to mumble, and then winced from the pain of his broken jaw.

"Yo, who the fuck is this?" Sheed spat, clearly not recognizing the voice. "Put Pooky on the phone."

"I gant," Beaver Bushnut slurred.

The wiring that was holding his jaw in place was restricting his speech.

"What?" Sheed asked, barely understanding his words.

"I gant. Ooky got gilled."

"Pooky got killed? Yo, who the fuck is this?"

"Lithen, Ooky got gilled on Elhi Theet."

"Slow down," Sheed instructed him. "You said Pooky got killed on Delhi Street?"

"Yeth and Thontino gilled him!"

Chapter Nineteen

Sheed threw his phone against the wall, breaking the small device into pieces.

"Fuck!"

"Baby, what's wrong?" Jasmyn asked while sitting up in the bed. "Is everything okay?"

"Fuck no! Them bitch ass niggas killed my fuckin' brother!"

He hopped off the bed and put on his boxer briefs. He then ran to the closet and threw on a black Polo sweat suit and a pair of black Air Maxes.

Jasmyn slid up behind him and wrapped her arms around his waist. "Baby, you need to calm down and think for a minute. I can see that you're hurtin' right now, but you can't go out there actin' off of emotion. Somethin' bad could happen."

He pushed her arms away then grabbed his Desert Eagle from the Timberland box on the top shelf. He ejected the magazine, checking to see if the gun was fully loaded. Satisfied, he shoved the magazine back in the handle, and then cocked a bullet into the chamber.

"Jas, I ain't try'na hear that shit right now."

She reached out to bear hug him, but he mugged her in the face. She fell to the carpet, but defiantly hopped back up and wrapped her arms around his legs.

"No, you're not going!" She screamed while holding on for dear life. "I love you Rasheed, and I'm not gonna stand here and watchchu throw your life away!"

Tears began falling from his eyes and his hands began to tremble. Not only was Pooky his older brother, he was his best friend. Ever since the day their parents died in a car accident, he was the only true blood relative that Sheed had left. He looked down at the beautiful woman who held the key to his heart, and he understood her fears and concerns. Unfortunately, if Pooky was truly dead his only option was revenge.

He reached down and helped her stand to her feet. "I love you too Jas, but if my brother's really dead I gotta ride for him," he said in a compassionate voice. "I'ma do everything I can to make it home in one piece, but if I don't it's a canary yellow Corvette parked out front. It's paid for so if you want, you can sell it and keep the money for you and your daughter."

"No Rasheed, I don't want your money," she broke down crying and rested her head against his muscular chest. "All I want is you."

He ran his fingers through her silky hair, and kissed her on the forehead. "I'm sorry Jas, but I ain't got no other choice."

He kissed her one last time, and then grabbed the keys to her Mazda and left the apartment.

***

In South Philly

It was 7:40 p.m. when Little Angolo walked inside of his restaurant on 14th and Porter. He shook hands with the maître d' and handed the man his trench coat.

"Michael," he addressed him. "Did Carmine get here yet?"

"Yes, Mr. Gervino," he pointed toward the back of the dimly lit dining room where Carmine and Alphonso were waving him over, "He's right there."

"Good," Angolo nodded his head. "Bring us a bottle of Merlot."

As he headed toward the back of the restaurant the patrons smiled at him and waved. He smiled back and continued toward Carmine and Alphonso. He felt good to be back home in South Philly. Here, the Italian community treated him like royalty. Ever since his father *Big Angolo* established *The Gervino Crime Family* back in the 1940's, the only Italian who was more recognized in Philly was Rocky Balboa, and technically the man didn't exist.

At the age of seventy three, everything about Little Angolo screamed one thing, mafia. From his tailor made Brooks Brother suits to his oversized square framed glasses, he was every bit the old school mobster. He moved through the restaurant with the grace of a don and when he reached their table, one at a time they held his right hand and kissed the diamonds on his pinky ring.

"So, how was your flight?" Carmine asked as he stood to his feet and pulled out a chair for him.

"A little jet lag, but I'll be fine," Little Angolo replied as he took a seat.

He reached across the table and grabbed one of the bread sticks that were piled on the appetizer tray. He took a bite and enjoyed the savory flavor.

"So, what's the problem boss? Why was I sent for?" he joked with his grandson.

"It's this shit with the Moreno's," Carmine complained. "That fuckin' Grip is really tryin' my patience. I mean the nerve of this moulie. He leaves the country with the docks up for grabs and the second I make a play, he crosses the fuckin' line."

Little Angolo glanced around the restaurant, and then gestured for him to lower his voice. Carmine nodded his head and continued talking in a lower voice. "And to make a bad situation worse, he whacks Romey Noodles and hangs his burning body from a fuckin' bridge."

The maître d' approached the table with a bottle of Merlot clutched in his hands, and Carmine stopped talking. The maitre d' could see they were going over business so he sat the bottle on the table and left without saying a word.

"So," Little Angolo resumed the conversation. He opened the bottle and poured himself a glass of wine. "Why am I here? I'm supposed to be in South Beach right now. Just me and an 18 year old broad with tits the size of volleyballs," he chuckled. "I'm friggin' retired ova here."

Carmine sighed. "Listen gramps, I just need your advice. You've dealt with this moulie in the past and you know he operates. Tell me what I need to do to get rid of this fucker."

Little Angolo took a sip of his Merlot, and then looked at Alphonso. "You're the underboss, what do you think needs to be done?"

Alphonso looked at Carmine, then returned his gaze to Little Angolo. "I think we need to go at him with everything we got."

"Bingo," Little Angolo smiled, and then looked Carmine square in the eyes. "In the meantime, I'm gonna talk to Clavenski. He's responsible for some of this shit, and you need to hold him accountable."

Chapter Twenty

Later That Night...

After discovering Pooky's ransacked Range Rover and the partially blood stained sidewalk, Sheed, Rahman, and Jihad were in Allentown, Pennsylvania. They were sitting in front of Breeze's house in Rahman's MPV. It was 10:35 p.m., and they'd been there for the past hour.

"Lil' cuzzo, you sure this nigga ain't in there?" asked Rahman. "It's a Hummer in the driveway," he pointed at the large SUV, and then pointed toward the second floor of the house, "and one of the lights is on."

Sheed shook his head from side to side. "Naw Rock, that nigga be ridin' around in a Maserati. When I was locked up they used to always send me pictures to keep me in the loop. Breeze drives a Maserati. Egypt and Zaire got twin Panameras and Rahmello be ridin' around in an Aston Martin." He pointed at the H2. "That's his baby mom's car. She's probably the only one in the house right now. Her and the baby."

"I'm sayin' though," Jihad spoke up from the backseat. "How the fuck don't none of y'all know where the bul Sonny be layin' his head? That was ya man right?"

Sheed shrugged his shoulders. "That's how the nigga be movin' these days. Ever since his bitch got killed, he won't let nobody near his family except for Breeze and Rahmello. He moved his mom off of Reese Street, and the only mutha'fucka who knows where they live and who we can get to right now is Breeze. That's why we goin' at him first."

"A'ight, but what about the young bul Rahmello?" Rahman asked. "I heard he's from 24th and Somerset. What they be callin' it now?"

"24th and Bloodline," Sheed answered.

"Yeah that's it," Rahman nodded his head. "Niggas be sayin' the young bul about his work. I'm thinking about g'tting' his ass out the way a.s.a.p!"

He reached inside of the glove compartment and pulled out an ounce bottle that was halfway filled with dust juice. As he twisted off the lid and tilted the bottle, they heard the powerful humming of Breeze's Maserati. The silver sedan cruised pass them, and then turned into the driveway. Sheed wasted no time. He hopped out the passenger's side door and crept toward the Maserati with his Desert Eagle discreetly tucked behind his leg.

As Breeze climbed out the car, he noticed that Sheed was walking up the driveway. He was never informed about the murders of Pooky and Mar-Mar, and therefore, he had no reason to suspect that him and his family were in danger. He smiled at him.

"What's poppin' Blood? Whatchu doin' all the way in Allentown?"

Instead of responding, Sheed swung the Desert Eagle and hit him on the left side of his forehead. Breeze fell against the back left fender and slid to the pavement. Dazed and confused, he looked at Sheed in disbelief. "Yo, what the fuck is up witchu Blood?"

"Pussy, shut the fuck up!" Sheed snarled. He cracked him on top of his head with the massive handgun, knocking him out cold. Rahman and Jihad ran up to the Maserati, and quickly began the process of tying Breeze's hands behind his back. Sheed scooped his key ring off of the pavement, and then headed for the front door. After trying a couple of keys, he found the right one then cautiously opened the door. He glanced around the living room and there were no signs of Erika and the baby. He looked over his shoulder, "Yo, pick that nigga up and bring him inside."

Rahman hoisted Breeze over his right shoulder and followed Sheed inside of the house. He laid him on the suede sofa, and then gestured for Jihad to lock the front door.

Sheed looked at Jihad. "Stay here and watch this nigga. Me and Rock gon' go upstairs and see what's up wit' his bitch."

In the master bedroom, Erika was laying on their king sized bed in nothing but a pair of cherry red thongs. She was eating sunflower seeds and watching a re-run of *Love and Hip Hop Atlanta*. Her eyes were glued to the 50" screen and she was spitting sunflower shells into a plastic cup.

"Ahn ahn! K. Michelle is a mess!" She laughed at the scene where the R&B star and Carly Redd were arguing in the middle of a restaurant. "This bitch is shakin' the table!" She continued laughing as she repeated K. Michelle's infamous phrase. The bedroom door creaked open, but she was too caught up in the drama to take her eyes away from the television. Assuming it was Breeze, she said, "Bae, your dinner's downstairs in the microwave."

"I'm not hungry," Sheed replied in a cold voice.

"What the fuck?" she said, immediately recognizing that the voice didn't belong to Breeze. She quickly turned her head toward the door and covered herself with the bed sheets. "Sheed?" She looked at him skeptically as he stepped inside of the room. "What the fuck are you doin' in my bedroom? Where's Breeze?"

Sheed smiled at her, but didn't respond. Rahman walked up behind him. "He's a lil' tied up at the moment."

When she laid eyes on the light skinned man with the Sunni Muslim beard, she reached for the .25 that was stashed underneath her pillow, but Sheed tackled her before she could reach it. She struggled against his brute strength, but all he did was squeeze tighter. "Stop it Sheed! Get off me!" she screamed, waking up the baby who was sound asleep in his crib.

"Waaaaah! Waaaaah!" the infant cried out.

"Bitch, shut ya stupid ass up!" Sheed snapped. He punched her in the face, and then looked over his shoulder at Rahman. "Grab that lil' mutha'fucka and take him downstairs." He landed another blow to Erika's face, and then snatched her off of the bed and threw her limp body over his shoulder. After carrying her down to the living room, he held her body against the wall of the staircase and told Jihad to keep her in that position. He looked around for something he could use to tie her up, and settled on an extension cord that was balled up on the side of the television. All the while, the baby continued to cry as Rahman held him in his arms. He rocked the little boy and gently patted him on the back. "Settle down lil' man. Settle down. Uncle Rocky's got you."

As the little boy began to calm down, Sheed grabbed the extension cord off of the floor, and went to work. He walked halfway up the stairs, and stuck the cord through the bars of the banister. He tied it in a square knot and left both ends dangling down the wall. After descending the stairs, he approached Jihad who was still holding Erika against the wall face first. Jihad lifted her body, and one by one Sheed tied the ends of the extension cord around her wrist causing her body to dangle from the banister.

"Haddy, go in the kitchen and grab me a butcher's knife and a bottle of vegetable oil," Sheed ordered his large companion. He then walked over to the sofa where Breeze was stretched out and profusely bleeding from his forehead. About a minute later, Jihad returned from the kitchen with a butcher's knife in one hand and a bottle of olive oil in the other. He handed the knife to Sheed, and sat the bottle of oil on the suede ottoman that sat in front of the sofa.

Sheed examined the large knife, and then crouched down and sliced the back of Breeze's left ankle. "*Agh! Shit! Yo, what the fuck?*" Breeze screamed as the pain in his Achilles tendon shot through his body. His loud screams startled the baby, and Erika regained her consciousness.

Sheed scowled at the baby, then looked at Rahman.

"Take him in the kitchen and calm his lil' ass down." He flexed his jaw muscles, and then returned his attention to Breeze. "Ahn hun! This some real shit now!" he tormented him. "Y'all gon' kill my brother over some nut shit, and now y'all niggas gon' join him!"

Breeze could barely see. The blood from his forehead was dripping in his eyes, and the pain in his Achilles was so intense that his nervous system was on the brink of shutting down.

"Sheed, I can't see. Gimmie somethin' to wipe my eyes," he moaned. He was so out of it that didn't even realize the imminent danger his family was facing.

Sheed removed a red bandana from his back right pocket and used it to wipe the blood out of Breeze's eyes. "Yeah nigga, I want you to see every bit of this shit!"

"Yo Sheed, what the fuck is you doin'? I don't even know what's goin' on right now," Breeze continued moaning. He looked up and saw Erika hanging from the banister, and his body temperature elevated. "Hey, yo Sheed! What the fuck, son?"

"Nigga shut the fuck up!" Sheed snarled through clenched teeth. In a fit of rage, he swooped down and sliced the Achilles tendon on Breeze's other leg.

"Agggghhhh!" Breeze grimaced from the pain. His loud cries sent Erika into a frenzy. She jerked her body from side to side, desperately trying to free herself. She bucked, wiggled, and squirmed, but none of these movements seemed to help her cause. Defiantly, she attempted to get her feet on the ground but she was so high up on the banister that the tip of her toes couldn't even touch the carpet. She broke down crying and rested her forehead against the wall. "Sheed, why the fuck is you doin' us like this?"

He ran toward her and violently smacked her across the back with the blade of the butcher's knife.

Whack! Whack! Whack!

"Agggghhhh!" she screamed. "Sheed stop! Please*!*"

"Bitch, shut the fuck up!"

Whack! Whack!

Despite the fact that Breeze's hands were tied behind his back, he rolled off the sofa and attempted to stand. Unfortunately, the wounds to the back of his ankles wouldn't allow it. Frustrated, he laid on the carpet face first, cursing himself for not being able to help his family.

Erika continued screaming, and Jihad removed the .9 mm that was tucked in the small of his back. He cocked back the hammer, and placed the lips of the barrel to the side of her face.

"Bitch, you scream one more time and I'ma blow ya fuckin' brains out!"

She stopped screaming and her body went limp. She looked at Sheed and cried uncontrollably. "Why is you doin' us like this? What did we do?"

He looked at her, and then scowled at Breeze. "Ask ya punk ass baby daddy. He know what the fuck he did."

Breeze looked at him with a confused expression.

"What the fuck did I do?" he shouted. "I ain't did nothin' to you, Blood!"

"Y'all faggot ass niggas killed my brother!" Sheed shouted back.

"What?" Breeze screwed up his face. "Scrap, I swear on my mutha'fuckin' flag that I don't know nuffin' about that shit! My word! I don't know nuffin' about Pooky gettin' killed!"

Sheed shrugged his shoulders and lowered his voice. "Maybe you do, and maybe you don't. Either way Sonny and Rahmello was behind this shit, and the only way to get to them niggas is by goin' through you. So now," he walked toward the sofa and stood over him, "if ya ass wanna live, and you care about the well being of ya bitch and ya son, then I suggest you tell me where these niggas be layin' they mutha'fuckin' heads at."

Tears poured from Breeze's eyes, and he shook his head in disappointment. He heard the cries of his son, and at that point all the love and loyalty that he had for Sonny went flying out the window. "He lives in Montgomery County. In the same mansion that his pops bought for him and his moms back in the day."

"What's the address?"

"I don't know the address. I've only been over there one time, and that was last year when they first moved in."

Sheed shook his head in disbelief. "See, this the shit I be talking 'bout." He looked at Jihad, then reverted his attention back to Breeze. "I gotchu tied the fuck up and bleedin'. Ya bitch is hangin' from the banister, and ya stupid ass got the nerve to be playin' games." He grabbed the bottle of olive oil from the ottoman. He twisted off the top, and then poured the warm liquid in his right hand. He then pulled out his Desert Eagle and lathered up the six inch barrel.

"See, I tried to be diplomatic about this shit," Sheed continued. "But now you forcin' my hand." He walked over to Erika and snatched off her thong.

"No!" she screamed. "Sheed don't do this! He's tellin' you the truth!

"Bitch, don't start that screamin' shit again," Jihad warned. "You ain't gon' do nothin' but make me squeeze this mutha'fuckin' trigger." He held the gun in front of her face, and her brown eyes nearly popped out the sockets. She lowered her head and continued sobbing.

"Come on Blood! You ain't gotta do this!" Breeze pleaded. "I told you everything I know!"

"Naw nigga, you think this shit's a mutha'fuckin' game! But I'ma show you!" He placed the triangle shaped barrel between the crack of her ass and shoved it inside of her rectum. "Ummm!" she cried out, desperately trying to muffle her screams.

Sheed smiled at Breeze and plunged the massive barrel in and out of her rectum. "Is you feelin' me yet? This stankin' ass bitch of yours is feelin' me." He chuckled, and then looked Erika in the face. "Ain't that right baby? Ahn huhn, yeah I know," he nodded his head up and down. "You feelin' me like a *mutha'fucka*."

"Come on, Blood! Chill da fuck out!" Breeze shouted at the top of his lungs. "I told you everything I know!"

Again, Sheed shook his head in disbelief. "See, there you go fuckin' around! You really think this shit's a game." He shoved the barrel deep inside of Erika's ass and squeezed the trigger. Her body jerked violently and a fountain of blood burst from her stomach and splattered against the wall. He slowly removed the blood covered barrel from her rectum, and a thick glob of bloody fecal matter fell to the carpet. Her head lollied to the side and the energy of life eased from her brown eyes. Breeze cried like a baby. "What the fuck Sheed? This shit ain't right, Blood. I told you everything I know."

Sheed towered over top of him and aimed the barrel at the back of his head. "Nigga, I'ma ask you one more time. What's his fuckin' address?"

"I swear on my flag," Breeze sobbed. "I don't —"

Doom! Doom! Doom! Doom!

The .50 caliber slugs ripped through the back of his skull, and his warm brains decorated the bottom of the sofa. His body convulsed, then calmly came to a stop.

Disgusted, Sheed kicked him in the ass, and then looked at Jihad. He held up the smoking gun. "Find me somethin' I can use to wipe this jawn off." He gestured toward Erika's dead body. "This nasty ass bitch got blood and dookie all over this mutha'fucka."

Jihad looked around the living room and settled on the yellow baby's blanket that was lying on the sofa. He tossed it to Sheed, and Sheed wiped down the gun. He tossed the dirty blanket on Breeze's body. "Let's go in the kitchen to see what's up with Rock."

When they entered the kitchen, Rahman was pacing back and forth trying to get the little boy to stop crying. Sheed stepped to him and exchanged his gun for the baby. He hoisted the baby in the air and smiled at him.

"Your dada's so stuuupid," he cooed in a baby's voice. "Uncle Sheed told him to give up Sonny's address, but him wouldn't tell Uncle Sheed what him wanted to know. Him so stuuupid!"

The little boy stopped crying and giggled at the sound of his voice. Sheed carried him over to the stainless steel oven, and then leaned forward to open the door. He removed the top rack and gently placed the little boy inside of the oven. When he closed the door and reached for the keypad that controlled the heat, Rahman reached out and grabbed him by the arm.

"Nah cuzzo," he shook his head from side to side, "he's just a baby."

Sheed looked at him like he was crazy, and then snatched his arm away. "Fuck that! Them bitch ass niggas killed my brother, and now I'ma kill everything they fuckin' love." He pressed the keypad until the digital screen read 375 degrees. "And I know whatchu thinking," he said to Rahman. "You hopin' that I leave the kitchen first so you can turn the oven off while I'm walkin' away." He shook his head from side to side. "Well that's not happenin'. So please," he gestured toward the back door where Jihad was waiting for them to make their exit, "after you."

Chapter Twenty-One

The Following Morning...

Clavenski was sitting at his desk drinking a cup of Columbian roast, and going over the Title III wiretaps where Sonny and his team were discussing everything from drug distribution to murder.

SONTINO MORENO: A'ight, so this is the situation. [Brief Pause] From here on out we're changin' the way we conduct business. Instead of coppin' the usual 100 bricks at the beginning of the month, I'ma start coppin' 200. I'ma drop y'all consignment price from $30,000 to $25,000 so therefore y'all can keep y'all prices at $35,000, and make an extra $5,000 off of every brick. At the same time I'ma start frontin' y'all 50 bricks instead of the usual 30 so y'all gon' have to step y'all game up. [Brief Pause] At the end of every month I'ma need $1,250,000 from each of y'all. Can y'all handle that?

BRIAN PENDELTON: Yeah we can handle it.

Clavenski highlighted Sonny's statements, and then took a sip of coffee.

"I'm gonna get this son of a bitch," he said to himself, and then continued reading.

SONTINO MORENO: Now, for the second order of business. [Brief Pause] This nigga gotta die tonight and as a favor to Poncho we gon' be the ones to park him. According to Poncho this nigga pissed off the wrong people and now he's gotta go. As we speak, I've got people watchin' his every move and we need to have him parked by the mornin'. No mistakes.

Clavenski exchanged his highlighter for a pen, and then jotted down Sonny and Poncho's name. He then drew an arrow between the two names and wrote, *Possible Drug Connect?* He laid the pen on his notepad then lounged back in his swivel chair and locked his hands behind his head. Technically, this was more than enough to secure an indictment against Sonny and *The Block Boys*, but he wanted more. He wanted Grip.

Up until now, he never had the airtight case that was needed to get the *Black Mafia* don off the streets. In the late eighties and early nineties when he was Philadelphia's District Attorney, he did everything in his power to dismantle the infamous *Moreno Crime Family,* but the slippery Grip would always escape his wrath. Witnesses to his crimes were too afraid to testify against him. On the rare occasions when a witness wasn't afraid to cooperate they were found dead, belly up in the Delaware River. Evidence against him and his organization would turn up missing, and if somehow it did manage to make it inside of a courtroom, Grip's high powered attorneys would find a way to have the evidence suppressed.

As Clavenski leaned forward to continue reading the transcripts, he heard a soft knock on the door. He looked up and cleared his throat. "Come in."

Agent Long walked through the door with a blank expression on his face. He was dressed in a Mitchell & Ness Pittsburgh Steelers jacket, a matching fitted hat, a white T-shirt, and a pair of Levis. The iced out lion's head that hung from his platinum necklace shined bright, and the five carat diamonds that decorated his ear lobes did the same. He closed the door behind him and approached Clavenski's desk.

"What's up, Andy? What's that?" He pointed at the stack of papers on the desk.

"The Sontino Moreno transcripts," Clavenski smiled. "Monica dropped them off about an hour ago. She also provided me with the file on Ervin Moreno. Speaking of which, do the state guys have any suspects in that case?"

"Nah," Agent Long replied while sticking a piece of bubble gum in his mouth. "I spoke to Detective Sullivan on the way over here, and according to him the PPD aren't too concerned. To them, he's just another dead drug dealer."

"Well what about the funeral?" Clavenski asked. "Did the family make any arrangements?"

"I believe so," Agent Long nodded his head in the affirmative. "Yesterday while conducting our surveillance, me and Monica followed Sontino and his mother to the *Baker Funeral Home* on Broad Street. So we're pretty sure that Baker's is the location."

"Okay, what about Gervin? Did he make any appearances on our surveillance footage? I mean, after all this was his son."

"Nope, not yet," Agent Long stated. "Hopefully he'll show up at the funeral, and if he does we'll need him to interact with Sontino. That would definitely bolster our conspiracy charge."

Clavenski downed the rest of his coffee, then lounged back in his swivel chair. "I need you to get as close to Sontino as possible. Because I'm telling you right now, if he's anything like his grandfather," he gestured toward the wiretap transcripts, "these won't mean a goddamned thing." He reached down and grabbed the leather briefcase that was lying on the floor beside his chair. He laid it on the desk and popped it open, revealing the rubber banded stacks of hundred dollar bills.

"This is the $350,000 that you formally requested. Now listen up closely, this is a lot of money right here. You make the buy and bring the cocaine straight to me. Do I make myself clear?"

"Absolutely," Agent Long nodded his head.

Clavenski pointed at the red rubies on his lion's head pendant. "And make sure those cameras are rolling when you make the buy. It's imperative that we have this transaction on tape." As he closed the briefcase, his Samsung vibrated on the desktop.

Vrrrrrm!

He picked up the phone and examined the screen. "Goddamnit!" The caller was the very last person that he wished to speak to, Angolo *Little Angolo* Gervino, the former boss of *The Gervino Crime Family*. He slid the briefcase across the desk and dismissed Agent Long with the flick of his left hand.

Agent Long scowled at him, but accepted the briefcase nonetheless. As he turned to leave the office he heard Clavenski say, "Mr. Gervino! How's the Miami weather treatin' ya?" The name caught him off guard, causing him to walk a little slower than usual. *You gotta be shittin' me*, he thought to himself while heading for the door. *I know this mutha'fucka ain't talkin' to Little Angolo.* He stepped into the hallway and with the door slightly ajar, he eavesdropped on Clavenski's conversation.

"Cut the shit Andy! Besides I'm not in Miami. I'm back in South Philly. What the hell is goin' on up here? I got a call from Carmine sayin' that you fucked up the situation with Smitty. Carmine's pissed Andy. He claims to have a legitimate beef. You're not holdin' up to your end of the deal."

"A beef?" Clavenski bitched up. "With me? For what?"

"This younger generation, fugget about it! They have a thirst for blood that hasn't been seen since the days of Roy DeMeo. He's frustrated Andy, and honestly I don't blame him."

"Mr. Gervino I'm doing the best that I can! Smitty was supposed to have testified before the grand jury, but Gervin whacked him!"

"I don't give a shit!" Little Angolo shouted through the phone. "You had the perfect opportunity to finish this nigger once and for all, and you friggin' blew it!"

Clavenski sighed. "But he's always two steps ahead of me."

"Bullshit! We started you, Andy! My *Family's* the motivating force behind your success! We had to pull a lot of political strings to get you where you are today, and this is how you friggin' repay us?"

"You've gotta believe me, Mr. Gervino! I'm trying!"

"Well you're not trying hard enough!" Little Angolo continued shouting at him through the phone. He took a deep breath and calmed himself down. His family and Clavenski's family shared a long history together, dating all the way back to the 1940s when they controlled Cuba. His father and Clavenski's grandfather were business partners, and together they built a criminal empire that generated millions.

"Listen Andy," he lowered his voice a few octaves. "Carmine's my grandson, but most importantly he's the boss of this *Family*. There's only so much I can do to hold him back."

"I understand that, but just hear me out. Gervin has a grandson, and from the information that I've gathered so far, this kid is the key to bringing him down. I've got him on everything from drug distribution to murder. Now here's the kicker, because he's a Moreno, everything he does I can connect it to *The Moreno Crime Family*."

"Listen Andy, I'm not calling the shots anymore," Little Angolo said. "That's up to Carmine. He's losing his patience, and he feels as though you're forcin' his hand. I've said everything that I could possibly say. You've been warned."

Click!

***

On the other side of the cracked door, Agent Long shook his head in disbelief. "This no good rotten son of a bitch!" He said to himself. "It's cool though. I know just how to handle this shit." He looked down at his lion head pendant, and then walked away.

***

In Upper Dublin, Pennsylvania

As always Sonny was awakened by the soft kisses that Daphney and Keyonti were placing on his face.

"Up, up dada! Wakey up, up!" The little girl demanded as she softly caressed his wavy hair. He wiped the sleep out of his eyes, and then sat up, resting his back against the padded headboard. He noticed that they were already dressed so he glanced at the alarm clock on his nightstand. "Damn, it's 11:40?" He yawned and stretched out his arms. "Where's my mom? She good?" He knew that his mother was still devistated from Easy's murder, and he wanted to make sure that she was okay.

Daphney removed a piece of lint from his hair, and then kissed him on the lips. "Considering the circumstances, she seems to be doin' okay. She's been runnin' around the house cookin' and cleanin' all mornin', but how 'bout you? Are you okay?"

"I'm a'ight." His lips were smiling but his eyes told a different story.

"Are you hungry?" she asked.

"Yesh!" Keyonti interjected, and then ran her hands up and down his abs. "Him want eat, eat," she looked at Daphney, and then returned her focus to Sonny. "Right dada? You want eat, eat."

Sonny and Daphney fell out laughing. He picked her up, and climbed off the bed. He kissed her chocolate cheeks, and then handed her to Daphney. "Take her downstairs and keep an eye on my mom for me. I need to hop in the shower and get dressed."

She sighed and looked at him with a concerned expression. "Okay, but you're sure you're alright?"

He kissed her on the forehead, and then tapped her on the ass. "Yeah ma, I'm good. Just keep an eye on my mom for me."

As Daphney and Keyonti headed for the door, he grabbed his iPhone and called Rahmello.

Ring! Ring! Ring!

"Yo bro," Rahmello answered. "What's poppin'?"

"You already know," Sonny replied. "I was callin' to make sure y'all cleaned up that mess from yesterday."

"Yeah bro. That's a dead issue."

"A'ight, now what about the young buls? Did they hold it down?"

"Yeah, them lil' niggas played they part, especially Heemy. I ain't gon' talk crazy over this jack, but from here on out we callin' that nigga *Leather Face*," Rahmello chuckled. "You shoulda seen the way his lil' ass was goin' to work wit' that chainsaw!"

"More or less," Sony replied halfheartedly. "But on another note, how you feelin' about this pops situation?" He knew how close Rahmello and Easy had become over the past year and a half, and he needed to make sure that his younger was okay. Rahmello just sighed. "I ain't gon' hold you brozay," he paused and searched for the right words to express himself. "A nigga kinda fucked up right now. As soon as me and pops got tight," he snapped his fingers, "just like that he was gone. It's almost like our bond wasn't even real. Like it was only a figment of my imagination."

"Nizzaw," Sonny quickly corrected him. "That shit was definitely real, bro. Pops loved you and don't you ever forget that."

"I won't," Rahmello sighed. "But dig bro, I'm goin' back to sleep. I'ma holla at you later."

"A'ight, lil' brozay. Just be easy you heard? I love you."

"I love you more."

Click!

***

Rahmello laid the phone on his nightstand, and continued running his fingers through Olivia's silky hair. Her head was resting on his chest and she was quiet. She was too quiet. Her warm tears were pelting against his skin and he could feel her body trembling.

"What's wrong mami? Why you cryin'?"

His concern for her well being made her cry even harder. She desperately wanted to tell him the truth about his father, but she couldn't. Her loyalty to her family wouldn't allow it.

"Damn Oli," he sat up to get a better look at her face, "tell me what's wrong."

"I feel so bad for you and your family," she sobbed. "I hate to see you hurting like this."

"Don't even worry about it, mami. We'll be okay."

"No," she shook her head defiantly. "You don't understand. I'm so confused and afraid!"

"Afraid?" hHe screwed up his face. "Afraid of what?"

"My papi,'" she continued sobbing and placed her hand on her stomach. "He can never find out about this baby."

Rahmello placed his hand over her's. "Listen Oli, you love me right?"

She looked at him like he was stupid. "You know I love you. I've loved you since the first time I laid eyes on you! Ever since then, I knew you were the one for me. But it's papi," she shook her head from side to side, "he'll never accept you."

"Well, if you love me the way you say you do, then marry me. If we get married ya pops won't have no other choice but to accept and respect our relationship."

She silently weighed her options. Either she could marry the love of her life and complete their family union, or she could honor her father's demands to only marry within her race. She wiped away her tears, and then looked him square in the eyes. "I love you Mello, and there's nothing in this world that would make me happier then to be your wife. But this is something that could never happen. There's no way I can disappoint papi. I'm sorry."

***

When Sonny entered the dining room, he spotted a plate of food at the head of the table, but the room was empty. "Yo Daph! Mom! Where y'all at?" he called out.

"We're in the white room!" Daphney replied in a shaky voice.

When he stepped into the large room, he was immediately greeted with the demands of Keyonti.

"Up, up dada! Up, up!" She extended her arms toward him and he scooped her off of the white carpet. He carried her over to the white suede sectional where Daphney and his mom were sitting in silence. "Why y'all lookin' like that?" he asked, immediately taking notice of their distraught facial expressions. "What happened?"

Daphney began to speak, but Annie held up her hand, signaling for to be quiet. She then looked at her son and slowly shook her head. "Sontino, it's Brian. I just got off the phone with his mom, and she told me that his house was burned down and that they found him, Erika, and the baby. They're dead."

He lowered his head, and sat down beside Daphney. "Damn," he said to himself as he closed his eyes and massaged his temples. Warm tears trickled down the sides of his face, and Keyonti kissed him on the cheek. She said, "Fat-Fat lub dada. No cry dada. No, no cry." She used her small hands to wipe away his tears, and then rested her head on his shoulder and rubbed his back.

Sonny returned his attention to his mother. "So whatchu sayin'? Did they died in the fire? Like was it a freak accident or somethin'?"

"No baby," Annie replied with tears in her eyes. "They found Erika hanging from the banister, and the baby," her voice cracked, "somebody stuffed that lil' boy inside of the oven, and burned him alive. That's what they're started the fire."

"Fuck! Fuck! Fuck!" Sonny snapped, and then broke down crying. Annie took Keyonti from him and handed her to Daphney. "Take this child upstairs. She ain't got no business seeing her daddy like this."

Daphney nodded her head, and then carried Keyonti out of the room. Annie returned her gaze to Sonny. "Sontino look at me."

He wiped away his tears, and looked into her eyes. "What's up, mom?"

"I don't know what the fuck you got goin' on out in those streets, but this shit is gettin' outta hand," she spoke to him sternly. "First it was your father, and now it's Brian and his family. They're fucking dead." She pointed toward the hallway. "Now your wife, she's a very strong woman, and although she probably won't admit it, that girl's scared to death. So whatever's goin' on out there.you need to put an end to this shit. Do you understand what I'm tellin' you? Make it stop!"

He took a deep breath and slowly nodded his head.

"Yeah mom, I understand."

Askari

Chapter Twenty-Two

Back In North Philly

Heemy was awakened by the soft taps on his bedroom door. This was the first time in over a week that he actually slept in his own bed, and he was glad that he could finally occupy his personal space without Pooky bothering him.

"What?"

"Raheem open the door," Treesha stated from the hallway.

"Whatchu want? I'm sleep."

"I need to talk to you. Can you open the door?"

Damn, man, she's always burnin' me the fuck out, he thought to himself as he climbed out of the bed and unlocked the door. As she stepped inside of the room, he sat down on his bed and picked up the remote control to his television. She leaned against his dresser and folded her arms across her chest. "I need to tell you something."

"And what's that?" he asked without looking at her. He turned on the television and switched the channel to ESPN.

"I need to talk to you about your father."

"My father? Ain't dude doin' life upstate? Whatchu need to talk to me about him for?"

She approached his bed and sat down beside him. "When I was seventeen, my high school sweetheart was arrested for murder. A week later I found out that I was pregnant with you. I wrote him letter after letter, but they all came back, *Return To Sender*. Apparently, he was locked up under an alias and I didn't know the name.

"About six months later, I received a letter from him sayin' that he wanted me to move on with my life, and that he wanted nothing to do with me because I would only add more stress to his situation. I was crushed, and it was around that time that I started gettin' high."

"I'm sayin' though," Heemy shrugged his shoulders, "why is you tellin' me this shit? This nigga's been in jail my whole life, and he's never comin' home. Fuck that nigga."

This was a defense mechanism that he developed at an early age. Whenever he was confronted with the issue of his missing father, to ameliorate the pain of not having him in his life, he would sike himself out by saying, *Fuck that nigga or Fuck dude*. But in all actuality, his natural instincts yearned for the love and affection of a father.

Treesha took a deep breath, and then sparked up a Newport 100. After taking a deep pull and exhaling a cloud of smoke she said, "He came home last year."

"He came come?" Heemy perked up. "How? I thought you said he had a life sentence?"

"He did have a life sentence, but his brother paid some really good lawyers, and they beat his case on appeal."

Heemy smiled at her and hopped off of the bed. "Well, where he at? Why he ain't come through to check on us?"

"He did," she answered in a shaky voice. "But when he saw how cracked out I was he despised me. I was so caught up in my addiction that I didn't even give a damn. I never even told him that you were his son," she confessed, and then broke down crying.

"A'ight, well what's his number?" Heemy asked, while grabbing his cell phone off of the dresser. "We can call him right now."

Treesha's face turned bright red and she lashed out in full force. "We can't call him!" she screamed in his face. "You fuckin' killed him! You killed my man motherfucker!"

"What?" Heemy asked, completely dumbfounded.

"Pooky!" she continued screaming. "He was your father and my first love, and you fuckin' killed him!"

His cell phone slipped from his grasp and fell to the carpet. *How the fuck was Pooky my dad?* he questioned himself. *This shit don't make no mutha'fuckin' sense. Just as* he was about to ask her for clarity, two brown skinned men appeared at his bedroom door. Both were strapped with pistols and the barrels were aimed at his face.

"Sir, I'm gonna need you to turn around and place your hands behind your back," Detective Sullivan stated in an authoritative tone. "You're under arrest for the murders of Raheem McDaniels and Jamar Christie."

Heemy scowled at the two detectives, and then looked at his mother. "What the fuck is this? You called the cops on me, and had 'em hidin' in the hallway all this fuckin' time?"

"I had to," Treesha cried. "I needed to protect you. What if his brother comes around here lookin' for you? Them boys will kill you. I'd rather visit you at somebody's jail then visit you at somebody's cemetery. This was the only way for me to protect you."

Heemy shook his head in disbelief. "You triflin' bitch!"

"Sir!" Detective Sullivan shouted. "I said turn around and place your hands behind your friggin' back!"

Heemy thought about going for the Glock that was srashed under his pillow, but he remembered what Rahmello said about their high powered attorneys. Beads of sweat trickled down his forehead, and his anxiety caused him to bite down on his bottom lip. His eyes shifted from the pillow, to his mother, and then settled on the two gun toting detectives. *Fuck, man! This nigga Rahmello better not be bullshittin' about these fuckin' lawyers!*

"I'm not gonna say it again!'" Detective Sullivan warned.

Heemy shook his head from side to side, then reluctantly turned around and held his hands behind his back.

***

Around The Corner, In The Fairhill Projects...

Twany was sitting at his kitchen table eating a bowl of Apple Jacks when he heard a loud boom!

"Yo, what the fuck was that?" he asked himself as he hopped up from the table and ran for the Mack 11 that was laying on top of the refrigerator.

"Police! Get on the fucking ground!"

The first Swat Team member to storm inside of the small apartment was halfway through the living room when he saw Twany running toward the refrigerator. "Get on the fuckin' ground! Now!"

Twany grabbed the Mack 11, then spun around with his finger squeezing the trigger.

Bdddddoc! Bdddddoc! Bdddddoc!

The hollow tipped slugs ripped through the officer's body armor, sending him tumbling to the floor with his AR-15 spraying wildly.

Pdddddat! Pdddddat!

The bullets missed Twany and burned through the refrigerator and wooden cabinets. Twany crouched down and continued his assault.

Bdddddoc! Bdddddoc!

The second Swat Team member stormed inside of the apartment, and hopped over his comrade's dead body. As he glided through the air, he let off a succession of gunfire.

Pdddddat! Pdddddat! Pdddddat!

His bullets knocked Twany backwards and spun him around 360 degrees. He dropped the Mack 11 and crashed into the back wall. As he slid to the floor, the only thing he could think about was retrieving the Mack 11 from the kitchen floor. He reached for the gun, but the police officer was already squeezing his trigger.

Pdddddat! Pdddddat!

Every bullet twisted Twany's body in a different direction, leaving him wedged in between the refrigerator and back wall. The officer stood over the top of him and aimed the barrel at his face. Twany looked at him with a shocked expression as if he couldn't believe what was happening. He gasped for air, and then looked toward the ceiling as his soul left his body.

***

Sonny, Rahmello, and the twins were at *Donkees*, sitting in his office in total silence. An hour had passed since Sonny broke the news about Breeze and his family, and the energy inside of the room was a mixture of pain and frustration. As Sonny sat behind his desk trying to come up with the right words to encourage his team, his iPhone vibrated on the desktop breaking the uneasy silence.

"Yo?" he answered.

"Hey yo Sonny, this shit is bad bro!" Nipsy cried through the phone.

"Nipsy?"

"Yeah it's me, bro! They killed Twany and locked up Heemy for that Pooky and Mar-Mar situation!"

"Who? The cops?"

"Yeah bro! They ran down on Heemy while he was at his mom's house, and then they kicked down my front door lookin' for Twany! He musta thought they was Pooky's peoples because he blazed one of 'em before they killed him!

This shit is bad, bro! I don't know what the fuck to do!" Nipsy continued crying.

"Damn!" Sonny whispered, eliciting the concern and speculation of Rahmello and the twins.

Rahmello hopped up from the sectional and approached his desk. "Damn brozay, what the fuck happened now?"

"It's Nipsy. He said the cops killed Twany and locked up Heemy for that shit wit' Pooky." He returned his attention to Nipsy. "Listen scrap, just calm down. Tell me where you at and I'ma have the twins come scoop you up."

Nipsy wiped away his tears and regained his composure. "I'm in the projects at the playground on 11th Street."

"A'ight, my nigga, the twins is on they way. For now, I just need you to be easy."

After disconnecting the call, he lounged back in his swivel chair and cracked his knuckles one by one. It was hard for him to mentally process everything that was happening, but he knew he had to step his game up and be the general that Mook had raised him to be. He opened the cigar box that was positioned at the front of his desk and removed a Cuban cigar. He then reached inside of his desk drawer and pulled out a gold lighter and a gold cigar cutter. After clipping off the ends of the cigar, he nestled the wrapped tobacco leaf in between his lips, and then used his solid gold lighter to ignite the tip of the stogie.

After taking a deep pull and blowing out a thick cloud of smoke, he glanced around the office, and one by one looked his homies in the eyes. "Aight my niggas this is how we gon' move," he removed the cigar from his mouth and wedged it between his thumb and index finger. "We gon' tighten the fuck up and hold this shit down like *Block Boys*. I know we had some major setbacks, but we gon' bounce back accordingly.

"The first order of business is Sheed and them bitch ass niggas he runnin' wit'. Them niggas is the common denominator to all of our problems and these mutha'fuckas gotta go." He took another pull on the cigar and blew out a cloud of smoke.

"The second order of business is pop's funeral. As y'all already know, it's scheduled for Friday mornin' at the Baker's. It's a strong possibility that Sheed's gonna make a move so we gotta be on point. Not only my mom and grandmom, but Daph and the kids are gonna be exposed. So therefore, I need y'all to have y'all eyes on them at all times.

"The third order of business is the funeral for Breeze and his family. I already sent his mom enough money to handle all of the arrangements so we good on that end."

"The forth order of business is the young buls from Delhi Street. We gotta help Nipsy wit' the funeral arrangements for Twany, and I'ma holla at Savino about gettin' Heemy outta jail. Speakin' of which," he looked at Rahmello. "I thought you took care of that situation?"

"I did," Rahmello quickly replied. "I don't know how the fuck they chargin' him. They ain't got no bodies and the young buls ain't say nuffin' about no witnesses. Plus, I made sure that they cleaned up as much blood as they possibly could. I'm tellin' you bro, it's no way they can prove a murder beyond a reasonable doubt. I don't even know how they filed charges in the first place."

"A'ight," Sonny nodded his head. He stubbed out the cigar, and sat it in the ashtray. "They probably try'na shake him up to get a confession. It's either that or they got a witness. We won't know until Savino hops on the case. Hopefully, the lil' nigga's smart enough to keep his mouth shut. If he does, he should be good.

"Now, for the fifth and final order of business. After pops' funeral, we gotta get back to this money. We got a shit load of work to move, and we still gotta feed the corners. On top of that, my nigga from Pittsburgh is comin' through to grab 10 birds." He looked at Rahmello. "After the funeral, I need you to go to the stash house and grab 14 of 'em. Bring 10 of 'em straight to me so I can get Pittsburgh outta the way and the other 4 is for the corners. Drop 'em off wit' the caseworkers, collect the money from last week, and make sure everybody gets paid."

Sonny looked at Egypt and Zaire. "I need y'all to go through the projects and pick up Nipsy. Find out exactly we he needs for the funeral, and then bring him to see me."

Egypt nodded his head. "Say no more, Sonny. We on it." They saluted him and Rahmello, and then left the office.

Rahmello took a seat in the chair that was positioned in front of Sonny's desk. He took a deep breath. "Bro, I need to holla at you about somethin'."

Sonny stared into his blue eyes and noticed a sadness that he, himself once experienced. It was the sadness of a man who'd lost his first love. "It's Olivia ain't it?"

"Yeah," Rahmello admitted. "I know you told me not to fuck wit' lil' buddy, but when you told me that we was already fuckin' wit' each other."

"For how long?" Sonny asked.

"A little over six months."

"Six months?" Sonny shot back. "And you ain't never tell me?"

"Naw," he slowly shook his head. "She made me promise not to tell nobody. She wanted to keep our relationship a secret because she was afraid that Poncho would find out."

"So lemme guess, Poncho found out and he made her cut you off?"

"Naw, not exactly. I got tired of keepin' our relationship a secret, and I wanted to step to Poncho correct so I asked her to marry me."

"Marry you?" Sonny chuckled. "After six months? That Columbian pussy must be somethin' special," he continued laughing, trying to lighten up the mood.

"Naw," Rahmello cracked a smile. "Well yeah, this pussy's definitely official, but that's not the only reason I wanted to marry her. I wanted to get married because we found out she's pregnant."

"So what was her answer?"

Rahmello lowered his head. "She said she couldn't marry me because she didn't wanna disappoint Poncho."

"Damn brozay," Sonny reached across the desk and massaged his shoulder. "Look, after pop's funeral I'ma holla at Poncho and see if there's anything I can do to fix the situation."

Rahmello couldn't believe his ears. He assumed that Sonny would be mad at him but on the contrary, he was rocking with him.

"Yo, what's up wit' the sudden change of heart?" Rahmello asked him. "What happened to all that shit about stay away from her because she's the connect's daughter?"

Sonny lounged back in his swivel chair and locked his fingers together. "That's your problem now."

"My problem? What's that supposed to mean?"

"It means that after we run through this last shipment, I'm leavin' all the street shit to you. The weight. The corners. Everything. So therefore, if ya love for ol' girl is strong enough for you to jeopardize ya business relationship wit' her pops, then that's on you."

Rahmello thought it over, and for him the answer was an easy one. He thought about the love that he had for Olivia and a huge smile appeared on his face.

"I ain't gon' hold you, if I had to choose between the game and Oli. I'm chosin' Oli."

Instead of responding, Sonny just smiled. He was raised on principles, and one of those principles was to want for his brother what he wanted for himself. So therefore, if he desired to enjoy a peaceful life with his wife and their family then obviously he wanted the same for his younger brother.

"Yo, what the fuck is you smilin' for?" Rahmello asked him.

"I'm smilin' because I'm proud of you," Sonny said.

"Proud of me for what?"

"For you choosin' ya family over money. It ain't too many niggas out here that's willin' to do that." He looked at Rahmello with a newfound respect, and then he reached across the desk to shake his hand. "Family over everything?"

Rahmello accepted his gesture with a firm handshake. "Nothin' before family."

***

At Police Headquarters

Heemy was sitting in a holding tank that was known throughout the streets of Philly as *The Bubble*. It was a large holding cell with cream colored walls and a large plexy glass window that permitted the *Turnkeys* to monitor the actions of the detainees who occupied the cell. Three wooden benches sat in the center of the room, and three pay phones were screwed into the left wall. A broken toilet was positioned in the far right corner, and it filled the cell with a pungent odor.

"Damn, it stinks in this mutha'fucka," Heemy said to himself as he was beginning to lose patience.

His young eyes scowered the cell, taking in the slightest movements of the other detainees. This was the first time he'd ever been in custody, and he was nervous to say the least.

A frail white man who appeared to be a heroin addict was sitting on the first bench shivering and crying. He was obviously dope sick. He got up from the bench, and staggered over to the toilet stall. Heemy could tell from the nervous expression on the man's face that he was struggling with the decision of holding his bowels or releasing them in front of a room full of strangers. He anxiously shifted from side to side, and then staggered inside of the toilet stall. The walls on the stall were only three feet high and it didn't have a door. The man didn't care. He turned his back to the toilet and unbuckled his pants. As he lowered them to his knees and squatted over the toilet, a large black man who was sitting in the back row stood to his feet. "Mutha'fucka, you better sit ya ass back on that bench."

Terrified, the white man began to cry. "But mister, I'm dope sick! I have to take a shit really bad, and I can't hold it any longer!"

"I don't give a fuck!" the black man snapped. He stormed toward the toilet stall and stood in front of him. "It's already stankin' in this mutha'fucka! So what, I'm 'posed to just stand here and let you make it worse than it already is? Fuck dat!"

"I'm sorry mister, but I can't hold it!" the white man whined. He squatted over the toilet bowl, and began to release his bowels.

Enraged, the black man kicked him in the chest, knocking him backwards. As he reached out for the white man's neck, Detective Sullivan banged a pair of handcuffs against the plexy glass window.

"Knock it off!" he shouted.

The large black man scowled at him and flex his jaw muscles.

"I'm not fucking around," Detective Sullivan warned.

The man returned to his seat, and Detective Sullivan turned his attention to Heemy. "McDaniels! Front and center!"

Heemy stood to his feet and approached the large window.

"Turn around and place your hands behind your back," Detective Sullivan instructed.

Heemy did as he was told, and the detective opened the small latch in the door. He placed the handcuffs around Heemy's wrist, and then turned his head toward the officer at the front desk.

"Open the door to the bubble."

The door popped open and he guided Heemy out of the cell. As the door closed in front of him, Heemy noticed that the dope sick white man was standing in front of the toilet stall with a stupid expression on his face. He took a closer look and noticed that the front of his pants and sneakers were covered in diarrhea. *Damn that's fucked up*, he thought to himself. *At least this dick head detective came to get me 'fore I had to sit in there and smell that nasty ass shit.*

Detective Sullivan led him to the elevator and took him to the second floor where the robbery/homicide division was located. When they stepped off the elevator, they made a right turn and walked down a long hallway before making a left and approaching a brown door that had the words, *Interrogation Room*, printed on it in white letters.

Detective Sullivan opened the door and ushered him inside of the room. The walls were eggshell white and a small brown table was screwed into the wall. Two metal chairs were connected to both ends of the table and a surveillance camera was positioned in the top left corner. A large two way mirror was built into the wall that was adjacent to the table, and the only thing that Heemy could think about was the television show *The First 48*.

Detective Sullivan removed one of the handcuffs and motioned for Heemy to take a seat at the table. He then took the wrist that was still handcuffed and cuffed him to the metal chair.

"Just sit tight, Mr. McDaniel's. I'll be back in a couple of minutes."

Exasperated, Heemy sighed and laid his head on the table. "My own fuckin' mom lined me up," he said to himself as he sat there replaying the entire incident in his mind. He thought about Pooky and a tear slid from his right eye. "Damn man, that bitch shoulda told us."

For as long as he could remember, he yearned for the feeling of a father's love, and when he finally had the chance his mother robbed him of the opportunity. Now, all because of her he had to spend the rest of his life knowing that he murdered his own father.

"Damn!"

The door opened and Detective Sullivan reappeared with a brown folder clutched in his right hand. He laid the folder on the table, and then sat down across from Heemy. "So Raheem McDaniels, we have a lot to talk about young man."

He opened the folder and extracted the written statement that Treesha provided earlier that day. He slid the three page statement across the table. "I want you to take a look at that, and then tell me what you think."

Heemy picked up the statement and couldn't believe his eyes. Treesha had written down everything that happened all the way up until the point she passed out on the stoop. There was no mention of Sonny and Rahmello, and therefore the police were unaware that him and Twany were ever connected to *The Block Boys*. In their eyes, Heemy was just another poor black kid from the hood, that with the help of the Public Defender's Office, would get railroaded in the Philadelphia judicial system.

"Yo this is bullshit!" Heemy spat. "I never even heard of these niggas!"

"Oh I doubt that Mr. McDaniels," the detective smiled, trying to press his buttons. "Not only was Pooky your father, he controlled the drug trade on Delhi Street. Mar-Mar on the other hand, he was the one who actually sold the drugs. Now according to your own mother, you and your friend Twany killed the both of them in cold blood."

Heemy screwed up his face. "Man, that smokin ass bitch is lyin'! Me and Twany ain't do shit! If you don't believe me, just ask him! We don't even know these niggas!"

"Ask who? Antwan?" Detective Sullivan continued smiling. "I can't. He's friggin' dead!"

Heemy's brown face became tight and flustered. "Dead? What the fuck you mean he's dead?"

"You heard me!" Detective Sullivan raised his voice a few octaves. "He's friggin' dead! Pooky and Mar-Mar's crew killed him," he lied, desperately trying to push Heemy's buttons. "And now they're lookin' for you."

Before Heemy had the chance to respond, the door swung open and Mario Savino stepped inside of the small room. His gray Ferragamo suit was tailor made, and his powder blue dress shirt and yellow necktie added an elegant touch. His diamond cufflinks shined bright, illuminating the, *MS*, that was stitched on each sleeve, and his diamond bezeled Yacht Master, a gift from Sonny, shined even brighter. His hair was trimmed to perfection and with a clean shave, he appeared to be more mafioso than attorney. He smiled at Heemy, and greeted Sullivan with an ice grill. "Excuse me detective, but this interrogation is over. My client has nothing to say in regards to this matter, and as of right now, Judge Rogers is reviewing my *Motion To Dismiss*."

Savino reached inside of his jacket pocket and pulled out a copy of his motion. "Here," he handed the paperwork to Sullivan. "As you can see, pursuant to the United States Supreme Court's decision in <u>Inre vs. Winship</u>, the court will have no other choice but to dismiss these charges due to a lack of evidence."

Heemy and Sullivan both looked at the dapper Italian. "You can say whatever you want," Detective Sullivan scowled at him, "but your client is going down for murder."

"Bullshit!" Savino snapped. "Don't waste my time detective. You haven't a scintilla of evidence that my client is guilty of these alleged crimes. Moreover, given the fact that the Commonwealth has yet to produce a body for either of these gentlemen, there's nothing to suggest that these alleged murders even took place."

Detective Sullivan was confused. "How do you know all of this? We never even—"

"Detective!" Savino interrupted him. "As I've previously stated, Judge Rogers is reviewing my motion, and you have about," he glanced at his Yacht Master, "72 hours to produce a body or anything else that would link my client to these alleged crimes."

Heemy sat in his chair smiling from ear to ear. He could barely comprehend the words that Savino was using, but understood enough to know that the dapper attorney was about to get him out of jail.

Detective Sullivan scowled at Heemy, wondering how he got the money to hire such a stellar attorney. He then returned his gaze to Savino. "Well if nothing else, we have DNA evidence and a material witness!" he propounded.

Savino chuckled. "First of all, detective, I have a DNA specialist who will verify and testify that the amount of blood that was discovered at the scene isn't enough to establish a murder. Secondly, your so called witness is a crack whore with a criminal record longer than Broad Street. I mean come on," he shook his head from side to side, "really!"

Detective Sullivan hopped up from his seat and stood toe to toe with Savino. He scowled at him for a few seconds, and then looked down at Heemy. "Boy you better hope those bodies don't turn up because if they do," he returned his gaze to Savino, "I'm gonna have you and this fake ass Robert Shapiro standing in front of a jury sweating like a Boy Scout at the Neverland Ranch!"

Savino flexed his jaw muscles and squinted his eyes. "Trust me detective, I'm the last son of a bitch you want to see inside of a courtroom. My cross examination is so good that when I'm through with your stupid ass, your wife is gonna want a divorce, and your own mother will deny the day that she gave birth to you." He winked his eye and smiled at him. "Trust me, I'm really that good."

Enraged, Detective Sullivan grabbed his folder from the table, and then stormed out of the room. Savino smiled at Heemy and nodded his head. "Don't you worry about a thing. I'll have you out of here by the weekend. Monday at the latest. Just so you know, your family said to tell you they love you."

Heemy smiled, knowing that Savino was referring to Sonny and Rahmello. "Tell my family that I love 'em even more."

Chapter Twenty-Three

Two Days Later...

It was the morning of Easy's funeral, and the weather outside of the *Baker Funeral Home* was a chilly 42 degrees. Dark rain clouds turned the bright blue sky into a somber gray, and the mellow   rumbling of thunder, coupled with the sporadic images of lightning, was a clear indicator that a storm was approaching.

A procession line of cars were lined up and down Broad Street, from Norris Street to Susquehanna Avenue, and every windshield was decorated with a fluorescent orange *Funeral* sticker. At the head of the procession, a black Mercedes Benz hearse was waiting to be loaded with Easy's gold plated casket, and directly behind it was a black 2015 Mercedes Benz Sprinter van.

Sonny was standing beside the bulletproof van. He was holding Keyonti and talking to Daphney when someone walked up behind him and rested their hand on his shoulder. He glanced at the light skinned hand, and then noticed the uncomfortable look on Daphney's face. An eerie feeling came over him and his body temperature elevated. *Naw it can't be him*, he thought himself, hoping that the hand didn't belong to his archenemy and estranged grandfather. He spun around and was relieved to discover that the hand belonged to Poncho.

"Sontino, how ju doin'?" Poncho asked with a fraudulent concern. He extended his right hand.

"I'm just rollin' wit' the punches," Sonny replied as he looked hands with the old Columbian. He glanced over his right shoulder where Rahmello and the twins were strategically positioned around his the Sprinter van. They each had an H & K MP5 tucked inside of their Burberry London trench coats, and their eyes were scanning up and down Broad Street, looking for any signs of Sheed and his cohorts.

As the pallbearers exited the funeral home and began loading Easy's casket in the back of the hearse, Poncho took a deep breath and shook his head in disappointment. "Ju poppa was fine man, Sontino. It's a shame he died so violently."

"Yeah," Sonny agreed, feeling slightly uncomfortable. "But you can bet ya bottom dollar that whoever killed him is gonna face a thousand deaths. And after that, I'ma murder they whole family," he continued with his voice full of determination.

Poncho cracked his knuckles and gritted his teeth. "Dis is to be expected of ju. I made de same exact vow when my Angelo was gunned down." He fixed his eyes on Keyonti. "Is dis ju daughter? She is beautiful Sontino." He reached out to caress the little girl's face, but she cringed and started to cry. Sonny kissed her on the cheek, and then handed her to Daphney. "Wait for me in the van."

She nodded her head, and then stood on her tippy toes to give him a kiss. As she opened the van's side door, her intuition kicked in and she looked at Poncho suspiciously. She'd never met him before, but there was something about his body language that rubbed her the wrong way. After climbing inside of the van and settling into the black leather seat, she gazed out the tinted window and studied the interaction between Sonny and the strange Columbian. *I don't know exactly what it is, but somethin' about this dude ain't right*, she quietly suspected.

On the other side of the tinted window, Poncho could feel her energy. He stared at her silhouette for a few seconds, and then returned his attention to Sonny. "I know dat dis is a bad time, but I never received de gift dat ju promised."

"The gift?" Sonny looked at him skeptically. "What gift?"

"De gift from Mexico. Ju don't remember?"

"Damn that's right," Sonny nodded his head. "My pops was supposed to have dropped that off to you the night before they found his body. They musta got him before he had the chance to come see you."

"I figured dat," Poncho confirmed. "He call me and tell me he comin', but he never show up. Now, my friends in Mexico are askin' all types of questions, and I have no answers."

Sonny shrugged his shoulders. "Just tell 'em it's a done deal."

"No papi, it's not dat simple. I cannot say such a thing without having any proof. How can I be sure dat dis was even handled?"

"You can be sure because I'm standin' here tellin' you," Sonny shot back, feeling slightly disrespected.

Slowly, Poncho shook his head from side to side. "I don't know about dat, Sontino. For all I know, de gift could be in Hawaii on a beach enjoing de sunset. Most importantly, me and my brother gave you—"

Sonny held up his right hand, stopping him mid-sentence. "Stop right there, Poncho. I can see where this is goin', and trust me that's what we *not* gon' do!" he continued in a calm voice. "You and ya brother asked me to handle a situation for y'all, and it was handled. My soldiers put their lives on the line, and with all due respect," he shrugged his shoulders, "y'all ain't give us a goddamn thing. We *earned* those bricks and that's that."

Poncho's face became red with anger. "Is dat right?"

"Absolutely," Sonny maintained his position.

Poncho quickly suppressed his anger and displayed a fraudulent smile. "Ju know what Sontino, I have always known ju to be a man of ju word, and I was outta line for questioning ju integrity. Especially at a time like dis," he gestured toward the hearse. "Please accept my deepest apologies and give ju family my condolences."

"I appreciate that," Sonny replied half heartedly.

Truth be told, he didn't care if Poncho believed him or not. He'd already decided that the extra 100 keys that Poncho was referring to, belonged to him and his team. So basically, Poncho had two choices, respect it or check it.

"Okay Sontino, it's time for me to go. Ju need time to take care of ju family." He waved his left hand in the air, and signaled Estaban who was parked up the block in a triple black BMW 760. "When ju ready for ju next shipment, just gimmie a call and I'll take care of ju as always."

"Well since you brought it up," Sonny said, "my lil' brother Rahmello's gonna be handling that side of the family from now on. So he'll be the one contacting you."

Poncho looked at him like he was crazy. "No, Sontino. I deat wit' ju and ju only, not Rahmello."

"Well fuck it," Sonny shrugged his shoulders in a nonchalant manner. "I guess we'll have to take our money elsewhere. I'm sure the Italians in South Philly would love to do business wit' him."

"Well I guess it is settled." Poncho shook Sonny's hand, and then glanced at the Mercedes Benz hearse. "Sleep well my friend."

Estaban pulled up beside the hearse and Poncho climbed in the passenger's side. He shut the door, and then looked in the backseat where Chee-Chee was clutching a cell phone in his right hand. "Just relax Chee-Chee. Not yet." He looked at Estaban and gestured for him to pull off. "Vamanos."

Estaban made a U-turn in the middle of Broad Street and cruised up the block. He pulled into the McDonald's on Diamond Street, and parked in the first parking space facing

Broad Street. He immediately noticed that six men were posted in the parking lot, standing beside three Yamaha R1s. Each motorcycle was jet black, and the six men were dressed in black riding suits and black helmets.

"What the fuck is up wit' these niggas?" Estaban said to himself.

The six men were clearly out of place, and the tinted visors on their black helmets bolstered his suspicions. Poncho noticed them as well. He tapped Estaban on his shoulder. "Who de fuck is dat?"

"I don't know."

The six men hopped on their Yamahas, revved their engines, and then filed out of the parking lot in a single file line. Each motorcycle was carrying a rider and a passenger. Unbeknownst to Poncho and Estaban, the passengers were strapped with Uzi submachine guns, and their sole mission was to murder Sonny and Rahmello.

***

At the intersection of Broad and Berks, Sheed made a wide left turn, nearly sideswiping a white Mercedes Maybach. A black ski mask was covering his face and two Desert Eagles were resting in his lap. Rahman was sitting in the passenger's seat and Jihad was seated behind him. Both of them were strapped with an AK-47.

***

Inside of the white Maybach, Malice was sitting in the passenger's seat ice grilling the Mazda MPV that nearly sideswiped the front of their car. "Mr. Moreno, did ju see dat?" she cautioned. "De guys in dat van were wearing skimasks."

"Yeah, I seen 'em," Grip replied from the backseat. He removed the nickel plated .10mm that was tucked in his shoulder holster and cocked a bullet into the chamber. "Muhammad stay close to that mini-van," he instructed. He looked to his right where Murder was reaching for the two Mack 11s that were wedged in between her Ugg boots. "If these mutha'fuckas stop anywhere along this procession line we're gonna hop out and go to work."

Murder looked at him, and held up the Mack 11s. "Si, Mr. Moreno."

***

Agent Long and Agent Brown were sitting behind the tinted windows on their Ford Excursion. They were the fifth vehicle in the procession line, and just like the rest of the people who attended funeral, they were waiting for Sonny, Rahmello, and the twins to hop in their Sprinter van so they could drive to the cemetery and finally lay Easy to rest.

As they sat there surveying the scene, three motorcycles cruised by and Agent Long instantly recognized that the passengers on the back of the bikes were strapped with Uzis. "Ain't this a bitch!" He reached underneath his seat and retrieved his Glock 19. He looked at Agent Brown. "No matter what happens Monica, stay in the truck." He hopped out the Excursion and took off running behind the motorcycles. "Yo, Sonny watch out! It's a hit!"

***

Sonny had one foot inside of the Sprinter van when he heard the humming of the motorcycles and someone yelling, "Yo, Sonny, watch out! It's a hit!"

He looked over the roof of the van and saw Kev running behind the motorcycles with his gun aimed in their direction.

As the first bike cruised pass the van, the passenger aimed his Uzi and Kev fired his Glock from behind.

Boc! Boc! Boc! Boc!

The bullets hit the passenger in his back, but they didn't deter him from letting off a spray of gunfire.

Tttttat! Tttttat! Tttttat!

Sonny, Rahmello, and the twins took cover behind the bulletproof Sprinter van as the rapid gunfire rocked it from side to side. Kev continued shooting as the passenger on the second bike opened fire.

Tttttat! Tttttat!

Sonny pulled out his FNH .45, rolled off of the back left fender, and returned fire.

Bdddddoom! Bdddddoom! Bdddddoom!

Rahmello and the twins followed suit.

Pdddddat! Pdddddat! Pdddddat!

The driver of the first motorcycle was struck several times. He lost control of his bike and crashed into the MPV that was driving up the block. His passenger was thrown from the motorcycle, and he slammed into the MPV's windshield face first.

Crash!

The passenger on the second motorcycle was riddled with bullets, and he fell off the back of the bike. His driver switched gears and gunned the R1 down Broad Street with the third motorcycle hot on his trail.

Despite being severely wounded, the passenger who fell off of the second motorcycle aimed his Uzi at Kev who was still shooting at the fleeing motorcycles.

Boc! Boc! Boc! Boc! Boc! Boc!

Just as the wounded passenger was about to squeeze his trigger, Sonny peeped him out the corner of his eye. "Yo Kev, watch ya back bro!" He swung his FNH in the direction of the wounded passenger and squeezed.

Bdddddoom!

The .45 bullets blazed through his helmet and visor, laying him out flat. Kev looked at Sonny, and wiped the sweat from his brow. "Good lookin' Ike."

Sonny responded with a head nod.

The intersection of Broad and Norris was nothing short of pandemonium. Spent shell casings and broken glass littered the street. The smell of burnt gunpowder hung in the air, and the rapid succession of gunfire left a foggy mist. The cars in the procession line were attempting to flee, causing traffic jams and minor accidents. For those who couldn't drive away, their only option was to abandon their cars and run for cover.

***

As soon as the gunfire stopped, Sheed, Rahman, and Jihad hopped out of the MPV and picked up where the shooters on the motorcycles left off.

Brrrrroc! Brrrrroc! Brrrrroc! Brrrrroc!
Doom! Doom! Doom! Doom! Doom!

Sonny, Rahmello, and the twins dipped behind the Sprinter van again. Their ammunition was depleted and with their family was trapped inside of the van, they saw no way out.

"Damn brozay!" Rahmello shouted over the gunfire. What the fuck we gon' do?"

"I don't know!" Sonny shouted back. He looked to his right and saw Kev running toward them. "Damn Kev, you ran outta bullets too?"

"Yeah," the undercover agent replied. "This shit is fuckin' crazy!"

Inside of the van, Daphney quickly realized that they ran out of bullets. She cracked the side door and shouted, "Hurry up y'all! Get in the van!"

***

Grip, followed by Murder and Malice, hopped out of the Maybach and got busy. They ambushed Sheed and his crew from behind.

Moc! Moc! Moc! Moc! Moc!
Bdddddoc! Bdddddoc! Bdddddoc!

A hail of bullets ripped through Jihad's muscular frame killing him instantly. Rahman ran to take cover behind an abandoned Audi, but a succession of bullets danced up his back, and spun him around. "Agggghhhh!" he grimaced in pain as he crashed into the Audi's back fender. "Lil' cuzzo, I'm hit!"

Sheed aimed his Desert Eagles at Malice, but when he squeezed the trigger nothing happened. Confused, he looked at both of his pistols and discovered that the hammers were locked back. "Fuck!" he shouted in frustration. He was so caught up in his emotions that he forgot the number one rule when it came to a shootout, keep a count of the number of bullets fired. He looked at Malice who was swinging her Mack 11s in his direction. She wasted no time.

Bdddddoc! Bdddddoc! Bdddddoc!

The bullets missed their target as he dove behind a bullet riddled Lexus. He looked to his left and saw Rahman lying on his side. "Lil' cuzzo, I can't breathe!" he cried out. Thick globs of dark blood were pouring from his nose and mouth, and Sheed realized that there was nothing he could do for him with two empty weapons. He spotted Rahman's AK-47 lying on the ground beside him, and he crawled toward it. He was centimeters away from the assault rifle when Rahman shouted,

"Sheed watch out!" He glanced over his shoulder and the only thing he saw was the smoking barrel of Grip's .10mm.

Moc! Moc! Moc! Moc!

"Nooooo!" Rahman screamed as the back of Sheed's head burst open and his brains splashed against the pavement. He reached for his AK-47, but a sharp pain shot through his chest and he quickly pulled back his hand. He coughed uncontrollably and a thick glob of blood shot from his mouth. His insides were burning and his lungs were growing weaker by the second. He heard sirens in the near distance and silently prayed that the police arrived on the scene before his adversaries had the chance to finish him off.

Grip, Murder, and Malice heard the sirens as well, and realized that they had to move quickly. Grip and Malice ran toward his Maybach, and Murder hopped up on the hood of the Audi. She aimed her Mack 11s at Rahman's baldhead. "Hey punta!"

He looked up.

Bdddddoc!

She jumped off the Audi and ran toward the Maybach where Grip and Malice were safely inside. As she settled into the backseat, Muhammad threw the transmission in *reverse.* He backed the car halfway down the block, and then whipped it around and headed south on Broad Street.

***

Seconds later a plethora of Philadelphia police cruisers arrived on the scene, but due to the massive traffic jam they were forced to stop at the corner of Broad and Norris. They hopped out with their guns drawn, and couldn't believe the carnage that lay before them.

***

Inside of the Mercedes Sprinter van, the women and children were huddled on the floor, and the men were staring at one another in disbelief. They would have never imagined that Grip would be the one to save their lives. Had he and his people not taken action when they did it would have only been a matter of time before the high caliber bullets decimated the van's bulletproof exterior.

Sonny looked out the back window and saw the police cruisers at the bottom of the block.

"Damn, we gotta stash these burners 'fore the cops come," he said while removing his suit jacket. "Here," he handed the jacket to Zaire, "use this to wrap up all the guns." He handed over his FNH, and Egypt and Kev did the same. "Mello give him ya' burner."

No response.

He looked to his right and couldn't believe his eyes. Rahmello was stretched out on the back seat, and his trench coat was covered in blood. His eyes were rolled into the back of his head and he wasn't moving. "Naw brozay! Not you too!" Sonny shouted as he pushed Zaire out of his way and knelt down beside him.

Upon hearing this, his mother, grandmother, and Daphney got up from the floor and rushed to his side. Annie checked Rahmello's pulse, and then looked at Sonny. "He's still breathing," she cried. "But we need to hurry up and get him to the hospital."

Sonny gathered his composure and once again looked out the back window. He spotted two police officers running in their direction, and then he looked at Zaire who was stashing their weapons in the van's hidden compartment. The back door swung open and he was greeted by the barrel of a 9 mm. "Show me your fuckin' hands!" The first of the two police officers shouted.

Sonny held up his hands in a defenseless posture and quickly pleaded his case, "Yo my family's in here. This was my pop's funeral and my lil' brother got shot."

The officer peeked his head inside of the van and saw Rahmello stretched out on the backseat with his head cradled in Annie's lap. He also spotted Daphney who was consoling a crying Keyonti, and Sonny's grandmother who was holding Dayshon. He lowered his firearm and activated the walkie talkie that was clipped to his left shoulder. "We need an EMT at the *Baker Funeral Home* on Broad Street. We have a victim who's suffering from a gunshot wounds and he needs medical assistance."

***

In the midst of the drama, Agent Brown, acting on the orders of Agent Long was crouched down in the backseat of the Excursion. When she realized that the gunfire had stopped, she peaked out of the window and spotted a crowd of police officers scattered throughout the block. Two of the police officers were standing beside Sonny's Sprinter van. Cautiously, she climbed out of the Excursion and made her way toward the van.

As she approached the vehicle, the two police officers looked at her skeptically. The younger of the two held up his right hand and motioned for her to stay away. "Ma'am, this is a crime scene. You need to back up."

***

Up the block, sitting in the McDonald's parking lot, Poncho, Estaban, and Chee-Chee were shocked and confused. Between the shooters on the motorcycles and the shooters who hopped out of the MPV and the white Maybach they were completely dumbfounded.

Poncho looked at Estaban and asked him, "Was dat ju work?"

"Nah papi, I don't know what's goin' on," he quickly answered.

Poncho gritted his teeth, and then looked in the backseat where Chee-Chee was sitting with a blank expression on his face. In his right hand, he was holding a cell phone that was programmed to detonate the bomb that was placed in the cargo compartment of Easy's hearse. Poncho looked down the block and spotted a beautiful Black and Asian woman walking toward the van that was carrying Sonny and his family. He then reverted his gaze back to Chee-Chee and slowly nodded his head. The frail Columbian held up the cell phone and pressed the *CALL* button.

***

"Ma'am this is a crime scene. You need to back up," said the police officer.

Sonny looked at him. "Naw, she's okay. That's just Suelyn, my accountant."

She ignored the police officer and looked directly at Sonny. "Is everybody okay?"

"Naw Sue, them pussies shot Mello."

"Well is there any—"

Ka-Boom!

The unexpected blast lifted the hearse off of the ground and sent shards of metal flying through the air. The effects of the blast were so devastating that it shattered the Sprinter van's windows and rocked the large vehicle from side to side.

Sonny and his family dropped to the floor as the broken glass covered their bodies. Dark smoke filled the van, and the intensive heat from the blast made them feel as though they were trapped inside of a sauna. Their eyes were burning and their eardrums were ringing. Dayshon and Keyonti were coughing and gagging and Sonny was livid.

Thump!

A large object slammed into the roof of the van and everyone ducked for cover. Sonny looked around and to his astonishment nobody was hurt during the blast. In the corner of his right eye, he saw something dangling in the crushed frame of the back window. He took a closer look and sadly he shook his head. A flaming Christian Louboutin pump that was connected to a burning leg was hanging off the back of the roof. It was then that realized the source of the loud thump. It was Suelyn's dead body.

Chapter Twenty- Four

Later That Night...
At The Eaglesville Rehabilitation Center

Aside from Nahfisah and the black woman who was sitting in the corner nodding off from a methone shot, the recreation room was empty. Nahfisah was sitting in front of the television, flicking through the channels when a picture of Easy appeared on the screen. She turned up the volume and listened closely.

"This was the funeral of Ervin *Easy* Moreno," said a young white woman. She was standing in front of The Baker Funeral Home, and the microphone she held in her right hand prominently displayed the Channel 9 logo. Her curly blonde hair was slightly blowing in the wind, and the bright lights from her camera crew illuminated her tanned face. "According to the Philadelphia Police Department, Ervin Moreno, an alleged drug kingpin, was the victim in a gangland murder. A week ago, Philadelphia police officers, responding to a 911 call, discovered a burning Jaguar on the corner of 5th and Cumberland. Upon further investigation, they discovered Mr. Moreno's dead body in the trunk of the car. He was badly burned and multiple gunshot wounds covered his face and chest."

She positioned herself in front the decimated Mercedes hearse, and continued her broadcast. "Unfortunately, the violence surrounding his death carried over to his grieving family. According to eyewitness reports, after his casket was placed in the back of this hearse, his family was ambushed by a gang of shooters who were riding on motorcycles. An estimated two hundred and fifty rounds of gunfire rained down on his family, who were sitting in this Mercedes Sprinter

Van," she said as she gestured toward the taped off vehicle. "In the aftermath of the shooting, a bomb that was secretly stashed in the cargo of Mr. Moreno's hearse, was detonated, killing fedearal agent Monica Brown. A total of nineteen people were injured during the ambush, with six of them, including Agent Brown, being pronounced dead at the scene. It was also confirmed that Mr. Moreno's son was critically wounded during the attack.

This is Jessica Summers, reporting to you live from North Philadelphia. Back to you Herm."

Nahfisah dropped the remote control and shook her head in disbelief. "No," she whispered to herself. "This can't be right." She assumed the reporter was referring to Sonny, and her blood began to boil. Her yellow face became a flustered bergundy and warm tears flowed from her blue eyes. As she broke down crying and slumped to the floor, the only thing she could think about was the first time she'd met her big brother.

February 1st, 1996

Nahfisah was laying in her bed watching Martin, when she heard someone outside of her window crying. She climbed out of the bed and looked out of the window. Across the street, a little boy was leaned against the fence that lined the basketball court. She squinted her eyes to get a better look, and noticed that the little boy was the new kid from school. She tied a scarf around her head, and then went outside to check on him. She walked across the street and entered the basketball cage. As she walked toward him, she noticed that his hand was bleeding.

"Are you okay?" she asked in a soft voice.

"Yeah," Sonny lowered his head. "I'm a'ight."

"You don't look a'ight." She pointed at his left hand. *"You're bleeding."*

He looked at his hand and spotted a gash between his thumb and index finger. She grabbed his hand and examined it closely.

"Eeeewwww, that's a nasty cut." She scrunched up her face and released his hand. *"Come on."* She turned around and began walking toward the opening in the fence. *"Follow me to my house so I can clean your hand and get you a BandAid."*

"Naw I'm good," he quickly replied. *"What I look like going over your house? I don't even know you."*

She stopped walking and spun around to face him. She placed her hand on her bony hip and snapped her neck sistagirl style.

"Boy, you better stop playin' wit' me. My name is Nahfisah Thompson and your name is Sontino Moreno. I know that's your name 'cause you're the new boy at my school. All the girls at my school know your name. So there, now we know each other. She grabbed him by his wounded hand and led him inside of her row house.

After grabbing a bottle of peroxide and a box of BandAids, she grabbed his hand and began the process of cleaning his wound.

"Nahfisah," her grandmother said as she entered the living room. *"Chil', whatchu down here doin'?"* She pointed at Sonny. *"And who is this boy?"*

"This is Sontino, granny. He's a friend from school," she quickly replied in an innocent voice. *"He cut his hand and I was putting a BandAid on it."*

Her grandmother looked back and forth between Nahfisah and Sonny. *"Humph, you hurry on up then get back to bed. You got school in the mornin'."*

"Yes ma'am."

As her grandmother went back upstairs Sonny said, "Damn, ya grandmom look mean as shit."

Nahfisah laughed at him. "Naw she's okay. She's been takin' care of me every since my mom started runinn' the streets."

After she thoroughly cleaned his wound and covered it with a BandAid, she led him to the front door. She asked him, "Will I see you at school tomorrow?"

He looked at his bandaged hand, and then stared into her blue eyes. "Yeah I'm goin', but you're chillin' wit' me at recess."

She giggled. "We can chill. I'm warning you, Sontino, you better not go around sayin' I'm your girlfriend. 'Cause if you do," she smiled at him and waved her fist in front of his face. "I'ma sock you in the eye!"

Sonny laughed at her. "Girl, you better get outta here."

As she closed the door behind him, her grandmother her from the second floor. "Nahfisah!"

"Yes granny!"

"Come on up here. I need to talk to you."

"Okay," she replied, and then ran up the stairs. She walked inside of her grandmother's room and plopped down on the bed. "What's up granny?"

The old woman looked at her, and then reached forward to straighten out her scarf. "It's about that boy," she said. "Don't you go around callin' ya'self likin' him."

Nahfisah blushed. "Granny, I don't like that boy."

"Umm hmm. That's whatcha mouth say. I seen the way you was lookin' at him, and I'm tellin' you right now you don't be likin' that boy!"

Nahfisah was confused. "But why?"

"Because," her grandmother mother stated with authority. *"That lil' boy is ya brother."*

"My brother?"

"Umm hmm. Y'all got the same good for nothin' daddy. That goddamn Easy Moreno."

"Easy Moreno?" Nahfisah said. *"I heard my mama sayin' that name before. He's my daddy?"*

"Umm hmm. But don't you go around sayin' nothin', ya hear? That's one of those things we just don't talk about."

Nahfisah began to cry. *"But if he's my brother and we he got the same daddy, shouldn't I tell him?"*

Her grandmother shook her head. *"Didn't I just tell you that's one of those things we don't talk about?"*

"Yes ma'am."

"Good. Now go to bed. You got school in the mornin'."

Back To 2014

"Nahfisah! Are you okay?"

She looked up and saw her counselor, Ms. Mary, rushing toward her. The Puerto Rican woman knelt down beside her and pushed the hair out of her face. "Sweetie, what's the matter?"

Nahfisah sobbed and pointed at the television. "Somebody killed my dad, and now they're try'na kill my brother!"

***

At Poncho's New Jersey Estate

Olivia was lying on her bed crying her eyes out. She'd just finished watching the six o'clock news, and the segment about Rahmello and his family left her completely unglued.

"Papi did this. I know it," she sobbed into her pillow.

The night before she called Rahmello and told him that not only did she decide to keep their baby, but that she would also marry him. In turn he insisted that she tell Poncho about their relationship. After disconnecting the call she went straight to her parent's bedroom and told them about Rahmello and the baby.

Poncho was furious. He was already debating on whether he should kill the rest of Easy's family to avoid any possible retaliation, and now that Olivia confirmed his suspicions about her and Rahmello, he vowed to show no mercy. Disgusted, he contacted Estaban and Chee-Chee. He instructed them to meet him at his bodega in North Philly, and together they devised a plan to ambush Easy's funeral and kill his entire family in the process.

Marisol, Olivia's mother, was walking down the hallway when she heard the cries of her daughter. She placed her ear against the door. "Oli, its mami. I'm coming in."

She opened the door, and found Olivia curled up on the bed. She sat down beside her and rubbed her back. "Just give him some time, Oli. Ju papi is as stubborn as a mule, but when it comes to ju, he can be as soft as cotton," she consoled her only daughter. "He only wants de best for ju."

"I hate him mami! I hate him so much!" she whined, unaware that Poncho was walking down the hallway a couple of feet from her door. He stopped walking and stormed inside of her room.

"So ju hate me?" he shouted, catching her and Marisol off guard. "Ju ungrateful bitch of a daughter!" He ran toward her and snatched her off the bed by her hair. "Ju are a disgrace to dis family and I want ju outta my house!" he continued shouting while dragging her toward the hallway.

"Adios mio! Mami help me!" Olivia screamed. She reached out and wrapped her hands around Marisol's ankle. "Help me mami! Please!"'

Poncho pulled on her hair with all of his might. The force was so strong that her soft hair ripped from the scalp and he fell into the hallway. Marisol ran toward him and pleaded for the safety of her daughter and grandchild. "Poncho please! Dis is ju daughter. She's carrying a baby!"

Her words only added fuel to the fire. The thought of his only daughter lying with a black man made him want to scream. He jumped to his feet and quickly removed the leather belt from his trousers.

"Poncho please," Marisol begged him for mercy. "What are ju doing? Dis is ju daughter!"

Whack!

The leather belt landed across Marisol's face, and she crumbled to the floor.

"Dis is all ju fault!" Poncho shouted as he stood over top of her. "Ju raised dis little whore!"

"But Poncho," she cried.

Whack!

He landed another strike and Marisol curled up in the fetal position. The pain was intense, but she was more than willing to take the whipping rather than watch her daughter be subjected to his anger.

Estaban walked inside of the house, and immediately heard the commotion on the second floor. He ran up the spiral staircase, and saw his father whipping his mother. He ran toward Poncho and tackled him to the floor. "Papi, calm down!" he pleaded with his father. "We have big trouble!"

Marisol got up from the floor, and then quickly locked her and Olivia inside of the bedroom. Poncho stood to his feet, and looked at Estaban skeptically. "What are ju talking about," he quickly   inquired. "Trouble like what?"

"The bomb," Estaban blurted out. "That woman who died from the bomb was a federal agent. Papi, we need to leave," he suggested while back peddling toward the spiral staircase. "Uncle Juan is at the airport waiting for us. He's takin' us back to Columbia."

***

At The Aramingo Diner

Agent Long was sitting in the last booth with a blank expression on his face. After the funeral, he received a call from Clavenski telling him to meet him at the diner. Apparently, he wanted to speed up the indictment on Sonny and Grip. He insisted they go over a few details before presenting their case to the grand jury that following Monday.

As he sat there sipping on a glass of root beer, the only thing he could think about was the ambush at Easy's funeral. Images of the man who fell off the back of the second motorcycle made his blood boil. He could have sworn the bullets that he fired into the man's back was enough to kill him, but unfortunately he was wrong. The entire scene was running through his mind in slow motion. He aimed. He squeezed his trigger.

Muzzle flash. *Boc!*

Muzzle flash. *Boc!*

Muzzle flash. *Boc!*

The man fell off the back of the motorcycle. He fixed his aim on the fleeing rider, and squeezed his trigger.

Muzzle flash. *Boc!*

Muzzle flash. *Boc!*

He heard Sonny shouting at him. His words chopped and screwed like a mixtape from Houston, Texas. "Yooo Keeev, waaatch yaaa baaack brooo!"

He glanced to his left. The man that he shot off the motorcycle was aiming an Uzi in his direction. Sonny fired his FNH.

Muzzle flash. *Doom! Doom! Doom!*

The tinted visor on the man's helmet exploded. His body jerked. His muscles released. His head lollied to the side. He was dead.

"Damn," he whispered. He hated the fact that he was deceiving the man who undoubtedly saved his life, but he had no choice. He had a job to do and his every intention was to fulfill his obligation. As he gulped down the rest of his root beer, his cell phone vibrated on the table.

Vrrrrm! Vrrrrm!

He glanced at the screen and saw that the caller was Detective Sullivan. *This pussy mutha'fucka*, he thought to himself as he accepted the call.

"Sully, what the fuck happened to you? You were supposed to have met us at the funeral. What happened?"

"My daughter woke up with a fever this morning, and my wife insisted that we rush her to the hospital," Detective Sullivan explained, completely blindsided by Agent Long's demeanor.

"Well maybe it's a good thing you weren't there," Agent Long acknowledged. "These son of a bitches had Broad Street looking like Baghdad."

"I heard about Monica," Detective Sullivan sighed. "Are you feeling okay? I know how close the two of you were."

"To be honest with you Sully, Monica's the last thing on my mind at this point."

Askari

"Is that right?" Detective Sullivan asked. Something about this conversation was rubbing him the wrong way. Agent Long was way too calm for a man who just witnessed the murder of a close friend. His voice carried a harsh undertone, and he appeared to be a completely different person.

"Alright, well I was just calling to check on you buddy."

"I appreciate that Sully. Thanks."

"Oh yeah," Detective Sullivan continued. "I spoke to Detective Phoenix, and we've made a positive identification on one of the shooters. From the funeral that is."

"Do tell."

"Is Sontino caught up in a beef with the Italians in South Philly?"

"Not that I'm aware of," Agent Long stated. "But you never know."

"Alright, well, does the name Paulie Rizzo ring a bell?"

"Paulie Rizzo, absolutely," Agent Long confirmed. "He's a soldier in *The Gervino Crime Family*. Are you saying the Italians were responsible for the hit at Easy's funeral?"

"That's exactly what I'm saying."

Agent Long gritted his teeth. The more he thought about it, the more it all made sense. He looked toward the front of the diner and spotted Clavenski walking through the door. "Hey Sully, lemme call you back."

When Clavenski walked through the front door, he was surprised to see that the small diner was relatively empty. A beautiful Spanish woman was standing behind the cash register, and she was speaking in Spanish to another woman who appeared to be a waitress. In the back of the diner, seated in the last booth, he laid eyes on Agent Long, and began walking in his direction.

"Terry, did you prepare the video footage like I asked?" he said as he sat down across from him.

"Not yet," Agent Long replied, while holding up the iced out lion's head that was connected to his platinum necklace. The red rubies that represented the lion's eyes were actually hidden cameras, and he'd been using them to record his interactions with Sonny. So far he had the footage from *Donkees* where he and Sonny were negotiating cocaine prices, and most recently he recorded the events from Easy's funeral.

"Well, you need to have that taken care of by the morning," Clavenski dictated with a smug attitude.

He then waved his hand in the air, signaling for the waitress to come over and take his order. The beautiful Spanish woman approached the booth and smiled at him. "Can I get ju somethin', papi?"

"Yes, I would like a hot cup of coffee, and a blueberry Danish."

After jotting down his order she asked, "Is dat everything? Ju don't want nothin' else?"

"No that'll be all," he said, and then dismissed her with the flick of his hand. He returned his attention to Agent Long. "I was going over the transcripts from the Title III wiretaps and I noticed that Sontino keeps referring to a man named *Poncho*."

He laid the brown folder on top of the table and flipped it open.

"Is that the complete file from the Moreno case?"

"Yes," Clavenski clarified. "The copy machine in my office was giving me problems so I decided to take the file home, and just make the copies there. "We're scheduled to appear before Judge Arroyo and the grand jury on Monday morning. This is why I need you to hurry up and convert that video footage to a USB."

"I'll have it ready by the morning," Agent Long assured him. "Now, back to those Title III transcripts. You mentioned the name *Poncho*. What's that about?"

Clavenski flipped through the paperwork and held up a black and white photograph.

"This is Poncho Nunez, a major cocaine distributor from Columbia. In the mid-eighties, Poncho and his brother Juan, were sent to America by Pablo Escobar. They were originally stationed in Miami, but eventually made their way to Philadelphia. This was during the, *Cocaine Cowboy Era*, when all we cared about was Pablo Escobar and Griselda Blanco. The Nunez Brothers were so discreet in their endeavors that they managed to slip through the cracks. I'm not certain, but I've gotta hunch that Poncho Nunez is the *Poncho* that Sontino's was referring to on the wiretaps."

Agent Long took a deep breath and cracked his knuckles. "Alright, first and foremost, I need to make the buy from Sontino. The only problem is that due to the events at his father's funeral, he's probably gonna hold me off for another week or two. Shouldn't we focus on securing our strongest evidence before presenting our case to the grand jury?"

"Not at all," Clavenski replied. "The date's already been set for Monday morning, and that's final."

"Come on Andy, cut the bullshit. Why are you so determined to take down *The Moreno Family*? I mean come on, let's keep it real. Who's putting you up to this shit?"

"Excuse me?" Clavenski retorted.

"Just keep it real," Agent Long challenged. "I already know that you're working for *The Gervino Crime Family*. I've got you on tape talking on the phone with Little Angolo."

"Wh—what?" Clavenski stuttered. "Just who in the hell do you think you're talking to Terry?"

Agent Long's nostrils began to flare and his hands trembled with anger. "You know what, I'm sick of this shit anyway." He reached underneath the table and grabbed the P89 that was lying on his lap. He cocked a bullet into the chamber, and then aimed the barrel at Clavenski's face. "Murder and Malice," he called for the waitress and the woman behind the cash register. "It's time to go to work."

Clavenski's eyes nearly popped out of his head. "Terry, what the hell is going on?"

"Pussy, you tell me!" Agent Long barked at him.

Clavenski jumped to his feet and Agent Long squeezed the trigger.

Boc!

The .9mm slug ripped through his stomach and flipped him into the next booth. Agent Long looked at Murder and Malice. "Take his punkass down to the basement."

He grabbed his cell phone off of the table and called Grip.

Ring! Ring! Ring!

"Hello," Grip answered.

"Uncle G, its Gangsta. Where you at?"

Askari

Chapter Twenty-Five

The emergency room at Temple University Hospital was filled to capacity. People with injuries of all kinds were waiting to be seen by the medical staff, and for obvious reasons they couldn't keep their eyes off of Sonny. His white Ferragamo dress shirt was covered in blood and he reeked of burnt sulfur. The bling in his Presidential Rolex shifted with his every movement, and for the past hour he'd been pacing back and forth from one side of the room to the other.

"Yo who the fuck is comin' at me like this?" He said to himself while cracking his knuckles one by one.

He knew it couldn't gave have been Sheed because him and his shooters were dead before the blast. Moreover, he knew Sheed like the back of his hand and he was well aware of his capabilities. This type of drama was of another caliber. Deep in his heart he suspected Poncho, but he couldn't connect him to a possible motive.

"Could it be the Italians from South Philly?" He briefly considered, but quickly dismissed the notion. "Naw that nigga Carmine ain't stupid. He knows that mob shit don't hold no weight in the hood."

No matter how hard he tried he couldn't decipher this dangerous enigma, and for the first time in his twenty five years of life he felt completely vulnerable. He had to figure out the identity of his enemy. The lives of his family and team depended on it.

Vrrrrm! Vrrrrrm!

His iPhone vibrated in his slacks interrupting his train of thought. He retrieved the phone from his pocket and saw that the caller was Daphney.

"What's up ma? Y'all good?"

"Yeah daddy, we good. What about Mello?" she inquired. "Is he outta surgery yet?"

"Naw, they're still workin' on him."

"Well what about you?" she asked with a deep concern. "Are you okay?"

"Yeah I'm good," he sighed. "I'm just worried about Mello. I done lost too many of my niggas as it is. I ain't try'na lose him too."

Warm tears trickled down her face. She desperately wanted to be by his side, but he wouldn't allow it. After the drama at the funeral, he sent her and their family back to their estate in Montgomery county. He also sent the twins and gave them strict orders to hold everything down until he returned.

"Just be strong daddy. Everything's gonna be okay, "she replied in a soft, comforting voice.

Sonny took a deep breath and used his free hand to massage the back of his neck.

"A'ight ma, I gotta go. Kiss the kid for me and tell my mom and my grandmom that I love 'em."

"I most definitely will," she confirmed. "Just keep us updated on Mello's condition."

"You already know."

"And Sontino," she blurted out at the very last second.

"What's up, ma?"

"I love you."

"I love you more."

Click!

As he placed the phone back in his pocket he noticed that every eye in the room was glued to the television in the far left corner. They were watching the six o'clock news, and the room was so quiet that if you listened closely you could hear a cockroach pissing on a cotton ball. When he looked up at the screen and saw a picture of Suelyn a lump formed in the back of his throat. Directly above her picture the caption read, *DEA Agent Murdered By Car Bomb.*

"A DEA agent?" he questioned, while squinting his eyes at the screen. "Yo what the fuck is this?"

Almost immediately, her picture was replaced with the gory scene outside of the *Baker Funeral Home.* Roland Rushin was standing in front of the Mercedes Sprinter van that saved the lives of him and his family. The reporter was holding a microphone in his right hand, and eloquently speaking to the citizens of Philadelphia.

"It was here, directly outside of this funeral home, where Agent Monica Brown was blown to pieces, and where seven men were savagely gunned down in a hail of gunfire.

"According to the Philadelphia Police Department, the bomb that killed Agent Brown was placed underneath this Mercedes hearse," he announced while positioning himself in front of the decimated vehicle. "The DEA's office has yet to issue a formal statement, but a spokesperson did in fact verify that at the time of this incident, Agent Brown was participating in an undercover operation."

The middle aged black man paused for a moment, and then placed his left hand on his earpiece. He nodded his head up and down, and then returned his gaze to the camera.

"Okay, it was just confirmed that one of the victims in this incident was Rahmello Moreno, the twenty one year old grandson of Black Mafia crime boss, Gervin *Grip* Moreno."

Pictures of Grip and Rahmello appeared at the top of the screen as Roland Rushin continued his live broadcast.

"For those of you who don't know, *The Black Mafia* also known as *The Moreno Crime Family* has plagued the streets of this city for over five decades. But from the look of things, it appears as though they've attracted some serious enemies, and I'm assuming that these gangland murders are the beginning of something far worse. This is Roland Rushin reporting to you live from North Philadelphia. Back to you Jenny."

As Sonny stood there thinking of all the evidence the federal government could possibly have against him, a short white man dressed in green scrubs entered the waiting room. A stethoscope was dangling from his neck, and a brown clipboard was clutched in his right hand. He glanced at the clipboard, and then looked around   the room.

"Rahmello Moreno!" he announced. "Is there anyone present on behalf of Rahmello Moreno?"

The people in the room recognized the name *Moreno* from the news, and they all looked at Sonny. His light skin, chiseled face, and wavy hair were a dead giveaway. The resemblance between him and the pictures of the two men that were just displayed on the television was inescapable, and they didn't doubt for a second that the young man in the blood stained shirt was related to the infamous Moreno Family.

"Yeah," Sonny stated as he approached the Jewish looking man. "I'm Sontino Moreno. Rahmello's my little brother."

The doctor extended his right hand, and Sonny accepted the gesture with a firm handshake.

"My name's Dr. Levy and I'm the surgeon who operated on your brother." He glanced around the room full of spectators, and then returned his gaze to Sonny. "Do you mind if we go to the back so we can have some privacy?"

"Naw not at all," Sonny replied, then followed the doctor through the doubledoors. As soon as they were alone, he began his interrogation. "So what's up wit' my brother, doc? Did he make it?"

Dr. Levy sighed, and then said, "Your brother suffered a single gunshot wound to his left leg, and the bullet severed his femoral artery. The bullet was recovered during surgery, but as a result of him losing so much blood, he slipped into a coma. We did everything that we could do for him at this point."

"A'ight, but will he survive?" Sonny asked with tears in his eyes.

The doctor lowered his voice a few octaves.

"It's touch and go at this point. Like I said," he shrugged his shoulders, "we did everything we could do for your brother. The femoral artery is one of the main elements that the body uses to circulate blood. To be honest with you, it's a good thing that you got him here as fast as you did. Had you got him here a few minutes later he would have bled to death."

Beep! Beep! Beep!

The doctor looked at his pager, and then returned his gaze to Sonny.

"Listen Mr. Moreno I need to get going, but I'll be checking on Rahmello throughout the night to evaluate his improvement or lack thereof."

"A'ight doc, but how long do these comas last? And is it okay for me to see him?"

"I've seen comas last anywhere between a few hours and a couple of years. In this particular case, your brother lost a substantial amount of blood. At this point, the only thing we can do is have patience. Now as far as you seeing him, that's not a problem. Just check with the receptionist at the front desk, and she'll provide you with all the necessary information."

When Sonny returned to the waiting room he noticed that Grip was at the receptionist's desk inquiring about Rahmello. He stopped in his tracks and took a deep breath. There was so much bad blood between the two of them that he honestly didn't know how to address the situation. *Damn, I wanna kill this mutha'fucka so bad. But if it wasn't for him, me and my family would be dead right now*, he thought to himself as he stood there in full gangsta regalia. He was ice grilling the man who undoubtedly turned his world upside down.

Grip spotted him out the corner of his eye and turned to face him. "Sontino how are you?" Grip asked. "Is everybody safe?"

"Yeah we a'ight," Sonny confirmed while staring in his blue eyes.

"What about Rahmello?"

A warm tear slid down the left side of Sonny's face.

"He's in a coma, and the doctor said he might not make it."

Grip stepped in closer and wrapped his arms around him.

"Grandson, will you please forgive me? I love you and there's nothing I wouldn't do for you and our family."

Sonny broke their embrace and took a step backwards. He wiped away his tears, and then glanced around the emergency room where everyone was watching as if his life were a movie. Grip looked up at the television and noticed that the news was broadcasting from outside of the hospital.

"Come on Sontino. We need to get out of here."

"Get outta here?" Sonny screwed up his face "I'm not leavin' my lil' brother in this mutha'fuckin' hospital. Somebody's try'na kill us, and I gotta be here to protect him."

Grip took a deep breath and slowly nodded his head.

"Yeah, we definitely have a powerful enemy," he agreed, catching Sonny off guard by using the word *we*. He fiddled with the diamond ring on his right pinky, and then said, "Don't worry about Rahmello. He's safe."

"Safe?" Sonny retorted. "He's laid out in a coma. Anybody can creep in here and finish what they started."

310

Instead of responding, Grip nodded his head toward the two black men who were strategically positioned by the entrance. He then gestured toward the front row of chairs where another black man was sitting at full attention. They each had a clean shaved face, a neatly trimmed haircut, and were dressed in black suits with red bow ties.

The man who was sitting in the front row had a Final Call Newspaper lying on his lap, and underneath a nickel plated .45 was clutched in his right hand.

The two men positioned by the entrance had expressionless faces. Their dark, cold eyes scowerrd the large room, and their body language personified discipline heads straight, shoulders squared, and their hands were folded in front of them, right over left.

After studying the three men Sonny returned his attention to his attention to Grip.

"They witchu?"

Grip nodded his head in the affirmative.

"Now come on, it's imperative that we leave this hospital."

As they left the emergency room and stepped into the chilly December weather they were immediately bombarded by flashing lights and news cameras. News reporters from every local station were crowding the walkway, and they all wanted a piece of *The Moreno Crime Family.*

"Mr. Moreno! Mr. Moreno!" Roland Rushin called out as he positioned himself in front of the crowd. He held his microphone to Grip's face. "Do you have anything to say about the recent attacks on your family?"

Grip scowled at him, and continued walking towards the parking lot where Muhammad was standing beside his Maybach with the back door wide open. Directly behind the large sedan, a black Escalade was parked with the engine running.

"Mr. Moreno!" Jessica Summers, the young white woman from Channel 9 News called out. "Is this your other grandson, Sontino Moreno? Is he the new boss of *The Moreno Crime Family*?"

Sonny too stopped walking and looked at her with a sinister glare.

"Yo, where the fuck is y'all gettin' this shit?"

The young woman stood firm.

She held her microphone up to his face and asked him, "Aren't you Sontino Moreno?"

"Yeah I'm Sonny Moreno," he quickly confirmed, "but I never even heard of this so called *Moreno Crime Family.* Y'all mutha'fuckas is trippin'."

He pushed the microphone away from his face, and then climbed inside of the Maybach. The multitude of flashing lights illuminated the car's plush interior, causing him to close the curtain on his window. He looked out the corner of his left eye and saw Grip reclined in the white lambskin seat. He was fiddling with the diamond ring on his right pinky and flexing his jaw muscles.

As Muhammad pulled out of the parking lot with the Escalade close behind, he peeked in the rearview mirror and noticed that Sonny was cutting his eye at Grip. Muhammad didn't say a word. Instead, he reached inside of his suit jacket and calmly removed the .45 that was nestled in his shoulder holster.

Sonny could feel Muhammad's energy. He looked into the front seat and locked eyes with the old man through the rearview mirror. Disgusted, he shamefuly shook his head, and then reclined back in his seat. *Damn yo, if only Mook could see me now.*

"Sontino," Grip spoke in his deep voice. "You okay?"

"Naw," Sonny shook his head disdainfully. "What the fuck is *The Moreno Crime Family*? And how these mutha'fuckas got me mixed up in it?"

Grip sighed. "It's a long story."

"A long story?" Sonny repeated. "A'ight, well go 'head, I'm listening."

Grip nodded his head, and just as he was about to explain the legendary bloodline that ran through his grandson's veins, his Samsung vibrated in his pants pocket. He retrieved the phone and looked at the screen.

"Hold on Sontino. I need to take this call." He held the phone to his ear. "Hello."

"Uncle G, it's Gangsta. Where you at?"

"We're just now leaving the hospital. It's Me, Sontino, and Muhammad. Ahmed and Mustafa are riding behind us."

"Sontino?" Gangsta questioned, wondering how Grip was able to pull off what seemed to be impossible. "That's a good thing. It's time for him to know what's goin' on, anyway."

"I agree," Grip said. "Where are you?"

"I'm at *The Aramingo Diner,* and I've got Murder and Malice wit' me.*"

"Did y'all get to the bottom of this shit?"

"Absolutely," Gangsta confirmed. "Little Angolo and Carmine was behind this shit. That punkass Clavenski played a roll in this shit, too. It's cool through," he continued, and then looked down at the wounded prosecutor. "I've got him right here, and I'm about to tune his ass up somethin' nice."

"I fuckin' knew it," Grip hissed through the phone. "I *knew* my brother was behind this shit. Now, as far as Clavenski, you just keep him nice and warm for me. We'll be there shortly."

Click!

Grip looked into the front seat. "Muhammad, take us to the garage on 22nd Street. We need to switch cars."

Muhammad nodded his head, and then turned left on Erie Avenue.

Sonny was confused. He looked back and forth between Muhammad and Grip. "What the fuck is goin' on?" He asked his grandfather. "You know who killed my pops and shot up his funeral?"

"I do," Grip confiirmed. "It was *The Gervino Crime Family*. We're officially going to war."

Sonny screwed up his face. *"The Gervino Crime Family?* I ain't never bump heads wit' them niggas so why would they be comin' at me?"

"Because," Grip replied, "you're a Moreno."

"Yo, here you go again wit' this Moreno shit!" Sonny snapped. "What the fuck is *The Moreno Crime Family?*"

Grip rolled up the partition, and then looked Sonny square in the eyes. "What's the definition of knowledge?"

"The definition of knowledge?" Sonny continued his rant. "These mutha'fuckas murdered my pops and tried to blow up my family, and you got the nerve to ask me this dumbass question?"

As calm as still water, Grip stared at him with a blank expression. "Just answer the question."

Immensely frustrated, Sonny shook his head and flexed his jaw muscles. "It means to know somethin'."

"Not exactly," Grip corrected him. "The definition of knowledge is to comprehend the reality of something as it truly exists, with certainty. Now, with that being said, do you know who you are?"

Sonny was speechless. He looked into his grandfather's blue eyes, and then shamefully lowered his head. How could a question so simple embody such depth.

"I'm Sonny Moreno," he answered while slowly raising his head. "A North Philly Block Boy."

"Certainly not." Grip checked him. "You're my grandson. You're Sontino Moreno, a worldwide boss."

Again, Sonny lowered his head. His brain was moving at the speed of light, and mixed feelings permeated his heart. The newfound respect that was developing for his grandfather was conflicting with his feelings of hatred and contempt. He desperately tried to keep it together, but everything was hitting him at once. His chest became tight and his own tears betrayed him. He was doing the unthinkable. He was crying in the presence of his enemy.

"Sontino," Grip addressed him. His voice was so deep and regal it reminded Sonny of James Earl Jones. "Tighten up and walk like a champion." He reached out and placed his hand on Sonny's left shoulder. "Did you hear what I said?"

"Yeah," Sonny sniffled and wiped away his tears. "I heard you."

"Good," Grip replied in a compassionate voice. "Now, let's try this again. Do you know who you are?"

Sonny took a deep breath and continued to flex his jaw muscles. "Man, I don't fuckin' know."

Grip chuckled and removed his hand from Sonny's shoulder. "And that's something that I *do know*! Why? Because in order for you to truly know who you are, first you need to know who *I am*!"

"Oh yeah," Sonny challenged him. "And who the fuck are you?"

Grip's face turned to stone, and he looked his grandson dead in the eyes. "I'm Gervin Moreno and I was born to be a gangster..."

Askari

To Be Continued...
Coming Soon
Blood of a Boss III: The Reckoning

Coming Soon From Lock Down Publications

GANGSTA CITY

By **Teddy Duke**

STREET JUSTICE **II**

By **Chance**

A DANGEROUS LOVE **VI**

By **J Peach**

BONDS OF DECEPTION **II**

By **Lady Stiletto**

LOVE KNOWS NO BOUNDARIES **III**

By **Coffee**

BURY ME A G **II**

By **Tranay Adams**

BLOOD OF A BOSS **III**

By **Askari**

DON'T FU#K WITH MY HEART **II**

By **Linnea**

BOSS'N UP **III**

By **Royal Nicole**

THE KING CARTEL **II**

By **Frank Gresham**

LUV IN THE CLUB

By **Sa'id Salaam**

SILVER PLATTER HOE

By **Reds Johnson**

LOYALTY IS BLIND

Askari

By **Kenneth Chisholm**

Available Now

LOVE KNOWS NO BOUNDARIES **I & II**

By **Coffee**

SLEEPING IN HEAVEN, WAKING IN HELL **I, II & III**

By **Forever Redd**

THE DEVIL WEARS TIMBS **I, II & III**

By **Tranay Adams**

DON'T FU#K WITH MY HEART

By **Linnea**

BOSS'N UP **I & II**

By **Royal Nicole**

A DANGEROUS LOVE **I, II, III, IV, V**

By **J Peach**

CUM FOR ME

An **LDP Erotica Collaboration**

THE KING CARTEL

By **Frank Gresham**

BLOOD OF A BOSS

By **Askari**

STREET JUSTICE

By **Chance**

BURY ME A G

By **Tranay Adams**

BOOKS BY LDP'S CEO, CA$H

TRUST NO MAN

TRUST NO MAN 2

TRUST NO MAN 3

BONDED BY BLOOD

SHORTY GOT A THUG

A DIRTY SOUTH LOVE

THUGS CRY

THUGS CRY 2

TRUST NO BITCH

TRUST NO BITCH 2

TRUST NO BITCH 3

TIL MY CASKET DROPS

Coming Soon

TRUST NO BITCH (EYEZ' STORY)

THUGS CRY 3

BONDED BY BLOOD 2

Askari

Made in the USA
Columbia, SC
17 February 2021